PRAISE FOR JUGGLER FROM REAL READERS

I067145b

Pulled me in from the first page!
Amazon Reader Review

A delightfully multi-faceted novel! Dry and sometimes dark/ironic humor! A 5-star book!
Amazon Reader Review

This book, from one unlikely turn to the next, kept me laughing harder and harder all the way to the unbelievably bombastic script-reading climax! But underneath the gut-laugh worthy situations, the funny stuff is also heart-warming and moving. A great read if you're looking for humor with truth and heart!
Amazon Reader Review

Well-drawn characters and beautiful sense of place. Excellent. Five stars!
Amazon Reader Review

I've had to explain the awesomeness of this book to most of my coworkers so they know I'm not dying of laughter at my desk like I've completely lost it. Fresh and fun! Easy to read and so enjoyable!
Amazon Reader Review

Wonderfully funny and touching
Amazon Reader Review

A five-star book I hope everyone will enjoy!
Amazon Reader Review

Sick. Twisted. Hilarious.
Amazon Reader Review

ABOUT THE AUTHOR

Rich Leder's screen credits include eighteen produced television films for CBS, Lifetime, Hallmark, and others; and feature films for Lionsgate Entertainment, Paramount Pictures, Tri-Star Pictures, and Left Bank Films. In addition to movies, he writes the *Kate McCall Crime Caper* series and other funny books.

He has been the lead singer in a Detroit rock band, a restaurateur, a Little League coach, an indie film director, a literacy tutor, a magazine editor, a screenwriting coach, a commercial real estate agent, a wedding guru, and a visiting artist for the University of North Carolina Wilmington Film Studies Department, among other things, all of which, it turns out, were grist for the mill. He resides on the North Carolina coast with his awesome wife, Lulu, and is sustained by the visits home of their three children.

RICH LEDER BOOKS

Workman's Complication (The First Kate McCall Crime Caper)
Swollen Identity (The Second Kate McCall Crime Caper)
Emboozlement (The Third Kate McCall Crime Caper)

Juggler, Porn Star, Monkey Wrench
Let There Be Linda

RICH LEDER

JUGGLER
PornStar
MONKEY WRENCH

This is a work of fiction. All names and characters are either invented or used ficti-
tiously. The events described are purely imaginary or fictionalized based on real oc-
currences—unless they were precisely true or sort of true, in which case they weren't
purely imaginary in the first place.

ISBN: 978-0-9911769-8-4

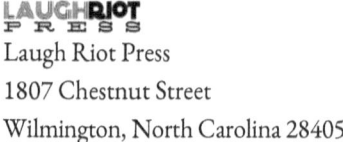

Laugh Riot Press
1807 Chestnut Street
Wilmington, North Carolina 28405

DEDICATION

For the late great Stu Robinson, my first agent in LA, a world-class Hollywood gentleman with a splendid sense of humor, who put me on the ladder and encouraged me to climb.

ACKNOWLEDGMENTS

For many years, while living in the fantastical San Fernando Valley, I wrote movies for the networks and studios, whose offices and campuses I visited by snaking through the canyons into LA. I toiled in the trenches beside a battalion of smart and talented executives, producers, directors, actors, and other awesome filmmakers—all of us fighting the good fight. I was young and impressionable, and the town took me under its crazy wings and gave me the ride of a lifetime. There are too many to mention by name, but I am indebted and grateful to them all for their tutelage. This book is a result of their influence, of the hilarious and improbable adventures we shared. They are complicit in whatever the hell it is I've done here.

Rich

JUGGLER

PornStar

MONKEY WRENCH

A WORD BEFORE YOU START

My name is Mark Manilow. I'm a screenwriter and now a novelist. If you were hoping for some kind of lesson to be learned from my implausible LA love life and dubious romantic escapades, if you were wondering whether or not such a lesson exists in this book, the answer is: I think so. But in the end, that will be up to you as much as it is up to me. Either way, I thought I would offer a word before you start, a leg up as far as lessons go, so that you won't get halfway in and say, "Jesus Christ, Manilow, isn't there any goddamn thing to be learned here?"

When I was eight years old, my father was the coach of our Little League team. We were the Lawn King Weedwackers. Our uniforms were emerald green and two sizes too large. I was number eleven. There was a kid on our team named Scott McSween. His father was an ophthalmologist. Scott was number sixty-six, a bizarre baseball number and certainly a mistake by the uniform company. He was skinny, and the huge numbers wrapped all the way across his back and around his rib cage. His entire head vanished inside his hat. On the occasion of our first game, he chose to wear black dress shoes instead of cleats.

It was a wet and muddy Saturday morning—a good day for baseball. Mud on a clean uniform is one of life's little pleasures, and we were chomping at the bit. Some of us were even sliding before the game to get the mud off the ground and onto our pants.

The foul lines were packed with parents sitting on folding lawn chairs and blankets, holding umbrellas, taking pictures. The mayor showed up to throw the first pitch. A high school marching band played the National Anthem while younger siblings ran wild between babies in strollers and hard-of-hearing grandparents. There were sponsor signs and American flags and red-white-and-blue streamers strung along the outfield chain-link fence.

My mother and some of the other moms served sodas and hot dogs at the cinderblock concession stand, organizing the candy in colorful lines, chilling the Yoo-Hoo, popping the popcorn.

My father, wearing an emerald green Weedwacker T-shirt, gave us a pep talk, told us our positions, and sent us running out to the field for the top of the first inning. Scott strolled out to right, took off his glove, sat in the grass with his back to the game, and searched for four leaf clovers. He would not turn around for all the tea in China.

Time out was signaled and a conference was called at home plate. Everyone agreed that it would be too traumatic for the uncooperative outfielder to be hoisted up off the grass and ceremoniously removed from the field in front of all these people. The poor kid would never live it down. The umpires, coaches, and parents decided to play on with an extra right fielder. Scott would be allowed to express his free-spirited approach to defense, and another boy would watch his back. The umpire said, "Play ball," and the game began.

Dr. McSween and his wife stood by the right field foul line and begged Scott to face the game. "You don't have to put your glove on, honey," his mother said, "but there are four leaf clovers behind you. I can see them from here. Please, Scott . . ."

There was no measuring Dr. McSween's blood pressure. His face was on fire. While his wife tried every trick to get Scott to be a team player, the eye doctor took this opportunity to deliver a pitch-by-pitch account of the action and turn the embarrassing situation into a learning experience. "Low and outside, Scott. It's two balls and one strike. There's a man on first, so where's the play if it's hit to you?"

Scott's response, which he delivered without ever looking up, was to recount the important cartoons he was missing in order to sit in the grass and pick clover. "I don't like baseball. I like cartoons," he said calmly and often.

It was a suburban battle for control in a public arena. Other parents felt pity, I'm sure, in a kind of there-but-for-the-grace-of-God-goes-my-messed-up-kid manner.

Scott never swung at a single pitch the entire game, just stood straight up and down at the plate with his bat on his shoulder, and we played every inning with two right fielders, one to protect him from his inevitable beaning.

His parents eventually accepted the situation and watched the game with their friends, drinking coffee and discussing the newest proposal to improve the deadly Route 4 and 17 interchange.

In the last inning, Scott turned and picked clover while facing home plate. Everyone cheered for him like he'd hit a homerun. He tried not to, but he smiled. I'm sure this moment saved him from a life of misery. There were way worse eight-year-old things he could have done than sit with his back to the game. A severe eating disorder or lighting matches in the living room while Mrs. McSween prepared dinner, for instance, were other you're-not-the-boss-of-me choices available to him at the time. But his line in the sand was hunting for outfield clover and not his father or my father or the mayor or the umpire or the high school marching band or anyone anywhere could make him cross that line.

While writing this book, I thought of Scott in right field and his parents by the foul line and how after all their emotional cajoling and play-by-playing the end result was to sit in a folding lawn chair and let the thing ride until it was done.

It could have gone either way. At any time on that muddy Saturday morning, Scott could have put his glove on, stood up, and faced the game. He didn't, but he could have. There was nothing the McSweens could do to determine the outcome. It was up to crazy little number sixty-six all along.

So there it is, a leg up.

PART I
FOOLISH
BALL OF TWINE

1. MY LIFE IS A LOT LIKE MY HOUSE

The ground shook as I left my house and walked down the driveway to my car. I was headed to LAX and then Paramus, New Jersey, to visit my parents, and the Earth, with its jolt and roll, was reminding me that tectonic activity was underfoot at all hours of the day and night and would be waiting for me when I returned.

I didn't need reminding. There is no solid ground in LA. The place is always shifting. That's why it's plausible to build houses like the one I own, a 1,700-square-foot California ranch that hangs ridiculously over the edge of a steep Coldwater Canyon cliff. A sliver of my house is constructed on level land. The rest is suspended in midair, supported by thin wooden beams supposedly cemented to the craggy ravine wall one hundred feet below my bedroom. My neighbors' homes are similarly situated. We live in our houses without care because we know it wouldn't matter if they were built in the flatlands of Northridge; the ground moves, and no one is secure. And since no one is secure, anything goes, which is the first singular truth of LA: It's all good.

My life was a lot like my house. The day before everything changed, I was twenty-two, living in Hackensack, and had written a screenplay that an agent at William Morris thought had commercial potential. The agent's name was Mike Lerner.

He said, "Mark Manilow, Mike Lerner. William Morris. I read your script. Your life is going to change, babe. Get on a plane right now. Take the red eye. You have to be here in the morning. Make it a one-way ticket."

My script was called *Full Force*. It was the story of two hardcore army sergeants in Vietnam who use their platoons to wage a war within a war, fighting each other and the Viet Cong at the same time. It was violent and action-packed with crisp dialogue and deeply drawn, emotional characters that you care about and root for. I wish. At the time, I didn't know character arc from Noah's Ark. It was violent, anyway.

"What about my job?" I said. I had been working for a commercial real estate developer in Fort Lee, leasing corporate office space, which is even less fulfilling than it sounds. My heart was pounding like a jackhammer, so I could barely hear his reply. He was at his desk in Beverly Hills but sounded so distant he could have been calling from outer space (though many people equate the two).

"My opinion? You're never going back. I'm ninety-nine-point-nine percent sure I'm going to sell your script tomorrow. Mid-six figures against one point two. It's a gold mine. See you in the morning. I'll have your contracts ready. Here's Jason. He'll set it all up."

He passed me to his assistant, Jason, and I quit my job and took the red eye, but I never met Mike Lerner. He and Jason were fired ten minutes after they got off the phone with me. My script vanished with them. No one at William Morris had ever heard of it.

I had no idea where I was, where I was going, or how I was going to get there. I had no return ticket, no job, and nowhere to stay. I had no car, no friends, no bank, no credit, and no agent. I was planning on using some of the one point two to help me settle in, but that train left the station along with Mike Lerner.

LA is the easiest place to get lost in—physically, spiritually, emotionally, and intellectually. Luckily, it's also the easiest place to *be* lost in. The sun is shining, the women are gorgeous, and the camera is rolling. I'd find another Mike Lerner. I was a screenwriter now with a hot script in my hands. How many of me could there be?

Plenty, it turned out. One of the peculiar facts of Los Angeles is that if you stop ten people on the street and ask them how their script is coming along, nine of them have an answer. It's in turnaround, I'm stuck in the second act, it's in pre-production, my agent loves it, my agent hates it, my agent was fired ten minutes after he said he'd sign me, and so on. This is the second singular truth of LA: Everyone knows two things, their job and how to write a movie—meaning how to write *your* movie.

For the next twelve years, I parked cars, washed cars, gassed cars, sold cars, tended bar, flipped burgers, stocked groceries, checked groceries, drove a cab, drove a tow truck, drove a school bus, tutored, temped, waited tables, moved furniture, and dug ditches (which, in its way, is just like writing movies).

Throughout it all, I studied my craft (screenwriting gurus grow in LA like corn in Kansas) and wrote scripts—dramas, comedies, dramedies, romantic comedies, sophomoric comedies, teen comedies, family comedies, action, adventure, action-adventure, thrillers, sci-fi, and westerns. I acquired an agent (several agents), wrote a few television movies for money, pitched my stories to studio, cable, and network executives, and stumbled forward through the smog.

At the start of my thirteenth year in LA, I was at the farmers' market on Fairfax writing a coming-of-age movie about a North Carolina boy who accidentally invents an anti-gravity gel. All kinds of crazy hijinks ensue and the boy, his parents, his siblings, the mayor, the barber, the barber's talking dog, and the traveling salesman with the heart of gold learn important life lessons. I was drowning in the second act when I heard her laughing, which, in retrospect, was the beginning of the beginning of the end.

2. JUGGLER

Laughter is the great aphrodisiac that no one talks about. I was thirty-five, and I had never been in love. The joy in her voice as she laughed at something she saw in a magazine while sitting in the sun on Fairfax changed all that in a single heartbeat. I crossed the open courtyard and stood before her. "What's so funny?" I said.

"Fashion. It's hysterical. Look at this and tell me your sides don't split."

It was a photograph of some supermodel walking the runway in a sheer silk blouse that was open to her waist. "Why wear the shirt at all?" I said.

"Exactly," she said. She had soft brown hair pulled casually to the side, chocolate eyes, a touch of blush on her cheek, a hint of red on her lips. "I have great tits, and I wouldn't be caught dead wearing an outfit like that."

"You do have great tits," I said. "What's your name?"

"Julie Bowers. What's yours?"

"Mark Manilow."

"Like Barry?"

"Except Mark."

"Do you really think I have great tits?"

"I'm sure of it."

She was from Easton, Pennsylvania, a small, almost-charming town directly across the Delaware River from Phillipsburg, New Jersey. She was reared on The Hill, which is where Lafayette College sits. I had graduated from Lafayette before I took the corporate real estate job in New Jersey.

"I can't believe you lived in Easton," she said. I had carried my coffee and notepads to her table and was sitting across from her.

"Small world," I said, "though I wouldn't want to have to paint it." She laughed again; it sounded like music. "So what are you doing in Hollywood?" I said. "How's your script coming along?"

"You mean like a movie script? I'm not writing one. I don't write movies."

Within a month, I had moved out of my place and into hers. Two months later, we were engaged. Two months after that, our families flew in, mine from New Jersey, hers from Chicago, and we were married on the beach in Santa Monica on one of those perfectly clear days that demonstrate without question that the weather is a harbinger of exactly nothing.

We honeymooned in Antigua and returned to Dickens Street in Sherman Oaks to start our new life. Sherman Oaks is a pleasant town in the San Fernando Valley, which is a suburb of Los Angeles that cascades down the north side of the Santa Monica Mountains and spills across Ventura Boulevard until it runs out of steam. The Valley, as it's commonly called, is renowned for its smog, which is as brown and ubiquitous as a UPS truck and veils the low-rising mountains that rim the northern edge of the vast valley. Sylmar is one of the towns out there. It might as well be New Guinea, it's so far away.

On certain days, few and far between, the sooty haze dissipates, and residents who live along the southern rim of the valley can see the northern mountains with their naked eyes. *"I didn't know there were mountains there"* is an oft-repeated statement on the streets of Sherman Oaks, Studio City, Encino, Tarzana, and Calabasas on such days. Further and even fewer between are the days when the sky clears to a dazzling blue and the mountain range *behind* the mountains of Sylmar becomes visible. Car accidents along the 101 are commonplace on such days. Hospital emergency rooms fill with disoriented citizens, their geographic reality altered forever with the knowledge that there are mountains behind the mountains. The Mountains of Brigadoon, Julie called them.

She was supportive of my screenwriting, brewed me green tea to energize my inner artist, and made sure I had plenty of private time to make magic out of words on paper. She even told her friends that I was a magician, and that—it turned out—was the harbinger of everything.

We were happy as clams for exactly three weeks, and then Warner Brothers decided it was time to make a war movie about two grizzled sergeants with a deep personal disdain for one another that would tragically and explosively play itself out in the fiery jungles of Vietnam. Out of nowhere, *Full Force* was a go project.

They paid Bruce Willis all the money in the United States Mint to play one of the sergeants and electronically transferred all the funds in Fort Knox to a bank account in Switzerland belonging to Arnold Schwarzenegger so he would play the other.

A seventeen-year-old European cameraman, who had shot two fast-paced music videos, was hired to direct. Though he was sketchy on the war's longitude and latitude, he knew the location of the Caribbean and bought an island there with his paycheck.

I received enough cash to buy my Coldwater Canyon house on stilts and live modestly off the interest of what was left for more or less the rest of my life.

For Julie, success meant pressure, and she cracked after we closed on the house. Before we even moved in, six months after our romance had begun, she was gone.

It turned out that her innermost secret, her most profound belief, her deepest dream, revealed for the first time by my sudden success, was that she was born to be a juggler. Her life was without meaning until and unless she mastered the art of juggling.

I'm not half bad with words, especially when they're coming from my heart, but no amount of professing my love for her could stop the packing of the suitcase, the marching through the house, and the disappearing down the driveway in a cab.

I called her father, Dr. Bernard Bowers, a psychiatrist, but there was no medication he could prescribe, and he blamed me for pushing her over the edge.

"This is all your fault, Mark."

"How do you figure, Bernie?"

"Your newfound money and power represent a penis the size of Rhode Island. Julie can't cope. Juggling is simply a metaphor for her sidestepping your enlarged member. You changed the rules, and Julie is juggling your testicles to find her footing."

"Metaphorically?"

"She won't come back until your genitalia have returned to normal size."

"How will I know when they have?"

"Own your guilt, Mark."

Even more than I felt like killing him, I often felt like killing myself after speaking with Julie's father. That's how I knew he was a real psychiatrist.

I left for Canada, which doubled as Vietnam, Washington D.C., Miami, Mexico, Nebraska, New Orleans, and a dozen other *Full Force* locations. For six months, the time it took to shoot the film, I ate craft service muffins and burned through thousands of cell phone minutes trying to locate my wife. She was nowhere, and I gained ten pounds.

Willis and Schwarzenegger were brilliant as the war-crazed sergeants. And the European director blew up everything in Canada that resembled a Far Eastern jungle, which is to say anything green. He used real explosives because the producer was able to hide them in the massive tax rebate that he then pocketed. Canada rebuilt the decimated landscape into golf courses, so everyone was happy except me.

After *Full Force* wrapped (and immediately imploded in post production), I moved back into my Coldwater Canyon house alone, heartbroken and confused. The harder I tried to find Julie, the further away she seemed to get. I worried myself sick that some terrible wickedness had befallen her.

She's found someone else was a thought I couldn't shake. She's living in Romania, the center of the juggling universe, with a hairy man who can juggle flaming animals eating fresh fruit. (It makes no difference whether he's the one eating the fresh fruit or if it's the flaming animals, he can still juggle them.) His name is Bela, and he makes love to her three times a day.

These thoughts drove me crazy. I had a recurring dream of Bela and my beautiful Julie discussing the secrets of juggling over the green tea she had brewed for him to bring out his inner magic. She was telling her new Romanian friends that he was a magician. She was wild-eyed, her hair wind-blown, wearing gypsy clothing and trinkets, juggling madly in the town square. In the dream, while she juggles, she tells passersby that she has great tits. If this is not a nightmare, then what is?

I called her friends; maybe they had heard from her. They had not. I went to the ad agency she worked at. The people there had no idea where she was. When I returned home from the ad agency, there was a message from her on my voicemail: *"Have faith in me, Mark. The course of our lives is beyond our control. We must follow our paths to the end no matter where they lead. My father says your penis is gigantic. It doesn't matter. I'm a sail in the wind. Bela says hello."*

I only imagined the part about Bela.

I went into a tailspin that lasted more than two years, right up to and including me walking down the driveway to my car as the ground shook, on my way to LAX and then Paramus, New Jersey. I had hope that this trip home would ground me, reset my compass, and put me back on track. Instead, my life, like a foolish ball of twine, rolled off the table and entirely unraveled.

3. BROKEN BONER

So I was thirty-eight years old and on my way to Paramus for the first time since I'd left the Garden State for the Promised Land sixteen years earlier. I was flying home because my mother's Aunt Ida was dead as dirt at the age of ninety-four. She was a prodigious cigarette smoker, feared for extinguishing her lipstick-stained butts on any forearm left exposed and within reach. This wasn't because she was careless or daft or far-sighted but because she didn't like you, even if she didn't know you. She had no money and so lived off her relatives, who she never thanked and endlessly castigated. There was some vague uncertainty as to whether or not she was an actual blood relative. *"There was no Aunt Ida and then suddenly there was,"* my mother once told me.

My flight to Newark Airport was memorable because of a conversation I had with a fat man who helped himself to half my first-class seat.

"You in the movie business?" the fat man said.

I was working on a script. "Yes."

"Me too. What do you do?"

"I'm a writer."

"Perfect. I'm always looking for writers." He reached into his pocket, fished out a business card, and handed it to me with fingers as long and round as cigars. "Ken Moynihan. Great Dane Entertainment."

I took the card and shook his hand, which was thick and meaty. "Mark Manilow."

"What kind of movies you make, Mark?"

"Features. I've had one produced, but it's tied up in a legal mess that's never going to unwind. It's called *Full Force*."

"Who was in it?"

"Bruce Willis and Arnold Schwarzenegger."

"No shit. That's great. I make porn."

There was nothing outlandish in his tone of voice. He might just as well have said: *"No shit. That's great. I make cutlery."* He saw the surprise on my face.

"People who live in glass houses, Mark. Know what I mean? Porn's bigger than Hollywood now. It's leaner, it's meaner, and it has hot naked women getting it on like the sky is falling. Everybody's making money. Nobody's getting hurt. Customers couldn't be happier. Porn is the biggest win-win in the world."

"I don't live in a glass house. I live in Coldwater Canyon. My house is on stilts."

"Good for you. I shot a movie in Coldwater Canyon. *The Pool Boy*."

"What was it about?" I couldn't stop the question from falling out of my mouth. Ken had a big laugh. His whole face shook like a bowl of Jell-O. "I mean, I know what it was about," I said, belatedly.

"Sure you do. Everybody does. That's the kicker. The audience is in on the joke. We all know what the movie's about. In this one, Dallas Westcott holds her pool boy hostage, screws his lights out, and then calls her friends over to do the same. Did someone say orgy? How much money you think I made?"

"I'm guessing plenty."

"Cost me eighty grand to shoot, one fifty to market. Try again."

"Three hundred thousand."

"Add a zero."

"No way."

"I'm rich. I guess you figured that out. Know what I do with my money?"

"Anything you want."

He laughed again. A great hearty roar. No shame. Not even a hint of guilt or regret. "I like you, Mark. When you get tired of Hollywood kicking your balls in, you call me. We'll do some business, you'll make some money, and I'll get you laid. Let me tell you something, you've never met anyone in your entire life who can make you happier than I can."

"I can't write porn."

"Listen carefully to this next sentence. It is the single greatest secret in an underground, multi-billion dollar industry that has evolved into the biggest subculture in the history of humankind, including every race, creed, and color in the rainbow. Here it is: anyone can write porn."

"I wouldn't know where to start."

"Let's see. Okay, I got one. Two nurses and a doctor go at it with a patient in the operating room. Patient's in a full body cast. He's got one hole for his tongue, another for his pecker, and all kinds of pulleys and shit to move him around in a dozen positions. Call it *Broken Boner*. We'll get Dallas Westcott to play one of the nurses and make a boatload of cash. What do you say?"

I had no idea what to say. "I've got your card." That's the best I could do.

4. ONE ISSUE AT BAT, ONE ON DECK, AND ONE IN THE HOLE

I rented a car at Newark Airport and drove to my parents' house in Paramus. Route 4 had changed in a way that I didn't think was possible: it had gotten worse. Gargantuan shopping malls of all shapes and sizes had lined every inch of both sides of the highway when I first left for Los Angeles. In my sixteen-year absence, city planners had somehow folded time and space in on themselves to create heretofore-undeveloped parcels of land upon which they then commissioned and constructed even more stores and shops. The impossible truth of Paramus is this: there is nothing for sale in the world that you can't buy on Routes 4 and 17, so traffic crawls all the way from Ridgewood to the George Washington Bridge, giving countless cars ample time to turn into the next strip mall or the next one after that and so on for miles and miles.

Here's a typical Paramus experience: the Johnsons are in the market for a labradoodle. While dad puts it on plastic at PetSmart and mom buys an iPod at Best Buy, Junior picks up a drum set at Sam Goody, and the twins slip into the latest jeans at the Super Gap, all in a cockeyed strip mall wedged between a Target and a Lowes on one side and a Grand Union, a Costco, and a Filene's Basement on the other.

The entire strip mall is jammed between a mega-monster Walmart and an IKEA the size of Jupiter, and all of that is crammed between the Garden State Plaza, an epic indoor shopping continent, the Bergen Town Center, its evil twin, Paramus Park, the granddaddy of indoor malls, and the Fashion Center, an upscale experience for those who can't spend enough money. In Paramus, the food courts have food courts, should you get hungry crossing from the Sbarro to the Starbucks.

My father, Arthur Manilow, DDS, was still an orthodontist. My mother, Diane, was still selling residential real estate part-time. They lived in the house where I grew up, a center hall colonial on three-quarters of a wooded acre with huge planting beds of pachysandra and a screened porch in the back with white wrought-iron furniture and bird-patterned cushions. The cushions flew south to the basement at the end of every autumn and returned in early spring; you could set your clock to their migration.

When I was growing up, my father would grill flank steak for sandwiches that we would eat on the porch, mosquitoes massing on the outside of the screens. We drove them all mad. *"It's the only revenge we get against the little shits,"* my father would say.

As I pulled into the driveway, he was pushing a leaf sweeper across the front lawn. My mother was weeding the pachysandra.

Dad pushed the sweeper in immaculately straight lines, back and forth across the grass. If the spinning brushes missed any leaves, he would continue to the end of the row, make a tight u-turn, travel back down the already swept ground and shoot for the misbehaving leaves again. If he missed even one, it was down to the end of the row and another straight-as-string reversal. When the difficult leaves were finally swept aboard, only then would Dad move on and begin his next perfect row. I'm sure I don't have to tell you how he ate corn on the cob.

It wasn't by accident that he became an orthodontist. His father, my grandfather, was an administrator for the New York City public school system. Dinnertime conversation in their Washington Heights house centered night after night on my grandfather's struggle to put things in order, to straighten out the mess. On those days that he was successful, happiness hung in the air. Disorder played out as frustration and discontent. If things weren't straightened out, happiness was unattainable. My father was taught this lesson early and often. He learned it well, though my mother's nature was the perfect counterpoint to this logic and so, I think, my father was happier than his father. Or perhaps it's just that teenage teeth are easier to straighten than the New York school system.

My mother works the pachysandra as if her chaotic approach itself will propel the weeds out of the earth. There is no rhyme or reason to her system. Left first, then to the right, then turn and grab some behind her, then move to an altogether different area and begin there, leaving the area she had been working incomplete and messy.

When they were first married, this intuitive, unplanned schematic for gardening—and eating corn—drove my father crazy. He could barely glance at her plate during dinner on the back porch. His flank steak sandwich, potato salad, and neatly eaten corn were each assigned specific locations on his plate. Crowding was impermissible. My mother's plate was an artist's palette. Steak and potatoes all intermingled, corn eaten in some kind of indecipherable code. My father's frustration matched that of the mosquitoes buzzing insanely beyond the screen.

But her gentle laugh and easy smile at the weeds and kernels she left behind proved comforting to him over time. Life was balanced, he reasoned, if both sides of the equation were given equal weight. My mother agreed and delighted in my father's orderly ways.

I smiled at them and thought this kind of compromise is what makes a marriage work, but I may not have been the best judge. My wife was flashing her tits to Romanians while juggling bowling pins and carving knives.

They stopped their lawn work as I climbed out of the car and grabbed my suitcase from the trunk.

"There he is," my father said. "How was the flight?"

I still had Ken Moynihan's business card in my pocket and visions of *Broken Boner* in my head. "Fine."

We met on the brick path and embraced.

"You feel thin, Mark. Are you eating?" my mother said.

"When I'm hungry."

"There are things we can do to increase appetite," my father said.

I had been home exactly one minute and forty-seven seconds, and he was straightening me out. "I was kidding, Dad. I'm always hungry."

"There are things we can do to fix that too. And if you're eating all the time and still not gaining weight, that's something else altogether. I'll call Ben Greenberg. You can see him while you're here. It's better to deal with it head-on than to let it stew."

"Ben Greenberg from Little League?"

"He's a doctor now," my mother said.

"He played second base. No arm," I said. I could picture him throwing slow-motion pop flies from second to first. "He couldn't hit either."

"So what," my father said. "He's a gastroenterologist at Hackensack Med."

"Married with three kids," my mother said.

"Lives in River Vale," my father said.

"I'm fine, really. I don't need to see him," I said.

"We'll keep an eye on it," my father said.

We were still on the front path, not even at the door, and there was already one issue at bat, one on deck, and one in the hole. The issue at bat was my inability to take care of myself. It was a miracle that I knew to come in out of the rain. Neither of them, I'm sure, were surprised to find I couldn't feed myself at the appropriate times on any given day.

I didn't have to be a fly on the wall to know the content of that evening's bedtime talk. I would be in my childhood bedroom, in the same bed, and they would be down the hall. My father would shut the door, turn out the lights, and stand at the foot of the bed in the dark, hands on his hips. My mother would already be under the covers.

"He's wearing tennis shoes, Diane. And dungarees."

"I know, Arthur. California clothes."

"He's thirty-eight years old."

"He's a writer. That's the only explanation."

"Take him shopping. We live in Paramus, for Pete's sake."

"Maybe Bloomingdale's."

"There's no way we can eat at the club."

"We'll get him khakis in the morning."

"I have shoes he can borrow."

"Yes. The brown loafers."

"Start cooking now, Diane. He's got to put on five pounds before he goes back."

The issue on deck was my choice of career and the lonely, unacceptable life it had led to. Little Benny Greenberg with his weak-ass arm had gone on to become a doctor, a substantial and steady way to earn a living. I, on the other hand, was subsisting on magic. Even when I cashed my check, bought my house, and set up an income-producing fund that would sustain me, albeit at a minimal level, for the rest of my life, my parents wondered aloud in every one of our conversations when I was planning to get a real job and thus a real life —like no-hit Benny with three kids.

The issue in the hole was that I lived three thousand miles away instead of in the next town over, where I could be expected to attend all holidays and they could keep an eye on me. I'm sure they saw this as some kind of rejection. One minute I was leasing corporate office space in Fort Lee, the next I was in Los Angeles chasing a dream. What had they done wrong to so seriously screw me up? Nothing, it turned out. The blame was all mine.

We stepped up onto the porch.

"Your sister's coming for dinner," my mother said.

"With Phil and the kids?" I said.

My father nodded. "Driving in from the city to get a gander at the movie man."

My mother squeezed my arm and kissed my cheek. My dad took my suitcase and smiled with joy, if not pride. My trials and tribulations aside, they were happy to have me home. But I was even happier to be here.

5. LIFE MOVES FORWARD WITH THE GENTILITY OF A BULLDOZER

I thought the house would fit me like an old sweater, but I was wrong. It was tight and scratchy, and it had an unfamiliar musty smell, as if someone else had been wearing it around town. I knew the rooms like the back of my hand, but even that didn't help me. I couldn't get comfortable. It wasn't my house anymore. I grew up here, but the years had changed us both. I was older, and my life experience had expanded my vista for both better and worse. The house was older, too, but the years had caused it to grow smaller. I couldn't believe how small it was. The dining room table, once the size of a football field, sat ten adults when fully extended. I had remembered dozens of people feasting for hours around its mighty circumference. I would lie in bed after a festive dinner and imagine my father installing two phones, one at either end, so guests could check in with friends on the far side of the table during the meal.

I stood at the bottom of the stairs and looked up. Gone was the perilously steep cliff from my childhood, replaced instead by an ordinary flight of stairs.

When I was eleven, I'd answered the phone one Saturday morning and told the caller that my father was at work. It was his tennis partner, a radiologist named Dr. Leibowitz, confirming their match. He expressed mild surprise that my father hadn't called to cancel and disappointment that they would miss their game and then asked me to relay the message that he, Leibowitz, would find another morning match. I hung up and my mother entered the kitchen and asked who had called. I gave her the message. She turned on a dime and went back upstairs. I went into the den and clicked on the television. Three minutes later, my father's voice roared from the second-floor landing.

"Mark."

He didn't have to say anything else. His furious baritone thundered down the stairs and reverberated through the house.

I walked into the foyer, stood at the bottom of the stairs, and looked up. My father stood on the second-floor landing, a mile away. I was at the bottom of the Grand Canyon, and he was the God of Tennis, in his perfect whites with rackets at his feet, at the top of Mount Olympus. He was home all along, and I had blown his morning match, the one and only time of the week that he got to play. My mother had told him the truth to soften him up. He had called Leibowitz to try and catch him, but was too late. The radiologist had already made another match. My father's Saturday game was gone.

"What the hell did you do that for? Why didn't you just say, 'Let me check?'"

I had no idea he was home, no idea why the hell I did that, and no idea why I didn't just say let me check. I was eleven. I had no idea about anything, really. It was Saturday morning. Cartoons were on.

"All you had to do was walk up the stairs and say, 'Dr. Leibowitz is on the phone.' Now you can walk up the stairs and park your behind in your room. You're grounded." I began the long climb. It took me two hours to reach the second floor where my father was waiting.

Though remembering the event made my legs cramp out of muscle memory, I had finally figured it out. It was the stairs all along. They were the reason I didn't check for my dad in the first place. The vast amount of time involved in undertaking an expedition to the second floor and back would have made even Lewis and Clark think twice. It was simpler to believe he wasn't here than to search for him.

I wondered if the stairs had suffered the same fate as the dining room table, began the long climb, counted four seconds from bottom to top, crossed the upstairs hall, and discovered that my room was gone.

What I found was a gym. My parents had not simply redecorated my room; they had changed its use. There was no evidence to suggest I had ever slept here. My bed, my dresser, my desk, my easy chair, all of them had been sold for pennies at yard sales. They had torn up the navy blue carpet and put down shiny, faux-wood flooring. There was a stationary rower, a recumbent bike, a digital treadmill, and a universal gym. One wall was entirely mirrored, with an exercise bar for ballet stretching. Another wall showcased a flat screen television. Beautiful framed photographs and their accompanying inspirational sayings had replaced my posters of major league baseball players. I wondered where I could purchase a membership. But mostly I was sad.

It's unreasonable for us to expect that our parents will leave our rooms untouched forever and ever. Life moves forward with the gentility of a bulldozer. Our childhood bedrooms aren't meant for preservation like museum exhibits. My parents were right to move on. I did. We all have to.

Unfortunately, right and wrong aren't part of the equation when it's your heartstring childhood memories in the spotlight. There were photographs of me scattered around the house, but where was the hardscrabble proof of my young life? Where were my army men? My Encyclopedia Britannica? My baseballs? My comic books? My initials carved in the wood of my bottom dresser drawer with a ballpoint pen?

My youth had vanished into the ether. Gleaming exercise gear occupied the space where my memories should have been. There's no reconciling this kind of loss. You carry the weight and walk away—in this case downstairs, where my sister Leslie was arriving like a Cape Fear hurricane, husband and children pouring into the foyer behind her like an eighteen-foot storm surge.

6. ISN'T IT ALWAYS SUNNY WHERE YOU LIVE?

"Where is he?" Leslie said. "I won't believe he's here until I see him for myself."

"Hi, Les," I said. I was halfway down the stairs.

"Oh my God. I thought everybody in California was in great shape."

"Everybody but me."

My sister exercises with a vengeance. She's a triathlete who hates to swim, bike and run. She gets no enjoyment from her seven-days-a-week, three hundred sixty-five days-a-year, two-hours-a-day training sessions. She's far too thin, but has no eating disorder. Rather, she has a living disorder, though you would never notice from a cursory glance at a middle school soccer game in Central Park, say, or an insurance industry dinner-dance at The Pierre with her husband, Phil Hirschman.

Phil and the kids, my twelve-year-old niece, Janice, and my four-teen-year-old nephew, Danny, all watched my descent with wonder, as if I were a walking catfish, gills and mustache dripping swamp water on the foyer floor.

"You're white as paste," Leslie said. We hugged for the first time in ten years. "Isn't it always sunny where you live?"

Leslie is two years older than me, so she was forty at this moment in time. Despite our relative closeness in age, we did not interact as friends while growing up in Paramus. Her circles and my circles nowhere near intersected. That kind of disconnect has always been emblematic of our relationship.

She is my father's daughter, but without the counterweight of my mother for balance. She has his voice and his looks and his insatiable desire to set things right. As is evidenced by my father, this is not necessarily a highway to unhappiness. The antidote, as it is for many ailments, is perspective. Leslie has none.

She went to college and graduate school at New York University, married a New York insurance agent in a New York temple, worked as a high-powered New York efficiency expert for a profitable New York consulting firm (streamlining other New York firms) until she had New York children at a New York hospital, then retired to be a stay-at-home New York mom. Other than two weeks in the Hamptons when the weather was nice, one week in the Berkshires when it wasn't, and Sunday trips across the George Washington Bridge to showcase the grandchildren and eat flank steak sandwiches on the porch with my parents, Leslie had not ventured off the island of Manhattan since she was seventeen years old, except once, a disastrous vacation to San Diego when Danny and Janice were four and two respectively.

"You remember Phil?"

"Vaguely," I said, and everyone had a good laugh.

"It's okay. I don't remember you at all," Phil said.

We laughed because we collectively knew it was meant as a witty rejoinder to my "Vaguely." But it wasn't funny. He said it as if underneath the joke he meant for it to hurt me somehow. We shook hands, and I remembered why I never liked him.

"Good to see you, Phil."

"Likewise, Marky."

No one else in the world ever called me Marky. Not even as a schoolboy. I hated it. What's worse is that early on in his relationship with Leslie I pulled him aside and told him I hated it. He laughed it off and has never called me anything else.

"Hi Uncle Mark," Danny said.

"You I remember," I said. "And Janice too."

They were just babies when Leslie and Phil took the trip to San Diego, an excellent city for vacations with children, on the advice of one of Phil's clients. I drove down from LA and met them at a pre-arranged location in the parking lot of the world famous San Diego Zoo.

The only thing larger than the San Diego Zoo is the San Diego Zoo parking lot, an ocean-sized tarmac that requires binoculars and a map to locate the zoo entrance if you arrive too late in the day at the wrong time of year.

It was mid-afternoon, way too late in the day, and it was the height of tourist season, absolutely the wrong time of year. Phil and Leslie had chosen the outermost edge of the vast parking lot as a meeting place (in all fairness, we would have had to park there anyway as only a handful of spaces were available even out here in the hinterlands).

It was unusually hot and humid for San Diego, ninety-six stifling degrees in the shade, and Phil, thinking he would rent a nifty stroller once inside the zoo, had left their stroller in the hotel room.

The kids were starving and over-heated and had missed their naptime, which, it turns out, was precisely when we were asking them to travel miles and miles of steaming macadam to a zoo they didn't believe existed and didn't want to see.

Four-year-old Danny suffered the first meltdown, screaming and crying his brains out while falling to the ground and rolling like a runaway Lincoln Log under the cars of complete strangers, somehow always out of the reach of Phil, who was on his hands and knees trying to get control of him.

One look at her brother losing his mind and two-year-old Janice went ballistic, rolling under cars like Danny, but in the opposite direction. Phil and Leslie were beside themselves with anger and frustration at each other (for ever leaving Manhattan) and at their children. They were crawling through the parking lot, screaming at the kids, cursing the zoo and the city of San Diego, sweating through their clothes, scraping their knees, becoming filthy and ragged, looking like a homeless family on the loose at the zoo. I joined in the hunt and can tell you that trying to coerce an imploding four-year-old out from under a pick-up truck when the four-year-old has no intention of ever coming out is no bar of chocolate.

It was late enough that some people were already leaving the zoo, and these people stopped and stared. Some took pictures. We were *that family* that all these people would talk about when remembering their trip to the zoo that fateful day. We were more entertaining than the monkeys, I'm sure, who were sitting in the shade, hiding from the heat.

Though I hadn't seen Janice since she was two and rolling under parked cars, I had seen photographs through the years, so she wasn't a stranger. Even still, her dark beauty took me by surprise. "I know you have to sell insurance when you grow up," I said to her, "but if you ever want to be a movie star, just let me know."

"I want to be a movie star," she said.

"No you don't," Leslie said.

"What do you remember?" Danny said.

"Everything," I said. "I keep your box scores in a scrapbook. I have every game you ever played."

"No way."

"Every game."

"What position do I play?"

"Left out. Kidding. Center field. Unless you're pitching. Even Mickey Mantle couldn't do both at the same time."

Danny nodded and smiled at me. It was a good answer. Fourteen-year-old nephews need proof of connection before they'll offer up any real kind of communication. I had followed his career through my father, who had sent me the box scores of Danny's baseball games for many years. I kept them in a scrapbook. I was a ballplayer too, once upon a lifetime ago.

"Unless he was loaded," Phil said. As usual, he had found the most negative aspect of the conversation, Mantle's alcoholism, an aspect no one else would have thought to interject, given the tone and context of the conversation, and made that his point of view.

"But then he wouldn't know he was doing both at the same time," Leslie said.

"But technically he'd still be doing both at the same time," my father said.

"But he wouldn't know it," Leslie said.

"What about Willie Mays?" my mother said. "Could he do both?"

"It sure seemed like it," my father said.

"Mickey Rivers had no bones. He's the only one who could have done it," Phil said. Rivers was also once a centerfielder for the Yankees. No bones, but lots of spine.

Leslie didn't like the general direction of the conversation. There was no clarity to it. "But would he have known he was doing both at the same time?"

Now my father didn't like where it was heading. He had thought this question was boxed up and put on the shelf. "It doesn't matter.

He would still have been pitching and playing centerfield simultaneously."

"Whether he knew it or not?"

"It's irrelevant, whether or not he knew."

"He wouldn't be able to do both at the same time without knowing it," Leslie said. "Not only is it relevant, it's central."

"You're arguing about something that no one can do," I said. "It's the reality of it that's irrelevant. Like selling insurance." Everyone laughed.

Phil was born into a multigenerational New York insurance family. They had endless money. He was probably the worst insurance salesman in the history of insurance but was worth ten million without selling a policy. "Pays the bills, Marky."

This was the tenor of my relationship with my brother-in-law. Dig and dig back. It was how we said: *"We're not really related; you bag of shit."*

7. THE MOVIE BUSINESS IS HARD FOR NORMAL PEOPLE TO UNDERSTAND

We ate dinner in the dining room at the shrunken table. My mother made baked ziti with salad and garlic bread. My father sat at the head of the table, I sat directly to his right, my mother sat at the other end. Leslie sat across from me, Phil was next to her, and Janice was next to him, to my mother's immediate right. Danny was next to me. I could easily converse with any of them without using a telephone.

Aunt Ida's funeral had been cancelled. It had been proven at the eleventh hour, beyond all doubt, that the evil witch was never a blood relative of the Manilow clan. The pronouncement was taken with mixed emotions. The good news was that Aunt Ida's mean streak was not part of our DNA. There was significant relief that a Manilow infant, born or yet born, was not genetically preparing to burn future generations with his or her spent cigarettes. Also good news was the obvious: no one would have to travel all the way to Smithtown for the burial. The Long Island Expressway could be murder any time of day.

The bad news was the emotional repercussion of having been duped by the devil for forty-eight or so years. It would take generations to recover from this family tree failure. The money and time spent on Ida was as heavy on the Manilow mindset as the scars on our arms. One hundred years from now, when the story of Aunt Ida was being passed down, it was likely that those Manilows who were responsible for her inclusion would suffer in the telling of the tale, possibly titled: *Hoodwinked For All Time*.

Still and all, we were now free to discuss other things. We talked about the kids' school, Janice's horseback riding, Danny's earned run average, Leslie's triathlons, Phil's insurance, my father's approaching retirement, and my mother's real estate listings and sales. Each topic was neatly opened and bandied about until it was under control and laced up like a dress shoe. But all of it was prelude to the main event, the real subject on everyone's mind—my screwed up screenwriting life.

"You have to get over it and get on with it," Leslie said.

"You don't really believe the whole juggling thing, do you, Marky?"

"She's in Romania right now," I said, "or Yugoslavia or someplace where juggling is very important. Armenia, maybe."

"Why did she leave?" Janice said. There was no malice in the question. She hadn't inherited the asshole gene from her father.

"He doesn't know. If he did, she wouldn't have left him in the first place." My sister could always be counted on for compassion and empathy.

"I agree with Leslie. It's time to move on," my father said. "Find someone else and start your life over. It's not too late to still have a real life. You're only thirty-eight."

"I have a real life."

"Where are you hiding it?" Leslie said. When you're born into a family, you're given a special knife to use on your siblings. Leslie's knife came with instructions that read: *Stick in Mark's back. Stab hard, twist savagely, repeat often.*

"I hope she's happy," my mother said. "And then I hope she gets hit in the head with a brick."

"Mom, she's still my wife."

"Not for long, Marky," Phil said. "It has to be an affair. The juggling story's a quacker. If it looks like a duck and talks like a duck and smells like a duck—"

"It's an insurance salesman." I couldn't help myself. It was like hitting the side of a barn. "She left because she couldn't accept the success of my movie. She wanted to blaze her own path, not walk down mine." I was answering Janice because I didn't want this discussion to be a defining moment in her adolescence: *"I'm a lesbian now, Mom, because your idiot screenwriting brother wouldn't give me a straight answer why his wife left him. I've determined that all men are as duplicitous and evasive as Uncle Mark and so I will only love women. Especially women who juggle."*

"Oh," Janice said. "Pretty hardcore." I had made some future high school boy the luckiest little shit in town.

"Exactly," I said.

"The success of your movie, that's the part I don't get, Marky. If nobody ever sees it, how can it be a success?"

Not surprisingly, my father felt the same way. "I don't think any of us get that, Mark. It's a little bit frustrating, to tell you the truth."

"The movie business is hard for normal people to understand," my mother said. "Don't take it personally. We don't hold it against you."

"Julie did," Leslie said. *Stab hard, twist savagely, repeat often.*

"Can you explain it, Uncle Mark?" Danny said.

"It starts with an idea," I said. "Just some idea that floats into your head from nowhere."

"The movie business, you mean?" My father had to have the premise of the answer straight from the get-go or it was no-go. "You're saying the whole movie business starts with an idea?"

"Yes," I said.

"Must be a big idea," Phil said.

"Not necessarily," I said. "Most of the time it's a really small idea. Just a thought somebody has that they think would be a good movie."

"So the whole movie business depends on writers having ideas that can be movies? Don't you think that's just a writer's point of view? Don't you think directors and producers and people who work for the big studios would have something to say about that?" Leslie said. Even when we were children, she never gave me half an inch to breathe. It's true that we love our siblings with all our hearts, but it's also true that we sometimes don't like them very much. You can't choose your family. It's life's greatest crapshoot. All of human history has been determined by who was born where and at what particular time.

"Anyone can have the idea: a director, an actor, a producer, a studio or network executive, your plumber, your haircutter," I said. "Even a writer, if he's lucky."

"Then what?" my father said. The braces were on, now he needed the rubber bands, but where, exactly, to put them was still unclear.

"People in power have to agree that the idea has merit. That they could make money off it if it were turned into a movie," I said.

"I'd have been good at that job," Phil said. His wife and children rolled their eyes. He was a good and loyal provider, but he was also a dickhead. Deep inside, I suspect they thought so too. But they were a family and were bound and belonged to each other and so they loved him despite his dickheadedness.

"The tricky part is that only one idea in a thousand is given the go-ahead," I said.

"Pretty steep odds," my father said.

"The steepest," I said. "It's almost impossible to get started."

"So why do people do it?" Janice said.

"It's a mystery," I said. "But once these people in power decide this is the one-in-a-thousand idea they've been waiting for, they hire a writer, if one isn't already attached to the idea, to flesh it out and make a story out it."

"That's you, Uncle Mark," Janice said. It was worth the trip east just to see her— the dark shining eyes, the gorgeous smile, the open innocence, the non-judgmental nature of her twelve-year-old soul. If I could bottle her spirit and sell it to devious, burned out Hollywood producers—the vile producer of *Full Force* came to mind—I would make a killing.

"I wish you were a vice president of Warner Brothers," I said, and everyone laughed. "Yes, that's me if I'm lucky."

"I'd rather be lucky than good," Phil said.

"You are, Dad," Danny said, busting his father's balls. Everyone laughed, even Phil, who had a pretty good sense of humor for an insurance dickhead.

"So some writer makes a story out of the one in a thousand idea," I said, "then writes a screenplay, which is then rethought by committee and rewritten over and over until all the creative life and soul is beaten out of it, and then that script is sent to movie stars, who are offered mountains of money to star in it and, if you're extremely fortunate, one of them says yes."

"What are the chances of getting a movie star?" my mother said.

"One in a thousand," I said.

"So a one in a million idea gets a movie star attached. That about right?" my father said. It was the perfect kind of conversation for him, and I hoped this might be the moment he finally understood what I was doing with my life and why.

"Yes," I said. "Somehow, no one knows how, a famous actor says he or she will be in the one-in-a-million movie and then hundreds, sometimes thousands of people are hired, dozens of giant tractor-trailers filled with unbelievable amounts of equipment are moved halfway around the world, and tens of millions of dollars, sometimes more than a hundred million dollars, sometimes way more than a hundred million dollars, are spent turning the words the writer wrote into filmed images of actors actually speaking the words out loud . . . what are we talking about again?"

I knew Leslie would remember. "How you can possibly consider your movie a success."

"So the odds of any of that falling in place are improbable at best. But *Full Force* fell into place—one in a million. I had the smallest idea, turned it into a script, the people in power wrote huge checks, hired an army of workers, and actually *made* my movie with two global stars and a great supporting cast. On top of that, I got paid enough to live more or less comfortably for a very long time. I beat all the odds and made good money. Feels like success to me." I put a forkful of baked ziti in my mouth as if to say: *Period.*

"But nobody's ever going to see it," Leslie said. "So the perception of success is yours alone. It's based entirely on process, not product. The public never gets to pass judgment. So whether or not the process was successful can't truly be determined because the success of the product can't be determined. Your success is completely subjective, Mark. Sorry to burst your bubble."

"You should have gone to law school, honey," my mother said to me.

"New England School of Law would have been perfect for you," my father said. I had applied to that one and only law school and been accepted. But I had a heart, so I knew I couldn't be a lawyer. I framed my acceptance letter and presented it to my parents before taking the mind-numbing commercial real estate job. They had never recovered.

"How many movies a year does Hollywood make? Phil said.

"Five hundred, more or less, from all the American film companies, including the Independents. But probably more like two fifty or so from the Hollywood major studios and mini-majors," I said.

"So two fifty," Phil said. "Basically, they start with two hundred and fifty million ideas and after this long and impossible process, they end up with the stuff we get to see in the theaters?"

"Right." I had never thought of it that way. A chill went through me. All of us were thinking the same thing.

"That's the best they can do?" my mother said.

"There are five good movies a year," Leslie said.

The mediocrity of it all was shattering.

"Why are most movies so . . . run of the mill?" my mother said.

I wanted to tell her it was because writing by committee only works when the committee is in for the long haul, like the staff of a sitcom or an hour-long drama, where the cacophony of voices have time to coalesce into a unified sound. A one-shot story needs a solo voice at the wheel in order to find a focused point of view and a single sensibility. Adding writer after writer more often than not creates chaos and confusion, usually on deeply subconscious levels that translate as vibes on the screen and in the theater and are not easily evident or even explainable in a studio meeting. But I was still shaken by the numbers: five good films out of two hundred fifty million ideas. Even if it was overstated by a ton, there was no escaping the shock of it. I said nothing.

"I could make a movie out of the phone book that's better than the junk they put out there," Phil said.

"Daaaad," Janice and Danny said.

"What?" Phil said. "It's all in there. White pages, yellow pages, every person, every business, every product, every story in America is in the phone book. Let your fingers do the walking."

"It's just information. There's no beginning, middle or end," I said.

"I'd make it up," Phil said.

"You need a powerful protagonist and an antagonist that's his equal," I said.

"There's eight million people in the Manhattan phone book. I'd pick one for the good guy and one for the bad guy."

Phil had a way of burrowing under my skin that no one else, not even Leslie, had mastered. "You can't make a movie out of the phone book, Phil."

"Maybe *you* can't, Marky," Phil said. "But somebody can and somebody will. I smell a blockbuster."

The conversation drifted after that, and I was glad it did. When your insurance selling, millionaire, dickhead brother-in-law gets the best of you in a screenwriting debate, it's time to eat your garlic bread and shut the hell up.

8. THE CAUSE OF WORLD FAMINE

The rest of my trip home was more of the same. My parents expressed their concern for my broken marriage, my lackluster career, my teenage taste in clothing, my uncanny ability to make poor life choices, my health, my income, my car, my house hanging over Coldwater Canyon, and the general waste and malaise that defined me in their eyes. I could feel myself cracking under the withering expression of their love and worry. They were correct: *it wasn't too late to right the ship.*

I could still go to law school. I'd be forty-one when I graduated. Plenty of time to fill a pension fund, find a wife, and raise a Bergen County family. I could sell my house, move to Paramus, and live with my parents while I attended law school in the City. I could sell my 1970 Mustang convertible too. My parents played bridge on Tuesdays with Len Rosenberg, owner of the largest Volvo dealership in North America. Len would happily help me out. I could join a gym, take up golf, get a haircut, and learn to play bridge. Len would welcome me into their Tuesday game with open arms. My wife would adore the Rosenbergs. My kids would thrive in the Bergen County school system. My father, retired by the time they were born, would oversee the straightening of their teeth by Len Rosenberg's son, Andrew, who was my father's junior partner and had a contractual agreement to buy the practice when my father hung up his braces for good. My mother would pass down her recipes to my wife, and they would cook Sunday dinners side by side, laughing about last

Tuesday's bridge game or the silly things my kids were doing. I would be a real estate lawyer because of my experience leasing office, tech, and warehouse space. My practice would thrive, and I would buy a house in Ridgewood or Woodcliff Lake. My parents would come to my house on Sundays, and I would grill them flank steak sandwiches and serve them red wine and a tossed salad and corn, which my father would eat in razor-sharp lines like my son and my mother would eat helter-skelter like my daughter. We would all attend Len Rosenberg's funeral and sit Shiva with Andrew, who was my closest friend and the straightener of my children's teeth.

The attraction was strong. We discussed the color of my Volvo, the names of my children (Henry and Justine), and who would sit where at their bar and bat mitzvahs. But as I was calling a San Fernando Valley realtor to put my house on the market, my parents took me to their country club for dinner, and I was saved.

Riverside Country Club is where Bergen County Jews who suffer from Golf go for treatment. Golf, as everyone knows, is a disease, not a game. *"Do you have Golf? I'm so sorry"* is the correct conversation starter. It is a serious condition requiring many, many thousands of dollars and countless hours to control. Sadly, there is no cure. Once infected, it is a lifelong debilitating illness, not unlike Skiing. If you're smiling now, you should stop. There is nothing funny about Golf.

We ate dinner in the enormous ballroom. They once hosted two huge weddings simultaneously within these walls and neither wedding knew. There must have been a thousand Jews at the giant buffet. They were truly a tribe. They all shopped at the same stores, did their hair and nails at the same salons, drove the same cars, wore the same clothes and watches and jewelry, and laughed at the same jokes. I was overwhelmed. How many times can you see the same sweater and slacks combination before losing your composure? The measurement of their happiness was off the charts. Their joy was uncontainable. I lost my inner balance. Too much happiness all at once is destabilizing, like a four-year-old spinning and spinning and spinning on the front lawn, then stopping and falling and flailing about, unable to see straight or stand up, but laughing like a hyena at his own dizziness—even as he's vomiting.

Everyone knew me. Even people who didn't know me knew me. A few asked about my life in LA, but most by far wanted to know where in the City I was going to attend law school. Len Rosenberg had my Volvo picked out and washed. In a matter of minutes, I would be wearing the same sweater and slacks as the rest of them. Italian loafers would be slipped on my feet without my knowledge. I moved to the buffet to escape their joy and discovered the cause of world famine.

How could millions of Africans find food when all of it was here —served by young Irish waitresses and Hispanic men with tall chef hats? There were twenty different salads. Twelve soups. Five cooks preparing fresh pasta with half a dozen different sauces. There were carving stations, sauté stations, and grilling stations offering seafood, steak, veal, chicken, and lamb. There were potatoes and rice and vegetables in every imaginable combination. There was a sushi bar and two huge sizzling woks. There was Thai food and Indian food and a pizza oven. There were ice sculptures surrounded by fruit carved into flowers decorated by flowers shaped like fruit. There was one wall of nothing but dessert.

There was tremendous eating and laughing and gossiping. My ears were buzzing, and my vision was blurred. I could see that though grandparents dominated the group, there were plenty of younger members as well. I was introduced to single women as a soon-to-be-divorced future real estate attorney. Apparently, that arrangement of words is a turn-on in this part of the country because I could have had sex with any one of them in the locker room with just a wink of my eye. I could have proposed and been married on the spot. A wedding planner and a rabbi were on hand, just in case.

Throughout it all, I couldn't shake the thought that if the golf course had lights, these people would still be playing and all this food would have gone to waste. I realized that these culinary displays were part of the treatment and the only reason that there was no such illness as Night Golf.

I never loved my parents more. They knew that I had been thrown for a serious loss by Julie's departure. They could see my confidence had been shaken and decided to save me. They dragged me to Riverside for a full exposure to the life I could have chosen, and it had replenished me by scaring me half to death.

Accepting that we are who we are is the port where safety lies. It's the dark uncharted waters of who we could have been, given this choice or that one, where unreasoned regret lies in wait with fear and terror. If it's paralysis you're looking for, travel home sixteen years later and plot anew the course of your life.

I told them I was going back to LA, and they smiled sadly and said they knew I would and that they believed in me in spite of everything. My father shook my hand as he carried my suitcase to the car and told me he was proud of me. Even if he didn't mean it, I glowed for weeks. I promised that it wouldn't be so many years until I visited again and drove away.

In the mirror I saw my father lift a rogue leaf and drop it in the pile at the curb. The huge municipal vacuum truck would be by to suck them all up on Wednesday.

9. OFFICER DOWN

On my way to the airport, I stopped at the elementary school I had attended so many years ago. It had suffered the same fate as our dining room table. It was not just smaller; it was Completely Smaller. It was once my universe, holding all my friends, all my thoughts, all my laughter and dreams and secrets, and now it wasn't. I had no idea where my grade-school friends were or what had become of them. They were teachers and gynecologists and electricians' wives. They had attained great wealth or died young, tragic deaths. They were lost to me, and my youth was lost with them. I sat in the rental car and began to weep.

The weight of my journey home had become too heavy to carry. Where was I? Did anyone know where I was? Who could find me? My bedroom was gone. My parents were old. My sister was hardened by the narrowness of her own life. Where was my anchor? How did I get here? Where was I going? My wife had left me, and my career was drowning. I was unrecognizable to even myself. You can't reclaim your childhood when you've lost it in the tall grass. That's why we hold onto our memories so dearly. That's why we keep close contact with our friends. We can find our lives in their eyes and in their laughter. The meaning of us is secure in their hearts and minds. They know us now, and they knew us when. We never see ourselves more clearly than we do with our childhood friends. Our journeys are traceable, step-by-step. Our senses of humor, the food we eat, the clothes we wear, how we arrived at this moment in time as the people we are, it's all mapped out in our friends so we won't get lost as we move forward. We are our childhood friends in the most primal of ways and they are us. I had no friends from my childhood. I had misplaced my youth and now it was gone and there was no getting it back. Not ever. The tears poured out of me.

As I left the school parking lot, I ran a stop sign and was pulled over by a Paramus policeman, my eyes and cheeks wet with remorse.

"License and registration," the cop said.

There was something in his voice that struck a chord so deeply buried inside me that I hardly heard it. "What did I do, officer?" I said as I fished for my wallet.

"You drove straight through a stop sign in a school zone," he said. I opened the glove compartment, retrieved the rental contract and whatever else looked official, and handed the whole stack to the cop. I did this without glancing up at him because I was still in quick recovery mode from my emotional outburst at the school. I was wiping the tears from my eyes while trying to put a finger on the vaguely familiar feeling that had resonated inside me when the cop spoke again.

"Mark?"

I looked at him. "Gibby?"

"Jesus Christ. Mark Manilow. I can't believe it."

He was Tom Gibson, the starting left tackle on our high school football team. We weren't friends, but Gibby played first base on the baseball team too, and I was the shortstop. We were high school teammates who had never spoken one word after graduating. We drank beers together at parties from time to time, but he was something of a lug nut back then and aside from the normal high-school-locker-room banter, I wasn't interested in forging a friendship. I'm sure he felt the same way. "Wow, Gibby. You're a cop."

"Since after high school. I could retire if I wanted to, I got twenty on the job, but I like it."

His father had been a cop as well. I imagined the bond between them was strong, whereas the bond between my father and me was harder to categorize. If I had become an orthodontist, our relationship might have been different, maybe even as strong as Gibby and his dad. It's possible that the Manilows and the Gibsons could have been a foursome at the Paramus Public Golf Course Father and Son event. Afterwards, we would all have had beers at a sports bar. The orthodontists and the cops shooting the shit, watching a ballgame on the big screen after a competitive eighteen holes. "That's great, man. You look good."

"So do you." He glanced at my license. "You live in California?"

"Los Angeles."

"Get out."

"I'm visiting my parents."

"Your dad straightened my daughter's teeth. I married Patty Golembuski. Remember her?"

"Of course I do. Congratulations. That's fantastic." I had only the dimmest picture of Patty Golembuski in my mind. Huge breasts, that's all I could get my hands on, so to speak.

"Our kids go to the same schools we went to. We got a son, too. Going to be bigger than me. He's in eighth grade. He's a monster."

Gibby was the size of a minivan. Monster was probably the perfect word for his mammoth middle school son. I was still in the car, sort of twisted sideways and looking up at the block of granite in the blue uniform. Short, sandy hair, eyes spread so far apart they were closer to his ears than to his nose, huge teeth with large gaps between them, incongruously cute freckles on his cheeks. The years had dulled his features, but it was Gibby. I had the fleeting desire to take infield practice.

"What do you do in LA, Mark?"

"I write movies, Gibby."

"No kidding. So do I."

In a flashing microsecond, all other emotions were thrown from the boat so it wouldn't capsize and sink. "Really?"

"I bought Final Draft and wrote three scripts so far. They're action stories. Cops and car chases and gunfights. No blood, though, and no sex. Going for the PG13."

Final Draft is a package of script-writing software that automatically formats typed words into industry standard screenplay style. Everyone can be a screenwriter, so everyone is.

"I got an agent," he said.

That was enough for me. I hit the gas and burned rubber down the street, choosing a life on the lam for evading a traffic ticket over a life in LA writing films that no one would ever see. It was in all the newspapers and there was a nationwide manhunt for me. But I was in Panama, living under an alias, working the night shift on the canal, letting water rise and fall in the locks—all of that in half a heartbeat.

"Me too," I said. "What are you working on now?"

"It's called *Officer Down*. It's about a cop who specializes in crimes where other cops have been shot. If there's an officer down, this guy is on the scene kicking some major bad-guy butt. Saving lives, taking names, that kind of thing. He's got a kid at home, needs an operation. Don't know for what yet. What do you think?"

"You'll figure it out." I knew he meant what did I think of his movie, but I didn't want to have that conversation. His movie was as good as my movie, as good as any movie. Maybe his execution wasn't as crisp as mine, but who knows, maybe it was.

"What's yours about?" Gibby said. He was leaning against my car and his holstered gun was front and center in my face. I wanted to grab it and shoot him so I wouldn't have to answer the question, but I didn't. It was hard enough being on the run in Panama for a traffic ticket. Imagine if I was trying to stay one step ahead of the law for killing a cop. Imagine if the guy from *Officer Down* was after me.

"It's about a married couple that wants to get divorced, but can't because if they do, then neither one of them will get their uncle's inheritance. The only way out of the marriage while still getting the money is if one or the other of them is declared insane. They spend the movie trying to drive each other nuts. It's called *Crazier Than Thou*."

"Funny stuff. Good luck with it."

I had made the whole thing up that second. I hadn't written anything since Julie left me. "Thanks. You too."

"Maybe we could write one together."

"We probably could."

He gave me a whopping ticket and told me to have a good trip home. I told him to say hello to his big-breasted wife and his colossal kids and left Paramus a smaller man than when I arrived. Humility is a virtue unless they drop a dump truck of it on you. Then it's as crushing as concrete.

10. A DREAM OF INFINITE PROPORTION AND HYPER-BRILLIANT COLOR

My house had not fallen into the canyon while I was away. That's the best thing I can say about my return to Los Angeles. My neighbor had collected my mail and waiting for me in the stack was a letter from Julie. Actually, it was a torn piece of a paper bag. There was postage on it and my address, obviously, but the part written for me was written right there on the bag for anyone to read. Why would the post office deliver something so clearly not a letter? It broke all postal laws. It practically broke all laws of nature.

It read: Mark, I am in the Amazon. There is an Ancient Juggler here. He is traveling on intergalactic paths. Ours may never cross again. Or they may. We must do what we must do. My guide gave me this wisdom. He has been eaten by a lion. Regards, Julie.

What in the world was she doing in the Amazon? She hated bugs. You would find her perched atop a chair, screeching like an animated elephant at a mouse, if a platoon of ants were marching across the kitchen floor. A housefly was cause for a counterattack far more severe than simply swatting it out of the sky. It would have to be de-winged and then crushed with the heel of a boot and then flushed down the toilet twice. The Amazon was home base to every bug in creation. Bugs no one had ever heard of were living there by the billions. I would have bet my life that she would never set one foot in the Amazon.

I called her father, seeking his perspective, and read him the letter. "I can't hear you, Mark," he said. "Your penis has grown so large that it's blocking your sound waves from entering the phone. You're choking on your own genitalia. Embrace your heritage. The Ancient Juggler did not condone your circumcision." He was crazier than his patients, as all psychiatrists are.

Julie's torn paper bag with a stamp was devastating, no doubt, but there was a single ray of sunshine contained within its contents. Bela, the cuckolding Romanian juggler, was dead or at the very least eaten by a lion. Even a juggler of his European prowess would be hard pressed to juggle without arms. Bela the foot-juggling Romanian didn't have the same impressive ring to it. It served him right. He had stolen my wife and introduced her to the Ancient Juggler. I was a screenwriter who had introduced her to TIVO.

The paper bag pushed me over the edge. Blitzkrieged by jet lag, I fell into a sleep so sound, so unmoving, that reality and dream state flip-flopped and leapfrogged until all dimensions were lost and my mind spun into a dream of infinite proportion and hyper-brilliant color.

I tumbled through space and crashed into the sea where I began to sink, weighed down by my melancholy, which acted like rocks in my pockets. As I was giving up the ghost, a passing ship threw me a line and towed me aboard. It was a Hawaiian Princess Cruise Line ship and island women were dancing topless to a reggae band. My mother put a lei around my neck, and my father handed me a piña colada. A line dance began, and Leslie and Phil, waving a phone book above his head, swept me into it. We danced off the deck and down the plank to my elementary school in Paramus, where all my lost childhood friends were waiting, and Gibby and Patty and their kids were loung-ing in my bedroom, inexplicably positioned at center court in the gym, bleachers full of fans, who were cheering as Len Rosenberg rolled my new Volvo through the doors while pulling Dr. Leibowitz, my father's MIA tennis partner, into view with a long leash. I puked saltwater on Len's shoes, kissed Leibowitz full on the mouth, and realized that all was not lost, just my marriage. I awoke that Monday morning and filed for divorce.

Of course, it was overwhelming sadness that had nearly done me in. True love is the profound interweaving of two souls into one without either soul being lost in the conjoining. It is a bit of human magic and cannot be duplicated or falsified if it's to be real. Brief though it was, what Julie and I had was a bona fide connection. There were trillions of threads involved in the forming of our union and their untangling was as painful as a death in the family.

In essence, that's just what it was. The Mark-Julie life that was born in the farmers' market on Fairfax was dying a bewildering death, was even already dead, and I couldn't get over the idea that I had somehow failed her, not the other way around, and in so doing had failed myself. Confusion on all sides is the by-product of a broken heart. Worse things can happen to you, but it doesn't seem like it.

I took the divorce papers home, signed them on the kitchen counter with a ballpoint pen—like the one I used to carve my initials in the bottom drawer of my childhood dresser—and resolved to leave them there in the hope that she'd show up some sunny day and either countersign them, a thought that left me sick to my stomach, or toss them in the trash and set them on fire, a little wish I indulged in whenever I was stuck in traffic, so five or six times a day. Despite these tiny shreds of dreamy hope, I knew there was nothing left to do but press on, which, if you think about it, is a pretty good plan for most situations.

11. WRITE ME SOMETHING I CAN SELL

My father had said that it wasn't too late to still live a real life. He was right, to a point. It was time for my second draft. The phone rang, and I heard the voice of Cathy Burns, my wound and wired agent.

"How was your trip?" she said.

"Good," I said. "Saw my family, my old school . . . memory lane."

"I was there once. Didn't care for it. Personal history is almost always sad. And since today is already a part of history, all we have is tomorrow and the day after that."

Her phrasing sent me back to Paramus High. I thought to share the journey with her. "I had a science teacher in high school," I said. "Mr. Jackson. He used to give us Words of Wisdom at the beginning of every class and tell us to remember them forever and a day, *for if the world should end tomorrow, you shall have but one day to remember them.*' He's part of my personal history, and he isn't sad at all. His brother played for the Globetrotters back in the '60s."

"You should write a movie about him."

"You think so?"

"No."

"Oh."

"Mark, we're having a hard time selling you as a feature writer."

"But I am a feature writer. I wrote a feature with Bruce Willis and Arnold Schwarzenegger."

"We're having a hard time."

"I've been pitching."

"No one's buying. The business is changing. If you can't write martial arts, you've got no future."

"I've got a martial arts movie."

"What's it about?"

"Two boys at a prep school in New Hampshire in 1942. They discover a tunnel that leads through the Earth to China and unwittingly release a demon ninja that threatens the balance of world power. Using a potion that gives them extraordinary skills, they fight explosive martial arts battles while working through their college applications. It's sort of *A Separate Peace* meets *Crouching Tiger*."

"You made that up this second, didn't you?"

"Yes."

"It's not just us, Mark. All the big agencies are letting writers go."

"You're letting me go?"

"I can't afford to spend any more time on you. The returns aren't there. I have to focus on the writers who make money."

"What are they writing?"

"Martial arts, comic books, theme park rides, and sequels."

"What about comedy?"

"Only if it's lowest common denominator."

"I can do that."

"No you can't. You're too smart. That's what everyone says. Mark's got talent, but he's too intellectual, too emotional, too real."

"What about funny? I'm funny."

"If you think about it, yes. But without having to put any effort, zero thought into it, no, you're not that funny. Sorry, Mark. You're not lowest-common-denominator funny. You can't dumb it down."

"What can I do to change your mind?"

"Write me something I can sell, something with comic book heroes, something that doesn't require a shred of intelligence to enjoy, something based on something else, nothing original, something without meaningful emotional content, something that doesn't make a statement and avoids all controversy, something with excessive violence and naked women, blow things up, bridges and office buildings, smash some cars, make sure there's a gay character, put in some farting. Do all that and then call me."

"No problem, Cathy."

"Good luck, Mark."

"You, too."

I try to be a glass-half full person. But sometimes the glass isn't half full or half empty; sometimes there's just nothing in it at all. And then other times, like when your wife leaves you to be a juggler and you're a foreigner to your family and your agent drops you and you can't write a sentence to save your life and your career is in cardiac arrest, then you can't even find the damn glass.

I put my hand in my jacket pocket. Something small and thin brushed my fingers in a seductive manner. I took hold of it and brought it to my face. It was the business card of Ken Moynihan, president of Great Dane Entertainment, and scribbled on the back were these two words: *Broken Boner.*

12. 1415 DESHAYS STREET

"Great Dane Productions," the receptionist said. Her voice was perky and professional. I was expecting something huskier with a more moaning-with-pleasure quality.

"Hi," I said. "Mark Manilow for Ken Moynihan."

"One moment, please."

A handful of seconds slipped past, plenty of time for me to consider the depths to which I was sinking. *"Hang up the phone, Mark,"* I said to myself. *"If you take the next step, all is lost. Hang up, Porn Boy, before it's too late."* "What did you call me?" I said back to myself. *"Porn Boy,"* I said. The moniker rang around my head like big, fat, bonging bells . . . *Porn Boy, Porn Boy, bong-bong-bong.*

"Hollywood kicking your balls in?" It was Moynihan. No hello. No small talk whatsoever. It was as if we had been close personal friends for years and years and could bypass the cocktail franks and cut right into the porterhouse.

"I found your card," I said.

"Of course you did. Come to the house, Mark. Let's get you going."

This is why porn had surpassed Hollywood. What had taken Moynihan half a minute to accomplish would have taken the studios half a year: Who is Mark Manilow? Is he approved? What has he written? Call his agency. Have them send samples. We should read him and then discuss whether or not we like his writing. We'll have to discuss it because we can't know for sure what we think until we find out what everybody else thinks. Once we've figured out what we think, we'll have another meeting to discuss whether or not he fits in the big picture. Since the big picture is shifting on an hourly basis, we may need to read him again and then meet again to make sure we still think what we think we think, or if we need to re-think what we think we think. We'll need more samples. What else has he written?

"Great," I said. "When?"

"Half hour."

"I'll be there. Where am I going?"

"Encino. 1415 DeShays Street. The gate code is 6969. What else, right?"

"See you in thirty minutes."

Taking a meeting with a porn producer was a slippery slope. I knew I shouldn't go. Some actions are irrevocable. There's no explaining them away over baked ziti, salad, and garlic bread.

And yet I had to go.

No one in LA was giving me a second look, and if I couldn't make money as a writer, then I wasn't really a writer. If I wasn't really a writer, then I was every bit the fraud my family thought I was. Worse, I was wasting my life doing nothing, possibly the most frightening self-realization a person can have. Even someone who writes porn doesn't have to face that mirror. At least they're doing *something*. Hundreds of millions of people around the globe were experiencing sexual sensations because of the scripts porn writers had penned. *Hundreds of millions!* No one, zero people, had seen a single frame of *Full Force*, and no one ever would (thanks to the deadbeat lying producer).

And that was the crux of it. I wanted a script I had written to be funded, shot, and then seen by an audience, even if that audience was masturbating while they were watching it. Good for them. There are a lot worse things you can do with your life than help people get their rocks off.

Encino is another enormous community in the San Fernando Valley, further east than Sherman Oaks, but still rolling down the Santa Monica hills and spreading north past Ventura Boulevard a good long ways. DeShays Street was a curvy road running along the bottom of the foothills, south of the Boulevard. Whoever lived here, probably plastic surgeons and cosmetic dentists, had big bucks. The houses you could see from the street were gigantic, with wide manicured lawns and fountains and esoteric sculptures that shouted: *We have money, so it doesn't matter if we have taste.*

But there were also houses you couldn't see, monstrous mansions hidden from view behind impressive gates, tall walls and iron fences. I came to 1415 DeShays and pulled up to the ten-foot teak doors. There was a gorgeous garden planted along the fence line that could have been the cover of *Lawn & Landscape* magazine. It was lush and green and exploding with color. I could hear the irrigation system delivering a cool drink. If the garden on the exterior gate looked like this, I could only imagine how brilliant the grounds were on the inside. A keypad was positioned beside a sign that read: *No Soliciting*. I punched in 6969, and a voice resonated from a hidden speaker. "Yes."

"Mark Manilow. Ken told me to come to the house." Just the thought of it, a producer inviting me to his house, where he lived, where his real life was, his family photographs, his high school yearbook, just the thought of it uplifted my spirits. As impersonal as Hollywood had become, porn was entirely personal. It had to be by its very nature. I was being welcomed into a new world, and my first stop was coffee and cheese Danish at Ken's kitchen counter. What better place to discuss *Broken Boner*?

"Pull all the way in and park behind the sky-blue Jag."

"I'll do it," I said. Ken had a butler, naturally. He was rich as Midas. Everything he touched turned to X-rated DVDs that sold like hotcakes and made millions. At some level, success is simply success.

The huge gates swung open, and I drove through them into what could only be described as Eden. The grounds, as I suspected, were botanical garden quality. Everywhere I looked were bursts of Technicolor on green-green backdrops. Fountains and birdbaths and rock gardens and lovely private patios with small ponds filled the landscape as far as I could see. The property had to be ten acres just here in the front. The driveway was slate and meandered gently through the grounds, bordered on both sides by colorful perennials, as if Ken wanted his guests to unwind on their drive through his glorious private park.

It was working. I could feel the tension falling off my shoulders. I approached what I thought was the house. It was a very large French country chateau, shingled top to bottom, with a dark slate roof that had a deep sloping line. It dawned on me that this huge two-story structure was the garage. There were ten doors for cars, each of them a work of art unto itself, complete with etchings and carvings and stained glass—on the garage doors! There were huge French windows upstairs that swept the length of the building. *That's where the help lives*, I thought, *maids and cooks and butlers and groundskeepers and nannies and tutors and drivers all on the Moynihan porn payroll and living in a garage that could be a five star bed and breakfast.*

I turned past a thick grove of tall palms and facing me was the most beautiful home I had ever seen. Like the garage, it was a French country chateau, only much larger, twelve thousand square feet at least, and spectacular in every detail. There was a large circular motor court in front of the house, and I rolled slowly past a showcase of fine European automobiles—Mercedes, BMWs, Audis, Range Rovers,

Bentleys, Rolls—until I saw the sky-blue Jag. I parked behind it, got out, and walked past it on my way toward the front door. It was a convertible, like my Mustang, and the interior was custom sky-blue leather. It had whitewall tires in which the whitewall part was also sky blue. The license plate read: *DWPS*.

The front entrance area was a courtyard with tables and chairs, like a small Parisian café. I rang the doorbell. A woman with a headset answered, and my reality was turned upside down and inside out forever.

13. PORN STAR

The entrance foyer behind her was huge, and the polished hardwood floor was covered with cables. There were lights and cameras and other filmmaking equipment within easy view as well. "You're Mark?" the headset woman said.

"Yes."

"I'm Trisha. Follow me."

I stepped into the house, and Trisha shut the door behind me. I followed her across the long wide foyer. I could see massive rooms—parlors, dens, and libraries—shooting off hallways in all directions. Asian rugs, expensive furniture, original paintings, and stone sculptures were displayed throughout the house. There were several pianos and countless books. There were cables and generators and banks of lights everywhere. At the end of the foyer was an extra-wide double doorway. Trisha stopped here to let what lay beyond it properly sink in.

It was a Great-Great Room, perhaps five thousand square feet, with twenty-foot ceilings. The entire back wall, one hundred feet long, was French doors and huge windows from end to end and top to bottom. The fenced yard beyond the incredible wall of glass included an immaculate swimming pool, two tennis courts, a stable and riding corral with horses, a putting green, and several barn-like outbuildings.

Inside the Great-Great Room were numerous, well-defined areas. There was the bridge of a space ship, a restaurant kitchen, a lawyer's office, a grade school classroom and a medieval bedroom. They were movie sets. There were lights and screens and cables and cables and cables.

Fifty people were making a movie. It was a soundstage with a real live crew of filmmakers. Grips and electricians and camera crews and carpenters and painters and sound engineers and craft service were all at work, which on a movie set translates to standing around waiting. It wasn't *Full Force* with its many battalions and motorcades, but it was impressive and right in front of my face. I could reach out and touch it.

"First time on a porn set?" It was Trisha. I had completely forgotten her.

"Yes."

"I'll keep an eye on you. You wouldn't be the first guy I had to carry out of here." She must have seen my eyes go wide. "I'm kidding," she said. "You would be the first one. Ken's waiting for you in the saloon."

"The saloon?"

She gestured toward a far corner of the room where an authentic Old West saloon had been built and was being lit. The set was buzzing with activity as the crew made last-minute adjustments. "We don't do Westerns very often. But this is a good one. It's called *Hung Like A Horse Thief*. Watch your step. There's cable everywhere."

I entered the Great-Great Room and crossed carefully to the saloon where Ken was talking with a very tall man with spiky, improbably white hair. "Ken," I said, stepping over a large coil of cable.

"Mark. Come over here and say hello to Guy."

We were standing in front of the bar: a fat man in Armani, a tall man with blinding white hair, and a lost little bar mitzvah boy.

"Mark Manilow, Guy Fuchs. Guy Fuchs, Mark Manilow." His name, naturally, was pronounced Fucks. He was flaming gay.

"Ken tells me you're going to write our next epic," he said.

"Broken Boner," I said.

"I love it," Guy said. "Don't tell me another word. Just write it and let me make magic."

"He's my number one director. You're starting at the top," Ken said.

"Good place to start," I said.

"Not really. No place to go but down," Ken said.

"Going down's not so bad in this business," Guy said, and we all laughed. Why the hell I was laughing I had no idea.

"Actors on the set," someone yelled, and a man and a woman crossed the saloon and joined our group. They were dressed in Wild West outfits with chaps and boots and vests and spurs. The man was just under six feet tall, trim and fit. He hadn't shaved and his clothes were black, apparently signifying that he was the bad guy. He was in his thirties. The woman was younger, late twenties, and five feet five or so. She was dressed like the sheriff, with a badge and double six-shooters. She had blonde hair and lots of it. I had never seen such beautiful hair. She was pretty, but overly made up for the camera. She had one brown eye and one eye that was sky blue.

"This is Sheriff Dallas Westcott," Ken said. "And this is Long Ron Dong, our horse thief who's about to meet his match. Say hello to our new writer, Mark Manilow. He's the real deal from Hollywood. Wrote a movie for Bruce Willis and Arnold Schwarzenegger."

I shook hands with Long Ron Dong who in an effort to stay in character and be funny at the same time said, "Howdy, *pardner*," and then I shook hands with Dallas.

"You and I will talk later," she said. She held onto my hand for a long time. "We're going to be friends."

"Places, please," said the first assistant director, and Ken moved me to the side, near a saloon table and chairs. There were two director's chairs waiting for us and he sat me down in one and took the other for himself. Guy was fifteen feet away, seated in front of a monitor, wearing headsets, looking at the script. Dallas and Long Ron took their positions at the bar. The director of photography made last-minute lighting measurements. The camera crew went through their preparation checklists. Makeup and hair did touch-ups.

"This is the scene where Dallas finds Ron alone in the saloon. He's the most wanted horse thief in the West, and she's the sheriff who always gets her man. It's the first time they've come face to face. That's funny, right? Coming face to face. You'll love porn. It's a laugh riot all the way to the bank."

"Do you live here, Ken?" I said. It was a somewhat odd question given the circumstances, but *"Are they going to fuck right in front of me?"* got stuck in my throat.

"Bel Air. Randy Newman on one side. Nicolas Cage on the other. I've been trying to get Randy to do my music for years. He won't budge, the goofball. I could make him a fortune in money." On the set, hot now with lights, Long Ron and Dallas were rehearsing their lines. Ken nodded at Guy that the whole thing looked good to him and continued talking. "This is my office. I bought it for two-eight six years ago. It's worth eight and half, maybe eight-seven. The good news is I put nothing down. The better news is the movies pay the mortgage. I made six million bucks getting laid in the hot tub. My kids are going to any college they want. Harvard. Stanford. What a life."

"Mark." I looked up, but they were slating the scene. "Scene forty-two. Take one." The clappers slapped together, and I remembered what a beautiful sound that was. Dallas and Long Ron were totally in character, as if they were really going to act. "Rolling."

Ken sat back in his chair and smiled. At that precise moment, he was probably the happiest man in America. Except, of course, for Long Ron Dong.

14. THERE'S A HARD DICK IN THE HOUSE

"And . . . action," Guy said.

I remember the dialogue, but it was inconsequential. There was Western-sounding lingo about rustling horses and hideouts and hangings, but then Long Ron said, "Maybe you'd like to see what I'm packin'," and Dallas said, "You gonna take me for a ride, cowboy?" and I knew, like everyone else, that the fun was about to begin.

Dallas and Long Ron started kissing at the bar. His hands were all over her. You could hear them slurping and swallowing each other's tongues and then you could hear this: "Take her shirt off, Ron. I want your face in her tits in ten seconds. Nine. Eight. Seven . . ." Guy Fuchs was watching the monitor while periodically glancing up at the action. His voice was the only sound besides Dallas's soft moaning.

Long Ron had her shirt off and perfectly spectacular breasts in the open air in exactly ten seconds. They were unbelievable breasts. The most amazing boobs I had ever seen anywhere at any time.

"Jesus," I said. It was a whisper that slipped out without permission.

Ken nodded. "Only God can make them like that. They don't stick out like whorehouse water balloons. She was born with them. One in a million as far as knockers go. And I've seen a few."

Whorehouse water balloons? I didn't know what the hell whorehouse water balloons were and right now it didn't much matter.

"Close on the tits, please," Guy called out. "Suck, Ron. You've been out on the trail for six months stealing horses. You're very hungry for her tits. Let me see hunger."

The hand-held camera was moved closer to the action. Any closer and the cameraman could have sucked her tits himself. I had the conscious thought that he had the best job in the world. Again, except for Long Ron.

"That's good. Very hot. Take his pants down, Dallas. Don't touch the chaps, just the pants. That's right, sweetheart. You have never wanted to suck a horse thief's cock as much as you want to suck this one now."

What kind of words were these? What kind of sentences were they forming? Dallas removed Long Ron's pants and out fell the largest penis in recorded history. It was as if he had surgically removed the cock of one of his stolen horses and had it transplanted onto his groin.

"Now that's a dick," Ken said.

"Mmmmm," Guy said.

Dallas went to work. Focused and moaning and slurping and sucking like the biggest thing in the universe was Long Ron's dick, which it almost was.

"Camera, please move in. More. That's good. No one in the gang sucks dick like this, Ron. None of the homies can get you hard like the sheriff. This is what you've been waiting for. Let her know, big boy. Let her hear it."

Long Ron made sounds of pleasure, and Dallas kept at it, glancing up at him, making eye contact. Eye contact! They were acting during the blowjob!

"You look hard, Ron. Are you hard?"

Long Ron somehow, I had no idea how, had the presence of mind to nod in such a way that the camera would think the nod was part of the acting, part of the blowjob. It was a brilliant moment for theater of any kind.

"Get her up on the bar, Ron. Take her pants off, and get her pussy nice and wet."

He lifted her like a Russian ballet dancer and sat her on the bar. She was completely naked, and she was perfect. She had the body of a Los Angeles Lakers cheerleader only better, sleeker, fitter, more curves in more of the right places. She was a Goddess and she was spread eagle on the bar, positioned in such a way that the camera could get a full view of her throwing her head back and thrusting her pelvis while Ron licked her vagina, which he did, by the way, with great purpose.

"Makes you wish you were a cowboy, doesn't it?" Ken said.

"Absolutely," I said. It came out of my mouth as a reflex action, like a doctor tap-tap-tapping your knee with his little hammer. No matter how hard you try not to let it, your knee jerks spastically when he hits the spot.

"I need to see your clit, Dallas. Clit, please." Dallas spread her legs, repositioned her ass and her hands and Long Ron's head all in one effortless motion while maintaining a steady stream of erotic racket. I was awestruck.

"That's good, hold that. Lick, Ron, baby, lick her good," Guy said, and then he lifted his eyes from the monitor and addressed Ken and me. "She's got the best clit in the business," he said.

"Bar none," Ken said.

It was surreal. There was a film crew watching them have sex on a fake saloon bar in a Great-Great Room in an Encino mansion in the middle of the day and no one, not one person in the crew, seemed particularly turned on. It might well as well have been an episode of *Friends*. At the craft service table, people were eating bagels and cream cheese.

"Okay, let's keep rolling and move to the table," Guy said.

Like the crew of a nuclear aircraft carrier during war games, grips moved lights on the fly to pre-marked spots on the floor. Camera adjusted accordingly. Hair and make-up moved to the actors. *Holy crap,* I thought, *two seconds ago Dallas Westcott's naked orgasmic ass was on the bar groaning with ecstasy and now her lipstick is being reapplied.*

"Let's go, let's go, let's go, people. There's a hard dick in the house. Let's not waste it," Guy said.

Long Ron was focused on his cock. It was the size of a steel girder. I was terrified of the thing. I can only imagine what Julie's father would have made of it.

At one point, Ron looked over at me and winked. Butt ass naked with the exception of his chaps, his dick stretching all the way to the Santa Monica Pier, the man had the temerity to turn and wink at me. Was he attracted to me? I had heard that many porn stars were bisexual, but I wasn't, was I? Was I giving off vibes I wasn't aware of? He had to be used to people staring at his dick. It could cast a shadow on Pasadena. Maybe that was his way of saying: *"It's okay, Mark. Even I know it's out of this world."*

"All right, here we go, still rolling," Guy said. "Dallas and Ron, I want to see some serious fucking. I want everyone to know why they called it the Wild West. Let's rewrite some history."

Using the table and straight back chairs as props, Dallas and Long Ron began to screw each other's lights out in a way I had never imagined was possible. Position after position after position he would pound into her with the brute force and fury of a cyclone and then seemingly without warning, just when you thought she was blindsided and ready to cry uncle, she would institute a flawless reversal and ride him until I thought his cock would break in half. They were indefatigable! I could feel the ground shaking. They were ten feet in front of me putting on the most impressive physical display of strength and stamina I had ever witnessed. You want ratings? Put this on live network television and one hundred million people would watch.

It wasn't sexual intercourse. It couldn't be defined as either sex or intercourse. It was a mad crazy cross between professional wrestling, *Dancing With The Stars*, and no-rules Rugby. It was sex as competition. Sex to the death.

"Someone's going to get hurt," I said.

"They're professionals," Ken said. "They'll take it right to the edge."

They were groaning with pleasure while Guy Fuchs shouted out instructions that seemed superfluous to me. "Left leg, Dallas. Good. Slow it down, Ron. Long, easy strides. Nice, nice. Pick up the pace, that's fine. Just like that. Do me a favor, cowboy. Grab her left tit, please."

And then Guy stood up and said the following words: "How much longer, Ron?"

"Minute thirty," Long Ron said.

"A minute thirty to what?" I said to Ken.

"Lift off," Ken said.

"Jesus Christ on a crutch," I said. Papa Shelley, my father's father, used to say it all the time. I had never once said it until now. It seemed right. Ken lit a cigar. He was the Red Auerbach of porn.

"Dallas, I need you to have a real one," Guy said. He moved onto the set, out of the shot, but close to his actors. "You have sixty seconds. I'm here for you, honey."

My brain separated from my brain stem and spun inside my head like a gyroscope, throwing off questions at warp speed, questions that raced around my skull like atoms in a super conductor. How could this be happening? How could these two Herculean athletes, after a triple overtime marathon of this magnitude, co-conspire to orgasm at precisely the same second as calculated on the inner stopwatch of a horse thief named Long Ron Dong?

And yet that's exactly what happened. Long Ron and Dallas reached a real and volcanic climax at the same moment, and Guy Fuchs said, "Cut. Print it."

I expected to hear the popping of champagne, like a World Series locker room with Bob Costas interviewing the combatants while being hosed with Moet, but there were more scenes to shoot, and it occurred to me that after sex like that, any celebrating would be anticlimactic, so to speak, for Dallas and Long Ron. Guy viewed the replay on the monitor, conferred with his DP, and said, "Moving on."

15. FEATURE FILMS ARE DEAD

The actors were given white terrycloth bathrobes and made small talk with the crew. Ken leaned toward me, his cigar creating huge wafts of gray smoke. "Twenty-five grand in a shoebox," he said. "And all the pussy you can screw."

"In a shoebox?" I said. This is how I always imagined deals were made. A producer with power and money would make a decision on the set and offer you a job.

"Cash money. What's your answer? I know it's yes, but let me hear you say it."

"Yes." There it was. I had crossed a line I had never considered approaching.

"Beautiful," he said, lifting his great weight out of the director's chair. Almost immediately, assistants who required his opinions, decisions, and directives surrounded him, orbiting like moons around a planet. He swatted them aside and smiled. "See you in a month, kiddo. *Broken Boner's* going to be huge. That's funny, right, a huge broken boner? What a laugh riot. You'll need a name. I'm thinking Dick Dental; it's got a ring to it." Then he vanished in a whirlpool of pornographic policy making.

Dick Dental. Ken had christened me, and there was no going back. I sat in the chair and stared at the saloon. I couldn't stop thinking about what I had just witnessed. It was like a fantastical collision of two trains traveling at great speeds in opposite directions on the same track. You know it's wrong to watch, but you can't turn away.

Something compels you to wait it out, to witness the thunderous crashing and see if survivors crawl from the wreckage. NASCAR is porn without the sex. So is boxing. We need a national referendum to redefine our positions on these topics. *We should let Ken have a crack at them*, I thought. *He has a way with words.*

"You ready, Mark?" It was Trisha. Her voice was cold water in my face.

"Ready."

She escorted me to the front door. I found out she was a UCLA Film School graduate. "There's no good work," she said. "Feature films are dead." Then she handed me a shoebox. "Twelve thousand five hundred. You get the other half when you deliver the script." She smiled and shut the door.

The afternoon Encino sun was hot and bright. As I crossed the Parisian Café entrance courtyard to my car, I finally understood its purpose. This was where visitors, including me, had to leave our innocence before entering Ken's playhouse. All were free to retrieve it on the way out, but I couldn't recognize mine anymore, so I resigned to leave it at 1415 DeShays Street and live the rest of my life without it.

As I opened my car door, I heard a voice. "Mark, wait." It was Dallas Westcott. She was still in her terrycloth bathrobe. She was barefoot. She crossed the courtyard and came right up to me. She smelled like sex and coconut oil body lotion, and I nearly passed out at her proximity. "What did you think?" she said.

What is the appropriate response when the hottest porn star in the universe, the very one you've just seen fuck the living daylights out of a notorious horse thief, inquires as to your opinion of her performance? She had washed off the stage make-up and her hair was pulled back in a casual ponytail. Her robe was loosely tied and I could almost see down the open top. For the first time since the camera started rolling, she was sexy as hell. "Amazing," I said.

"Thanks. I'm taking a workshop with Colonel Bill Curry. I think it's starting to pay off."

I paused to let the sentence sink in. Colonel Bill Curry was a Hollywood acting coach of bizarre renown. He had been a Denver, Colorado, clinical psychologist with a large private practice specializing in owner-pet therapy, but was summarily drummed out of the business for utilizing off-the-wall techniques to create harmony in the relationships of his clients and their dogs, cats, birds, reptiles, and fish. Spontaneous public nudity was a recurring theme for Dr. Curry as was sexual role-playing, ingesting pharmaceuticals, unusually loud singing, and excessively suggestive dancing.

He was on and off the American Medical Association radar when on one occasion he utilized all his systems and methods at once with a librarian, her German shepherd, a telephone salesman, and his parrot in the main concourse of the Denver Airport. When the judge decreed that Curry's license was null and void forever on any planet in any solar system, the psychologist legally changed his name to Colonel Bill and rededicated himself to improving the human condition through his manic modus operandi.

The question was: Where could he find a large pool of people insecure enough to consistently need and engage his special services? What subset of humankind had the deepest, most powerful, most subconscious, and never-ending desire for attention, approval, and guidance at any cost? The answer was actors. So he moved to Hollywood, ran an ad in the trades, and was back in business within weeks.

It was her acting that Dallas was asking about, the quality of her acting. Not the sex, the acting. "It really is," I said. "Paying off big time."

She moved closer to me and slipped her hand in my pants pocket. "That's my hand in your pocket. I'm giving you my card. I want you to call me. I want to talk to you about movies and acting. Will you call me, Mark?"

Her hand was rubbing around ever so gently down there in my pocket. My reaction was entirely palpable and reasonable too, under the circumstances. "Yes," I said.

"Good." She removed her hand, smiled up into my eyes, then reached up and kissed me on the cheek. "I can't wait."

She smiled again and then turned and walked back to the house, giving me one last anticipatory look over her shoulder before disappearing inside. The air where she had been standing still smelled like coconut oil. I breathed it in and then fished her card out of my pocket. It was sky blue and had *Dallas Westcott Porn Star* printed on one side and her phone number printed on the other. I flipped it over and over a few times to make sure it was real. Was it my imagination or did it smell like coconut oil? I climbed into my Mustang, put the shoebox on the passenger seat, and turned the engine. Before I pulled out, I caught sight of the sky-blue Jag's license plate. DWPS. Dallas Westcott Porn Star.

I drove slowly through the private park to the huge teak doors that opened to facilitate my exit. As I rolled through them, the No Soliciting sign by the front gate keypad passed by me at eye level. My final thought was this: Ken Moynihan must be the funniest man in America. Here at 1415 DeShays Street, porn people are always welcome, but sellers of vacuums or hairbrushes or bibles or cosmetics are told to take a hike. Unless Mary Kay wants to bend over a couch, there's no way she's getting past these gates.

16. LEAVE ME A MESSAGE AND SOMETHING GOOD WILL HAPPEN

Somewhere around the time Julie left me, my head began to hurt. It was a dull throbbing pressure that came and went on its own volition and would appear in whichever of the cerebral sections suited its fancy. I didn't want to see the doctor. Who does for brain-related issues? It's not like the neurology ward is Good News Central. The chances of a neurologist saying *"Mark, congratulations. We discovered an entire lobe of untapped information. You now speak Mandarin and play the bassoon. Don't be surprised if you start writing sonnets or inventing organic fuels"* is remote. More often than not, the news is bad or worse than bad, but I had never had a concussive event and brain tumors were a non-factor in my genetic history. I knew I had to go if for no other reason than to confirm that it was nothing serious.

When I was in Toronto for the filming of *Full Force*, I made an appointment with a Canadian doctor and went in for an examination. The doctor looked in my eyes and ears and up my nose, had me perform a series of touching and balancing exercises, drew my blood and took a CAT scan of my brain.

Most of what he said I don't recall because his sentences sounded like this: "Mark, the bulbous cerebral cortex is composed of convoluted grey matter internally supported by deep brain white matter. The two hemispheres of the brain are separated by a prominent central fissure and connect to each other at the corpus callosum. A fully developed cerebellum is found at the back of the brain. Brain stem structures are almost completely enveloped by the cerebellum and telencephalon, with the medulla oblongata projecting through the foramen magnum to merge with the spinal cord." If I had listened to him long enough, I would have had a concussive event as a result of smashing my head against the wall.

But my CAT scan was clear, my balance was fine, and my blood work was normal, so he sent me home. There was a ninety-nine point nine percent chance that what I was experiencing was stress related, he said. Once this emotional transition had passed, the sensation of pressure in my head would disappear.

The problem was that the emotional transition didn't pass. The pressure in my head kept pace with the pressure in my life, ebbing and flowing as determined by phases of the moon, journeys to Paramus, and letters from the Amazon.

I went to two more doctors in Los Angeles who re-confirmed and re-re-confirmed that there was nothing clinically wrong with my head, that my CAT scan was clear and that it was emotionally based stress that was causing the symptoms. They each sent me home with a prescription to buy a dog or tropical fish.

I chose the fish and spent hours looking at them. For a while, their mindless circles around the tank were soothing to me. Even my life was better than theirs. But for the past week, these expensive fish were nothing but a reminder of the stress they were intended to relieve because the reason I was spending my waking hours staring at them was that I couldn't write *Broken Boner*. I was completely blocked. I couldn't write porn to save my life.

Story, character, dialogue, rhythm, and tone were spirits in the night. I couldn't find them. Who was the patient? What kind of accident would land him in the hospital in a full body cast except for the hole at his dick, which jutted out like a mainmast and the holes at his mouth, eyes, and nose? Who was the doctor who diagnosed his condition and recommended such a peculiar cast and such remarkable traction? Who designed and built the erector set that would eventually allow this patient to be hoisted around in all the various Kama Sutra positions? How could the patient survive the movement without excruciating pain? What kind of nurse would have sex with a man in a full body cast? And to make a threesome out of it? Who were these medical professionals? How did they arrive at this moment in time? What were their names? What were their hobbies? Who were their medical center associates, and did they know about the hospital escapades? How could anyone get away with this? Wouldn't someone hear the orgy hullabaloo? A wandering janitor? The hospital Chaplain on late-night rounds of mercy? A clown visiting the children's ward? Would all of them end up entangled in sexually contorted positions, riding the faceless man in the full body cast with a cock the size of Idaho? My mind lurched this way and that like a skiff in a storm.

If I couldn't write a story in which the only reality is the unreal sex, then I was even lower than the writers who could. I had to deliver or all was lost. I had been paid. I had taken the money in the shoebox, which theoretically should have given me the freedom to create but instead had trapped me in a no-name hospital in a no-place city with no-scruples doctors and no-morals nurses and patients with life-threatening injuries that could fuck for hours and predict their moment of orgasm to the second. I couldn't get off the dime. I had to find help. But who could I call that would understand the delicacy of my situation? Who had knowledge of superhuman sex, an appreciation of filmmaking, and real-life screenplay exposure? Who would know that I was only dabbling in porn, that my day job was professional screenwriting, and that my career was only on hold, not over and out and so would proceed with subtlety and discretion?

Taped to the glass of my fish tank was the business card of Dallas Westcott. I put it there for inspiration, though the memory of her banging Long Ron Dong was more jarring than arousing. She had asked me to call her. She had said, beside the Courtyard of Lost Innocence, that she wanted to discuss movies and acting. Of course, she had said these things while wearing a tiny terrycloth bathrobe with her hand massaging my package, but she had said them nonetheless.

It was crazy, and I knew it. I was a Little Leaguer from Paramus, New Jersey. I had no business calling an international porn queen and inviting her over to my house to talk about the script I was writing for her to star in. That's not how I was raised. That wasn't my life. I couldn't do it. I wouldn't do it. I took her card off the fish tank with the intent of tossing it in the trash. It still smelled like sex and coconut oil.

I picked up the phone and dialed the number.

"Hi, this is Dallas. If you have this number, you're somebody special. Leave me a message and something good will happen."

"Dallas, it's Mark Manilow. I met you at Ken's place in Encino. I watched you and Long Ron, uh, play a scene in the saloon. I'm the one writing *Broken Boner*. You said you wanted me to call you so we could talk about movies, so here I am calling you. I mean, obviously I'm calling you, it's me leaving this message." It got worse from there. After rambling on about professionalism in the porn industry, inquiring as to how she and her co-stars stay in top physical condition, and wondering aloud if she'd ever performed with Ken's horses, I left her my contact information—phone, address, email, cell, fax, social security number, Writers' Guild ID, birthday, high school batting average, SAT scores, favorite food, mother's maiden name, and plenty of other unnecessary information in a ninth-grade voice still pushing through puberty. I hung up knowing she'd listen to the message and regret forever her hand in my pants pocket.

That night, I had a horrendous dream. I was nominated for an Oscar for Best Original Screenplay for *Full Force* despite the fact no one had ever seen it. Seated at my table was Phil wearing a sandwich board that said *Phone Book, The Movie*, Bela, who was missing both arms and was being fed by the lion from the *Wizard of Oz*, Andrew Leibowitz, my father's partner in orthodontics, and the fashion model from the magazine Julie was looking at when I first met her at the Farmer's Market on Fairfax. The model was wearing the same see-through blouse with no buttons that she had on in the photograph that brought Julie and me together. Ken Moynihan was the emcee.

He had a bell that he rang as an exclamation mark at the end of every sentence. I was one of the nominees; Gibby was the other. His family was seated at the next table wearing Paramus Police uniforms. He was nominated for *Officer Down*. Ken announced my name as the winner, but not for *Full Force*. Instead, I had won the Oscar for *Broken Boner*. As I walked to the stage, everyone in the audience began to strip naked and have sex except for Gibby's table, where everyone had changed into horse thief clothes and were firing six-shooters in the air with reckless abandon. Long Ron Dong appeared nude in a spotlight and sang "Here She Comes, Miss America." Ken rang the bell over and over while he handed me my Oscar, which was a living, breathing statuette of Dallas Westcott wearing a terry cloth robe and waving her teeny-tiny business card in my face. And then I was in a full body cast on a gurney, and Trisha was rolling me through the massive orgy, saying, "Feature films are dead." People shook my dick to congratulate me as I went by, and Ken kept ringing his bell, ding-dong, ding-dong, ding-dong...

I sat up in bed, a little panicked and a little out of breath, and heard my doorbell ringing. It was past midnight. I went to the front door and looked through the peephole. Dallas Westcott was waiting for me.

17. I WANT TO BE AN ACTRESS

"One minute," I said. I pulled on a pair of jeans and a Steely Dan T-shirt and opened the door.

"I love Steely Dan," she said.

"Me too," I said. And those were the only words I could find. She was wearing skin-tight black leather pants and a black sweater. Her hair was down around her shoulders, and her lips were just the smallest bit pink, her cheeks just gently rouged.

"You called me," she said.

"I know."

"It's not too late, is it? I'm not good with time."

"No, it's fine. I wasn't doing anything."

"You were sleeping."

"Except that, yes."

Then we stood there. *How is it possible*, I thought, *for someone to smell that good in the middle of the night?* Sex and coconut oil. If I lived to be a hundred years old, I would never get over that smell.

"This is a very nice front door area."

"Thank you. I get a lot of use out of it." I winced, though I suspected there weren't many men who would have done better.

"You have fish." She gestured over my shoulder at the tank in my living room.

I turned to look as if I had never seen them before, as if the tank were a complete surprise. "I have fish," I said.

When I turned back, she had taken a step toward me and was very close. I'm sure she could hear my heart beating.

"Mark. You should invite me in."

"I know. Want to come in?"

I gave her a midnight tour of my house, which took us through the living room, into the dining room, into the kitchen, through the glass sliders onto the back deck, and past the Jacuzzi to the rail overlooking the pitch-black canyon. We stood by the rail, listening to the Coldwater Canyon night.

"I want to be an actress."

"You are an actress."

"Thanks, Mark. I knew I liked you." And then she put her arms around my neck and we kissed, me and Dallas Westcott, kissing on my back deck like I wasn't a kid from New Jersey and she wasn't an international porn star. I put my arms around her waist.

The kiss ended, and she smiled. "That was nice. I like how you kiss me."

"I'm too nervous to know what I'm doing."

"Why are you nervous?"

"Because I think you're going to ask if my bedroom is part of the tour."

"Is it?"

"Yes. And I think we may have sex in there."

"Is that why you're nervous?"

"I'm not a horse thief. I'm just normal."

She put her finger on my lips and said, "That's not real. Most women don't want to be pounded with a sledgehammer until they can't walk. Porn is about what men like."

"What do you like?"

"I like normal."

The tour continued to my bedroom where Dallas Westcott re-defined normal for me until five fifteen in the morning.

We had coffee and toast on the back deck and watched the sun rise over the canyon. I asked her about her life. She was from Garden City, Michigan, a blue-collar suburb of Detroit. Her father worked in a warehouse packaging auto repair tools for shipment across the continent. Her mother answered phones for a roofing company. She had two older brothers. The younger of the two was a professional security guard; the older one rebuilt transmissions. No one in her family went to college, but all of them were comfortable beneath the hood of a car, even her mother, and happy to spend five hours there on a Saturday or Sunday, particularly if there was a case of cold beer and a Tigers game on the radio. She was an under-achieving student. Numbers were her weakness. She was a middle school cheerleader, she said, because she liked wearing the very short skirt that showed off her legs. Besides that, her childhood memories were dim and faded with a vague sense of dissatisfaction and claustrophobia.

As she grew older, boys liked her, and she received a ton of attention. In her junior year of high school, she discovered the drama club. Acting was a revelation. On the stage she could be anyone from anywhere but *Garbage City*, as she called her hometown. She wanted to be an actress and announced it at dinner. She wanted to be bigger than a greasy garage weekend listening to Bob Seeger, bigger than this cold, gray town in the shadow of Dearborn, bigger, even, than Detroit. Her dreams were belittled and dismissed out of hand. She was told to marry a master mechanic, buy a house down the street, and fill it with grandkids. And she should stop talking so much. She vowed to herself that some day she would show them.

One night, after too many shots of peppermint schnapps, she entered a wet T-shirt contest at a bar on Telegraph Road and won. A representative for a lingerie company was in the crowd, and she was discovered. Her modeling career took her to LA, where one day she was posing in bikinis, one day she was posing nude, one day she was posing nude with men in suggestive positions, and one day she was having sex on camera.

Her films were wildly popular. She was a porn star with a sky-blue Jaguar and fans around the globe. She could talk all she wanted to anyone except her family, who had disowned her upon seeing her first film, *Car Trouble*, in which she played a helpless woman with a broken down vehicle that gets towed to a garage with three horny mechanics. There was no part of the car that she didn't have sex on. Her family was mortified. It was a Chevy in the film.

"What's your real name?" I said.

"I can't tell you."

"Why not?"

"When I entered the wet T-shirt contest, I used the name Dallas Westcott, and I won and everything good happened. It would be bad luck to let anyone know my real name."

"You're superstitious?"

"A little."

I told her I was struggling with *Broken Boner* and asked if she would help get me going. We talked about porn films and porn actors and porn producers and porn directors. We talked about the man in the body cast and the nurse who first decides to fix his broken boner. We talked about the doctor who walks in on them and joins in the fun, and that's the word—*fun*—I was missing.

"Look, no one thinks this is real sex. It's supposed to be hot and bothered and fun more than anything else," she said.

Fun more than anything else. I could do that. I had written plenty of fun movies. Now I would write one with sex in it. My mind was already solidifying a storyline. Characters and dialogue were forming in my subconscious. There was rhythm to it now, and a tone of voice.

"You helped me a lot," I said.

She snuggled up to me and kissed my neck. "I'm glad," she said. "Now you can help me."

"I will. What can I do? Name it. The world is your oyster."

"Write me a movie. A real movie, not a porno. I want to be an actress who doesn't have sex on screen. I want you to write me a Hollywood movie."

"You mean just make one up and write it for you?"

"Yes, and then raise the money and produce it." She swung her leg over my lap and was straddling me, kissing me, running her hands through my hair. I was kissing her back, and she was still talking. "I know you can do it, Mark. I believe in you. I knew when I met you. I had a feeling. And now it's true. Say yes. We'll do it together. We'll be a team. Say yes, baby. Say yes . . ."

What was happening between my legs was very different than what was happening between my ears. My brain was telling me that of all the impossible undertakings in the world, negotiating peace in the Middle East, for instance, or putting hot lava back into a volcano, writing and producing a legitimate feature film for Dallas Westcott was at the top of the list. Any assentation or acquiescence on my part would be misleading at best.

"Yes," I said. "Of course I will."

We had sex again, right there on my back deck, where neighbors on their decks across the canyon could catch a free show if they were so inclined, then Dallas put on her clothes, hopped in her Jag, and drove off.

Los Angeles is the funniest place to live on Earth. Not funny ha-ha funny, funny are-you-fucking-kidding-me funny. How do I know? I had just committed to writing and producing a legitimate Hollywood feature for Dallas Westcott in exchange for sex.

18. MARCUS WELBY IS TOO SMART FOR PORN?

The script was good. I liked the characters. There was Nurse Brittany from Philadelphia, with a wicked sense of humor and an insatiable desire to help her patients. There was Dr. Longfellow from Scarsdale, an expert in groinal medicine, both Eastern and Western, including massage and sex therapy. And then there was the patient, a mysterious man known only as Patterson. What a crew! There was a subtle underlying humor to the piece, a sort of tongue-in-cheek homage to television medical dramas throughout the years. And there was sex. Nurse on patient, nurse on doctor, nurse on nurse, patient on nurse on nurse, nurse on doctor on nurse on patient, and so on.

It wasn't as easy as I thought it would be to write the sex scenes. I needed guidance from Dallas to fully understand the intricacies of the various and sundry positions. She insisted on tutoring me and did so several times daily. Whereas sex with Julie felt good in my heart, sex with Dallas felt good in my head. I was completely cognizant of her body and my body and all our tangled undulations. It was intellectually as well as physically explosive sex, immensely satisfying to think about afterwards. It was sex with a worldwide porn star for whom I would write a real movie when the porn movie I was already writing for her was complete. Despite the reality of it, it was eminently unreal to me in a whirling, swirling, out-of-body sort of way, and so my heart sat on the sidelines much of the time. Her heart was in Hollywood. But we were having fun, and fun is porn, and the script was done in three weeks.

I emailed *Broken Boner* to Ken and waited. I imagined my future and was surprisingly pleased. I would write a dozen of these things, and then Ken would let me direct—which is every writer's dream, whether or not they admit it, even in porn. I had watched Guy Fuchs direct a saloon scene and was confident that I could match his skill and passion. I would make new friends, porn friends, who would come for dinner at my house, and we would listen to Tom Waits and Dr. John and Ray Charles and eat sashimi and drink beer and watch our movies and laugh and then have giant orgies that went all weekend. I would explain the new course of my life to my parents who would be stunned to silence but would also see how happy I was, how my Hollywood training had actually been preparing me to write and direct a new breed of porn films, and realize that I was finally a success. There would be awards, and my sister and her husband would fly in from New York to share them with me. Poor Phil would still be trying to sell me on his phone book idea, but I would be beyond that now. Leslie would have to eat her words because my professional sexual marathons would have chiseled my body to a rock-hard-writing-directing-porn-star-fucking-award-winning-shit-eating-grin-little-brother-with-a-path-of-his-own. Life could be better than that, I suppose, but it could also be worse. You take the road your car is on; that's the answer.

Ken called me the next day. The next day! "Mark. Ken Moynihan. I read the script."

This is why he was rich. He didn't waste time, money, or words. It wasn't unusual for a writer to wait four months for a Hollywood producer to read their script. I resolved right then and there to keep this porn gig quiet. Half the writers in the Guild would sign up for porn if they knew their scripts would be read in a day and cash money would be handed over in a shoebox. "What did you think?" I said. In my mind, I had narrowed his responses to: *"If I had found you ten years ago, I'd be even richer than I am now"* or *"Once in a lifetime script from a once in a lifetime writer"* or *"Hottest thing I ever read"* or *"Rent your tux, kiddo, you're going a win your first porn award."*

It felt wonderful to feel wonderful.

"Good try is what I think. It doesn't work the way it should. We're going to have to rewrite you."

My brain sent an urgent message to my mouth saying that there had been a major miscommunication received by my ears and I was to immediately inquire again. "It doesn't work?" I said.

"Not the way I want it to."

"What's wrong with it?"

"It's too smart. You can't think about porn. You just watch it."

"It's not too smart. I intentionally wrote it so it wouldn't be too smart."

"You can't help yourself. First thing you see is Welby Hospital. Right off the bat you got us thinking, "Hey, Marcus Welby, I remember him."

"Marcus Welby is too smart for porn?"

"He might as well be Einstein. It's all downhill from there."

"I'll do another draft. I'll fix it."

"No you won't. You'll make it smarter. Now you'll be thinking about thinking about not thinking, which is worse than thinking about not thinking, which is how the thing reads now. See what I'm saying? It takes twice the thinking not to think. That's two times more thinking than porn can handle. You think with your brain, Mark. Can't have that in porn. Have to avoid the brain altogether. That's the only way it works. It's a cock-driven medium. You have to think with your schlong."

"I can do that."

"I don't think so. Your pecker's not leading the pack. Some people have it, some don't. Guy Fuchs will do the rewrites. I'm sorry, Mark. I'll send somebody with the rest of your shoebox. You'll get the writing credit; so don't sweat that. Send me the name you want to use. I still like Dick Dental, but I need it in writing. You're just not a porn guy, kiddo. Sorry to have to be the one to tell you."

And then he hung up.

There's nothing colder than pure incredulity. I stood there frozen in it for a good long while before I thawed enough to sit on the couch and look at the fish. My heart was beating, and I was breathing, but all other Manilow mental and physical faculties were suspended in thick amber goo.

19. TANGO JOE

I sat there long enough for it to get dark and then drove out into the Valley. I was headed to Foster's, a bar that catered to depression, frustration, disappointment, and anger and so was a favorite haunt of Hollywood filmmakers. Located in a deadbeat strip mall in Canoga Park, it was there that I had drunk rum and cokes for six hours after being informed by the lying dirtbag producer of Full Force that the film was forever shelved.

I parked in the sad and sagging strip mall and headed for Foster's dirty stucco exterior. The front door was standard issue glass with stained and faded vertical blinds to prohibit low-rent shoppers from staring at the feckless filmmakers drowning their sorrows at the bar as they passed by on their way to the Mexican consignment shop or the vacuum repair store or the Chinese take-out place or the sleazy check cashing joint. There were several cars parked in the vicinity of the bar, including some upscale European sedans. There's no bank account big enough to hold back bitterness and despair if they have a mind to come in. *Misery isn't picky*, I thought.

The bar was dark and musty, no small feat in the bone-dry air of LA. *There must be a special setting on the air conditioner*, I thought, *high, low, dank*. I sat on a stool, and the bartender crossed to me. It wasn't Foster. There was no Foster anymore. He was a sitcom director who lost his sense of humor, his job, his agent, his house, and his mind. He opened the bar, worked it until his resentment ran dry, sold it to a director of photography who had developed inoperable cataracts, and moved to New Zealand, where it was rumored that he was now a shepherd who had possibly married one of his sheep. In headier times, there could be a black comedy in there somewhere.

"Rum and Coke," I said.

"No Coke," the bartender said. "Dr. Pepper okay?"

"Big glass," I said.

I lined up my empty big glasses as a new measure of time. I had been here five and one half glasses when someone sat beside me.

"Hey *mon*," he said like a Rastafarian. "How's the acid? You tripping the light fantastic?" He was drinking from a glass bigger than mine, and as he sat down the bartender filled it to the top with Wild Turkey. He put his hand out and said (in his normal voice), "Joe Hudson. I never forget a writer. Only their names."

I shook his hand. He looked as wasted as I felt. I'm certain he thought the same of me. "Mark Manilow."

He was of indeterminate heritage. European, Middle Eastern, and Asian bloodlines had co-mingled over the centuries, and Joe Hudson was the result. He was wearing a black-as-night, tight-fitting Zoot suit with a gorgeous black fedora and impenetrable black sunglasses. His hair was long and as black as his clothes. He was forty years old, thin and wiry, not thin and puny. His teeth were gleaming white and straight and smooth as Chiclets. "I remember you, too," I said. "You're a TV movie producer."

"Not anymore. That Joe Hudson's dead."

He had been a successful producer of television movies (Movies of the Week) when the major networks (CBS, NBC, ABC) were stamping them out like Fords in a factory before Les Moonves, Grand Marshall of CBS, changed the landscape, declared Long Form bad business for his stockholders, and shut down the assembly line. The other networks followed suit, closing their movie departments, or carving them hollow, leaving only Lifetime, Showtime, Turner, HBO, and a handful of others to fill the enormous gap. It was too massive a maw.

Thousands of people lost their livelihoods. Producers and directors and writers and actors and agents and managers and painters and carpenters and caterers and props and makeup and hair and sound and camera, not to mention network executives and all their marketing and support staff down the line, were all pink-slipped and sent scrambling for work. But there was too much overflow. Features, hour drama, and other venues couldn't pick up the slack. Only the very lucky survived.

Producers like Joe were as much to blame as Moonves and the executives. Together they had driven up the budgets of the movies to a price-point where the advertising dollars generated during their timeslot couldn't cover the cost of the films or left minimal bottom line bucks when they could. Big name actors were happy to take the exorbitant paydays but were shortsighted in their enthusiasm. The innate business structure of Long Form itself couldn't support the combined weight of the illogical network need for stars over story, the producers' greed for fabulous foreign sales, and the actors' and agents' steep ransom demands.

To try and make up the difference, time was shaved off the movies and sold for more ads. Television films that were once a click over ninety minutes were truncated to eighty minutes. This short-changing neutered their impact, made them less emotionally engaging, and tuned the audience out.

Bigger name stars with quotes through the roof were deemed the rational response. But no actor anywhere can save a half-told tale, one with clipped heartstrings and short-sheeted plotlines. Ratings sank like the *Bismarck*, and the sad cycle fed on itself until the business fell down dead. (Moonves wasn't wrong.) A handful of bloated and lumbering event-based movies for television and ridiculously low-budget films for cable were all that remained. Only a few deep-pocket producers had the desire and wherewithal to keep going. Guys like Joe Hudson were road kill.

He explained all this to me while drinking most of the tall glass of Wild Turkey. He took the final three fingers as a shot, downed it without losing his hat and then turned to me because there was simply no one else left to turn to. "It's like I was swimming in a pool, *mon*," he said. "The television movie pool. And every year the water goes down. The water goes down every year, but without fail, every year, somebody slips a hose in there and fills the thing back up. Up to the rim with Brim. So now the water's going down and then down and then down and I keep waiting for the hose until finally I'm standing on the bottom and can't reach the ladder to get out. It never occurs to me that they're draining the pool."

I had pitched him a true story I read in the newspaper about a grandfather in England who became a bank robber to raise money for his granddaughter's optic nerve surgery, then went on to rob more banks to help other sick children in need. The whole time he's dealing with his wife's senility and the evil Rest Home nurse, who suspects that something is awry with Grandpa's late night forays into London. There was a woman cop who broke the case, but kept it quiet and let the old guy go after he promised not to hit any more banks. He moved to Dover and held up jewelry stores.

The meeting was at Joe's office on Santa Monica Boulevard across the street from the ocean. It wasn't so much an office as it was The Museum of Joe. Framed photographs of him covered literally every inch of wall space: Joe running with the bulls in Spain; Joe deep sea diving with Great White Sharks off the Australian coast; Joe climbing mountains; Joe driving racecars; Joe skydiving; Joe hang gliding; Joe sail surfing; Joe big game hunting; Joe in an exploration submarine at the bottom of the ocean; Joe on the deck of a nuclear aircraft carrier; Joe on the set or out on the town with dozens and dozens of television movie actors—Peter Strauss, Richard Thomas, Gerald Mc-Craney, Jo Beth Williams, David Hasselhoff, Kellie Martin, Michael J. Fox, Ellen Burstyn, Pam Dawber, Valerie Bertinelli.

Most every television movie actor had at some point in time posed for a photo with Joe Hudson, who always wore black from head to toe. There were framed posters of his television movies signed by their casts and crews. And, finally, there were endless pictures of Joe dancing. He was a world-class ballroom dancer, a competitive dancer with awards and medals and certificates, all framed and hanging so dense and close and tight to his other memories and achievements that the walls themselves had disappeared.

And now the office had disappeared too, he said. He had lost it in the fallout. He had lost his over-mortgaged mansion in Brentwood, his over-mortgaged beach house in Carpenteria, his Bentley, his Harley, his Cessna, and his polo horses. He was living on a friend's tugboat down in San Pedro. All his meetings were in restaurants and bars. Technically, our sitting together could be considered a meeting. I made a mental note to keep the receipt for my rum and Dr. Peppers so I could take them off my taxes. The note slipped out of my head in twelve seconds and was replaced by Julie.

It was when I was falling in love with her that I met with Joe. She had sent me off to the Santa Monica meeting chock-a-block with confidence. I'm a feature writer, I had told her, and had no intention of working in TV. I didn't know how to pitch a television movie. How does anyone pitch a story with commercial breaks for Pete's sake? *"Work is work,"* she told me. *"Writing is writing, and work is work. It's just one project, and if you sell it and write it, it will be the best thing on TV all year."* And then she kissed me so that I would feel all the love and pride that she felt for me. She loved the way I told stories, laughed at the jokes, and cried at the sad parts. I was her magician. I knew from the beginning how lucky I was to have her and knowing that made the pain of losing her much sharper, more debilitating. We get one great love in our lives—and mine was over. Bleak prospects for the future and insurmountable sadness are the terrible by-products of a busted marriage. Maybe that's not always true, but that's how it felt to me in Foster's. I ordered another drink.

Joe remembered me from the bank-robbing-grandpa pitch and said he wished he'd bought the project at the time. "Where are all the good stories?" he said.

"Not in Hollywood," I said.

"Independent film is where the action is now," he said, and he held up his glass as if offering a wedding toast. "Television is a graveyard." There was a handgun in his waistband. As if my life wasn't surreal enough, here was Tango Joe with a pistol.

I held up my glass too. "Features are dead."

We drank to each other's sorry pronouncements. I was exceptionally drunk and feeling angry at the entertainment industry. The rum had made me belligerent, like the pirate on the bottle. What had we figured out at the dinner table in Paramus? Five good films out of millions of ideas? I couldn't get arrested, and the theaters were filled with mediocre comic books and thrill rides and sophomoric jokes. I had written some great scripts, made up a hundred terrific stories. That I was drowning in the Hollywood rip tide was Hollywood's fault, not mine. The town was broken, not me. I wanted to say something profound, something that would shake Foster's like an earthquake and send ripples and aftershocks all across LA, something that would right the Hollywood ship and jumpstart my dying career.

"I could make a better movie out of the phone book than the crap they put out there," I said. It was official. I was a drunken idiot.

"You think so?"

"I know so. It's the phone book. It's all in there. White pages, yellow pages, every person, every business, every product, every story in America is in the phone book. Let your fingers do the walking. That's what I always say." I never said anything remotely like that. I didn't believe a word of it anymore now than I did when Phil said it. I made another mental note: never drink rum and Dr. Pepper again.

I lost that note too and ordered another one, and Joe ordered another Wild Turkey, and we shared war stories. At some point he was singing about crocodiles and lining up bullets on the bar. Certainly his name wasn't Hudson and probably not even Joe. He was an LA original. Unique to Hollywood. There were no Joe Hudsons, for instance, walking the streets of Pittsburg or Charlotte or Phoenix or Tampa. Only Los Angeles. We said goodnight in the parking lot. I have no memory of driving home.

It was a beautiful night, even if it was spinning. I stumbled to the back deck and laid down on the chaise where Dallas Westcott and I had had sex and talked about her prospects for a legitimate acting career. I would never hear from her again, and I didn't care. I closed my eyes and dreamed of my wife.

PART II
ELEPHANTS IN UTAH

20. ANY CRAZY THING IN THE WORLD

A rum hangover under any circumstances is a bad business, but when mixed with Dr. Pepper, the stomach reacts with confusion followed by discontent followed by vengeance. My head hurt too, though not from the alcohol. The stress-induced, vise-like pressure had recently returned, and though I knew my CAT scan was clean, I wanted the pressure to go away. Like all screenwriters, I kept an extra-large bottle of extra-strength headache pills in my top desk drawer and was reaching for them when I came upon the business card of Dr. Alvin Yee.

On my way to LAX, to fly to Toronto and witness the production of *Full Force*, I spotted Yee's card on the community bulletin board at the Starbucks on Ventura Boulevard in Studio City. It said he was a "New Age Neural Pain Management Professional." Whatever that meant, I couldn't tell you, and I knew that calling him was a ridiculous course of action since he was practicing a medicine I had never heard of and was referred by no one I knew.

Still, neural pain management was what I needed, and Los Angeles was the capital of New Age everything. Who's to say Dr. Yee wasn't the leading New Age Neural Pain Management Professional in the world? Then again, who's to say he wasn't the only one? Playing out both sides of the discussion in Starbucks with coffee so close at hand made my head hurt worse. And I had a plane to catch, so I took his card, went to Canada for *Full Force*, saw the neurologist there, came back to LA and saw two more, was told to relax, had sex with Dallas Westcott, got loaded at Foster's with Tango Joe, woke up with a headache, and discovered Yee's card anew in my desk drawer.

I took three headache pills and reached for the phone to dial Yee's number, but it rang as I put my hand on it.

"Hello."

"Hey, *mon*. You still among the living?" It was Joe.

"Still living, Joe. What are you up to?"

"I'm parked outside, *mon*."

"Outside where?"

"Your house, *mon*. I'm in your driveway. Are you on drugs?"

I don't know what was stranger, having a conversation with Joe's Rasta voice or knowing I was having that conversation while he was parked in front of my house. "Why are you in my driveway?"

"Because we have a meeting."

"What meeting?"

"Get dressed. We gots to boogie."

"Do people still say we gots to boogie?"

"It's the rum. That's your ticket to the future. Don't miss the bus. Your brother Joe's the one who knows."

The problem was that it's hard to read Tango Joe, partly because he's an outrageous, exotic bird—rare and endangered, colorful and squawking—and partly because you can't judge how seriously to take him. Ignore him and you run the risk of missing something. What, you can't say, but something.

His power of persuasion is oddly subtle and surprisingly effective. It shouldn't work, but it does. You tell yourself you're not going with him, that it's crazy to go anywhere with him, but as soon as you open your trap to protest, his hook is embedded in the roof of your mouth, and you can feel him reeling you in. You can't remove the hook, and a part of you doesn't want to.

It's his unpredictability that finishes you off, the palpable sense that any crazy thing in the world could happen to Joe, and if you're along for the ride, could happen to you too. You can't help but like him, that's the other problem. "Give me ten minutes," I said.

21. STRONG ANSWERS AREN'T NECESSARILY GOOD ANSWERS

He was wearing a black silk shirt with black slacks, low black boots, black cowboy hat and black aviator shades. There was no gun in his waistband. He was driving a Mercedes convertible, and the top was down. It was a spectacular day.

"Where are we going, Joe?" I said as he turned the Benz onto the 101 North, which actually runs west through the Valley before bending to the right at Calabasas.

"Santa Barbara. Montecito, actually," Joe said.

Santa Barbara is probably the most wonderful place to live in the United States, possibly the world. It is oddly set on the California coast in the sense that it is facing the Pacific Ocean from the north, not the east, and so is looking south at it, and not west.

The mountains here run east-west, the only range in America that doesn't run north-south, and rise practically right from the beach, which is soft and gentle and lined with palm trees. But not only palm trees. Because of its particular latitudes and longitudes and some strange confluences of ocean currents and jet streams, the weather is perfect almost every day of the year and every variety of flower, tree, grass, plant, and fern is at home in Santa Barbara soil, living harmoniously side-by-side. Something is always in bloom, and the result is breathtakingly beautiful.

From an outdoor cafe at the picturesque marina, San Ynez wine in hand, one can see the sailboats, the beach, and the mountains in one eye-popping shot. Old Spanish architecture dominates the landscape, with gentle pink stucco and red ceramic tile roofs. The Queen of the Spanish Missions is located in the foothills of the mountains, and the view from its rolling lawns is jaw dropping. It is home to the extremely wealthy.

Montecito is a beatific suburb of Santa Barbara—even more mind-bogglingly beautiful and absolutely drowning in money. The richest of the rich live here. Movie stars. Business barons. Oprah and Ty Warner, the Beanie Babies guy, call Montecito home.

"Any particular reason?"

"We're pitching a movie to an independent investor."

"What movie?"

"I'll tell you later. I want you to be fresh and inspired."

"You can't do that, Joe. You have to tell me now, so I can start thinking about it. I don't want to embarrass myself."

"You mad genius. Trust your brother Joe. Have I ever let you down?"

"We've never worked together. I pitched you one movie and got drunk with you at Foster's. Last night, in fact."

"So I've never let you down?"

"No."

"Smoke this."

He reached beneath his seat, and I spotted an ankle holster holding a large caliber handgun. He produced a fat joint and held it out to me.

"I quit, Joe. I haven't smoked in years." I had been a prodigious smoker through high school and college, but stopped when I began leasing corporate office space, precisely the time it would have helped me most.

"Why did you stop?"

"Smoke in your lungs is a bad idea."

"You live in Los Angeles, right?"

"Yes."

"I should have been on the debating team." He lit the joint, hit it big, smiled as he exhaled, and momentarily found his Rasta voice. "I'll supply the vibe, *mon*. You supply the movie. We'll be a great team. I shot the sheriff."

"Speaking of shooting the sheriff, Joe, you have a gun strapped to your ankle."

"Yes, I do."

"Are you licensed to carry a gun in public?"

"I think so."

"Not a strong answer."

"Yes I am."

"You are?"

"No I'm not."

"You're not?"

"Strong answers aren't necessarily good answers. Everyone in government knows this."

He put a CD in the player, *Primal Magic* by Strunz and Farah, and we rolled north past Camarillo and Oxnard and the city of Ventura. The Pacific was on our left, the air was dry and clear, and I imagined I had a contact high from Joe's joint. My head had stopped hurting, and I was happy just to be driving up the coast.

"Who are we pitching?" I said.

"Calvin Key," Joe said.

"Who is he?"

"You don't know who Calvin Key is?"

"No."

"Prepare to have your mind blown, young Skywalker."

"Are you going to tell me who he is?"

"He's a math teacher from San Jose."

"We're pitching a math teacher?"

"Who started a software company, wrote a program, built a business, and sold it for three point seven billion in cash and two billion in stock. Billion. With a B."

"Lot of money."

"No, my friend. Fifty million is a lot of money. Five point seven billion is something completely different than a lot of money."

"What is it?"

"The power to do, not dream, not think, but do or have anything in the world that crosses your mind. Buy an airport. Build a bridge. Own an army."

"Make a movie."

"Our movie. Exactamundo."

"And our movie is?"

"Not yet, *amigo*. Soon, though. I can hear your creative force field humming."

"What does his software do?"

"It counts."

"Counts what?"

"Anything that needs counting, which is everything on Earth. Cars, tennis balls, candy bars, sheets of plywood, trees in the northwest, seals in Antarctica, rolls of film, screwdrivers, bottles of root beer, shoelaces, people in China, boxes of chalk, dollars turned into Euros, Euros turned into yuan, grains of sand on the beach, galaxies in the universe. It counts forwards and backwards and sideways. It counts vertically or horizontally or perpendicularly. It counts in groups and columns and rows, by size and weight and color and name. It calculates and tabulates and formulates and does it all at the speed of light. It is the consummate counting package in the palm of your hand."

"Five point seven billion?"

"He wants to make an independent movie."

"How do you know him?"

"Ballroom. He's a closet dancer, not uncommon for high school calculus teachers. I've been giving him lessons, waiting for the right moment to make him an executive producer. Waiting for the right project, the right writer. Waiting for the stars to align in the Age of Aquarius. Waiting for you, *compadre*. You are my missing link."

"What are we pitching?"

"Magic," he said, and he turned off the 101 toward a deceptively sleepy beach town just south of Santa Barbara called Carpinteria.

22. WE'RE PLAYING FOR OUR NEW LIFE

Famous for their sweeping beaches and annual Avocado Festival, Carp, as locals call Carpinteria, is home to absurdly expensive farmland and strings of beach cottages that defy financial gravity. It's lovely and quiet, and wealthy Angelinos, many in the entertainment business, flock here on the weekends to their second homes, where campfires on the beach, outdoor showers, boogie boards, barbecues, and Fess Parker Pinot Noir await them. Julie and I had friends who lived here, and of all the places we wished we could live, Carp was at the top of the list.

Joe turned into a long private road, past a sign that read: *Treasure Cove*, another that read: *Residents Only*, and a third that read: *Security Cameras in Operation*.

"I thought Calvin Key lived in Montecito," I said.

"He does."

"So who lives here?"

"Me. Before I lost my house."

We arrived at the automatic arm restricting public access to the beachfront neighborhood. A white-haired man in a security uniform popped his head through a window in a small cabin beside the road.

"Joe Hudson," he said. His eyes twinkled with warmth and friendship.

"Mortimer, my friend. How are your testicles this fine day?"

"Never better, Joe. How about yours?"

"Dandy," Joe said. "Anyone home?"

"No. They're doing some work on it."

"Would you mind if I took one last dance around the living room?"

"What did you have in mind?"

"I was thinking a Samba."

"Would you consider a Bossa Nova?"

"Blame it on the Bossa Nova. You were always the smart one, Morty. Say hello to Mark Manilow, the world's greatest undiscovered screenwriter."

"You let him drive?" Morty said to me.

"He kidnapped me," I said.

Morty laughed out loud, his head bobbing up and down like an apple in water. "Don't dawdle, Joe. Painters have been in and out all week."

"Gone with the wind, *mon*," Joe said, and Morty lifted the automatic arm.

We parked behind a tasteful sea green cottage, exited the Benz, passed through a privacy gate, and strolled up a brick path toward the house.

"Nice house, Joe. Great spot."

"Belongs to a Pasadena plastic surgeon now. He rents it out for thirty-five grand a month to rich people who live in bad weather. He specializes in making your calves appear muscular."

"Not my calves," I said.

"Nor mine, Mr. Tibbs."

We climbed the steps to the back deck, which stretched the full length of the house. The entire rear wall was glass and so was the entire front wall. Looking through the house, from the back deck, I could see miles of the Pacific Ocean. Behind us were the mountains.

"Wow, Joe."

"Paradise lost," he said.

The French doors were open, and we walked into the house, which was being painted, though the painters weren't here. Drop-cloths and ladders and buckets and brushes and rollers and that wonderful blue tape that doesn't damage anything were scattered all around the one large living, dining, and cooking space, which was neatly sandwiched between the walls of glass. A doorway at the far end led to the bedrooms. There was another big deck on the front of the house, the ocean side, and a fire pit patio area built into the rock retaining wall toward the beach beyond that. From there, steps led down to the sand. It would take sixty seconds to be body surfing.

Joe moved across the room, stood at the glass wall, and took a deep breath. "Before they play a championship game, professional athletes picture the action in their mind's eye. Pele envisioned where his teammates would be, what he would do with the ball, what kind of shots he would put in the net. Gretsky did the same thing. Michael Jordon. Derek Jeter. Joe Montana. They all played the big game in their head before they went out and played it for real." He turned to me, black shirt, black pants, black boots, black hat, Pacific Ocean framed in the glass behind him, right ankle bulging a bit from the handgun. "They all had one thing in common. Something to play for."

"We're playing for your old house?"

"We're playing for our new life. We sell this pitch, we make this film, we do thirty million domestic, another thirty foreign, another thirty DVD, ten in ancillaries, it's a hundred million. We take our little piece and do nothing but make movies the rest of our lives. How does that sound?"

"It would sound a whole lot better if I knew what we were pitching."

He crossed the room, stood close to me, face to face. His eyes were still hidden behind the black shades. "You know what we're pitching. You've always known. Trust your feelings. Let the force be with you."

Without turning back for a last look at the ocean, he went through the doors and was gone. I followed him to the car, we waved farewell to Morty, merged back onto the 101 North, and exited again at Montecito in a matter of minutes.

23. CALVIN KEY

We turned onto Mountain Road, its endless fields of swaying grasses and greenery providing flawless backdrops for California oaks bathed in whites and pinks and yellows and blues, and Julie distracted me.

We had driven Mountain Road together on several getaway weekends, and I could hear her voice in my head. "Montecito is entirely too perfect," she said. "It's more perfect than nature, and that is a very dangerous proposition because nature is not perfect. It is, by its own design, imperfect. You can't defy nature and get away with it. There's a price to pay. And even Montecito doesn't have enough money to foot that bill."

She was right, as she usually was about such things. Montecito is perfect in a way that dazzles and impresses and overwhelms, but does not spiritually humble, as nature does daily, often on the sly and without effort. It's no accident that the richest of the rich and most renowned of the renowned reside here. Spiritual humility can be an inconvenience and a bore. "If they could whitewash the brush fires and mudslides," Julie said, "they would really have something."

The entrance gates to Calvin Key's estate were constructed of reclaimed barn wood from Vermont. They were twelve feet tall and attached to enormous flagstone towers, which were connected to a tenfoot perimeter flagstone wall covered with ivy.

"He's got fifty acres," Joe said. "In Montecito. Fifty acres. It boggles the mind."

The long curving driveway was lined on both sides by ancient oaks and the surrounding property was all rolling hills and wildflowers. Birds and butterflies added a pastel softness to the portrait.

"What are we pitching? It's time to tell me."

"Does anybody really know what time it is?"

"Don't do this, Joe. It's not funny. If this guy has money to invest in an independent movie—"

Joe cut me off as Calvin Key's house appeared. "If?"

It was a Spanish mansion of such grace and dignity that its immense size was an afterthought. The architecture was exquisite: curving sand-colored walls and sloping red tiled roofs, wrought iron railings that were works of art, stained glass windows, and bright ceramic staircases.

American Industrial Royalty had built it generations ago, their fortune made in oil and railroads. Silent film stars had bought it from them at the height of their success. A ship builder owned it after that and an arms dealer after that. Calvin Key paid cash for the estate and ensuing two-year restoration, somewhere in the vicinity of sixty-five million dollars. Inspiring is not often a word used to describe someone's house, but even a word of that magnitude didn't do the place justice. I was speechless, craning my neck like a third-grader as Joe rolled past the house and parked on the far side of the huge circular courtyard that wrapped around the grand marble fountain in which bright green lazy lily pads floated above speckled koi. It was known now as Casa Key.

"Last chance to tell me the movie," I said.

"Last chance for romance," he said.

We climbed out of the car and moved to the trunk. Joe opened it and removed a black briefcase with brass-plated clasps and combination lock. It was the briefcase of a traffic engineer or a claims adjustor or a low-level IBM research executive trying in vain to climb the corporate ladder, but it was not under any circumstances the briefcase of someone like Tango Joe Hudson. He must have sensed the incongruity of the thing because he looked at me and said, "I bought it just for this meeting."

"You think it will help?" I said.

"Sitting Bull does not think. He knows," Joe said, and we walked to the massive front doors.

It was on that walk that I reconciled the circumstances. *What's the worst thing that could happen?* I thought. *We meet Calvin Key, he looks at me, I have no idea what I'm doing here, I tell him just that, Joe instructs me to wait in the car, the drive back to LA is silent, and my life as a failed porn writer continues forthwith.* Not so bad, really. It was a nice drive, the ocean was fabulous, Key's house was once-in-a-lifetime magnificent, and Joe, for all his wackiness, was good company. Maybe we would stop on the way home and get something to eat.

"You ready?" Joe said. We were at the hand-carved front doors.

"Not even close," I said.

"Perfecto," Joe said, and he rang the bell.

The door opened, and a fifty-year-old man on a Segway Human Transporter appeared in the doorway. The man was thin but not skinny. It was hard to gauge his height because the Segway made him close to seven feet tall, but maybe he was six feet or so. He had thinning light brown hair and no tan. He wore an oxford shirt, blue jeans, and Sperry Topsiders with no socks.

If you think it's odd to be greeted by a man riding a Segway Human Transporter, you're right. The Segway is that self-propelled, two-wheel scooter-like vehicle invented by Dean Kamen that, when first presented, signaled a future in which Americans were finally too fat to walk and so had a machine to move them from Wendy's to Mc-Donald's to Taco Bell to Burger King at up to seventeen miles per hour by simply shifting their body weight. It's powered by an electric motor and uses computer chips to mimic human equilibrium. It works with weird gyroscope technology, tilt sensors, and voodoo, and upon its unveiling, it spooked people more than anything else and so was not immediately a success, though Calvin Key liked it enough to answer the door riding one.

"Calvin, you crazy man," Joe said, "Let me have your drugs before you get hurt."

Key smiled. "Come in," he said. "I've lost my butler."

We walked beside the Segway, which rolled slowly through Casa Key. The rooms were gigantic and had sixteen-foot ceilings, ornate crown moldings, huge iron-and-crystal chandeliers, Asian rugs the size of basketball courts covering authentic Spanish ceramic tile floors, priceless imported silk curtains, and fireplaces large enough to park a car in. The only thing more amazing than the mansion was the billionaire on the Segway—that and the fact that there was not a stick of furniture anywhere in sight.

"I haven't actually lost him," Key said. "I've misplaced him. He's having an affair with the cook, and they disappear together several times a day, though never in the same place twice and with an alternating disbursement pattern, so I can't predict where they'll be next."

"How long has it been going on?" Joe said.

"Seven months," Key said.

"He must be a terrific butler," I said, thinking that otherwise Key would have canned him long ago.

"Not really. He's lazy and disrespectful, but his girlfriend is a wonderful cook. If I fire him, she'll leave. She's made crab cakes and a citrus salad with chardonnay vinaigrette for lunch."

He had boiled the butler and maid's affair down to its most simple equation. One plus one equals two. Everything was a function of counting to Calvin Key. This did not bode well for the pitch, which didn't compute in any way, shape, or form.

We arrived in a room so large it could only have been a ballroom.

"This was the ballroom," Key said. "They used to have a twenty-five piece big band and three hundred guests. Tommy Dorsey played here."

The ceilings were twenty feet tall, and there were five enormous chandeliers. The floors were whitewashed oak with intricate cherry inlays, but again there was no furniture in the room. That is, except for a ping-pong table in the far corner, positioned like a green postage stamp on a white envelope.

We crossed to the ping-pong table and Key dismounted the Segway. He walked to me and put his hand out. "Well, I'm Calvin Key."

I shook his hand. "Mark Manilow."

"His cousin Barry is doing the music for the movie," Joe said while I was still holding Key's hand.

"Fantastic," Key said. "I've always wanted to meet him."

There are moments such as this in all our lives. Fish-or-cut-bait moments. Shit-or-get-off-the-pot moments. Put up or shut up. I had not had a moment like that in quite some time and this one, thanks to the Wild-Man-of-Borneo producer now playing air guitar with a ping-pong paddle, was a doozy. I wasn't related to Barry Manilow. Not even in my imagination. The response in my head was instantaneous: *That's not true, Calvin. I'm not related to Barry Manilow and even if I were, he's not doing the music for our movie because we have no movie because I don't have a single clue as to what our movie is about. Sorry to have wasted your time, but it turns out Joe is nuts.*

Key and I were still shaking hands. I knew I had to open my mouth, say those words, and extricate myself from Joe's fast-tangling web. It was an easy decision. What many people call a no-brainer.

"I'll set it up," I said. "He's pretty busy, but he loves the movie, and we've always been tight. He'd love to meet you too."

Joe broke into the chorus of one of my favorite songs by The Band. "I don't wanna hang up my rock and roll shoes." His new briefcase was on the table.

"I can't wait to hear the movie," Key said.

"Me too," I said. We stopped shaking hands.

Joe was still singing. "I don't wanna hang up my rock and roll shoes."

"Do you play ping-pong?" Key said to me.

In ninth grade, I entered the Bergen County Ping-Pong Tournament and placed seventh in singles. We had a table in the basement, and my dad and I played spirited games after dinner three or four nights a week. Not only did I play. I was good. At least twenty-two years ago I was good. "I do," I said.

"Let's play before lunch. Then we'll eat, and you can tell me the story," Key said. "That okay with you, Joe?"

Joe sang his answer. "I get a good time feeling every time I hear the blues."

"Excellent," Key said.

24. IF HE WAS KINKY, HE WAS HIDING IT

Key was good. He was a spinner, not a slammer, creating offense with slices and angles, putting his opponent on defense with his own defense, rather than with a loud and blustery offense. Our games were unassumingly competitive; neither one of us wanted to appear to be trying too hard, but both of us were perspiring, though not too much. As I expected, Key kept score better than anyone I had ever played with. The man could count like a wizard. We talked throughout our games.

He was from Santa Cruz originally, went to college there, got a masters degree in education, and became a high school math teacher in San Jose. I expected him to be kinkier. Santa Cruz is renowned for providing its citizens with a solid kinky foundation, and he had gone on to be a high school math teacher, which is an occupation to which only the kinkiest people aspire. But he was understated, not giving away anything I couldn't Google. If he was kinky, he was hiding it.

He had the kind of confidence that comes from having invented something so simple that anyone could have thought of it. But he was the only one in the world who had, and then he'd sold it for five point seven billion dollars. He was a little quirky, a little geeky, obviously smart, and apparently single. I don't think he was gay because he talked about a girlfriend living in Austin, Texas. She was a realtor who showed him property when he was in the market for a ranch.

On the advice of the realtor girlfriend, he had taken up ballroom dancing, which is where he met Joe, who outside of movies had a life and a half as an LA ballroom master. It was Joe who had lit his fuse for film.

"I never thought about producing a movie until I met Joe," Key said. "I didn't realize it was something you could just go do. That may sound naïve, but for most people, the film business is a complete mystery."

"Especially for the people inside the business," I said.

"All of life is a mystery," Joe said. He had put his new briefcase on the floor and was sitting on the narrow edge, watching us play. "Look at these three souls in this room right now, all of them bound for greatness and glory. How is it possible that our lives could lead us here to this very moment? How is it possible that of all the spirits on Earth, we have been chosen to join hands and produce a miracle that will be remembered for all time as a mirror and masterpiece of humanity? It is not our place to unravel the mystery. Our destiny is to become a part of it. It is, my brothers, the only way to enlightenment. Amen and hallelujah."

"Joe," Key said. "You may be the only person I've ever met who doesn't add up."

"I am the new math, Calvin," Joe said. "I am the Puzzle of Plenty."

"I don't know what that means, but I like the sound of it," Key said.

"Five minutes to lunch," said a voice behind us.

We turned to see a sixty-five-year-old black man in Bermuda shorts, no shirt, a blue blazer and flip-flops. His head was clean-shaven, and the chandelier lights bounced off his gleaming pate like laser beams.

"Cletis, say hello to Joe Hudson and Mark Manilow. They're in the film business, and they're trying to get me involved."

"Why would I care?" Cletis said, bluntly. "I ain't no movie star."

"They might make you one," Key said.

"Tell them to put it in writing. Do I look like I was born yesterday? You eating out by the pool. Don't be late. Crab cakes don't taste no good when they cold." Then he turned and left the room.

"Gentlemen. Cletis Oleander, my butler," Key said.

25. JUST ONE SOUL IN THE CITY OF ANGELS

The pristine Casa Key backyard was forty acres of oak trees and wild-flowers. There was a lighted tennis court at the end of a white pebble path on the far side of the pool, which was Olympic in size to match the house but elegantly designed to flow into the landscape, like a mountain lake in the wilderness. There was inexpensive, lightweight, rainbow-colored, outdoor-dining furniture set on the flagstone patio beside the pool. It was lowbrow, working-class, Jersey shore, poured-concrete-patio furniture made with soft strips of vinyl that you can strum like a summertime chair guitar, probably bought on impulse by Key, or maybe Cletis, at a Rite Aid or a Walgreens along with some Q-tips and Old Spice. The set included a round table featuring an imitation frosted glass top and a rainbow-striped umbrella that fit in a hole in the center of the table. There was also a matching serving cart.

We drank expensive champagne, which we poured ourselves, since Cletis was nowhere to be found. The crab cakes melted in our mouths, were impossibly delicious, and were expertly paired with the citrus salad and chardonnay vinaigrette. There was home-baked chocolate pecan pie with handmade coffee ice cream for dessert.

We talked about *Full Force* and the state of television movies, ball-room dancing, and insubordinate butlers. Key had been to Paramus and owned a piece of a company that owned a huge strip mall on Route 4. His father had been a pediatric dentist, so we had some common ground on that front. He was an only child, born when his parents were already in their late forties. They had both passed away before he re-taught the world to count.

He let on that he was looking for a challenge but nothing that would jeopardize his life. Hot air balloons and rockets to outer space had as much appeal to him as leading an expedition up Mount Everest or guiding a deep ocean submarine around the Titanic, which is to say no appeal at all. He was looking for a creative challenge, something that would make him feel emotionally engaged with the world around him, something that would reconnect him to humanity the way having five point seven billion dollars had disconnected him.

He seemed to have a reasonable sense of humor, a propensity for kindness, and a natural open-mindedness that was almost child-like in its curiosity. Underlying all of that was the unmistakable fact that he was a true genius, if the definition of true genius is the ability to see the world in one or all aspects with clarity so singular that the vision belongs to the genius alone. By that definition, it is no wonder that Calvin Key was disconnected. The five point seven billion was a symptom, not the cause. No one knew that better than Key, who had counted it all up long ago.

"I have to tell your cook. These crab cakes are *supremo*," Joe said.

"You probably won't meet Gloria," Key said. "She and Cletis disappear after lunch, and I usually can't find them until late in the afternoon, so this is as good a time as any to tell me your movie."

I can occasionally be a panic person, and I had a moment there at the poolside table where my heart skipped and my breath stopped. I had no idea where to start. But in that same microsecond, Joe reached down, lifted his new black briefcase, and placed it on the table. He opened the briefcase so that the contents were facing him, then looked at Key and smiled.

"All of life's meaning can be found in this briefcase," he said. He spun it around so that the opening faced Key and me. There was a single item in the briefcase: the Los Angeles phone book. "*Phone Book, The Movie*," Joe said. "Mark, tell him the story."

Chaotic rebellion in all its disturbing facets is what I was feeling. Screaming and shouting, the rending of garments, the pulling of hair, these are the reactions my internal controls were demanding. Emotional containment was out of the question. And yet there was Joe, smiling behind his briefcase, sucking me in like quicksand. I reached for the phone book, opened it to the white pages, and pointed to a name.

"Samantha Barnes," I said. "Just one soul in the City of Angels."

"Samantha Barnes," Key said.

"She is young, she is beautiful, and she is smart," I said.

"That's good. I like that," Key said.

"Amen, my brother," Joe said.

"She is a project manager for the communications conglomerate that publishes the phone book. Her research takes her to a forbidden file, a file to which she gains access with the help of . . ." I slapped the phone book closed and then threw it open to a different page. I had no idea what I was doing. I had the real-life physical feeling that I was falling through space, hurtling faster and faster to the Earth below. A horrid smashing death on the jagged rocks was certain. I pointed to another name. "Christian O'Connor."

"Christian O'Connor," Key said.

"Strong name for a strong man," Joe said.

"Yes," I said. "But strong in the most unexpected of ways. He is a blind bio-medical computer genius, creating a microchip that will process images from regenerated retinal lenses to the optic nerves of the human brain. Creating vision where none existed."

"Are they together?" Key said.

"Not yet," I said.

"Romance is the key to the castle," Joe said.

"In the forbidden file is the premise for a corporate conspiracy that calls for the destruction of the California coast. The clues to the conspiracy are hidden in the one book no one can decipher, yet grants universal access to the conspirators."

"The phone book," Key said.

"*Exactamundo*," Joe said.

I slapped the book closed. "It's all here. White pages, yellow pages, every person, every business, every product, every story in America is in the phone book."

Quoting my insurance-selling, dickhead brother-in-law Phil Hirschman for a second time gave a strange validity to his words, which in turn added a new layer to the psychosomatic sensation of falling to my death. I would now be nauseous when I crashed onto the craggy rocks.

"Let your fingers do the walking," Joe said.

The feeling of being quoted by Tango Joe was entirely out-of-body in a bizarre and unsettling way. It was like seeing a traveler from another time and that traveler is yourself—except you're not you, you're Joe Hudson. It was at this point I could feel tens of thousands of brain cells imploding all in a row like dominos.

"Joe's right, Calvin. All the great human stories are right here in this book, and Samantha and Christian will uncover the conspiracy, using the clues in the book itself, and in the process find love, adventure, danger, and enlightenment. And if they're lucky, if they're very lucky, they just might save the California coast."

"Who's the bad guy?" Key said.

As if the whole exercise hadn't already been a preposterous leap of faith, I opened the book to the yellow pages and pointed to the first ad I saw. "Diversified Propane Systems," I said. "A division of Jenkins Energy Corp. Marvin Jenkins. Energy tycoon. Billions and billions at his beck and call. Possibly the most evil man to ever walk the Earth."

"One mean mother," Joe said.

"Smart as a whip, though," I said. "Smarter than Christian."

"He has to be," Key said. "It has to seem like Sam and Christian can't win."

"They can't," I said. "It's going to take a miracle."

And then I closed the phone book and sat back. I was done. If Key asked me one more question, I would falter and have to tell him it was all a lie. I had nothing left. Joe sat down too, still wearing his black cowboy hat and shades. I wondered if he might pull the gun from his ankle holster and threaten to shoot Key if he said no or shoot me for screwing up a sure thing.

"Your distribution plan is the festival circuit and then a pick-up for cash with a piece of the action?" Key said to Joe.

"Sundance, Berlin, Toronto, Cannes."

'What's the budget, not including the marketing?"

"Start low, drive slow," Joe said. "Three million."

"Doesn't sound like enough," Key said.

It was business now, so it was Joe's show. I was the writer and summarily dismissed as a business idiot.

"It depends on cast. If we go for big names, no one will take us seriously, and the budget will climb like Hugh Hefner's blood pressure. We'll be Hollywood clones. I want us to be more than that. I want us to be under the radar. I want us to do something independent that makes people say: *Jumping Jesus, Granny get my gun; there's bears on the back porch.* To be more, we have to spend less. We have to be leaner and meaner and smarter than Wolfgang Puck."

Joe had a way of inserting similes that ripped your head clean off your shoulders. Aside from Hugh Hefner's blood pressure, Granny shooting bears on the back porch, and the allusion to Wolfgang Puck's uberintelligence, Joe had somehow, as he often did, found a way to make sound sense.

"No-name cast?" Key said.

"Not at all," Joe said. "Just not a name that comes with a million-dollar payday. Story is king, Calvin, and we've got the maestro directing the band."

I was the maestro. The fraudulent Porn Boy Maestro of Bullshit. I smiled and gave Joe a little salute.

Key took a breath, his eyes on the phone book. "I'm in," he said. "Let's make a movie."

If the rest of my life weren't out of alignment, these words would have been cause for high celebration. It isn't every day, or even every decade, that a billionaire becomes your producing partner in an independent film. It is akin to reaching nirvana for all aspiring filmmakers. I was now committed to write a movie about some crazy conspiracy to destroy the coast of California that somehow centered on the phone book. I couldn't have repeated the pitch for a million bucks. I could only hope that Tango Joe remembered the names of the characters and the basic premise I had just sold Calvin Key. It wasn't elation I was feeling as we lifted our glasses to toast our new partnership; it was a strange mélange of dread, astonishment, bewilderment, and disbelief.

On the walk back through Casa Key, Calvin gave us a little tour. The house had eighteen bedroom suites and twenty-two bathrooms. As we turned down one long hallway, we heard moaning and rhythmic banging coming from a linen closet. We stopped at the door. Calvin knocked. "My guests are leaving now, Cletis."

The banging stopped. Heavy breathing replaced the moaning. Oleander's voice came from behind the door. "What you want me to do, send up a damn flag?"

"That won't be necessary," Key said. "I just wanted you to know."

"Yeah, well, now I know. You mind?" Cletis said.

"Best crab cakes I ever had," Joe said to the linen closet door.

"Thanks, baby," said a woman's voice from inside the closet.

26. THERE'S A GODDESS IN YOUR DRIVEWAY

The ride back to Los Angeles was uneventful. I closed my eyes and listened to Joe talk on the phone. I was drifting in and out, but I know he spoke four or five different languages. I heard Spanish and Italian, some kind of Asian dialect, and something else I couldn't identify, possibly Martian. Nothing would have surprised me. If he had stopped the car in Oxnard and revealed himself to be an alien with a spacecraft made of tin foil (like Ray Walston's) hidden in a warehouse in Westlake, I would have taken it in stride: *Big deal, Joe. We just sold a movie about the phone book to Calvin Key.*

Like all active producers, Joe had dozens of projects he was shepherding along the trail. There was a reality show called *General Contractors Gone Crazy* for Home and Garden Television; a cooking show called *Battle of the Bulge* that featured fat chefs preparing gargantuan feasts; a game show called *Use it and Lose it* that awarded the prizes at the top of the hour but then put its contestants in threatening, compromising, and embarrassing positions with the proviso that if they use their prize to save themselves, they lose the prize and leave the show in shame; a detective series; a lawyer series; a doctor series; five sitcoms; and a newsmagazine show called *300 Seconds* in which trashy headlines would be broken and covered in no more than five minutes. "Giving people the news they want the way they want it," Joe said in several languages. But *Phone Book, The Movie* had leapfrogged ahead of the pack, and Joe was setting up a low Hollywood buzz to get us going. His buzzing put me to sleep, and the next thing

I remember was him shaking my arm, saying, "Wake up, young Sky-walker. There's a goddess in your driveway."

I opened my eyes, completely discombobulated. I saw my house and a sky-blue Jaguar parked in front of it. Dallas Westcott, wearing a low-cut evening gown, leaned against her car and looked as beautiful as Helen of Troy, if Helen of Troy had been a porn star in a form-fitting evening gown.

"I talked to Ken," she said. "I thought you might want a shoulder to cry on."

Joe and I got out of the car and walked to her. "Your gun is showing," she said to Joe as we arrived. His pants had gotten themselves hitched up on the ankle holster revealing his weapon. He shook them free and covered the gun.

"*Muchas gracias*, Senorita Snowflake," he said.

"Nice hat," she said. "You look like Richard Petty. He's a king, though, so that's a compliment."

"Joe, meet Dallas Westcott. Dallas, this is Joe Hudson."

"Nice to meet you," Dallas said, and they shook hands. Then she suggestively stroked my arm. "What about that shoulder, Mark? Is this a bad time?"

I looked at Joe and realized I had never seen his eyes and that probably no one in Hollywood ever had. "Joe—"

"Say no more, maestro. Just get to work on our movie. Samantha Barnes and Christian O'Connor save the California coast. You're a mad genius. I'll work out the details with Monsieur Billionaire." He opened the door to his car and smiled at Dallas. "Be gentle with him, Lady Macbeth. Maestros don't grow on trees."

"I'm not related to Barry Manilow," I said.

"Are you insane? Of course you are. It's in the documents. The fine print. I have agency access. Priority clearance." Then he popped into his car and drove away.

"You're making a movie with a billionaire?" Dallas said.

I wanted to tell her that I was too tired to talk, that I'd had a demanding day and really an exhausting couple of years and didn't have the energy to get into it. "It's an independent film. It's nothing yet. I haven't even written the script," I said.

She threw her arms around my neck and kissed me. "You did it. I knew you would do it, and you did it. You really did it."

"What?"

"You raised the money to produce a Hollywood movie for me to star in. I'm going to be Samantha Barnes. I love that name. Who is she, Mark? No, don't tell me. Just write the movie, and I'll do the rest. We're a team, baby. It's so exciting. Can't you feel it?"

My brain knew without hesitation what to say: Mark, it's very simple. Tell her this is not her project. Tell her you are only the writer and that Joe and Calvin and the director will make all the casting decisions and that this is not the movie that you are planning to one day write for her. She will understand, she will apologize for jumping the gun, and you will not paint yourself into a corner from which there is no exit. You will have behaved with honor and honesty and dignity and made everyone in Paramus proud.

No one in Paramus, however, had their hand down my pants the way Dallas did and so my dick felt it had a right and obligation to voice a paradoxical opinion: Fuck that noise, Mark. The world is your oyster. Do you not remember saying those words? You promised her that you would write her a real Hollywood movie. She asked if you would, and you said yes. What are you, a liar now? She's so hot, Mark. Tango Joe and Calvin Key will come in their pants when they find out you've got Dallas Westcott to play Sam Barnes. And if they don't, you will. Trust me, Porn Boy. She is inspired casting.

This debate took a fraction of a microsecond and after considering the pros and cons on both sides, the idea of coming in one's pants rang my bell with the most immediate urgency. "Yes," I said. "It's very exciting."

"What's it called? Can you tell me the name?"

"Phone Book, The Movie."

"I love it. I love it."

She kissed me some more and sent some inspired energy down to her hand, which in turn further inspired me. "I knew you would, " I said.

"What's it about?" she said as she led me into the house. "Is it romance or drama or action adventure?"

"Yes," I said.

"Oh good. I've really been working hard on that stuff in Colonel Bill's class."

I knew it was wrong. I knew, I knew, I knew, I knew, and I knew. But we went inside and had sex in the shower and then again by the fish tank—because Dallas wanted the fish to know I was the man of the house—and then we put on our clothes and Dallas said, "I have a surprise for you" as if having sex with the world's leading XXX porn star in my shower and then in front of my tropical fish wasn't enough of a surprise.

"What is it?"

"You have to come with me."

"Where?"

"That's the surprise."

27. YOU'RE A VERY SILLY MAN, MARK MANILOW

We drove out of the canyon in her sky-blue Jag, top down, wind blowing through our hair as the sun faded and millions of San Fernando Valley lights blinked on like stars. Dallas slid Kings of Leon into the CD player and turned it up.

It was a gorgeous night and after what had happened the only thought in my head was what would Julie say about all this? About Tango Joe and Calvin Key? About Ken Moynihan and Dallas Westcott and *Broken Boner*? About Cathy Burns bouncing me out of her agency? About receiving a moving violations ticket from Gibby, the screenwriting Paramus cop? About my hapless attempt to get on with my life without her in it?

You're a very silly man, Mark Manilow is what she would say. On our honeymoon in Antigua, there was an open-air corrugated tin café on the resort grounds but across the road and away from the action. It was a little rustic stop for coffee and bread with fresh fruit jam. We liked it because it was shaded and off the beaten path, and very few resort guests ventured away from the white beach and the blue water. Being from Southern California, we were in need of a break from the sun after a morning on the beach, whereas vacationers from North Dakota and New York soaked in as many rays as possible to sustain them through their long bleak winters.

We ate a light lunch there every day and were often the only customers. The first day it took one hour and twenty minutes to serve us scones and coffee. I lost my patience after thirty minutes of waiting.

How long could it possibly take to place two scones on a plate, pour coffee in two cups, and carry them to our table when there was no one else in the café but us? I questioned the waitress. I questioned the cook. I went for a walk around the café. I sat down. I got up. I sat down. I got up. I walked around the café. I questioned the cook. I questioned the waiter. I went for a walk around the café.

As I became increasingly agitated, Julie became even more wonderful. There were tiny little brown birds that chitter-chattered at our feet, seeking crumbs of muffins and toast. There were exotic plants and flowers growing wild on the hill behind the café. There was the colorful dress of the locals and the hypnotic cadence of their speech. There was the island music playing on the outdoor speakers. There was the glorious weather. There was everything to interest and occupy and elate and nothing to annoy or discolor or mitigate the moment.

"I'm busting a vein, and you're laughing at little brown birds and singing songs you don't know," I said.

"You're missing the point," Julie said.

"The point is we have been waiting seventy-seven, no, seventy-eight minutes for two strawberry scones and two cups of coffee. The point is we are the only ones here. The point is they have nothing else to do but bring us our lunch. It has now been seventy-nine minutes since they took our order."

"The point is that on a honeymoon time is suspended," she said. "There's nowhere to go and nothing to do. It might as well be seventy-nine seconds or seventy-nine years. All I am right now, at this exact moment, is in love with you. And everything I see, everything that happens, is an extension of that one simple feeling."

Then she kissed me and whispered in my ear, "You're a very silly man, Mark Manilow. Your gorgeous bride is sitting next to you, her tan is exquisite, her tits rule the world, and you are the one and only recipient of their goodness. Is that not enough to overcome your human burden of time? Before you answer, you should know that it is for me."

She kissed me again, and the scones and coffee arrived, and my reality was altered for the rest of the honeymoon. I never again cared how long we waited in that café. Julie was right about time and honeymoons and lots of other things. Part of missing her was not having her voice in my ear to smooth the rough road. Was Julie the only one in the world who could do that for me? That was the question that had me gazing at tropical fish at three in the morning.

Dallas took Van Nuys Boulevard north to Panorama City and parked in the gravel lot of what used to be a church, but now had a sign above the door that said *Colonel Curry's Acting Studio*. She turned off the car and put her hand on my thigh. "I want you to see my class, to see how far I've come. I told Colonel Bill about you, and he wants to meet you. Isn't this a great surprise?"

"Great," I said. But what I was thinking was, can't move legs . . . heart not beating . . . pain in head . . . can't breathe . . . need air.

28. COLONEL BILL

Colonel Bill Curry was six feet three inches tall in his socks. In his crocodile skin cowboy boots he was closer to six five. He had to be seventy years old, but he was hale and hearty and strong as a bull. He wore blue jeans and a tight-fitting black T-shirt upon which was printed: *I Hear Inner Voices*. He had a mane of golden hair swept back behind his ears that, in spite of his age, didn't look absurd. Rather, it made him look like General Custer, which was altogether appropriate given his outrageous demeanor and the slaughter about to befall the craft of acting.

When he first arrived from Denver more than a decade ago, the defrocked owner-pet therapist turned acting coach reckoned he needed a base camp, some simple structure that would accentuate the lofty ambitions and profoundly interwoven teacher-student relationships he meant to forge.

Coincidentally, the First Church of the Friends of Jesus was experiencing what they called *growing pains*. A sticky-fingered parishioner named Maureen was friendlier with Jesus than she should have been and absconded with one hundred and seventy-three thousand dollars from the petty cash drawer. Church officials decided not to press charges as even the most cursory of investigations would have uncovered a host of untoward activities, including a meth lab, escort service, and black-market weapons dealership. Instead, it was agreed upon to hastily vacate the building in the dark of night and vanish to the nether-reaches of the San Fernando Valley, where the Friends of

Jesus could reconstitute their worship under their new banner, the True Brothers of Christ, and seek retribution under their own sails.

Colonel Bill strode through the doors after the Friends of Jesus had vanished, took one look at the glorious light pouring through the long walls of stained glass, and agreed to a long-term lease with an option to buy.

Dallas squeezed my arm as we entered. "This is where I learned to act," she said. "I owe it all to the Colonel."

The church was gutted. A low stage was constructed on one of the long walls and a dozen chairs purchased at various and sundry yard sales sat in a semi-circle around it. More than half a dozen actors were seated in the chairs watching three other actors on the stage. There were minimal stage lights and a cluttered out-in-the-open office area off to the side. Changing and rest rooms along with a small kitchen were situated at the far end.

Dallas led me across the church toward the stage, and we silently took our seats so as not to disturb the actors, who faithfully reproduced the luncheonette scene from *Ghost,* in which Oda Mae tells Molly that she can hear Sam talking to her even though Sam has been murdered. Sam, of course, is sitting right there with them holding Molly's hand, dead as lead. The Colonel sat front and center in a navy blue La-Z-Boy recliner that was also elevated on its own small stage.

An actress named Lorraine played Molly, Sean, an earnest actor with vibrant red hair, played Sam, and a young pretty black girl named Turquoise played Oda Mae.

"Oh God," Lorraine said. "This is all so crazy. I can't believe I'm talking to you like this. I don't believe in these things. I don't believe in life after death."

"Tell her she's wrong," Sean said.

"He says you're wrong," Turquoise said.

"You're talking to him right now?" Lorraine said.

Turquoise cocked her head and raised her eyebrows. "What? You think I'm making it up?"

Lorraine looked around the imaginary luncheonette. "Where is he?"

"How should I know? It's not like I can see him. I just hear his voice."

Dallas was mouthing Molly's lines with Lorraine. The Colonel leaned forward in his La-Z-Boy, jutting jaw resting on his clenched fist.

"I'm holding her hand," Sean said, and he reached out and took Lorraine's hand.

"He says he's holding your hand," Turquoise said.

Lorraine looked pained, as if she wanted to believe it but simply couldn't. Dallas shared her disbelief. "I'm sorry. I don't believe you. Why are you doing this to me? I don't believe a word you're saying. Sam is dead. He's dead."

"I'm holding her hand," Sean said again.

"He says he's holding your hand," Turquoise said.

"We're missing something," the Colonel said. The actors stopped the scene and waited for instruction. "What are we missing?"

"Energy," said one actor.

"Voice," said another.

"Presence," Dallas said.

"All of the above," said the Colonel, and he bounded off his chair and onto the stage in two galloping strides. "Molly is crying out for contact, Lorraine. Her longing is what's missing in this luncheonette. Let's try something. This time, when Oda Mae tells you she can't see him, she can only hear his voice, remove your shirt and say, "If he's here, if he's really here, tell him to touch my breast.""

Whoa Nelly. My eyes shot open. I looked around the church. Was I the only one who heard him say that? No. The other actors were nodding in agreement, as if a topless Molly was what the scene had always been lacking.

"And Turquoise. Oda Mae is an earthbound angel. I want you to sing her words as loud as you can. Find a melody in your own soul and give it voice." He was strutting around the stage, sweeping his golden lion's mane aside with one hand while reaching up to the sky with the other, eyes closed, experiencing a brainstorm the size of a typhoon. "And Sean. Sam is the most sensitive of souls, do you agree?"

"Yes," Sean said. "I was going for sensitivity in death."

"I could feel the beginnings of it, but you didn't show me the emotion in your actions. This time, when you take Molly's breast in your right hand, reach out with your left and take Oda Mae's breast as well. Show us once and for all the deep wellspring of pain this murdered man is feeling."

"Should I take my shirt off too, Colonel?" Turquoise said.

"What do you think?" the Colonel said.

"I'm growing more attached to Sam."

"And you want to show him what's in your heart?"

"I think so. Yes, yes I do."

"A wise choice."

"What about my shirt?" Sean said.

"Only if you believe it," the Colonel said. "And I sincerely hope you do."

He started back to his La-Z-Boy. "And all of you stand up. The scene is static. Can you feel it? There's no electricity. You're no longer in a luncheonette. You're in a nightclub. Let me see you move. There are others in the club, some dead, some living, all in pain. Who are they? Where are they? Show me these sad souls. Break their chains and set them free."

Without any further prompting, three more actors jumped onto the stage and stood in the near background.

"In character now. All together. Energy, people. And . . . go."

"This is all so crazy," Lorraine said, except this time there was a sexual undertone to her words. The dancers began to bump and grind in the background. Turquoise hummed a throaty gospel that somehow seemed right. "I can't believe I'm talking to you like this. I don't believe in these things. I don't believe in life after death."

Sam literally ripped his shirt off, his face a road map of sensitivity in death. "Tell her she's wrong."

"Oh sweet child," Turquoise sang. "Oh sweet child he says you're wrong."

Those of us left in the audience began to clap like a choir in the South on Sunday.

"You're talking to him right now? Oh Lord right now?" Lorraine sang out, catching the gospel rhythm and melody.

"Yes," the Colonel said. "Yes."

"What? Tell me what? Tell me, tell me, *tell me* what? You think I'm making it up?" Turquoise sang.

"Where is he? Show me my murdered man," Lorraine sang.

"Good, good. Keep that energy. Make it work," the Colonel said.

The dancers seductively moved in and out and around the set. The rest of us clapped on the half notes. I felt my head bobbing to the beat.

"How on God's green acre should I know, should I know? How on God's green acre should I know?" sang Turquoise.

"That's your cue, Lorraine," the Colonel said.

Lorraine pulled her shirt off revealing a thin black bra. "If he's here. If he's really, really here. Tell him, oh won't you tell that man to touch my breast. To reach out and touch my virgin breast."

Sean reached out and held her right boob with his right hand. "I'm holding her breast," Sam sang. "Can't you see I'm holding her breast?"

The dancers gyrated and Turquoise removed her shirt. She had lovely tits and a slinky red bra. "Take mine too, Mister Sam. Take mine too," she sang.

"Watch me now, hey," Sean sang and took Turquoise's left tit with his left hand.

They were completely off script now, and it didn't matter one bit. I was standing and clapping and shouting amen as the actors danced and sang and made up words and lyrics and new plotlines. Beside me, Dallas was shaking and shimmying in her evening gown while the Colonel gave direction that took the scene further and further afield into still wilder and weirder places. Finally all the actors had their shirts off, Sean had removed his pants as well, and the original luncheonette scene from "Ghost," indeed the entirety of the film itself, was a distant memory.

"Cut," the Colonel said from his La-Z-Boy, and the actors paused, out of breath, lost in their sweaty rock gospel performance. "If the filmmakers had followed your lead, there's no telling where that movie would have ended up. You are a brilliant troupe, and I couldn't be more proud of your progress. Such energy. Such vitality. Such raw emotion. The gift and goal of every actor. Kudos and Hazzahs to you all."

The looks of pride and accomplishment on the actors' faces said it all. They would have followed the Colonel through the gates of hell if that were where the journey had led them. They were devoted to him, overjoyed with the spontaneity of their creation, the acknowledgment of their talent, and the thrill of professional progress that he had lavished upon them. It wasn't the Colonel's clients and their pets in Denver that had removed him from psychology. That much was clear.

"Now, let's try it again," the Colonel said. " In the nude this time."

29. WELCOME TO THE NEW WORLD

Despite her luminous skintight evening gown with the neckline that plunged all the way through the Earth, Dallas gave an earnest performance as Adrian in the empty ice rink scene from *Rocky*. She shuffled her feet across the stage to intimate skating while a young stud actor named Tyrone, a black man from the Louisiana bayou, jogged beside her with a pork pie hat on his head while wearing a Navy Pea Coat and bouncing a Spaldeen. His surreal rendition of the famous Philadelphia hoodlum-turned-boxer Rocky Balboa was beside the point because at the Colonel's inspirational urging the scene soon devolved into Dallas in her bra and panties riding Tyrone across the stage like a horse while whipping him and singing "You can get anything you want at Alice's Restaurant."

The actors were swept up in the Colonel's charisma. There was nothing they wouldn't do to earn his praise. Turn *The Godfather* into an alien slasher musical? Why not? Play *Hoffa* as a children's fable, Tyrone, again, in an otherworldly turn as Barney, the cloying purple dinosaur turned labor leader? *Absoluteamento*, as Tango Joe would say.

I have to admit it was exhilarating. Not acting, exactly, but some transcendental concoction of role-playing, orgiastic spiritual connectionism, unbridled stream-of-consciousness, and unconditional balls-to-the-wall insanity. Like all unorthodox, inspirational leaders, the Colonel was bat-shit crazy, everybody knew, and no one said a word. Inside all of us beat the drums of serious lunacy. What we're looking for is a preposterous pilot with no intellectual brakes, no log-jamming navigational gear, and no fear of failure to steer us clear of our own choking gears and fears. Reality is irrelevant in the wake of such a charismatic Commander in Chief. Colonel Bill Curry could have been Congressman Bill Curry if the Denver winds had blown east and not west.

But LA had won the Colonel Bill sweepstakes and the spiritual leader of The Church of Odd Acting was alive and well and mad as a hatter.

"Miss Westcott," the Colonel said as the class came to an end and the players toweled off and recovered from their acting orgy. "Is this the screenwriter you told us about?"

"Yes, Colonel. His name is Mark Manilow." She wrapped her arm around mine in a possessive he's-my-boyfriend-too sort of way that bothered me somewhere in the back of my head—though the brain-dust hadn't yet settled from the explosive absurdity of the Colonel's class—and I couldn't put my finger on why.

"I want to congratulate you, Mark Manilow, on your insight, hindsight, and foresight. It takes creative courage and inspired imagination to break the chains of command and travel the uncharted path." He shook my hand like a lumberjack. "Welcome to the new world."

"Thanks," I said. I had no idea what he was talking about. "Right back at you."

"In spades," he said. "There's not an actor among us who doesn't believe Miss Westcott is a legitimate leading lady."

Oh. That's what he was talking about. I glanced around for the door, but actors who thought little or nothing about removing their clothes while playing the pivotal scene in *Saving Private Ryan* had now encircled us. There was no way out.

"Tell us, Mark Manilow. What black magic are you planning for Miss Westcott? What trouble is brewing in her cinematic future?"

It's all been a terrible mistake. Those were the words lined up on my tongue. *It's all been a terrible mistake from the beginning, and this is the moment that I'm going to undo the damage before anyone gets hurt.*

"It's a barn burner," I said.

"Tell us," the Colonel said. "Hold nothing back."

"It's called Phone Book, The Movie."

"Gripping from the get-go."

"Dallas plays Samantha Barnes. She's a smart and sassy project manager for the corporation that publishes the phone book. She stumbles upon a conspiracy to wipe out the California coast, and the clues to the crime are hidden in the yellow pages. With the help of Christian O'Connor, a blind bio-medical computer genius, she has to break the code and save the coast while falling in love with Christian, who invents a device that regenerates his vision, so he can see her for the very first time on their wedding night."

"Bravo," the Colonel said, and the actors applauded. "Miss Westcott will immediately begin an advanced and focused series of introspective acting exercises to prepare her for the role."

"Oh, Colonel," Dallas said. She was blushing like a schoolgirl. "I'm honored. I'm really, really honored. It's all happening so fast."

Turquoise and Lorraine and Tyrone moved in and embraced her. Lorraine had tears of joy in her eyes, as if Dallas had just been crowned Miss Ludicrous Acting Student of the Year. "We're all behind you, Dallas," she said.

Yes they were. In various stages of undress, while making improvisational musicals out of murder mysteries, they were all together an ensemble cast.

The Colonel put his hands on my shoulders, held my eyes with his and everyone went silent.

"You are among friends, Mark Manilow. These four walls are your safe harbor. We have been waiting for a writer to guide us through the stars, and it is you. When your script is done, we will perform a staged reading here in the church. You have our hearts and souls. Do we have your word of honor?"

While the actors voiced their support and excitement, my brain ran though the growing checklist of reasons I should race from the building, grab a jet to Florida, and vanish into the Everglades for a good long while.

But there was something ethereal about the Colonel, something mystical and sincere and gentle and, yes, completely out of this world that was unavoidably uplifting. If my fish were grouchy and disobedient, I would hire Colonel Bill in an instant and carry them naked through the farmers' market on Fairfax at his behest. This was the Colonel's secret genius. He knew where the back door was and somehow had the key. Dreams and hopes and wishes and possibilities were the coin of his crazy realm. I was putty in his inspirational hands.

Besides, once Calvin Key had the chance to reflect on the tenuous nature of the project, the even more tenuous nature of the producer, and the most tenuous nature of the screenwriter, the odds of him actually coming up with the money were nearly nil. There would be no independent film, that was a given. At the same time, I was suddenly in a somehow unsettling relationship with a porn star, my head still hurt, and a space alien infiltrating humankind as an acting coach was offering me a staged reading of a ridiculous script for which I hadn't yet written word one. How much worse could it get?

"You have my word," I said.

"Brilliant," the Colonel said, and there was back slapping and hand shaking, and Dallas threw her arms around my neck and put her mouth close to my ear. "You and me forever, baby. I think I'm in love," she said.

30. WHERE'S THE SHOVEL?

I had plenty of reasons not to write *Phone Book, The Movie*. The fish tank needed cleaning. My Mustang needed a lube job at a car joint on the far side of Reseda. The bills needed paying. I was out of groceries. My Gold's Gym membership was about to expire. I needed office supplies. I had recorded Ken Burns' documentaries on the history of baseball, jazz, and the Civil War and needed to watch them one after the other, end to end. The dishes were dirty. There were clothes in the dryer that needed folding. I had to paint the dining room. There was a credit card charge that needed disputing. I had always wanted to learn bass guitar. My filing cabinet was a mess. I needed a haircut. What a beautiful day for a walk around the Tar Pits. I hadn't been to the Observatory in ages. I was hungry. I was tired. Maybe windsurfing in Malibu was my calling. It was time to reconsider going back to school for an MFA in creative writing. I was thirsty. I had to reread *The Sportswriter* by Richard Ford, *Dune* by Frank Herbert, *A Widow For One Year* by John Irving, and *Trust Me On This* by Donald Westlake. The Dodgers were playing the Mets in LA, the Giants were playing the Mets in San Francisco, and the Padres were playing the Mets in San Diego. There was a recipe for zucchini enchiladas I was anxious to try. There was an exhibit at the Getty I had to see. It was time to take up gardening. I hadn't been bowling since middle school. I needed new shoes. A mid-afternoon nap on the back deck sounded irresistible.

My head hurt.

The not-so-secret password for official entry into the ranks of writers around the world is *procrastination*. Ask anyone you know who writes if they would rather dig a trench to drain an overflowing septic tank or write the next pages of their project. *Where's the shovel?* is the answer you'll get more often than not. Where's the shovel, and I noticed your roof needed tarring, let me give you a hand with that when I'm done digging through the septic tank in your backyard, anything to avoid sitting before an empty computer screen or a blank sheet of paper.

But my head hurting was not an excuse to avoid work. It was inextricably woven into the fabric of the project itself. Turtle Waxing my car was a pretext for alleviating the pressure in my skull. Reorganizing the walk-in closet in my bedroom, usually my most soothing procrastination, made it worse—because hanging there beside my shirts and pants and jackets were the clothes of Dallas Westcott.

It started after I consented and committed to the staged reading of *Phone Book, The Movie*, when she'd whispered in my ear that she thought she was in love. Soon after that, a skintight pair of blue jeans, a micro-mini tennis outfit, and two pair of platform shoes she wore at work took up residence in my house. More clothes followed. Not all at once but steadily, like a light snowfall that sticks around and somehow dumps two feet on the roads, creating chaos and canceling school.

It wasn't long before I lost control of my medicine cabinet. Dozens of nail polish bottles and make-up containers and skin creams and lotions, including the impossibly intoxicating coconut oil, plus clippers, tweezers, files, cotton balls, and other items I couldn't identify jammed every inch of the narrow shelves. My things were relegated to the top of the toilet and the sides of the sink.

The shower fell next. My soap and shampoo were no match for the sheer volume of her reinforcements and had to camp out on the floor but in a far corner so we wouldn't trip over them when we fucked in there, which was her favorite morning activity—and not a terrible way to start the day from my point of view either.

However, most disconcerting of all was that the word *love* started working its way into more and more of her sentences. *"I love your Mustang, Mark." "I love the way you write." "I love your zucchini enchiladas." "I love your CDs." "I love your fish." "I love your kitchen cabinets." "I love that shirt." "I love the way you sleep." "I love the way you answer the phone when I call." "I love your eyes." "I love your hair." "I love your tongue."* Okay, I didn't mind hearing that one, but I knew I should have because her loving everything about me while thinking that she might also be in love with me, or was falling in love with me, or had fallen in love with me, was both troubling and frustrating.

It was troubling because I didn't now and never would love her back. I knew this very early on in our relationship from the disconnect in our senses of humor. We didn't laugh at the same things or in the same way.

Dallas thought Jay Leno was the funniest thing on two legs. While I think Jay is probably the nicest man in public life, he was only funny enough on the Tonight Show to make me smile from time to time. I'm sure he's far funnier without those network chains around his neck. Lewis Black, on the other hand, leaves me breathless. He's so funny it hurts me to watch him work. He is the sickest puppy in the litter and shares my twisted worldview on many important topics, candy corn at the top of the list.

I roar with laughter when I read or watch or listen to Lewis Black. I fall out of my chair and roll around the floor like a pre-school kid with a sugar rush, kicking my legs and gasping for breath, begging for more and for mercy at the same time. This is how I laugh when I think something or someone is hysterically funny.

Dallas doesn't do this. Her laugh, once small and cute and attractive, was no longer any of those things. It was a consciously controlled little snicker that escaped through the side of her mouth and evaporated almost immediately. I've seen smoke rings hang around longer than her laugh.

Julie threw her head back and laughed with the center of her soul. Hers was a complete surrender to the humor of whatever tickled her funny bone. No capitulation. No intellectualizing or qualifying the joke. No second thoughts. It was an exhilarating laugh, inspirational and reassuring.

It was frustrating because if you're not laughing about the same things in the same way, there's a better than even chance that you're not talking about the same things in the same way either, and Dallas and I didn't.

"Are you writing my movie?" She exited the bedroom, dressed for a day at Moynihan's porn palace: Detroit Tiger baseball jersey, sweatpants, and tennis shoes. She would do hair, make-up, and wardrobe at the set and then promptly remove her wardrobe at the first raised eyebrow of her co-star.

I hadn't written a single word, though a story meeting with Tango Joe and Calvin Key in two weeks was on the books. "Can we talk for a minute?" I said.

"What's Sam doing now?" she said as she sat across the desk from me.

"She just broke into Jenkins' office. Christian is monitoring her every move with a computer chip that tells him where she is and where she has to go and who else is in the building, and believe me, there are security guards around every corner."

"Oh man. Is she wearing black?"

"Head to toe."

"Covering her hair?"

"Her hair's pulled back in a French braid."

"You think of everything. I love that about you."

"That's what I want to talk about."

"What?"

"Our relationship, Dallas. Where's it going?"

"Anywhere we want it to."

"Yes, but is that a good idea, to leave it open-ended? Shouldn't we talk about where we want it to go?"

"That won't help."

"Why not?"

"Two reasons. First, it's bad luck to talk about a relationship when it's happening. You just let it happen. It's either going to work out or it's not."

"That's my point."

"So we agree on that. Second, relationships go where they're going. Talking about them never changes anything, so there's no reason to talk about them in the first place."

"Do you think our relationship is working?"

She interpreted my trepidation as fear that it wasn't working instead of fear that it would never end, leaned across the desk, and lightly ran her tongue up the side of my neck to my ear where she whispered, "It was working this morning in the shower."

"Yes, I know, but I need to talk about it."

"That's because you're a movie writer. My movie writer."

"Dallas—"

"Talk, lover boy. I'm listening."

She was, but now she had moved around the desk and was sitting in my lap, kissing my neck and face.

"I don't think it's working."

"I do."

"I'm not so sure."

"I am."

"Maybe we need to take a break."

"No break."

"Just a little break. Breathing space. Time to think."

"Sorry, baby. I'm not going anywhere. We're all wrapped up in each other, work and life and everything, and that's good luck. You'll see."

"Dallas, I'm saying I need time."

"And I'm saying you don't."

Not being able to laugh, not being able to talk, not being able to write, not being able to influence the direction and path of my life, which now included Dallas Westcott on multiplying and inexorable levels, all of this plus the bizarre reality of the independent film that I was chained to alongside Tango Joe Hudson, Calvin Key, and Colonel Bill Curry was creating pressure in my head that again and finally drew my attention to the business card of Dr. Alvin Yee, New Age Neural Pain Management Professional.

31. AT LEAST I KNOW MY CAT SCAN'S OKAY

With my CAT scan riding shotgun, I drove down Coldwater Canyon, turned left onto Ventura Boulevard, and took the scenic route, rather than the 101, to Reseda, turned right, and rolled on and on into the flatlands of the Valley, making lefts and rights through endless working class neighborhoods of weathered, 1950s California ranch houses.

Deeper and deeper into the Valley I drove, checking and rechecking the directions I had written on the back of Dr. Yee's business card, until finally I turned onto Constance Lane, a wide suburban street built as part of a gateless subdivision called Lake River Springs, which was a triple lie in advertising as there were no lake, river, or springs within one hundred miles. I drove to 2552 Constance Lane, pulled my Mustang to the curb, and saw Keanu Reeves mowing the lawn.

He was pushing a manual mower with rolling blades powered by the turning wheels, which turned as fast as the mower mowed. *Things in the film business must be tougher than I thought*, I said to myself, *if Keanu is cutting grass to make extra money.*

I climbed out of my car, CAT scan in hand, and walked down the front path, trying my best not to stare at the international movie star sweating bullets in the oppressive Valley heat. Our eyes met as I stopped to give him the right of way, and he smiled as if to say: *Just you wait, buddy.* "Don't knock. It's open," he said. Then the mower went by, and I continued to the front door, opened it, and crossed the threshold into the Twilight Zone of modern medical care.

The entrance hall and living room to my left were filled from floor to ceiling on all walls with thousands of books: textbooks, cookbooks, best-sellers, biographies, mysteries, histories, dictionaries, science fiction, nonfiction, books for children and teens and senior citizens, books about one thing, books about everything, self help and do-it-yourself, write a resume, learn macramé, books for dummies, and chicken soup books for every race, creed, and color. It was like stepping into the top-secret location of the Amazon mail-order warehouse.

To my right, the dining room was jam-packed with pots and pans and plates and platters and dishes and glasses and roasting racks and silverware and carving knives and gadgets and gizmos and mixers and blenders and choppers and graters and bottled sauces and jars of jam and hundreds of woks stacked one inside the other in tall towers that gave the room an old-time sci-fi feeling.

"We're in the kitchen," said a young woman's voice from deeper inside the house. "Come through the dining room."

Narrow paths had been carved through the mass of goods in both rooms for navigation. I entered the dining room, still recovering from Keanu the yardman outside the house and the unimaginable volume of stuff inside the house. At the end of the room, the path made a sharp left hand turn and spilled me into the large eat-in kitchen.

Food was everywhere, canned and packaged and wrapped right out of Ralph's. There were three large side-by-side refrigerator-freezers and dozens of canvas grocery bags filled to bursting and lined up on the floor. As I entered, Antonio Villaraigosa, the former mayor of LA, finished filling two bags with groceries, took a slip of paper from a thirty-year-old, drop-dead-beautiful Chinese woman, and exited out the back.

"Hello, Mark. I'm Caroline," the woman said as she crossed to me and shook my hand. "Nice to meet you."

She had long, straight, coal black hair and the smoothest skin I had ever seen. Her eyes were green and bright and shining, and she was slender and fit, and her handshake was soft but confident.

"This can't be the right place," I said. "But you're expecting me, so I'll stay."

She smiled a gorgeous smile and laughed out loud in a joyful, un-inhibited way that stopped my heart for a full moment.

"My grandfather will be happy to hear that," she said. "You can let go of my hand now."

"Sorry," I said, releasing her hand. "Your grandfather is Dr. Yee?"

"Yes."

"Is he here?"

She gestured behind me, and I turned around. Leaning against a kitchen counter was a vision I will never forget for the rest of my life.

"My grandfather, Dr. Alvin Yee," Caroline said, and then she said something in an arcane Chinese dialect that I assumed was, "Grand-father, this is Mark Manilow."

He was ancient, possibly ninety-five years old, maybe one hun-dred five, maybe one hundred thirty-five. He was five feet two inches tall and thin as a flagpole, but sturdy, not frail or fragile in any way. His hair was long and white and outrageously braided as was his beard, which was also white and long enough to reach his waist. He wore bright red Nike running pants and a Kobe Bryant Lakers jersey. His Air Jordans were as black as Caroline's hair, but his laces were as red as his pants. He wore a DreamWorks Animation baseball cap with Ray-Bans resting on the brim. There was bling around his neck.

He said something in Chinese to Caroline but never took his eyes off me.

"He'd like to see your CAT scan," Caroline said.

I handed him the large envelope, and he sat at the kitchen table, slid the CAT scan out, and held it up to the light.

"He doesn't speak English?" I said.

"Not one word," Caroline said. "My grandmother usually translates for him, but she's in China visiting *her* grandmother."

My jaw dropped open. "You're kidding?"

"Yes," Caroline said, and she laughed again. "She is in China though. One of her great grandnieces is getting married."

"Your grandfather didn't go?"

"Too many patients."

"That was Antonio Villaraigosa, right?"

"Yes."

"And cutting the lawn?"

"Keanu Reeves. He's a very good landscaper."

"Are they patients?"

"Yes. There's more head pain in Hollywood than anywhere else in the civilized world."

"That doesn't explain why the mayor is bagging groceries while Neo is mowing the lawn."

"My grandfather doesn't accept money as payment for his services."

"Credit cards only?"

"No credit cards."

"Bank checks?"

"No."

"Personal checks?"

"No."

"Travelers cheques?"

"None of the above. He's been a doctor for almost eighty years, and he's never accepted money for healing anyone."

"He must accept some money. He has a house."

"It belongs to a patient who is a real estate developer. His payment is that my grandfather is allowed to live here."

"For how long?"

"Until he no longer lives here."

"When he's done looking at my CAT scan, he can renegotiate my mortgage."

She laughed again, and there was a second where I couldn't breathe. And then I could, and I thought of all the books and kitchen gear and food. "Is it barter?"

"No. Each patient is given an obligation. A responsibility. Some patients bring things to the house—"

"Food and books and kitchen stuff—"

"Yes, and clothes. The bedrooms are filled with clothes and shoes and blankets and sheets and pillows and quilts. Other patients take things from the house and deliver them somewhere else. Mr. Villaraigosa delivers groceries to people who are hungry. Mr. Reeves mows the lawn. Miss Midler tutors twins in Alameda."

"Bette Midler?"

"Yes. The garage is filled with school supplies."

"What will I do?"

"It depends on what's wrong with your head."

The only thing wrong with my head at the moment was that it couldn't wrap itself around Dr. Yee and his peculiar new age neural pain management practice. I found myself staring at Caroline, and she caught me at it. She wasn't self-conscious or embarrassed or anything. For some reason, neither was I. We smiled at each other and waited for her grandfather.

"At least I know my CAT scan's okay," I said.

"I hope so," she said.

"You don't think it is?"

"How would I know? I'm a school teacher."

"I'm a screenwriter."

"No wonder your head hurts."

She laughed again, and I laughed too. "Seriously," I said. "I know my CAT scan's good."

Then Dr. Yee put the pictures of my brain on the kitchen table and said something to his daughter. Caroline looked at me and said evenly and without judgment, "Your CAT scan is not good."

32. SEE NOT WHAT ONE WILL NOT SEE

Three separate neurologists had told me unequivocally that there was nothing wrong with my brain. Still, no one wants to hear that their CAT scan isn't good, even if it is a fourth opinion from a five hundred-year-old Chinese rapper.

"Excuse me?" I said.

Caroline relayed my words to Dr. Yee, who responded immediately.

"Your CAT scan is not good. Big problem."

"Big problem? What's that supposed to mean? What kind of big problem?"

Caroline translated. Dr. Yee pointed to a section of my CAT scan that looked like spilled ink and said something that sounded bad in any language.

"Electron dysfunction," Caroline said.

I was as good as anyone when it came to panicking about health. Heart racing, blood pumping behind my eyeballs, ears plugged with anxiety, all of these symptoms and more I had learned, like a Jedi Master, to recognize from a mile away. I was conscious of a pick-up in the pounding of my heart. Panic was coming.

Dr. Yee said something to Caroline.

"My grandfather says don't panic," Caroline said.

"I'm not panicking. Who says I'm panicking?"

Caroline translated. Dr. Yee spoke for a very long time, giving me all the space I needed to go into full-throttle panic-mode. When he finished, Caroline turned to me.

"He says sit down," she said.

"That's it? That was the Gettysburg Address."

"You're right. Please sit down is what he said."

And then she smiled, and my panic subsided. I sat at the table across from Dr. Yee. Caroline sat at the end of the table, between us, forming a conversational triangle. If he sees electron dysfunction, I reasoned, he must know how to treat it. Chinese culture is five thousand years old. Certainly their old medical masters had encountered all kinds of electron dysfunction over the centuries. The Dark Ages must have had electron dysfunction off the charts. It would be nothing for Dr. Yee to prick me with needles or fill me with herbs or walk on my back in his Air Jordaned feet until my misbehaving electrons were neat and tidy and properly functioning.

"Okay," I said. "I'm sitting, and I'm not panicking. What is electron dysfunction?"

Caroline translated me for her grandfather and then translated him for me and went back and forth throughout our conversation.

"Think of your humanity as four distinct worlds, the physical, the spiritual, the intellectual and the emotional. These worlds are interconnected by a river of electrons that flows between them and carries dreams in its current for all the worlds to share. If the river is obstructed, then all the worlds are without dreams and so suffer gravely, each in their own way."

"So my river of electrons is obstructed?"

"I wish it were so, but there has been a crisis in your life, Mark, and this crisis has changed the very course of your river. It is a most unusual occurrence and means that the your condition is critical."

"Critical as in I'm going to die?"

"We're all going to die."

"Yes, but not all of us are going to die of a dysfunctional river of electrons."

"No, not all us."

"How come he can see the river and not one of the neurologists I went to can see it?"

"See not, what one will not see."

Now that I had confirmed Dr. Yee was actually Yoda, I sat back, let my life flash before my eyes, and got stuck immediately in Mrs. Morgan's first grade class.

I was six years old, and the funniest word in the world to me was *piglet* (a baby pig). This word would send me into instantaneous hysterics. Wild waves of insane laughter would overwhelm me. I couldn't hear, I couldn't see, I couldn't think, and I couldn't breathe. Say piglet and I was a goner. My parents often tortured me at home with this word until my uncontrollable laughter spread to them and even my sister and all of us would roar out loud.

Mrs. Morgan was an old lady who wore a beehive hairdo that was fire engine-red. She could not tolerate one moment of insubordination. Even then, I wondered why the heck she chose to be a first grade teacher anyway. She and I were mortal enemies as I could barely tolerate one moment of subordination, and the result was many meetings with my parents and much time spent in the corner. It's a miracle that my face isn't triangular in shape.

At the height of our epic struggle, we came to a chapter on farm animals in which there was a special sub-chapter on baby farm animals and a substantial sub-sub-chapter on baby pigs. Over and over, Mrs. Morgan read the word piglet—piglet this and piglet that and piglets and more piglets and a farm full of nothing but pink little piglets. I struggled not to laugh, which for a six-year-old is an internally combustible proposition.

Bobby Jensen, the boy who sat next to me, suffered from a bad case of contact laughter. He knew all about my piglet funny bone and detected my stifled laughter on his radar. Almost immediately, he commenced thrashing about in his chair, face even redder than Mrs. Morgan's hair, trying not to bust a gut. This, of course, made it worse. There was a ton of piglet TNT inside me, and Mrs. Morgan had lit the fuse. I lost my mind. I threw myself on the floor and rolled the length of the classroom, laughing hysterically, arms and legs flailing, until I bumped into Mrs. Morgan's chair.

"You find something funny about the word piglet, Mr. Manilow?"

As every first-grader knows, laughter is more contagious than chicken pox, and in seconds the rest of the class was hysterical as well. Thirty-two six-year-olds were bouncing around the room, throwing our piglet books in the air, going as crazy as monkeys on a banana boat.

Mrs. Morgan was apoplectic. She ran around the room grabbing random first-graders and tossing them in their seats, shouting commands of nonsense, trying to alter reality by the shrillness of her voice.

"There's nothing funny about the word piglet," she yelled over and over. "I order you to stop laughing whenever I say *piglet.*"

I jumped up on her desk and was dancing with laughter. From the back of the room, her hands full of first-graders, she turned and saw me.

She was so overcome with fury that she couldn't speak. She released the first-graders in her grasp and started for me, her face purple and throbbing with rage, her tall pile of red hair listing to the left like the Leaning Tower of Pisa. It was the funniest thing, next to the word piglet, I had ever imagined. All I could do was point at her and laugh and shout the word that started the whole thing. "Piglet," I shouted at her. "Piglet, piglet, piglet."

She grabbed a yardstick and raised it like a weapon, a samurai sword. It was no threat. If she couldn't silence me one way, she would silence me another—consequences be damned. But five feet from her desk, she had a heart attack and fell to the floor, dead as a rock.

Was this the crisis that changed the course of my electron river? Could my sad destiny have been decided in that Paramus first-grade classroom?

I saw Caroline and Dr. Yee staring at me. Three seconds had elapsed. Maybe two.

Dr. Yee said something. Caroline translated.

"My grandfather says welcome back. He hopes you had a nice trip."

If there's one thing I can't stand, it's a five hundred-year-old rapping Chinese new age neural pain management mind reader.

"Thank you," I said. "Please tell your grandfather I'm ready for my cure now."

"My grandfather says that the cure is not easy. It will require a special service performed over an extended period of time."

"Does the service cover the treatment?" I said.

"The service is the treatment and the payment at the same time, as it is for all my grandfather's patients."

"No acupuncture?"

Caroline translated. Dr. Yee responded. She smiled at me.

"Do you want acupuncture?"

"Not really."

"Then no acupuncture."

"What about shiatsu or aromatherapy? Shouldn't I be bathing in green tea?"

"My grandfather says you are a funny man. It's too bad about your electrons."

"My feelings exactly. What's the service?"

"What kind of car do you have?"

"1970 Mustang convertible."

And then Caroline and Dr. Yee had a long and somewhat heated discussion, an argument that Caroline lost.

"My grandfather wants to show me all around Los Angeles," she said. "You will be our driver."

"Excuse me?"

"I am only here for the summer. At the end of August, my grandmother returns from China, and I go back to San Francisco. My grandfather wants me to see Los Angeles, and you are going to drive us."

"When?"

"Every Sunday afternoon until your electrons are no longer dysfunctional."

"Just driving you and your grandfather around LA will correct the course of my electron river?"

"He hopes so."

"He hopes so?"

"Don't you?"

"Yes."

"So does he."

"Do I have to decide now?"

Caroline and Dr. Yee spoke Chinese.

"If you are here on Sunday at one o'clock, then your treatment begins. If you are not here, best of luck in the future. You'll need it."

Dr. Yee smiled, slid my CAT scan across the kitchen table while drilling my eyes with his, and said one last thing. Caroline translated.

"See you Sunday," she said. "We're going to Disneyland."

33. IT ONLY MATTERS IF YOU BELIEVE IT

The first thing that occurred to me as I stepped through the front door into the bright blue burning day was that Keanu Reeves really was a terrific landscaper. The yard looked clean and cut and edged and swept. I walked down the front path to my car, tossed my CAT scan on the front passenger seat, grabbed the door handle, and was stopped by Caroline's voice behind me.

"Mark, wait."

I turned to look at her and was taken, as I had been the first time I saw her, with her natural beauty. She stopped on the passenger side of the Mustang. I was on the driver's side. We spoke over the car.

"He wants you to bring some CDs," she said.

"Which ones?"

She read from a list. "The Allman Brothers Band *Live at Fillmore East*. *Hot Fuss* by The Killers, Mozart Horn Concertos, and anything by Snoop Dogg."

She handed me the list across the car. I felt a spark when our hands touched. Maybe she had dragged her feet across the carpet.

"Anything else?"

"Yes. I wanted to say I'm sorry about you having to drive me all over Los Angeles. It wasn't my idea. I'm sure you have better things to do with your Sunday afternoons."

"Actually, no, I really don't. Plus I have this electron issue."

"I heard about that." She smiled, and I felt the tension fall off my shoulders.

"Do you believe this stuff?" I said. "I know he's your grandfather, but rivers of dysfunctional electrons? I don't think they teach that in med school. Not even in China."

"Of course they do. Navigating the Electron River is a required course for all neurologists in China."

"You're kidding?"

"Yes," she said, smiling. "You're too easy."

"You have no idea," I said.

"It only matters if you believe it."

"The power of the mind?"

"The mind, the heart, the body, the spirit. The four worlds."

"Hard to argue," I said.

"He's helped a great many people in his lifetime, and all of those people have helped other people in order to be cured."

"It's a recipe for world peace," I said. "Have everyone with a headache in the Middle East—"

"Which is everyone in the Middle East," she said.

I nodded. Like that first time with Julie at the Farmers' Market, we were in sync. "Have them all deliver groceries and books and sheets and towels and pots and pans and wooden spoons to everyone else."

We smiled at each other, and then she turned and started back to the house. She turned again when she crossed the street and walked backwards a little ways down the front path. "See you Sunday, Mark," she said.

"See you Sunday, Caroline."

34. SEX NEVER LOSES

Successful screenwriting often comes down to nothing more than adherence to a creative system—the more complete and encompassing the system, the tighter and more readable the script, whether or not the thing has any merit as a story.

I had spent more than a decade developing a creative system that worked for me. It had given me the confidence to start a script, battle my way through it no matter how grim the going got, and find a way to write *Fade Out: The End*. All real writers have their own personal creative systems. I think that's what makes them real writers.

My system starts with the creation and formation of the beats that will give a grounding structure to the story, a dramatic three-act shape—clear, solid, causal beats knocking each other down from the first page to the last.

A beat is defined as the gist of a section of the storytelling and is very different than a scene, which is defined entirely by location and time. Any change of location and/or time is by definition a change of scene, though the beat may still be ongoing.

For example, one of the beats in *Phone Book, The Movie*, I thought, would be called *Samantha confronts Jenkins in his Office*. In that beat, Samantha will go from her car, one scene, to the darkened back alley entrance of the office building, another scene, to the inner loading-dock corridors, another scene, to the stairwell, another scene, and then scene after scene until she arrives at Jenkins' office and nails the evil son of a bitch but good. All of those scenes make up the beat.

As I'm creating my beats, I'm also envisioning three-dimensional characters with an unshakeable need to accomplish well-defined goals. These characters have habits and histories and unique points of view. They each bring an individual attitude to the story. An attitude they carried with them before the movie began, but they may or may not carry with them when it ends, if the unfolding events of the movie change their attitudes for the rest of their lives, as I hoped was the case with Samantha Barnes and Christian O'Connor. I try to hear the sound of their voices, the rhythms of their speech, and the vocabularies they accumulated through the living of their lives.

When I have all the beats and the characters are real enough to sit in my living room, feed my fish, and tell me I'm nuts to live in a house that hangs over a deep ravine, then I know I'm ready to write *Fade In*.

But my system had been worthless since Julie left me. *Broken Boner* notwithstanding, I hadn't written a word worth reading for a very long time. I hadn't been able to beat-out a single movie or create one memorable character. There was no dialogue ringing in my ears.

And then I met Caroline Yee. Nothing had happened between us and still I took the thought of her with me, back to Coldwater Canyon, and couldn't shake it. I knew enough about her to know I wanted to know more. I didn't see a ring, but maybe she didn't like to wear it when she was translating her grandfather's medical wisdom, which he apparently received via sub-atomic transmission from Pluto. Or maybe she didn't have a ring. Maybe she wasn't seeing anyone seriously. I'd find out on Sunday.

The energy behind that anticipation must have spilled over into my creative quadrant because for the first time since Julie had left, my system began to hum.

On the ride home from Dr. Yee's house in the Valley, I began to believe that *Phone Book, The Movie* would now take shape—beats would begin to fall into place, plots and subplots would begin to appear, rhythms would emerge, tone would solidify, and characters would come to life in my mind's eye. I would be a writer again very soon. I knew it in my bones.

And so, with my story meeting at Foster's fast approaching, I pulled into my driveway hoping Samantha Barnes would be waiting for me in my office. But Dallas Westcott was waiting instead.

"What did the doctor say?" she said. She was curled up on the couch wearing a red tank top and red boxers, her piles of blonde hair loose and spilling down below her shoulders. She was incredibly beautiful, yet all I could see was trouble ahead.

"I may or may not have electron dysfunction."

"I've heard of that."

"Really?" *How could anyone have heard of that?* I thought.

"I did a movie called *Brain Teaser*. I played a psychiatrist who had a patient who was a matador, and the electric currents in his brain got crossed when one of the bulls trampled on his head, and he became obsessed with sex. But the whole brain thing was that because of his crossed currents, he could read into your mind and turn you on without touching you. He was a brain teaser, and he couldn't stop himself."

"So what happened?" I said.

"He had sex with me and Tiffany Diamond, who played my nurse, but first he brain-teased us into having sex with each other. Hammering Hank Black played the matador. It was his breakout role. He played minor league baseball in Florida before he became a porn actor. It's not his real name, but he's black, so he thought that would be a good way for people to remember him. In the end, he sticks his penis into an electric socket, and it uncrosses the electricity in his head, and he loses his brain-teasing power, but now his penis becomes super-charged, so he has sex with four women at the same time."

"You don't see a lot of African-American matadors," I said.

"I don't know why," she said. "They're very fast runners. I think that's important in a bullfight. Plus they can jump if they have to. Those little Latino bullfighters, I don't think they can jump very high. But I love their outfits. I think Sam should wear one."

The truth was that I had no idea what the hell Dallas Westcott was thinking at any given moment. No one knows what anyone else is really thinking, of course, but at least you can hazard some kind of a guess. Not so with Dallas. Whatever her Michigan childhood had done to her had left her utterly unfathomable. But just because I couldn't read her thoughts didn't mean I wasn't aware of her motiva-tion, which was as clear as a Caribbean cove.

"Samantha Barnes?"

"She'd look great in a matador outfit."

"But why would she wear one?" I said.

She patted the sofa. "Sit next to me, and I'll tell you," she said.

I knew this was a bad idea. From across the room, her coconut oil aphrodisiac was only marginally effective, but up close it overwhelmed my free will. Sex on the couch was a given if I sat next to her.

"Come on, baby. I only bite a little," she said, motioning with her index finger for me to join her.

Dallas Westcott's comfort zone was sex. If bad luck was in the air and her life goals were veering off-track, a roll in the hay would set things straight. Sex was a way to keep the playing field tilted in her fa-vor. It was consciously calculated behavior, controlling and scheming but not necessarily mean-spirited. She didn't want anyone to get hurt; she just wanted what she wanted, which right now was a legitimate acting career, the ultimate look-at-me-now statement of self-worth shot like a cannonball all the way to Garden City. Orgasmic approval and agreement with whatever she was after were a constant affirmation that sex worked like a charm.

That wouldn't have been the worst news for me except that she was living in my house, and I was writing her a ridiculous movie, and I couldn't seem to stop either of those things from happening. Sex wins ninety percent of the time. The other ten percent it ties. Sex never loses. I knew I had to watch my step or I'd end up on the couch having sex, Samantha would be wearing matador clothing, and Dallas would never leave.

"If we're going to talk about the movie, I'm going to sit in this chair so I can concentrate," I said as I sat across from her.

She pouted for a moment but then sat up straighter. "You're worried about your electrons, aren't you? That they're not working right."

"There's no such thing as electron dysfunction," I said. "But I can't stop thinking that I might have it anyway. The doctor's a teeny tiny Chinese guy from outer space. About a million years old. Doesn't speak any English at all."

"Then how do you know what he said?"

"His granddaughter translated the conversation."

"Is she a nurse?"

"Schoolteacher. From San Francisco. She's visiting for the summer."

"What's her name?"

"Caroline."

"Is she nice?"

"Yes."

"Did they give you medicine?"

"No. I have to drive Dr. Yee and Caroline all around LA every Sunday afternoon until the end of August or until my electrons are good again. That's my treatment."

"Can I come too?"

"Dr. Yee didn't say I could bring a friend."

She pouted and said, "I just want you to feel better. Your life is pretty darn good, you know." She took off her tank top, slipped off her boxers, laid back on the couch and smiled her most seductive and beckoning smile. "Don't you think your life is good?"

Don't do it, I said to myself. *Don't do it, don't do it, don't do it, don't do it.* But I stood up and moved to the couch. She was one part manipulative, calculated, scheming succubus and one part innocent, dream-filled, small-town Michigan girl. It was as hard to like her as it was not to like her. Sex muddies all waters, even in the Caribbean.

Twenty-five minutes later, Samantha Barnes was an amateur bull-fighter with a closet full of swell-looking matador outfits.

35. ONE THING LEADS TO ANOTHER AND YOU NEVER KNOW HOW OR WHY

I spent the next week beating out *Phone Book, The Movie* and thinking about Caroline Yee. Dallas went to some kind of porn convention in Las Vegas where she would be crowned Queen of the Sex World. The house was quiet. I moved my shampoo back onto the shower shelf.

I began to envision *Phone Book, The Movie* as Film Noir, with Dallas Westcott playing Samantha Barnes as the private eye and the femme fatale at the same time, a collision of characterizations I couldn't stop and didn't want to. She was dreamy, strange, erotic, ambivalent, and cruel, which was how French film critics Borde and Chaumeton more or less defined Noir in the mid-1950s.

The truth is that Sam and the other characters began to see themselves like that. I was an innocent bystander watching it happen—as are all screenwriters once their scripts take on lives of their own. When the plot unfolds and the characters come to life, we are referees, relegated to ensuring that the game is played by the rules. It's our job to make sure a movie remains a movie and doesn't somehow morph into a stage play or a novella or a preachy essay, that characters don't suddenly decide they want to be someone else, that a comedy doesn't turn into a drama, that a drama doesn't turn into a mystery, that a mystery doesn't turn into porn.

As the beats materialized, I was stunned at the absurdity of the plot, the ludicrousness of the characters, and the preposterousness of the premise.

Marvin Jenkins owned propane processing plants and distributorships as well as air conditioning, trucking, and construction companies all over LA, each one with a different name and phone number. Christian O'Connor ran the phone numbers through the same software he was using to give sight to his damaged retinas. The code was broken one or two letters at time, like *Wheel of Fortune*, so it took most of the movie to figure out how Jenkins planned to blow up half of southern California, then buy the bombed-out land at an enormous discount and rebuild it for a profit in excess of two hundred billion dollars, making him the richest and most powerful man in the world.

The more I wrote the worse it got. I considered buying a one-way ticket to New Zealand and spending the rest of my life herding sheep under the name Sven Caginalp, but I didn't for two reasons, both of which hit me like cinderblocks while I was at the carwash talking to Toxic Bob Bloom, the heinous producer of *Full Force*.

Toxic Bob was a lawyer who never practiced law. He was also a human who never practiced humanity. He was tall and athletically good-looking, saw himself as a real-life playboy, and wore outrageous clothes that most men wouldn't be caught dead in (enormous Joe Namath fur coats, for instance) to fit the image.

Women liked him for his looks and vigor, but all discovered the truth of him at some point—he was utterly incapable of maintaining a primary relationship—and cut their ties, if they were lucky, before too much damage was done.

He hailed from the Midwest where his father, Charles Bloom, had made tens of millions in the manure business. The way it worked was

Toxic Bob's father bought the rights to all the pig, horse, sheep, goat, and cow shit in the middle of the country, and then sold it to the people on both coasts, whether they needed it or not, for more than he had contracted to pay for it. He was a shit broker and Toxic Bob grew up in the business. Selling people shit they didn't need was what he knew. It was in his blood.

He'd gone to law school so he could legally sell people even more shit they didn't need, but when it came time for him to take over the business, his father pulled the rug out from under him. The story was that Charles realized he couldn't trust his own son—and only child— with shit and excluded him from joining the firm. Toxic Bob never recovered from the slight.

He was considered one of the most emotionally bankrupt people in Los Angeles, an enormous accomplishment, and he was entirely void of whatever DNA component grants *homo sapiens* sympathy or empathy or any form of real connection or compassion. Naturally he chose an industry where product management on every level requires the most intimate understanding of those exact human traits: film-making.

But he had one high-energy characteristic that trumped his many shortcomings. It was this critical quality that allowed him to cover his deficiencies (like one of his gigantic fur coats) and make deals and films and money. He was a pathological liar.

In the land where selling shit to the masses had been elevated to an art form, like pruning bonsai trees, Toxic Bob optioned my script *Full Force*.

Actually, he never really optioned it. He wrote the contract himself and the mangled language hidden deep in the usually standard clauses was so convoluted that the Supreme Court couldn't decipher it. None of this was discovered until post-production. In the meantime, he acted like he optioned it, and that was good enough. He attached Willis and Schwarzenegger, promising them both the moon and stars, raised the money from an overseas hedge fund, hired the European director who spoke no English, paid himself an enormous fee, collected the Canadian rebate, and somehow got the movie made.

In all the conversations I'd had with him, he never told me anything that was true. But for several months, he was tolerable to be around for a few minutes at a time. He was reasonable company in small doses, as my mother would say, though it ultimately and always turned out you couldn't trust him with the snot from your nose.

The film was never released. There are dozens and dozens of contracts involved in the production of a feature film, and each of them was so muddled that all anyone could do was hire a lawyer and run for a lifeboat.

Willis, Schwarzenegger, the European director, every member of the cast and crew, the studio, the hedge fund, the distributor, the Canadian government, and an escort service in Toronto all filed massive lawsuits against Toxic Bob and each other, effectively sentencing the film to life in the can without parole. No one will ever see the movie, but everyone got paid, and the lawyers over-billed their clients as usual.

"Mark, babe, you've been on my mind," Toxic Bob said. We were waiting for our cars at the Studio City Car Wash on Ventura Boulevard. My Mustang wasn't dirty, but I needed a break from Sam and Christian and Marvin and the plot to blow up half of Southern California. There's only so much Noir-speak a man can take before his mind turns to mush.

"Hello, Bob," I said. All the money I had came from the big checks Toxic Bob had written me upon commencement and completion of production of *Full Force*, yet he was the last man on Earth I wanted to talk to. I had just taken a shower and would have to take another after our conversation.

"A little bird whispered in my ear that you've got a hot indie project with Joe Hudson. He's an old war buddy of mine. We fought the good fight in the TV trenches, side by side. It was the best of times; it was the worst of times. What's on the burner, babe? Talk to big Bob."

It was summer, and he was dressed like Buffalo Bill Cody: Western jeans, cowboy boots, fringed suede jacket, ten-gallon hat. There were two lies already in play. Three if you count that he wasn't a cowboy. The first lie was that he and Joe were old buddies. Joe had told me they met once at an Emmy party thrown by Peter Strauss to which Toxic Bob hadn't been invited but had crashed. The second lie was that Toxic Bob had worked in television. He never had. He was a feature producer all the way.

"I'd tell you," I said. "But then I'd have to kill you."

"Animal, mineral, vegetable?"

"Can't tell you, Bob."

"Comedy, drama, action?"

"I can't say."

"Cops, cowboys, talking fish?"

"A little of this, a little of that."

"Financing in place?"

"Seems to be."

"Anybody attached?"

"Nobody you know."

"I know everybody, babe. And everybody knows me."

"What are you working on?" I said.

"Show me yours, I'll show you mine? No problem. It's a romantic military sci-fi thriller. Hundred fifty mil. I got fifty committed overseas. I got Sony, Universal, and Disney on the hook for the rest. I got Tom Cruise and Matt Damon falling in love with Angelina Jolie and traveling through time to re-fight the war of the worlds, win her heart, and save her life before the aliens kill her, which they do over and over like *Groundhog Day*. Special effects up the wazoo. I got a hot director from Japan. He's going to burn it up. I'd give you the re-write, but the Japanese kid's doing it himself."

"Does he speak English?"

"Not really."

"Sounds great."

"It's a home run. Cruise, Damon, Jolie. I'm working on my Oscar speech."

"How's that coming?"

"Like a house on fire."

That's when the first cinderblock came flying through the air and smacked me hard in the back of the head. The more outrageous *Phone Book, The Movie* became, the better the chances were that it would fall apart before any of Calvin Key's money was spent and lost, before any more of our time was wasted, and before anyone got hurt or irreparably embarrassed.

I didn't have to lie like Toxic Bob to perform this great service of detonating *Phone Book, The Movie*. I could write it with all the honesty, skill, and talent I could muster, and it would disintegrate under the weight of its own nonsense. I could stop stressing. It had no future no matter what I did. Relief washed over me.

"I'll be rooting for you, Bob," I said.

Across the lot, one of the car wash guys held up Toxic Bob's car keys. He was finished with Bob's black Bentley roadster.

"One clue, babe. For old times' sake," he said, spurs jingling on the macadam.

"Look in the phone book."

"That's the clue?"

"That's it."

"I like it. Secrets within secrets within secrets. One thing leads to another and you never know how or why. Peace out, Mark. I'll be in touch." And then he was in the Bentley and on his way and the second cinderblock smashed into me.

Because of my failure as a porn writer, I became intoxicated on rum and Dr. Pepper and recommenced the digging of the hole out of which I couldn't climb; the hole I'd been digging since Julie left me, a hole made deeper when Tango Joe Hudson jumped in beside me with a wide shovel, made deeper still when Calvin Key joined us with billions of dollars of excavating equipment, and made even deeper when I committed to casting the thing with Dallas Westcott (including a staged reading by Colonel Bill Curry's crew) without telling anyone. I'd been dreading the project like a root canal, especially informing Joe and Calvin about Dallas, and that had reinvigorated the pressure in my head, which had led me to Dr. Alvin Yee and his beautiful and beguiling granddaughter.

One thing leads to another, and you never know how or why. I didn't have to dread *Phone Book, The Movie*. I could embrace it as a friend whose merciful death was coming soon and be grateful that it had introduced me to Caroline Yee.

36. THERE'S NO SIGN TO SAY WHICH WAY IS WHICH

Never was anyone dressed more appropriately for a day at Disneyland. As I turned the corner onto Constance Lane, Dr. Yee and Caroline were standing at the curb. Dr. Yee was wearing black cotton pants, black sandals, a black cotton T-shirt, and Joseph's Amazing Technicolor Dream Coat. It was a long kaftan kind of thing, with bright squares of fabric sewn together in quilt-like fashion. He could have led the Disney Electric Christmas Parade. His long white hair was in pigtails and so was his long white beard. On his head was an African skullcap as colorful as the coat, and his impenetrable Ray-Bans were protecting his ancient eyes from the hellacious Southern California sun.

Caroline wore a red sundress and red sandals. Her hair was pulled back and glistened in the sunshine. She had a straw hat to keep the sun off her face and sunglasses that were round, like John Lennon's.

She smiled and waved as I pulled the Mustang to the curb. I tried to read her eyes, but she wasn't giving much away. Possibly I was sensing an open-mindedness that matched the feeling I was feeling. Maybe she wasn't agonizing over an afternoon at Disneyland with her grandfather and one of his scramble-brained patients. Maybe she was looking forward to it with curiosity and hopefulness in the same way that I was. Maybe she had felt the spark when our hands touched just like I had.

Or maybe she'd spent the week pretending she had mononucleosis in the hope that granddad would let her take a pass on the Disney daytrip. Jesus, I was as nervous as a teenager driving his first date to the dance—with her chaperone from the Orion galaxy in the back seat.

They climbed into the Mustang, and I caught Caroline's eye. "You look great," I said.

"Thank you. This is my happiest dress. I thought it was appropriate. It's supposed to be the happiest place on the planet."

I took the 101 South (east through the Valley) to the 5 South. From there it was a straight shot to Anaheim and the Magic Kingdom. Dr. Yee sat with his hands in his lap, head bobbing to the Southern rock rhythms of Jamoe, Butch, and Berry. Caroline had a brief conversation with her grandfather and then turned to me.

"He wants me to ask you how your head feels," she said.

"Better. I had a good week. Tell him I was able to write for the first time in a long time."

She told him, and he said something, which she again translated.

"He says you have to thank him when you win the Oscar."

I laughed, and so did Dr. Yee. "Not for this one," I said.

"What are you working on?" Caroline said. "Can you talk about it?"

"Sure," I said. "It's a movie about the phone book, about a woman who works for the company that publishes it. She uncovers a sinister plot to blow up Southern California. All the clues to the crime are hidden in the phone book. She hooks up with a blind biomedical computer genius. They fall in love and save the coast."

I waited, but she said nothing. Her eyes were hidden behind her John Lennon specs. Her lips were lightly covered with pinkish lipstick that had a light sheen. They were turned gently upward, though not enough to know whether she was laughing at me or with me. "Do you think it's ridiculous?" I said.

"Do you?" she said.

"Yes. It's called Phone Book, The Movie."

"Why are you writing it if you think it's ridiculous?"

"It's hard to explain. No, that's not right. It's not hard to explain. It's hard to believe. That's what it is. Hard to believe."

I told her about drinking rum and Dr. Pepper at Foster's with Joe Hudson, our pitch meeting with Calvin Key, and my adventure with Colonel Bill Curry. I left out Ken Moynihan and *Broken Boner* and Dallas Westcott. Caroline listened intently, laughing wonderfully at the funny parts, but sensed the story was incomplete, which it was.

"How did you end up at Colonel Bill's?" she said.

It wasn't my failing at porn that I didn't want her to know about, it was my involvement with porn in the first place. No matter how absurd and hysterical porn is—and it's often more comedy than anything else—it remains a taboo topic, a negative opinion shaper, an embarrassment, and a source of shame and guilt. Anyone can talk about violence; it's front-page news most days of the week. Dead soldiers and crime victims and traffic fatalities are as commonplace as Campbell's soup. But porn is strictly a late-night, shades drawn, lights low, voices soft, door shut, kids asleep kind of thing. Definitely not something you share on your first date.

"An actor friend took me," I said.

She frowned a little, just barely enough for me to notice. In fact, she tried to hide it in a small smile.

"What?" I said.

"Nothing." she said.

"My mother's mother would say, 'It's not nothing. Nothing is nothing. This is something.'" I did an excellent imitation of my Nana Elly, who made English sound like Yiddish and Yiddish sound like Jewish immigrant rap.

"You didn't tell me you were seeing someone," she said.

"It's nothing," I said.

"Nothing is nothing. This is something." She smiled to make it a joke, but we had arrived at our first fork in the road. Go one way and I would remain one of her grandfather's patients. Go the other way and I would perhaps be more than that. The problem, as it is in all relationships, is that there's no sign to say which way is which.

"She's an actress. But I'm not really seeing her. I mean, we're involved, there is a certain involvement going on, but it's, well, it's dumb, and I'm trying to get out of it, but she won't let me. She won't leave."

"She won't leave?"

"Not yet."

Caroline thought about that for a moment, determined, I suppose, that it was truthful, and let her little frown dissipate. "Is she famous?" she said.

"For what she does, yes," I said.

"Should I ask what she does?"

"Please don't."

She turned to me and looked over the top rim of her John Lennon sunglasses. I looked at her too. Maybe she saw regret and embarrassment in my eyes. Maybe she saw someone who was lost and trying not to be lost but failing miserably at it. God knows that's how I was feeling.

"Okay. Will she ever leave?"

"I hope so. I've asked her to."

"No wonder your electrons are dysfunctional," she said, and her smile was warm again. We drove the rest of the way without talking, letting Snoop Dogg and The Killers say all there was to say until we arrived in Anaheim and Walt Disney took command of the conversation.

37. SOMETHING MAGICAL IN THE MAGIC KINGDOM

Actors wearing costumes of the Disney animated heroes—Mickey, Minnie, Donald, Goofy, Cinderella, Sleeping Beauty, and the rest—were waiting in the courtyard entrance area to blow the minds of children right from their first moment of arrival in the hope that after the hectic picture-taking, the families would be so overwhelmed and exhausted that before anything else happened, they would have to eat something to regain their strength. Food booths were strategically located nearby to facilitate this refueling. A pound or two of deep-fried dough covered with sugar and slugged down with a gallon of cola would have everyone up and on their way in no time flat.

Much of the chaotic focus was on Mickey and Minnie, the Adam and Eve of Disney mythology. Swarms of children, mouths agape, surrounded the rodents and reached their little hands out to touch them and make sure they weren't dreaming—that they really were in Disneyland and the mouse and his girlfriend were here as well. Nothing ever changed this Welcome-to-Disney routine. Every day of every year, the children squealed with incredulity and glee and the mice stole the show.

But when Dr. Alvin Yee entered the courtyard, the mob of little faces turned to him and fell silent. The entire courtyard was still. To these impressionable little minds, Yee wasn't a New Age Neural Pain Management Professional; he was the Emperor from *Mulan*. He wasn't constructed like the mice, but was flesh and blood, with real hair and a real voice and a face not frozen in a single expression for all of eternity.

Dr. Yee walked to the middle of the courtyard, the Enchanted Castle behind him in the distance, while the cartoon characters, the children, and their parents watched him, motionless, soundless. The adults were confused, happy in the familiar Disney-numb sort of way, but unsure of themselves.

A wife the size of a tour bus, with skin as white as Elmer's Glue, leaned in to her husband, a man who dwarfed her in height and girth.

"Honey," the wife said to the husband, "is that man part of Disney?"

"He has to be," the husband said, flipping through the Disney guidebook.

"Then why did he wait on line to buy a ticket?"

"I don't know. Nothing like this was in the brochure."

There was no confusion on the part of the hundreds of children in the courtyard. They knew something special was unfolding, something magical in the Magic Kingdom.

Yee must have known it too because he stopped, smiled, and held his arms out in a warm and welcoming embrace. With a rush and a gasp, the children abandoned the mice and the ducks and the various princesses and surrounded Dr. Yee, touching his pigtailed beard, his hot-wired kaftan, his thousand-year-old hands. They remained silent as he moved slowly through them, me and Caroline trailing behind him at a respectful distance, parents on the fringes, too stunned to take pictures, fake rodents and other cartoon characters as awed as everyone else.

We reached the end of the courtyard area, and Yee turned to the crowd and waved with both hands, and everyone waved back, including Mickey, Minnie, Donald, the Disney staffers and security guards, and the parents and the children. Then he turned again and walked into the park. There was one final moment of stillness behind us, as if Yee had a left a vacuum of real magic in his wake, and then all at once Disney-magic filled that vacuum with cardboard, wire, papier-mâché, and unblinking cartoon eyes.

38. LOVE AND LOGIC DON'T SPEAK THE SAME LANGUAGE

We traversed the Magic Kingdom, took the Small World boat ride, braved the Thunder Mountain railroad, laughed and cowered at the Pirates of The Caribbean, screamed in our rockets on Space Mountain, and arrived at The Matador when the line was long and included several school buses of first-graders, all of whom surrounded Emperor Yee to feel his magic up close.

Caroline and I stood to the side. We had sat next to each other on every ride because Yee had insisted on sitting alone and in the very front car if possible. Our conversations had been easy-going and flirty in nature. We shared an offbeat sense of humor and a somewhat cockeyed view of the world. I knew why my life-vision was skewed and imagined that growing up in whatever passed for normal in the Yee house had tilted hers as well.

I liked her a lot. I liked the way she smiled when she thought I was being silly about things. I liked the way she decided the food at Disney was just one ingredient short of being plastic. I liked the way she wrapped her arms around my waist on the Space Mountain ride. I liked the respect she paid her magical grandfather. I liked the way she didn't ask me about Dallas Westcott. I liked her silvery pink lipstick. I liked her slender body, her black hair, the certainty in her voice, the casual and generous quality of her laugh, the satiny smoothness of her skin.

She was levelheaded, she said, like her mother, but a bit of a gambler like her dad. Dr. Yee was her mother's father, and his name wasn't Alvin. When he first came to America, years after his children and grandchildren had arrived, his Chinese name was utterly unpronounceable in English. There was simply no translation for it. He was advised by his family to choose a more American-sounding name. He considered it for a week and then watched an episode of *Alvin and the Chipmunks*. He saw himself as the spunky and energetic little Alvin and snatched the name for himself. Dr. Alvin Chipmunk Yee, headshrinker from another planet.

"I know you think your personal life is strange and you don't want to talk about it, but I want you to know that mine is strange too," she said.

We were waiting our turn to ride the Matador. The line was long, and several children had gathered around Dr. Yee. His patience was infinite.

"You don't have to tell me," I said.

"I know. I don't talk about it very much. Most people wouldn't believe me."

"And you think I will?"

"I think you'll like me anyway."

She peered over the top of those John Lennon specs again and smiled.

"I know I will," I said.

"I was living in New York. The Upper East Side. Seventy-sixth and Second."

"I'm from New Jersey. Paramus."

"Must have been hard for you," she said. "There's no place to shop."

I smiled. "I still have the scars."

Dr. Yee was playing ring around the rosy with five-year-old strawberry blonde triplets, sisters who could've lit Los Angeles with the sound of their laughter. Their father was snapping digital pictures at a furious pace, and for these silly, joyous moments, Disneyland really was the happiest place on Earth.

"I was teaching calculus at Stuyvesant," Caroline said.

"Numbers are my Achilles heel."

"Writing is mine. Maybe we can help each other."

"That's what I'm hoping."

The zigzagging Matador line surged forward, and the ring around the rosy game ended. One parent asked Dr. Yee to autograph his Disneyland map.

"I met a man at a Knicks game."

"Who were they playing?"

"Portland. A friend of mine got four tickets from work. It was a double date."

"Was it blind?"

"Yes, a blind double date. My date was named Walter Rydell. He was a writer and a photographer. He did coffee table books. Big colorful hardcover books about motorcycles and diners and barns and tractors and baseball fields and sports cars. He took the pictures and wrote the stories. They're very good books. He's a wonderful photographer and a good writer."

"Nothing strange about that," I said.

"I didn't think so either," Caroline said. "He was smart and funny and talented and really nice. He was cute and successful, and we got along great."

"Still nothing strange."

"Not yet. He was in New York doing a book on boardwalks; Coney Island was one of them. We started dating, it got serious, and when he went home to San Francisco, I went with him."

"You left your job?"

"I left everything. Logic and love don't speak the same language."

Who knew that better than me? It was the only thing in the world I did know. "I'm guessing here comes the strange part," I said.

"I got a job teaching kindergarten at an inner city school, and we were living together near Haight Ashbury, and everything was going great, and then one day, maybe two months later, he told me he was seeing someone else."

"I'm a good guesser," I said.

She smiled as if she still couldn't believe she'd been reckless enough to drop her entire life in the East River for a West Coast relationship with a blind date named Walter. "That's not the strange part," she said. "He'd never met the girl he was seeing. They'd been writing letters for three years."

"Was she out of the country?"

"She was in prison."

The right response didn't come to me. I was hoping for something sympathetic, something warm and embracing that would demonstrate my sensitive side while simultaneously showcasing the measure of my inner strength and emotional generosity.

"You're shitting me," I said.

"That's not the strange part. The woman, Jenny Brann, was in jail for hiring someone to kill her husband. That's who he was in love with. A woman who hired someone to kill her husband."

"He told you that?"

"He introduced me to her. She got out of prison early for good behavior, apparently she hadn't hired anyone to kill anyone else in several years, and he brought her to our house on Haight and sat me down at the kitchen table and told me they were engaged and getting married in two days."

"Did her husband die?"

208 · RICH LEDER

"He worked construction. The guy she hired dropped a steel girder on him. Yes, he died."

"Sounds like Walter had a bit of a death wish." I was kidding, trying to find a ray of humor in an otherwise morose situation.

"Yes," Caroline said. "He told me he was sorry, but that he'd had a death wish for years, that Jenny was the perfect woman for him, and they were deeply in love, and he could only hope that that would change for the worse some day after they were married. She held his hand on the table and said she was sure it would. They both laughed, but I don't think they were joking."

"I'm sorry too," I said.

"As strange as that is, it's not the strange part for me. The strange part is that I never saw any of it coming. Walter walked in with Jenny Brann and said he had a death wish, and you could have knocked me over with a feather. I was upside down after that. I mean, how could you miss something so big? It's not exactly a confidence builder for forming future relationships."

My own relationship radar was damaged and defective. I felt what she felt.

"Not exactly," I said.

"But I like San Francisco, and kindergarten's fun to teach."

"Nobody hiring anyone to kill anyone else?"

"No, and it turns out I like kids."

"I do too." Julie and I had talked about having children. She could be raising a brood of Romanian jugglers by now, for all I knew.

"Anyway, you look at me like you could be interested if you thought about it, and before you make a decision about that, I wanted you to know that my personal life is strange too, and I'm still, like I said, a little upside down. I just want you to go slow, I mean, if you think you're going anywhere, with me, I mean."

The Matador line lurched again, an infinite series of switchbacks that forced us to walk ten miles to cover fifty yards. Dr. Yee was hiding one of the triplets in the folds of his kaftan while her sisters giggled and pretended not to know where she was. Caroline and I watched them for a moment or two in silence.

"You're part of my therapy, aren't you?" I said.

"I think you're part of mine," she said.

39. FAMOUS SPANIARDS DAY

The story meeting at Foster's was postponed for two weeks because Calvin Key was buying a diamond mine or an airline or the country of Finland or something that no normal citizen is able to buy. Joe stopped by to tell me about the rescheduled meeting and didn't remember exactly what it was that Calvin was purchasing, though I think Dallas, who was sunbathing nude on my back deck, distracted him.

"Tell me, Fernando Rey. Do you think she'd let us make a mold of her body?"

"Why, Joe?" He was wearing his sunglasses and black leather from head to toe. He had been dancing all night and had come straight from the ballroom. He wore a black and gold bandana on his head like a pirate. We were in the kitchen drinking coffee. Dallas was on the chaise soaking in the morning sun.

"Are you insane? We could market a body like that a hundred ways. Make enough money to bring back Elvis."

"Name one."

"Soda bottles. Can you imagine if they were shaped like her? Do you have any idea what that would do to sales?"

I pictured grocery store aisles of soft drinks bottled in Dallas Westcott's curves. For every prude in Omaha, every mother of small children in Salt Lake, and every Sunday school teacher in Wichita who would give up Gatorade and Sun Drop and Pepsi on the spot, there would be hundreds of adolescent boys and grown men who would increase their consumption tenfold. "Name another," I said.

"Dice."

"What dice?"

"Those that hang on the rear view mirrors of hot rods all over America. We've already got the original mold. We duplicate, replicate, and potentate it down to the right size, cast it in hard white plastic, paint the black dots in the right places, one on each nipple for instance, a deuce down below, a trey on each side of her ass, and sell them in carwashes from coast to coast."

"A potentate is someone who possesses great power."

"Yes it is, Tito Fuentes. Now repeat after me, 'Joe, you're a mad fucking genius.'"

"Joe, you're a mad fucking genius."

"Never forget it, and you'll be a rich man in more ways than one. Sweet baby Jesus, there's cornbread in the cupboard. Amen and hallelujah, my brother."

It was at this moment that I realized Tango Joe Hudson, who had built up a substantial life, had seen it blown to bits by the heartless Hollywood winds of change, and was furiously fighting the good fight to win it back, was my best friend in the business and maybe my best friend in the world. We left the kitchen and headed for my office to talk about the script.

"I've been talking to Barry's people," Joe said. "We've got a meeting in two weeks. He likes the idea, but wants to see the script before he'll commit."

"Barry Manilow?"

"Your cousin, Señor Wences. On your father's side."

"Barry Manilow likes the idea?"

"He'll tell you himself in two weeks."

Before I could internalize this disturbing data, Joe sat in my chair, put his feet on my desk, and said, "Is Toxic Bob Bloom a friend of yours?"

"No. He produced my movie *Full Force*. Why?"

"He calls me every day. 'Joe,' he says. 'It's your old buddy Bob Bloom.' He wants to know what project I'm producing, what script you're writing, where the financing is coming from, who's attached, who's distributing, who's directing. He wants to buy me lunch at The Palm."

"I saw him at the car wash the other day. He was all over me."

"He says De Niro owes him a movie. He'll attach him to ours if we make him a producing partner."

"Everything he says is a lie."

"He's got Meg Ryan and her new lips. He says we can have them in a package."

"The lips come separate?"

"Ryan and De Niro. Give me your drugs. You can't be trusted with them."

He opened my desk drawer and searched for illegal substances. If I'd had any, my desk is the last place I'd keep them. It's hard enough to put ten words together when you're straight as string.

"How can he attach actors without knowing what kind of movie it is? What if it was a slasher film?"

"Is it?"

"No. It's Noir."

Joe smiled. "They'll love us in Cannes. We'll stay on Bowie's yacht and eat oysters for breakfast."

I didn't bother asking him whether or not he knew David Bowie. There was no point; within minutes either the project would be a dead donkey or I would.

"I have to tell you something, Joe," I said. I still had never seen his eyes.

He stood up, reached behind him, pulled a pistol from a holster hanging just above his rear end, and said, "When I hear those particular words spoken in that particular tone of voice, I don't know what else to do but get my gun out. Here, you take it. I'm not to be trusted with bullets."

He handed me the weapon. It was the first time in my life I had held a loaded gun. I stood there like a fool, brandishing it like a wooden spoon. It was heavy and smelled like oil. It looked modern, like an automatic, or a semi-automatic. If you shot someone with it, they would be automatically dead; maybe that's where the name subconsciously came from.

"If this is bad news, I want you to shoot me in the heart," he said.

"Don't be melodramatic, Joe. I'm not going to shoot you."

"Melodrama is big business, Xavier Cugat. Look at Lifetime."

Today, apparently, was Famous Spaniards Day for Joe. Maybe he'd been up late watching a film by Pedro Almodovar or had seen something with Antonio Banderas or Penelope Cruz. Maybe he'd ordered paella for dinner or flan for desert. Maybe he was up all night doing the Samba with an older woman who'd carried a rose in her teeth. There was no reasoning your way through the thought processes of Joe Hudson. And besides, why not have a Famous Spaniards Day? Where was the harm?

"Joe, I should have told you a long time ago, but I promised Dallas the lead in *Phone Book, The Movie*. She's going to play Samantha. I'm writing it for her."

So there it was. The crazy ride that started when I met Ken Moynihan on my flight to Newark was over. Joe would be done with me now on this project, though I hoped he might consider me in the future for one of his TV pilots, and Dallas would put her clothes on and be out the door in five seconds flat. A person's entire life can turn on a sentence or two, and mine was about to make the hard left I'd been expecting and hoping for.

Joe stood there, leaning forward, hands on my desk, ponytail sticking out from under the black and gold bandana. Maybe it was the bandana that had inspired the Famous Spaniards Day. He said nothing. Not one muscle so much as twitched. I was suddenly glad to be holding the gun.

"She's a porn star, Joe. I couldn't help myself. That's my bad excuse."

"Correction, Picasso. She's the biggest porn star in the world."

"Yes," I said. "It's true."

"I see," he said. "You know what this means?"

Of course I knew what it meant. It meant the end of *Phone Book, The Movie.*

"What it means, Ponce de Leon, is that you and I are no longer making an independent feature film in search of distribution."

"I know."

"It means you and I are no longer making an independent feature film that critics will comprehend."

"I had no choice."

"It means you and I are no longer making an independent feature film that floats in the Hollywood mainstream."

"She sunbathes nude, for Chrissake, Joe."

"It means that you and I are no longer making an independent feature film, period."

And that was that. I held out the gun. He would either shoot me or shoot himself. Either way, I couldn't tolerate one more moment of his disappointment.

"What it means, Placido Domingo, is that we are making the must-see-movie of the year."

"What?"

"Repeat after me. I, Mark Manilow, am a mad fucking genius."

He took the gun, holstered it, came around the desk, and hugged me like a bear. I had zoomed right past the hard left and was doing ninety-five on the 405.

"In one orgasmic thrust of your long wet Willie, you have catapulted us past the rest of the pack, given us a marketing strategy Donald Trump's barber would envy, and made us as rich and fat and famous as dead Dom DeLuise before we've even shot a frame of film."

He bolted out of the office, adrenalin-flowing off him in iridescent waves, passed through the kitchen without his feet touching the ground, and landed again on the porch, in front of the chaise that held the buck-naked Miss Westcott.

"My darling Dallas," Joe said. "I have heard the news that you are to be Samantha Barnes and save the California coast from certain death and destruction. As your producer, I wanted you to know that this is the single greatest stroke of casting in cinematic history, except possibly for Kelsy Grammer in *X-Men*. That cat was born to be blue."

I was standing beside him, looking at Dallas, who shielded her eyes from the sun.

"Thanks, Joe. I've never been more ready to play a role in my life. I'm a legitimate actress now. I'll do a great job for you."

"And I'll do a great job for you," Joe said, and then he turned to me. "What about you, El Cid?"

No way, Joe, I thought. *Someone has to stop this train.* "I'll do a great job for both of you," I said.

Joe and Dallas shook hands as if she weren't nude, and he and I left the porch and walked through the house toward the front door.

"Where are you in the script?" Joe said.

"I finished beating it out. I just have to write it."

"You've got two weeks."

"There's more, Joe."

"Ninety pages. Fourteen days. Six and a half pages a day . . . there's more?"

"I committed to having a staged reading at Colonel Bill Curry's acting school."

"Perfect. We can bring Barry and do the meeting there."

"We can?"

"Can and will, Cortez. I'll set it up."

He climbed in his car and backed out of the driveway, already dialing his cell phone. Inside the house, my phone was ringing. *He's calling me,* I thought. *In his euphoria, he's forgotten he's at my house, and he's calling to tell me the good news.* Joe stopped before driving away and rolled down his window. "Stay away from Toxic Bob," he said. "He's the Grand Central Station of voodoo."

I nodded, completely out of words. Instead of stopping the project on impact, the news of Dallas' attachment as leading lady had propelled *Phone Book, The Movie* forward with enthusiasm, excitement, and momentum. I had two weeks to write the script before I introduced Barry Manilow, my new cousin, to Calvin Key, Colonel Bill Curry, and Dallas Westcott, who was suddenly standing behind me, still nude, gleaming with tanning oil, and holding out the phone.

"It's for you," she said. "Somebody named Julie Bowers."

40. THE GROUND IS MADE OF FROZEN WATER DOWN HERE

I took the phone from Dallas, who blew me a kiss before heading back to her chaise lounge on the deck.

I wasn't prepared to talk to Julie, so I walked down the driveway to my Mustang and leaned against the trunk. I felt like I was kayaking in white-capped water without a paddle. The river, in the mountains of Colorado, was raging, and there were jagged rocks and thick tree limbs at every bone-jarring turn. The sound of the rushing water was deafening, but there was a pounding in my head that I recognized as my heart, mad as fire, going boom-boom-boom-boom-boom. I couldn't hear myself scream as the kayak flipped over and then up and then over and then up again. I was spitting freezing mountain water and gagging on my own emotional turmoil.

"Hi," I said. "Where are you?"

"Antarctica. With the emperor penguins."

"You sound like you're next door."

"It's a satellite phone. It belongs to Greg."

"Who's Greg?"

"A man I met. He's the leader of the expedition."

"Expedition to where?"

"Antarctica. You're a very silly man, Mark Manilow."

Those were the words that could have saved me.

"Mark, are you there?"

"I'm here."

"The penguins are incredible. By the end of the summer, their breeding ground will be more than one hundred kilometers from the nearest open water. That's a hell of a long walk for a penguin. Or for anyone, really. Especially down here."

"I saw the movie."

"Forget the movie. Some people see the penguins as a metaphor for family values, monogamy, parenthood, sacrifice, but I think they're a metaphor for us."

"You do?"

"Yes. Emperor penguins are only monogamous from one season to the next. The mating cycle matches the reproductive cycle. If you look at it that way, the emperor penguin divorce rate is up around ninety percent."

"Julie, they're just birds."

"That's not why I called."

"What a relief."

"Don't be angry with me, Mark. It's hard to keep your balance when you're angry. It's bad for juggling and all sorts of other things."

"I'm sorry. Why did you call?"

"I had a premonition that something strange is going to happen to you. Maybe it's even happening now. Are you okay?"

"I have good days." That was true, but not the whole truth.

"Me too," she said.

"Are you coming back?" Jesus Christ, I thought, there was a catch in my throat when I said that. And, holy shit, there were tears in my eyes. I hoped the satellite somehow lost my heartbreak in the outer space transmission.

"Are you crying, Mark?"

"Not too often."

"That's good. Are you seeing anyone?"

"It's hard to believe."

"What is?"

"The answer to that question." There was squawking in the background, like a huge stadium crowd unhappy with the home team and giving them the business.

"Skip it then."

"Okay," I said. "Are you ever coming back?"

"The ground is made of frozen water down here. Let me put it that way. I'm pretty good with premonitions, Mark. If strange things are happening now, they're going to get stranger. Are strange things happening now?"

"Define strange."

"That's what I thought. They're going to get stranger. That's why I called. To tell you it's going to get worse and to wish you good luck. Greg, wait for me . . ."

I wanted to tell her I still loved her, that my affair with Dallas Westcott was a mistake I couldn't take back or even end, but was still a mistake. I wanted to tell her about Caroline and her magical grandfather. I wanted to tell her about the absurd film I was writing for the counting billionaire and about his butler and cook in the closet. And about Ken Moynihan and my trip home to Paramus, how my room was a gym and Gibby was a screenwriting cop, how I'd seen my niece and nephew for the first time in ten years. I wanted to pour my heart out in a way I hadn't been able to since she left me. I wanted to, but I didn't.

She was warning me that my life was strange, as if I needed a warning, as if I didn't know there was a naked porn star on my back deck waiting to screw me silly for good luck and a ballroom dancing producer and a madman shrink for dogs and cats and birds and fish turned lunatic acting coach all expecting me to behave as if things were fine. I didn't need a warning. It would defy physics for my life to get any stranger.

I walked back down the driveway and into the house. I saw Dallas on the deck, but turned into my office instead. I sat at my desk, turned on my computer, opened Final Draft, and typed these words: *Phone Book, The Movie . . . Fade In:*

41. CHICKEN FRIED STEAK

I hooked into the Noir spirit of the script—the language, the atmosphere—and closed my eyes so as not to see the outlandishness of the characters and the story.

What trash! Not great trash, not even good trash, but uninspired, middle-of-the-road trash, the kind of film that Hollywood does well and often. Not a cult classic by any means, but a low-brow, world-in-ridiculous-jeopardy, unlikely romance, none-too-thrilling thriller you might watch at three in the morning when you can't sleep because you don't have enough money to pay your bills.

You're channel surfing for a distraction and find *Phone Book, The Movie,* a film that promises to prove there are people in the world worse off than you, namely the guy who wrote the thing. So you stay up, regretting every minute, but watching all the way to the end, when busty Samantha Barnes, in the climactic finale, uses her bullfighting skills to sidestep the insanely evil Marvin Jenkins who, charging her like a bull, falls to his death from the helicopter pad at the top of his energy empire headquarters skyscraper.

But you're not really being honest. The reason you watched was because you recognized Dallas Westcott from her Moynihan classic *Two Balls In The Corner Pocket*, in which she played a pool shark who takes on Minneola Fats, a nickname earned by the outrageous circumference of his cock, which he occasionally uses—I swear to God —to make shots—played by an actor named Thad Whacker, who auditioned by dropping his drawers and sinking the nine ball with a flashy hip-thrust. Dallas and Fats wind up in half a dozen wild combinations together on the pool table, and at the high point (or low point), his testicles are literally in the corner pocket. As if you couldn't guess.

Throughout the two weeks it took me to bang out a first draft, my relationship with Miss Westcott took on an anomalous quality based on a decision I made the Monday morning after my Sunday afternoon at Travel Town with Caroline and Dr. Yee.

Dallas had showered and was ready for some good-luck sex before heading out to the deck to sunbathe nude. I slid away from her, sat up, and said, "We have to talk."

She was naked and her hair was still wet. She smelled amazing, just enough coconut oil moisturizer to make me weak. "I want you to fuck me like a freight train, Mark. Is that what you mean?" She tried to snuggle up to me, but I summoned a Herculean amount of self-control and held my ground.

"No, that's not what I mean," I said. My tone of voice was shaky, and I was afraid it would embolden her to continue with her morning constitutional seduction, but she stopped instead. It was a lucky break for me. I'm sure I wouldn't have been able to hold her off.

"About us?" she said, her mouth dropping ever so slightly into a frown.

"Yes."

"How long will it take, because I'm shooting a big scene in *Doggie Day Afternoon* at eleven thirty, and I want to lie in the sun and then cook breakfast."

"It won't take long."

She nodded. "Good."

"Dallas. I'm not going to have sex with you anymore."

Her sky-blue eye was confused, but focused. Her brown eye, however, had the quality of a sad, lost Michigan girl, unable to find approval from her father. I knew the look in her brown eye by heart.

"I understand," she said.

I stared at her blank-faced. "You do?"

"You need to concentrate on the script, like a boxer before a fight. I dated a middleweight once. He was Latino. He was training and wouldn't have sex with me. He said he had to focus with his body and his mind. Turned out it didn't matter. He got knocked out anyway. I learned two things. You should always have sex, and Latino guys should be bullfighters. But if that's how you really feel, I can wait. *Phone Book, The Movie* comes first. If you need to think about Samantha Barnes and not Dallas Westcott, I understand. Can we use a vibrator?"

She removed a massive penile-like object from the nightstand drawer, held it up, and turned it on. It shook and rotated and scared the crap out of me. When it wasn't giving her orgasms, it was carving tunnels through mountains.

"No, Dallas. No vibrator. It's not the movie."

She turned off the vibrator, put it back in the drawer, and said, "Are you sick? Are you dying? Because I've had sex with dying guys before. A last wish kind of thing. Don't be embarrassed if that's what it is."

It took me a moment to fully process that thought. Once I had, I immediately discarded it on the basis of its distracting carnal weirdness.

"I've met someone else, Dallas, and if I can't get disengaged from you, then I can't pursue anything with her."

"Who is she?"

"Caroline Yee."

"The nurse?"

"She's not a nurse. She's a kindergarten teacher. She's just helping her grandfather for the summer before she goes back to San Francisco."

She took a deep breath. She was among the most beautiful women on the face of the Earth and the most knowledgeable and willing sex partner any man had ever had in recorded history, and I had just told her that I wasn't going to screw her to the bedpost ever again.

It's reasonable to assume that a two-ton depression would already be crushing me, or that I'd be drowning in a dark, inky pool of remorse and regret. I had anticipated those reactions, but instead I felt good. I had been honest with Dallas about my feelings for Caroline and knew that after yelling and screaming and maybe even beating me with that Frankenstein vibrator, she would be packing her things and moving out.

"Oh, Mark," she said. "No one's ever said anything so wonderful to me in all my life."

"Excuse me?"

"Do you know how many relationships I've had?"

You would need Calvin Key's software to tally them up, I thought. "More than three?"

"Yes. And they all ended badly. But you care so much about me that you won't have sex with me while you're flirting with the nurse."

"She's not a nurse."

"If you didn't care, you'd just keep having sex with me anyway, like all the other men. But you do care. This relationship's a keeper, Mark. That's really what you're saying."

"No it's not. I'm breaking up with you here."

"You're cute, Mark."

"I'm not cute."

"Okay, you're the most handsome and rugged and macho screenwriter I ever thought I'd meet."

"I think you should move out."

She looked at me with pity in her brown eye and steely, calculating resolve in her sky-blue eye. "Oh, baby. I'm not going anywhere but to the back deck." She opened the nightstand drawer and again removed the battering-ram vibrator from hell. "You write the movie and have fun with the nurse, and when it's all over, we'll get serious."

She stood up. Joe was right. If we made a mold of her body, we'd be rich in a year. "You're not going to use that thing on the deck?" I said, a trace of hysteria finding its footing in my voice.

"There's an old man across the canyon who likes to watch me. He's got binoculars. It's good luck to do something nice for someone you don't know. I'll cook us some chicken fried steak and eggs for breakfast, and you'll feel better about everything."

And then she left, her perfect ass disappearing down the hall and around the corner to the kitchen, where she would cook me chicken fried steak and eggs despite the fact that I had told her ten times I didn't like chicken fried steak, that chicken fried steak was not something I liked to eat for breakfast (or ever), and that her chicken fried steak, in particular, was greasier and had more salt than I imagined chicken fried steak was supposed to have or would have if I liked to eat it in the first place.

But what she heard was: I love chicken fried steak, I can't get enough chicken fried steak, and please make me chicken fried steak five days a week for the rest of my life.

So far, I had no such communication problem with Caroline Yee. If I had asked her not to make me chicken fried steak, I feel sure she would have said fine, or asked why not, or told me it was good for dysfunctional electrons but at least would have responded to the words I actually said. I felt like that might be a good basis upon which to pursue a relationship. And so I did.

42. IT'S THE GAY GUY WHO FARTS

Griffith Park is the largest "municipal park with urban wilderness area" in the United States (not including Beverly Hills, the most extreme urban wilderness area in Los Angeles). More than four thousand acres of chaparral-covered terrain and landscaped parkland and picnic areas offer numerous family attractions and multiple educational and cultural institutions. The Los Angeles Zoo is here, as are the Autry National Center, the Griffith Observatory, the Los Angeles Equestrian Center, the Greek Theater, the Griffith Park Merry-Go-Round, camping grounds, swimming pools, soccer fields, tennis courts, golf courses, countless miles of hiking and horseback riding trails, and Travel Town—the destination of my second Sunday outing with Caroline and Dr. Yee.

Founded in the late 1940s with two little Los Angeles Harbor Department steam engines destined for scrap, Travel Town is now home to more than a dozen massive locomotives. There are long-retired passenger cars, freight cars, and cabooses to keep them company and old interurbans and motorcars for further historical reference. There are some trains made up for meeting space and other trains reserved for birthday parties. There is a gift shop with vending machines and grassy, shaded picnic areas. Peaceful and pleasant, an excellent scaled-down train circles the perimeter of the grounds, tooting its little horn and eliciting waves from the happy families that flock here on weekends.

As I turned into the Lake River Springs development, my cell phone rang.

"Hello."

"Mark, it's Cathy."

Cathy Burns. My agent before she dumped me.

"Cathy, hi. You're in the office on Sunday?"

"It's Sunday?"

"Yes."

"All the same to me, Mark. What's a weekend anyway? Know what I mean?"

"Not really."

She laughed like we had shared an old, personal, private joke. "Oh, that's too good. So listen, there's a reason I called. Toxic Bob Bloom was in my office yesterday, and he told me he was producing a project with you and Joe Hudson that I should know about."

I pulled to the side of the road so I wouldn't drive head-on into an approaching car whose driver would have no idea that our fatal collision was caused by the news that Toxic Bob had, in a stunning and complete and outlandish lie, attached himself to *Phone Book, The Movie*.

"He said he's producing?"

"With Joe Hudson. You're writing it, and the budget is in the bank. Hottest indie in town, he said."

"Did he tell you what it's about?"

"He said he'd let you do the honors."

I had come to expect this kind of mind-blowing dishonesty from Toxic Bob, yet the unmitigated gall of it, the infinite depth of his corruption, his limitless capacity for fraud and deception reminded me again of the sick and shameless state of his twisted soul. I had money because of Toxic Bob, but it was money he more or less stole to make a movie he didn't exactly own, and then he ruined it for everyone. He was poison.

"Mark, did I lose you?"

"I'm here."

"Can you talk about it?"

"All I can tell you is that it has a ridiculous premise, a brainless and contrived plot, paper-thin characters, melodramatic action, stilted dialogue, and a nonsensical resolution."

"That's the kind of movie I can really get behind. A satire of a satire. I like it."

"You don't understand, Cathy. It's based on every bad movie ever made."

"Translation: Huge opening weekend. Is there a gay character?"

I knew where this was going and understood there was no fighting it. "Flaming," I said. "There's some farting in there too. It's the gay guy who farts. Flaming farts, Cathy. I was thinking of you when I wrote it."

"I love it. Do you hear me? I love it like sex. Does it have sex? Tell me it has sex."

"Sex, excessive violence, and no meaningful emotional content. The truth is you don't need a shred of intelligence to enjoy it."

"I'm seeing something, Mark. You know what I'm seeing?"

"No idea."

"A blockbuster. An indie blockbuster like *Greek Wedding*."

"I want whatever drugs you're taking."

"Is it based on actual events? That helps us in TV."

"Not one word of it is true."

"So what? It sounds true, doesn't it?"

"Not really."

"Okay, inspired by actual events. Something must have inspired you."

"Yes, something implausible."

"That's all we need. I can rep this movie for you, Mark—domestic, foreign, DVDs, cable, Internet, new media, the whole shebang. Promise me you'll talk to Joe."

"I'll talk to Joe. Toxic Bob is lying, you know that, right?"

"Everybody knows that."

Everybody did know that. He countered this common knowledge by acting like his lies were true for long enough periods of time that people, as if bludgeoned into submission, accepted his lies as truth, even though they knew they were lies. That's how he lived his whole life.

"Do you hate this business as much as I do?" I said.

"Probably more. Is it really Sunday?"

"Go home, Cathy. Drink some rum. Try it with Dr. Pepper."

"This is the most exciting project I've heard about all year. You're back in the game, Mark. Dumb it down. Make it your mantra."

And then she hung up. I sat there dazed for a long moment. It wouldn't do a lick of good to call Toxic Bob and blast him. He suffered from the same hearing-to-comprehension disconnect as Dallas and would take that phone call as confirmation of his involvement. I would suggest to Joe that this time we ignore him. Maybe he would react like a barking dog on the other side of a fence that when you refuse to look, ceases to believe he exists.

Oh well, I thought, *at least I have an agent.*

43. MONKEY WRENCH

I pulled the Mustang back into traffic, continued on to 2552 Constance Lane, and checked the CDs that Dr. Yee had requested: *Gaucho* by Steely Dan, *Feeding Frenzy* by Jimmy Buffett, *Blood Sugar Sex Magik* by the Chili Peppers, and Holst's *The Planets*.

Caroline and her grandfather were waiting at the end of the front path. Dr. Yee was wearing a complete replica of Sandy Koufax's Los Angeles Dodgers uniform, number thirty-two. It was several sizes too large, and the short sleeves had to be rolled up a good ways and pinned, as did the pant legs. The hat had been taken in and pinned at the back so it would fit on Yee's head, and the extra material bulged out in a bulbous Dodger blue knob. Air Jordans, instead of spikes, were on his feet.

Caroline wore blue jeans, low baby blue Converse, a pink tank top, and a navy blue tailored shirt. Her hair was casually pulled back. Her lips were that effortlessly seductive shade of silvery pink that I'd been thinking about all week. Her eyes were bright and alert and happy to see me.

"What do you want to hear first?" I said to Dr. Yee. Caroline translated my question and then his answer.

"Jimmy Buffett," she said.

"Are you a parrothead?" I said to him.

"He says, 'Fins to the left, fins to the right.'"

I laughed and gunned the engine. We listened to Jimmy on the way to Travel Town, and Caroline glanced over at me every so often in much the same way that I was glancing over at her.

"How was your week?" I said.

"Never a dull moment with my grandfather. How about you? Did your actress friend leave or is there still a certain involvement going on?"

"She didn't leave."

"Too bad. I was rooting for you."

"Game's not over until the last out."

She smiled. "That's why they play nine."

My heart skipped half a beat, "You like baseball?"

"Big time. Do you?"

Julie had no feelings for baseball. We never went to a game. "Life-long love affair."

"Me too. We should go to a game one Sunday. I'll talk to my grandfather. Baseball's good for your head, I'm sure."

"How could it not be?" I said. "Dodgers or Angels?"

"Did you miss the uniform?"

There was something about the tone of her voice that implied there was more going on with the uniform than I had first noticed. I looked in the rearview mirror and inspected Dr. Yee more closely. His head was bobbing to *Cheeseburger in Paradise*. There were sweat stains on the hat and though the uniform was clean, it was . . . old.

"No way," I said.

"It was a gift."

"From Sandy Koufax?"

"He's an occasional patient."

"He's the best pitcher in the history of baseball."

As summer faded into fall in 1965, the Dodgers played the Twins in the World Series. Koufax, already a legend, was scheduled to pitch the first game, which coincidentally fell on Yom Kippur, the Day of Atonement, the highest and holiest day of the year for Jews everywhere, including Paramus.

Koufax, a Jew from Brooklyn, would not pitch on Yom Kippur. Jews across America, except, I imagine, for some diehards in Los Angeles, thrust their chests out with pride. Koufax came back to pitch blazing shutouts in games five and seven, with only two days' rest in between, and the Dodgers won the series in seven thrilling games. Koufax was the series' Most Valuable Player.

"Everybody in America loves Sandy Koufax," I said. "People he's never seen in his whole life probably tell him that everywhere he goes. They probably ask him to sign their newspapers or business cards or matchbooks or the palms of their hands. They probably tell him how great he was, relive the times they saw him pitch, talk about his no-hitters, his perfect game, his NL MVP, his three Cy Youngs. They probably congratulate him on being the youngest player ever elected to the Hall of Fame and remind him of that day in 1965 when they went to Temple instead of the ballpark. He must hear it every minute of every day of every year."

Caroline nodded. "I bet that's why his head hurts."

I took the Forest Lawn Drive exit off the 134, rolled past some horseback riders and some picnickers and some people selling flowers out of tall plastic buckets, made the left-hand turn to Travel Town, parked the car, and watched Dr. Yee's face light up like a sparkler.

If there's something to be said about the joyous inner child inside us all, Dr. Yee was saying it loud and clear, albeit in Chinese, from the first moment he arrived at Travel Town. Old steam engines were heaven for him. He went from one train to the next and then back and forth and then up into the locomotives and down to the cabooses and all through the dining cars and sleeper cars and stock cars and mail cars and tankers.

There was a birthday party underway for a brown-haired, six-year-old girl who saw Dr. Yee passing by, spontaneously jumped out of the birthday train, took his hand, and pulled him into the party.

His joy was contagious. The party went from blah-blah-blah-happy-birthday-to-you to an unforgettable event in the time it took him to rub a birthday balloon on Koufax's uniform and make his hair stand straight up. Parents with cameras in their cell phones and cell phones in their cameras took pictures of their children embracing this mystical, old-time baseball player.

Caroline and I were given cake and juice boxes and strolled to a nearby shady bench. The cake was chocolate with a light raspberry layer. I had apple juice with a tiny straw. Caroline had a juice called Berry Berry.

"Last Sunday, on the way to Disneyland, I wasn't completely honest with you," I said.

"I could tell you were holding back."

"I'm sorry. I don't want to hold things back. I want you to know who I am."

"Why?"

"Because I want to know who you are, and if I'm not honest beyond a certain point, then you won't be either. And I want to go past that point."

"You do?"

"Yes."

We were sitting beside each other on a bench beneath tall trees, off the main path, holding paper plates of chocolate cake in one hand

and juice boxes with little straws sticking out in the other. We looked into each other's eyes and then leaned in and kissed.

It was soft and warm and filled my entire body with extra-sensory goodness. It was the one moment in all of my life that I would choose to be frozen in, had I been given such a choice.

It was the best first kiss I had ever experienced, including my first kiss with Julie, which was all rockets' red glare and carried the power of a love-at-first-sight kiss. *How in the world*, I thought, *since it was not love at first sight for Caroline and me, could our first kiss surpass my first kiss with Julie?* The kiss ended before I arrived at an answer.

"That was nice," I said.

"Yes," she said. "I wanted to kiss you before you opened the flood-gates, in case I don't want to kiss you after that."

"Fair enough."

And then we kissed again, and it was even better than the first kiss.

"Okay, twice," she said. "But that's it."

I nodded and took a sip of apple juice. Its sappy-sweet coolness was instantly familiar, though I hadn't had any in probably thirty years.

"The actress friend of mine I told you about, the one I'm sort of, but not really involved with, the one I'm writing the movie for, the one who won't leave? She's not my friend. She's not even an actress. She's a porn star. Her name is Dallas Westcott, she's from Garden City, Michigan, and she's like a bad cold I can't shake. She moved herself into my house when I started writing the movie for her and even though I tell her it's over, she won't listen."

"She's a porn star?" Caroline said.

"Yes. But I'm not sleeping with her anymore."

Caroline drank from her Berry Berry box. "Is there more honesty on the way?"

"I'm a little married."

"Not to the porn star?" To her credit, she didn't rub the cake in my face.

"To a woman named Julie Bowers. But she left me to be a juggler. I haven't seen her in years. She's in Antarctica now with the emperor penguins and a guy named Greg."

I couldn't imagine what Caroline was thinking. If for no other reason, you have to try your best to live a normal-sounding life in the event that one day you have to explain it to a woman you're interested in knowing more about. If your life is abnormal-sounding, it's unlikely she'll be interested in knowing more about you.

"You don't look like the kind of person who could be this much of a mess."

"Thank you."

"You're welcome. Does a little married mean that you and Julie are also a little divorced?"

"The papers are on my kitchen counter. I signed them a long time ago. She had already hit the road."

"To be a juggler?"

"That's what she said."

"Is there juggling in Antarctica?"

"I don't think so. Just penguins."

"And Greg."

"Yes," I said with sagging shoulders. "And Greg."

Neither Caroline nor I had touched our cake since the honesty part of our conversation began. An argument could be made that there's such a thing as too much honesty. But I think honesty is less about quantity and more about timing and toothpaste. It's not that there was too much honesty on our Travel Town bench, it's that I may have squeezed the tube too fast. There may have been too much honesty all at once, blurted out and dumped between us in a problematic pile. Caroline needed to know it all, but maybe a tad less of the story on our second date would have sufficed. Sadly, like toothpaste, you can't put truth back into the tube.

"I didn't plan any of this," I said.

"I hope not, because if this was your plan, even my grandfather couldn't help you."

We both laughed. Even under the circumstances, her laugh was light and fresh and generous. Hearing it now produced a pang in my heart for I knew that the train, so to speak, had stopped here.

"We're not going to kiss again, are we?" I said.

She shook her head, not hard or resolute, but soft and sadly resigned. "No, Mark. You've got a juggler, a porn star, and a monkey wrench and—"

"You're the monkey wrench?"

"Don't you think?"

"I think you're the nicest person I've met in a very long time."

"I think you're nice too, but you have to resolve the porn star and the juggler before you can pursue a romantic relationship with the monkey wrench."

"Do you think we can be friends until then?" I said.

"Yes," Caroline said. "I think we can."

And then a funny thing happened. A valve somewhere inside me was loosened and steam poured out in a loud steady whoosh. As this interior pressure was released, my head, which had started to hurt in a dull, heavy, sad sort of way, lightened dramatically. I felt like my eyes opened a little wider and things came more sharply into focus. I felt like I could hear the sounds of Travel Town more clearly—the children, the parents, the whistle of the passing scaled down train on its endless loop around the park. I felt like I instantaneously lost ten pounds.

We ate birthday cake and drank fruit juice until Dr. Yee climbed out of the party train and approached our bench. He looked at us for a moment, focused particularly on me, and said something to Caroline. She translated.

"He says you look thinner. He thinks you lost weight since we arrived. He wants you to eat all your cake. He says don't lose too much too fast. There's plenty of time."

He rode the kiddie train around the park five straight times. Caroline and I disembarked after two trips. We went into the scaled down train station and read about the glory days of steam engines. We stood close to each other and never said a word. I couldn't remember the last time I was that happy.

44. HOLLYWOOD AND JUNIOR

I pounded out six pages a day and finished *Phone Book, The Movie* in two weeks. For those fourteen days, I let Dallas have the bed, and I slept on the sofa in my office.

She didn't like the arrangement—it skirted the boundaries of bad luck—and arrived in my office every morning, completely naked, already showered, skin glowing, golden hair wet, looking to fuck me like a cyclone.

Each time I told her no, that I had met someone else, and that she should really think about moving out, and each time she said that when I finished the script, I would forget about the nurse—who as far as Dallas was concerned was an extension of the fiction I was writing—and we would get serious.

I came to fear that sentence like no other. Did Dallas mean she would take me home to Garbage City and introduce me to the family that disowned her years ago?

That would be something, I imagined. Me and the Westcotts in the garage on a Saturday afternoon, Tigers on the portable TV with no sound, a couple cases of Pabst Blue Ribbon in the cooler, our noses under the hood of a rebuilt Impala, greasy rags in our hands, J Geils on the radio, a couple of big dogs, one mutt and one Malamute, chewing Frisbees in the yard, beef stew in a crock-pot on the workbench in case anyone got hungry before dinner.

"Dallas tells us you're a Jew," her father would say while re-greasing a gasket.

Her older brother, the tranny mechanic, a massive side of beef with cinderblock fists, would crush a can of beer while downing it one gulp, belch like thunder, and say, "A movie writer Jew is the way I heard it."

Mrs. Westcott, up to her elbows in motor oil, would smile to take the sting out and say, "Got nothing against Jews, Mark. Everybody ought to own one."

And the Westcotts would laugh like hyenas and slap me on the back with their greasy hands and make me drink two six-packs of Pabst and teach me the difference between a spark plug and a fan belt. They would like me because I could talk a blue streak of baseball, and I would like them—reservations about their underlying anti-Semitism aside—because they were simple folk, down to Earth, though dumb as paint.

Sure, they didn't understand the creative process and thought LA was a den of devils, but they were right about that. I wouldn't defend their daughter's career choice on a bet. I would simply try to explain that underneath it all she was still their little Detroit girl looking for attention, approval, and a blessing or two.

It would be her younger brother, the professional security guard, who would see through me like a screen door.

"You going to marry her or what, Hollywood?" That's what he would call me. Hollywood. His eyes would be narrow and dark and set deep behind a Neanderthal brow. His lips would be thin and unusually red, though not as red as his ears, which would be as big and floppy as flags. He would drink a case of beer in an afternoon and relieve himself in the side yard while yelling at the dogs to shut the hell up because they were barking insanely at the audacious time it took for him to piss.

"What's it to you?" I would say. I had to stand my ground against him if I was to have any chance at all with the Westcotts. Then I would smile like a tough-ass Hollywood punk, and he would nod.

"You're one ugly piece of shit," he would say.

And I would say, "Kiss my ass, Junior," and we would be friends for life—Hollywood and Junior—though I would never comprehend the time it took for him to empty his bladder and would hassle him mercilessly about it at Red Wings games and Lions games and Pistons games and Tigers games throughout our lives.

Dallas would be angry that I made her family like me. She would declare it to be the last straw and terminate our relationship at dinner, stomping out of the eat-in, floral-wallpapered, Formica-countered kitchen.

Her family would take my side and insist that I stay the weekend and drive the Impala down Telegraph Road to the Dairy Queen. I would gratefully decline, citing screenplay work back on the coast, but before I could stand and pack my bags, Dallas would reappear, ask once and for all for familial absolution, and beg me to marry her right there at the oak veneer table over chicken fried steak and potatoes.

I wouldn't be able to say no now that Junior was counting on me to be his wingman for the next thirty years, so I would be doomed.

I would never travel to Detroit. Not even in a dream.

45. THE SCRIPT WAS TERRIFIC

At ninety-four pages, *Phone Book, The Movie* was a lean, mostly cohesive, moderately acceptable screenplay. I had read worse movies in my life, though none more absurd. I wrote *Fade Out: The End* in the middle of the afternoon and, as was my long-standing tradition, had a shot of bourbon and played air guitar to *Back in the U.S.S.R.* with the volume cranked loud enough to rattle the windows.

I emailed the script to Joe on the boat in San Pedro and to Calvin Key in Montecito. Two days later, while Dallas was at work giving head to an actor named Meat Galore, who was playing the role of a nuclear scientist investigating an unusual radioactive reading emanating from Dallas's crotch, I received an email reply from Mr. Key saying the script was terrific and requesting that I drive to his house in the foothills of the San Ynez Mountains that afternoon for lunch. I accepted the invitation and called Joe's cell phone to see if we could ride together.

Joe was in Miami at a Tango competition. There was loud music in the background, apparently the semi-final round was about to begin, and he was scheduled to dance momentarily. He had not yet read the script, but had received it on his laptop and would read it on the overnight flight to LA, where he would arrive just in time to jump in his car, head north, and join me at Calvin Key's. "We'll drink champagne and talk about our rashes and hives. Rashes and hives, *mon*. Show me da hives." I missed him terribly.

I left Coldwater Canyon with the sun high in the sky, cruised onto the 101, and settled in for the ninety-minute ride up the coast. I would arrive at half past noon. I slid Dispatch's *Under the Radar* in the CD player and thought about the script.

The most nerve-wracking time for a writer is the time between when he or she finishes the script and when someone actually reads it. The time when no one other than the writer has seen the newly created words, sentences, dialogue, paragraphs, scenes, and sequences, when there is nothing to ground the project either this way or that. During this time, the writer lives in a gravity-free atmosphere for days or weeks or months on end, which sounds freeing and appealing but is in fact dizzying, discomforting, and wholly discombobulating—uninterrupted interior torture.

But two days later, Calvin Key had left me a message saying the script was terrific. That's the kind of grounding all writers are hoping for. Armed with the billionaire's proclamation of terrificness, I allowed myself the luxury of liking my script.

It was terse but descriptive, something all screenwriters strive for. When I introduced Marvin Jenkins, for instance, I wrote: *Standing behind the Diversified Propane Systems marble conference table, scotch on the rocks in one hand, Glock semi-automatic in the other, is the human brick wall named Marvin Jenkins (mid 50s), wearing a $10,000 custom-tailored suit of arrogance, as hard and unsympathetic a man as has ever lived.*

This is the trick of screenwriting, describing the essence of an action or a location or a character without describing the physicality of them at all. No mention of Jenkins' height or weight or hair color or skin tone, no mention of the brand of his suit. It was expensive, custom-tailored, and made of arrogance. Key had his own private picture of Jenkins in his mind's eye because I had painted the *kind* of person Jenkins was rather than the person himself.

The reasoning behind this, from a production point of view, is that the actor you finally cast may or may not look anything like the character you physically described, if you specifically described them, and worse, the actor you're trying to cast may think he or she can't play that character because he or she doesn't look like that character.

But what actor worth his salt doesn't think he can play a brick wall in a ten grand suit of arrogance? Even skinny Keanu Reeves, when he's done cutting Alvin Yee's yard, knows he could play that character, and he no doubt would, if he was cast.

Not that we were going to cast Keanu Reeves in *Phone Book, The Movie*. It was as unlikely as elephants in Utah that he would be willing to play opposite Dallas Westcott in a three-million-dollar indie.

But the script was terrific, even I thought so now as I passed the tall towers in Oxnard, and a terrific script meant Calvin Key might just increase the budget, as was his wish from the onset, and seek to attach more legitimate box office talent.

Naturally, Dallas would have to be cut loose to make room for an actress who didn't make her living giving blowjobs to Meat Galore. I would be there to soften the landing, but only so much. Her feelings for me, based on my betrayal—*hadn't I written the script for her?*—would turn on a dime and she would move out of my house and out of my life, leaving me free to focus on the juggler and the monkey wrench. To that end, it was a terrific script in more ways than one.

There was an action sequence in the middle of the movie that I thought might have special energy, blockbuster flare, and Experienced-Writer-At-The-Helm style, yet still fit within the low-budget constraints of the film. A piece of screenwriting I was becoming more and more proud of as I passed the city of Ventura.

Samantha and Christian smash straight through the gates of a huge, top secret, Diversified Propane processing plant and speed through the grounds taking pictures of Jenkins' illegal nuclear capabilities while being chased by two Diversified henchmen, Hatch and Piner, who are armed and dangerous and loaded with bad intent. During the car chase, Samantha has to switch places with Christian in order to snap the damning photos because Christian is still blind as wood and can't see what the hell he's supposed to be photographing.

But if he's blind, how can he drive Samantha's killer Mustang during a high-speed chase through a twisty, nuclear bomb-producing, propane-processing plant?

Exactly the question the audience will ask, except they, hopefully, will be on the edge of their seats while Samantha shoots the photos shouting *Turn left, turn right, turn here, turn there, faster Christian, they're right behind us* and other instructions until they blast through the gate on the far side of the plant, leaving Hatch and Piner in the dust as Christian, now enjoying himself behind the wheel, drives them home through LA traffic.

In between nearly crashing into explosive tanks of natural gas, not to mention a small arsenal of nuclear warheads, almost being shot by Hatch and Piner, and Sam's dire directions, there was smart and snappy dialogue about their previous failed relationships and the impact they might have should Sam and Christian date one day in the future—if they live.

It was only now that the writing was done and Calvin Key had said the work was terrific that I could appreciate the years of dedication and hard work I had put in and face the fact that I was something of an accomplished craftsman.

Inspiration is as fleeting as breath in winter and has no real relation to writing that I can see. It has as much to do with a finished script as the pilot light on a gas stove has to do with a finished feast. It is simply that moment of confidence in which you believe you can and should begin. All the rest is craft. If we are expert in our work, we are craftsmen and maybe even artists, the distinction between art and craft being shadowy even in the light of day.

As I pulled off the 101 into Montecito, I decided to tell my parents about *Phone Book, The Movie*. I hadn't spoken to them in some time and had never mentioned any of the insanity of the project—not Tango Joe, not Calvin Key, not Colonel Bill—to my parents, to my sister Leslie, or to anyone else I knew since I'd returned from Paramus. I also decided that I would leave my relationship with Dallas Westcott out of the story. She would be gone soon, and no one would ever have to be the wiser. We would skip that chapter entirely. Turning into the magnificent courtyard of Casa Key, I promised myself that I would call Arthur and Diane straightaway when I got home.

46. DARK RED RICE

Cletis Oleander opened the massive front door and looked at me like I was mud on his shoes, which today were out-of-this-world rattlesnake cowboy boots. He wore them with red sweatpants cut into shorts and the vest from a gray pinstripe three-piece suit. Once again, he was shirtless. He wore a watch on both his left and right wrists and a ten-gallon cowboy hat on his shaved head, a belated attempt to bring the ensemble together in a bizarre western way.

"You late," Cletis said.

"I don't think so. I'm right on time."

"How many watches you wearing?"

"One."

"Chump," he said, and that was the end of the discussion. He left the door open and walked away. Though it was an unorthodox beginning to my coronation, Mr. Oleander would soon be having sex with Gloria the cook in one of the two hundred Casa Key closets, and I would be rid of him for the rest of the afternoon. I shut the door and followed the butler through the house.

"How come there's no furniture?" I said. He was walking ahead of me, winding us through rooms I either hadn't seen the first time or had seen and couldn't recall. None of these rooms had so much as a chair or a couch or a table. He didn't even turn his head to answer.

"How come you late?"

"I'm not late."

We entered the gigantic ballroom. The ping-pong table was in its place in the far corner, the Segway Human Transporter parked beside it.

"Did I do something to you?" I said.

He stopped and faced me. "You mean besides be late?"

"I'm not late, Cletis."

He held up his wrists to show me both his watches and then turned around and started walking again. "How the hell do I know? Ain't my house," he said.

I was following him again. He was broad-shouldered with slightly bowed legs and a rhythmic bounce to his step that was all MTV Cribs and seemed superfluous in a Montecito mansion that, as he said, didn't belong to him.

"Yeah, well, it's not my house either," I said.

"You right about that, hoss," he said, and we passed through an arched doorway into a small, private dining room. There was a gorgeous tiled fireplace in the corner, and logs were burning and crackling in the hearth. More logs were piled in an opening built into the adobe wall beside the fireplace, and a row of candles flickered above the fire on the mantel. A cubist painting hung on the opposite wall. Its muted tones, burnt reds, browns, and blacks, matched the colors of the room, and its surreal and angular depiction of what appeared to be either a dinner party or an execution was a perfect counterpoint to the rose-colored Spanish walls. A Walmart card table with folding chairs was set for dinner. There were four place settings. The centerpiece was a high-tech telephone. There was no other furniture in the room.

Key was sitting at the table reading my script. He was wearing Levis, Docksiders with no socks, and a tailored oxford dress shirt, buttoned but untucked, with the sleeves rolled up. Only the color of his shirt had changed from the first time I met him. These were the clothes, apparently, that made him feel more human, less genius-freak-counting-billionaire. Like me, he wore only one watch.

"Take a seat. I'm re-reading the scene where Samantha meets Chris for the first time, and she doesn't realize he's blind. Very clever." He gestured at the seat across from him and then glanced at the doorway that led to the kitchen.

As I crossed to the table, a woman entered the room rolling a two-tier serving cart. It was the cart from the outdoor patio set by the pool. The day that Joe and I sold Key the movie, it carried crab cakes and a citrus salad with chardonnay vinaigrette. Today it was carting dark red rice flecked with green scallions, black beans with melted jack cheese, a bubbling casserole of chicken enchiladas in a jade green tomatillo sauce, and a wild greens salad with fresh pear dressing. The woman rolled the cart beside Key and transferred a still-steaming basket of homemade tortilla chips and generous bowls of guacamole and salsa from the top tier to the table. The aroma made my knees weak.

"Say hello to Gloria, Mark," Key said. "Gloria, this is Mark Manilow."

She was sixty years old with chestnut brown skin. She was a big woman, heavy-set, with wide hips and lots of meat on them, but she did not come across as overweight, though she probably was. She had big breasts and thick arms and strong shoulders. Most grown men would have no chance arm-wrestling her. Her eyes were a bright and shining brown, and her smile was broad and full and white-white-white. She had long braided hair, colored bright red and gold, pulled back in a kerchief, and wore a pale-yellow Hawaiian skirt and a blue work shirt with the sleeves cut off. She was barefoot. The AC/DC song "Whole Lotta Rosie" popped into my head as soon as I saw her.

"Hello, baby," she said. "Mister Calvin didn't say nothing about you being such a skinny little bird. You going to gain five pounds in the next ten minutes, I swear." And then she laughed aloud, and I thought I'd pass out. Her laughter was vibrant and alive and sounded like the perfectly clear and brilliant bells of a church in the mountains of Vermont, snow on the ridgeline, the sky a deep and icy blue. The kind of bells you can hear from miles and miles away, beckoning you onward, ringing: *Joy awaits you here.*

Cletis, who had been staring at me with an unpleasant mixture of contempt and revulsion, was a changed man when Gloria laughed. His frosty bitterness melted away and his eyes, generally narrow and filled with distrust, opened wide to fully take her in. I instantly knew why he was running off with her at all hours of the day and night.

"Nice to meet you, Gloria. Everything smells great," I said.

"You going to stand there sniffing at it or sit down so we can eat? Enchiladas ain't no good when they cold," Cletis said as he took the seat beside Key.

"Sit across from me, Mark. Cletis and Gloria are going to join us for lunch. Have a Corona." They were all three seated, and Gloria was piling plates high and heavy with her homemade Mexican feast. Key was squeezing a lime into a longneck Corona and handing it across the table to me. Cletis was drinking a Corona without citrus.

"Sit down, baby bird. Cletis is right. You want to get it while it's good and hot," Gloria said, and then she winked at the surly butler. "Ain't that right, midnight cowboy?"

"I'll see you later," he said, in a tone of voice that left nothing to the imagination.

"Behave yourself, old man," she said. "Not in front of the baby bird."

I took the beer from Key, sat across from him and disappeared into the most wonderful Mexican meal I may ever have eaten in my entire life. A wide array of flavors caressed me, teased me, and exploded in my mouth. I tasted cilantro and cumin and coriander along with garlic and juniper berry and Mexican oregano. These and other delicate spices worked together in perfect harmony with jalapeño, guajillo, and chipotle peppers, all of them impossibly fresh and magically coaxed into performing minor miracles. But it was the rice that floored me. There was something about the dark red rice that was sensual. Beyond good. Orgasmic. It was cocoa. There was cocoa in the rice, just enough to make the dish transcendent and not one teaspoon more.

"This is the best rice in the history of the world," I blurted out. "Everything's amazing."

Key nodded. "There's only one Gloria."

She was from Atlanta originally, the daughter of a roofer and a seamstress, but she had moved to New Orleans when she was still young, though old enough to know that school was not the road she was meant to travel. Like many great chefs, food was not sustenance for her, nor was it a career path—it was life.

"I been cooking everyday since I was sixteen, and I ain't never worked one day in my life," she said as my mouth melted and my heart soared.

She dropped out of school and went to work in the kitchens of many of the Crescent City's finest restaurants—Broussard's, Alex Patout's, Commander's Palace, Uglesich's—and for its most renowned chefs—Paul Prudhomme, the Sonniers, Frank Brigtsen, Emeril Lagasse. At each stop, she took the best of what she learned and made it her own, using joy and laughter the way others use sea salt and cayenne pepper.

Key had been on a business trip and had asked to meet the chef after eating a deliriously delicious meal at Brennan's. Gloria emerged from the kitchen and the billionaire offered her a job as his personal chef at an income previously impossible for her to imagine, many times her sous chef salary. Believing that the winds of the universe were blowing her westward, she accepted.

Cletis Oleander was from Charlotte, North Carolina, and had been a coast-to-coast truck driver all of his working life. Upon retirement, he moved into a trailer in Goleta, the town just north of Santa Barbara. He'd been married three times and had three children with three different wives at three different truck stops across the country. When his retirement stash ran low, he took a job corralling shopping carts in the parking lot of the Gelson's on State Street. This is where he first met Gloria.

She was pushing two carts piled to the sky with food for Casa Key, and he was rolling a snaky line of carts back to the store. Their eyes met as they passed on the tarmac. Their sexual attraction was instant and volcanic, hardcore proof that chemistry and mystery have more in common than either chemists or mystics are willing to admit.

Key, born with the kitchen haplessness of a techno-geek but the taste buds of a Frenchman, knew he was the luckiest man on earth—not for his billions, for his cook—and would do anything not to lose her. When Gloria came to him professing her love for Cletis and her desire to move out of Key's mansion and into the Goleta trailer, Key offered Oleander a ridiculous salary to be his butler and a room of his own to call home.

Cletis said he wasn't going to kiss Key's ass, no matter how much the billionaire paid him. He'd take the job, but wanted to live in his own damn trailer.

Key thought that was fair enough. He moved Oleander's trailer to a glade on the edges of the Casa Key property, Gloria moved in with Cletis but stayed on as Key's cook, Cletis became Key's disrespectful butler, and everyone was happy.

Except there was no time to get back to the trailer when the urge to screw each other's lights out arose during the work day, which it did twice every afternoon, and so Cletis and Gloria embarked on a mission to have sex in every closet in the castle before they grew too old to fuck, which if you asked them, wouldn't be for another thirty years.

Neither Gloria nor Cletis cared much for movies, Key said, but as we finished lunch, he also said, "I asked them to read the script, and they both had some interesting thoughts I wanted you to hear. Plus I had thoughts too. We'll patch Joe in telephonically. He was out all night dancing the Mambo with Miss Little Havana and missed his plane."

It was a set-up from the start. The Corona, the chips, the home-made salsa and guacamole, the enchiladas and the tomatilla sauce, the black beans with the jack cheese, and especially the dark red rice. It had blinded me, as he knew it would, from the two unshakable truths of the film business: there are always notes and everybody has them.

It wasn't a celebratory luncheon. It was a story meeting ambush. I was going to get notes on *Phone Book, The Movie* from the billionaire, the cook, and the truck-driving midnight cowboy butler who didn't like me.

47. I GOT A PROBLEM WITH THE BLIND DUDE

"Do you need a script?" Key said. From a stack on the floor behind his chair he handed me a freshly printed copy and then handed Gloria and Cletis their scripts. Their first names were written in large block letters with black magic marker across the top of the front page, and seemingly every page thereafter was either dog-eared or had a sticky attached. Across the top of the title page of Key's copy of the script, he had written *Executive Producer*. The stickies on his script were color-coded.

"I'll need a pen," I said, but Key was already handing me a red one.

"You did a great job, Mark. There are a just a few things we'd like to discuss, maybe clarify, and even change if we have to. As far as the story goes, there's a believability factor that we have to be careful of. It's a thin line and most of the time we're on the right side of it. But not all the time. There are character and dialogue issues too. And we have some questions about the pacing. But I think we should start with the story."

"Okay," I said. I had been in plenty of story meetings in my career and knew there was no stopping the notes from coming. I would have better luck holding back the tide with a teaspoon. "Where are we on the wrong side of the line?"

Key turned to Oleander. His cowboy hat was still on his head. He had unbuttoned his vest because he had eaten too much and could no longer fit into it. "Cletis, why don't you start us off?"

"I got a problem with the blind dude. No way she fall for him," the butler said.

"Why not?" I said. "He's smart, he's brave, he's nice, and he's handsome."

Cletis shook his head. "He blind. Can't see what the hell he doing. How he shave in the morning?"

I wasn't sure I heard that note correctly, but I was also fearful that I did. I looked at Key for guidance, but he was waiting for my answer as if the shaving note somehow had merit. "It's not really a movie about how Christian shaves, Cletis. What is it about his shaving that bothers you?" Even as I asked the question, I refused to accept that I was asking it.

"He going to cut himself all up and shit. Toilet paper be stuck all over his damn blind face."

"Are we really talking about shaving, Calvin?" I said.

"I think shaving's the metaphor, Mark," Key said. "Believability is the underlying issue. Cletis is a ticket-buying customer, and he's not signing on."

There are four kinds of notes: those that make the story better, those that make the story worse, those that are matters of taste and don't substantively change the story either way, and *Notes From Mars*, like the shaving note Cletis had proposed.

"Notes sort of come in two parts," I said. "The Problem and the Fix. Assuming for the moment that Christian's shaving is a problem, what do you think the fix is? I mean, I imagine there are women all over the planet, I'd guess in every country, who fall in love with blind men all the time."

"Three blind mice," Cletis said.

I had no idea what that meant. It didn't sound like a fix to me.

But Gloria nodded her agreement. Somehow she knew what Cletis meant. They must have developed a kind of nursery rhyme code to use when they were fucking in a dark closet. "Christian should have a housekeeper, baby bird, and Samantha should fall for the housekeeper. That's the fix."

"But Christian is the leading man," I said.

Key shook his head. "We're spitballing here, Mark. Run with us on this one."

I nodded, though I knew we were running straight off the edge of a cliff.

"Stevie Wonder blind. You think he shave himself?" Cletis said. "Come out on Soul Train, face all cut up and shit? I don't think so. People probably falling all over themselves to bang his housekeeper. People probably lined up outside his house right now."

"What people? Just people on the street? Just random people on the street lined up outside Stevie Wonder's house hoping for a chance to screw his housekeeper?"

"Don't be defensive, Mark. They're just notes." Key said. "I say we go with this idea of giving Christian a housekeeper. I think it's going to open the story up full-throttle, on an emotional level, I mean. Less linear. Less predictable. Let's give Christian a housekeeper and let Sam fall for him . . . or hey, wait a minute . . . *her*. We let Sam fall for her. It could be a woman, right? Why not?"

"Or why don't we let Christian shave with an electric razor and keep the story the way it is?" I said. "That might be easier than adding a new character and changing the emotional dynamic that drives the main subplot of the film."

"Baby bird, you missing the point," Gloria said. "It's very sexy, very hip. There are lesbians all over the world who would pay to see that movie."

Fantastic, I thought. We've identified a heretofore missing demographic. "So Samantha's gay?" I said.

Key smiled. "Now you're working with us, Mark. I like it. What do we think? Is Samantha Barnes a lesbian?"

"I say no," Cletis said. "Christian's the homo. Blind dude been in the closet all his life. 'bout time we let him out."

"That's good, cowboy. His housekeeper's a man and Christian wants to make love to him." Gloria winked at Cletis. He licked his lips to turn her on. All memory of the amazing meal was wiped away in that moment.

Key ignored them. "The housekeeper goes both ways, and he likes Sam because she's hot and bothered—"

"And the blind dude's face be cut up from shaving every damn day," Cletis said, interrupting.

"How come the bisexual housekeeper doesn't shave him in the morning?" I said, though I didn't recognize my voice phrasing the question.

"I like that," Key said. "We could have some tender moments between Christian, who's in love with the housekeeper on the one hand—"

"Damn homo," Cletis said.

"—and the housekeeper, who likes Christian as a friend, but is sleeping with Sam on the other hand, " Key said. "Now that's dramatic tension."

I wrote some notes down in the margins and took a moment to recap. The way I saw it, my blind, self-sufficient, wheelchair-bound co-hero was now a gay, incompetent, love-sick sap who wasn't smart enough to know there was such a thing as an electric razor and so spent his mornings covering his multiple facial shaving wounds with so much toilet paper that by the time he rolled himself in for breakfast, he was already too much of a bloody mess to love. No matter that he was a bio-medical computer genius about to cure his own blindness, not to mention blindness the world over, the guy couldn't even shave himself. We were only on page two, and I was exhausted.

The high-tech telephone in the center of the table rang like the bell at a boxing match. I debated throwing in the towel before the second round began. Key answered the call by hitting the speakerphone button.

"Joe, it's Calvin."

"Calvin Key, you crazy son of a sailor. Are you wearing your jockeys on the outside like I told you?"

"Not really, Joe," Key said, laughing.

"How about Mr. Stinky? You taking him out for a walk on the wild side?"

"Whenever I get the chance," Key said. "Joe, we're doing some terrific work with Mark. I've got Gloria and Cletis here, and we're going over the whole Sam, Christian subplot. It's come a long way."

"*Fantabuloso*," Joe said. "Where is it now?"

"I'll let Mark tell you. You were right about him, Joe. He's got the gift." Key gave me a smile and gestured at the phone like a Second Avenue Maitre d'.

"Hi, Joe," I said. "How's Miami?"

"Miami is insane. The entire city is checking into rehab and Ralph Kramden is driving the bus. It's a madhouse, I tell you. Shenanigans on every corner. Tell me good news, Sitting Bull."

"Well, Joe. We're changing the primary relationship in the script. Christian is now gay, and he has a bisexual housekeeper, a new character, who's torn between his friendship for Christian and his lust for Sam. We're only on page two, but I get the feeling we'll probably have to change the flow of the main line of action."

"*Perfectamente*. But I didn't catch the last line. Pick up the phone, Geronimo."

I looked at Key, who nodded that it was fine, and I lifted the receiver.

"I have only one question," Joe said.

"What is it?" I said.

"Have you lost your mind? I hear frustration. I hear irritation. I hear creative constipation. Think of me as ex-lax for your brain. You are sitting at a table with a billionaire who is going to personally write you a multi-million dollar check to produce the movie that you write. This is the happiest day of your life. It's a script, not a peace treaty. No one's going to die if there's a new character, even if he's a cannibal, which he might be. A bisexual housekeeping cannibal. Will your life substantially change if the bisexual housekeeper eats humans while Christian jerks off to gay porn he can't see?"

"No."

"Now you're cooking with gas, Cochise." Apparently, it was Famous American Indian Chief Day. "Put me back on the speaker and announce the name of the new housekeeper. Miracles are coming your way. It is written in the stars."

I put Joe back on the speaker and said, "We'll call the housekeeper Garrett DeYoung. He was a professional surfer before his bisexuality drove him into housekeeping. That's how he met Christian in the first place. At the beach. Christian likes to watch the waves break even though he's blind."

"We're going to make a fortune," Joe said.

48. GARRETT DEYOUNG

It took less than an hour for Christian O'Connor to disappear from the script altogether.

The blind—and now gay—bio-medical genius with blazing courage, a wry sense of humor, and a deep emotional commitment to Samantha Barnes became, in descending order, a deaf and gay shoe salesman, a gay quadriplegic librarian, a gay idiot savant, a wheelchair-bound busboy in the communications company commissary with gay tendencies, an LA detective with a limp just coming out of the closet, Sam's old, gay history professor at USC, and a gay homeless beggar who gets run over by a bus on page eleven. His complete deletion was inevitable. He was dead. He was gone.

The team was in love with Garrett DeYoung.

DeYoung's meteoric rise to the rank of leading man was diametrically opposed to Christian's demise. As the sun set on his bisexual housekeeping, he became, in ascending order, a former professional football player turned CIA operative, a former professional baseball player turned nuclear scientist, a former professional basketball player turned Navy SEAL turned hardnosed private investigator, a former professional soccer player turned Green Beret turned movie star turned astronaut, and finally, a former professional martial arts world champion turned NASCAR driver turned professional poker player turned international spy. Surfing became his hobby, and the only way to infiltrate Jenkins' Malibu mansion.

It was Gloria who suggested that Garrett and Samantha surf their way onto Jenkins' private beach in the dead of night, it was Cletis who brainstormed that Garrett take on and defeat a small army of private security men while Sam sneaks into the mansion to recover the next piece of the puzzle, and it was Calvin Key who added that budgetary overruns were of little importance when juxtaposed with such creative synchronicity.

We spent four hours on the phone with Joe. There were so many proposed changes that there was more red ink in my script than black. It would take me twice as long to do the rewrite as it had taken me to write the first draft. I would have to rethink the action and the characters and the dialogue all over again. It was hard enough to muster the energy to dive into that unlikely world in the first place. The thought of re-inventing it anew was daunting to say the least.

But it was the not-so-subtle change in the film's tone that bothered me more than the new characters and plot points. Joe had previously informed Key that Dallas Westcott would be our leading lady. Key's initial skepticism was a thatch hut on the beach, and Joe's enthusiasm was a tidal wave. Joe convinced the billionaire that casting Dallas as Samantha Barnes would separate us from both the Hollywood and Indie packs and ensure a distribution deal in every corner of the globe.

"It's the hope of what she might do, whether or not she does it," is how Joe put it. "It's like winning the lottery with a ticket you buy in an adult bookstore."

When I mentioned to Joe that adult bookstores don't sell lottery tickets, he laughed and said, "Then imagine our great good fortune, my brother."

But even imagining our great good fortune didn't alleviate my concern that the script had been driven to a racier place. More skin, more touching, more kissing, more sexual innuendo, more double entendres. Less Noir, more smut.

As I was preparing to voice my concern about the sexier turn we were taking, Joe casually informed us that he had spoken with Barry Manilow's people and coordinated and confirmed Manilow's appearance at the staged reading to be held at Colonel Bill's studio tomorrow evening.

"Sorry, Joe," I said. "But while I was counting my adult bookstore lottery money, I thought I heard you say the reading was tomorrow night."

"Strike when the iron is hot, *mon*," he said in his Rasta voice. "There's gold in them thar hills. The Colonel's troupe awaits only your brilliant second draft."

"I like it, Joe," Key said. "Every minute counts."

Counting minutes (or anything) was Key's special gift, so it was no surprise that he signed on, but there was the little matter of the massive rewrite still to be addressed.

"Well, about that second draft," I said. "I can't do it in twenty-four hours. I have Garrett and the beach battle at the mansion in Malibu and all these other changes."

Joe laughed. "Cinematic Swami that I am, I predict the second draft will take you seven hours start to finish. And I'm willing to wager twenty dollars."

"I'll take your action," Cletis said. "Six hours thirty minutes."

"Six hours fifteen minutes," Gloria said, and they both looked at Key.

The ultimate numbers man was flipping through the script and crosschecking it with the long list of notes and changes. "Five hours forty-three minutes, excluding lunch and bathroom breaks," Key said.

Joe sighed in a loud and exaggerated fashion. "Calvin Key, you co-coconut. Take my twenty dollars right now. I concede defeat." Everyone laughed except me.

"Joe, these are big notes," I said.

"And you're a big writer, maestro," Joe said. "We trust you to make the changes that need changing, adjust the plot that needs re-plotting, and create a Garrett DeYoung that Sam can love, and I mean physically, at least three times in the second act. Can I get a *you da man*?"

"You da man," Key said seriously, probably thinking it was some kind of break-a-leg ritual send-off that producers everywhere employed when writers went home to do their second drafts.

"You best not be da late man," Cletis said, showing me his watches.

"I wasn't late," I said.

"Late or not, baby bird. You da *only* man," Gloria said.

There was no way of explaining the impossibility of it. It was as if they thought screenwriting was water flowing through a faucet and that if the faucet were moved from the kitchen sink to the side of the living room couch, the water would still flow when the tap was turned. There was simply no understanding of the pipes behind the wall.

Calvin Key walked me through the mansion to the front door when we were finished with the notes. Gloria and Cletis were left with the dishes, though I suspect they quickly retired to an upstairs closet. Key wondered about the particulars of Garrett DeYoung's back-story, expressed excitement over the potential chemistry between Dallas Westcott and whatever stud actor played DeYoung, and said I should call him if I hit any roadblocks. Like everyone else in the movie business, Key now knew two things, how to be a software billionaire independent film producer . . . and how to write my script. But because of his special counting prowess, he also knew to the minute how long it would take to write it. (Not unlike Long Ron Dong, come to think of it.)

Eddie Gonzales, the man in charge of Key's cars (there were twenty-two of them) was polishing my hubcaps as I arrived. He had been instructed to wash, wax, and detail my Mustang while I was inside. I had never seen the car look better.

"I like Mustangs. They pretty slick." Eddie said, in a voice filled with Hispanic inflection that was high-pitched and very fast and reminded me of Speedy Gonzales. He was twenty-five years old. Skinny as a pipe cleaner. His hair was thick and straight and jet-black. He had dark eyes and a gold tooth in the center of his smile. He wore faded blue jeans with holes in the knees, a skin-tight San Antonio Spurs T-shirt, and low-top black Pumas with no socks.

His hoses and buckets and sponges and rags were neatly coiled and packed up. He was working on the front driver-side hubcap. It was gleaming, as they all were. He'd already polished them.

He was kneeling in such a way that he was facing me as well. "Thanks, Eddie. Looks good," I said. I put my hand on the door handle, but he kept looking up at me from his kneeling position, so I didn't open the door. "Am I done?" I said.

"Just a couple things, *hombre*," he said, and he stood and reached behind him. Rolled up in his back pocket was a copy of the script. *Eddie* was written across the top in black magic marker.

"On page twenty-four, when Sam get up to see who at the door, she got to be naked, *amigo*. A woman like that, she sleep in her birthday suit."

I was getting notes from the car kid. He had thoughts about the violence in the movie (there wasn't enough), the sex in the movie (not nearly enough), and the dialogue in the movie (not real enough).

"You be driving through all kind of propane tanks and shit, and the driver be blind? Damn *amigo*, you don't say shit like they say, about love and shit, you know what I'm saying? You be all like, 'Fuck this shit, man. We got to get out of this shit.'"

It went on like that for thirty minutes. Eddie was thrilled with the death of Christian O'Connor and the birth of Garrett DeYoung. He knew Dallas Westcott's work and was in concordance with Joe and Key and the rest of the team that she was a casting coup. He wondered if there would be a role for him.

I told him I would write him a part if I could, and then I climbed in the car and drove home. But first I screwed my head back on—it had fallen off when Eddie suggested he could be Garrett DeYoung's brother, who's been in prison and hasn't had a woman in five years, and so Garrett lets him have sex with Dallas.

There were two cars, Hertz rental sedans that I didn't recognize, parked in my driveway. I got out of the Mustang and walked to the front door. It was open, as in not locked, which made me hold my breath. I went inside and stopped breathing altogether.

Sitting in my living room were Arthur and Diane (my parents), my sister Leslie, her dickhead husband Phil, and Julie's psychiatrist father, Bernie Bowers. Theirs were the five most somber-looking faces I had ever seen.

Since I wasn't breathing, I couldn't speak. We stared at each other for five excruciatingly long seconds, and then Bernie stood up and said, "Mark, we're here for your intervention." There were tears of concern in my mother's eyes as she held up a DVD for me to see.

The photo on the box was of a familiar-looking naughty nurse in a white micro-mini uniform straddling a man in a full body cast with openings at his mouth and groin and a leering doctor in the near background with his stethoscope under the skirt of a Candy Striper. Superimposed on the image were the following words: *Dallas West-cott in Broken Boner*. Below them it said: *Written by Mark Manilow.*

PART III
WILD MEN
OF THE FRINGE

49. THE PURPOSE OF THIS INTERVENTION

Dick Dental. Ken Moynihan christened me with that pseudonym on the set of *Hung Like a Horse Thief*, saying the name had a ring to it. If it did, it wasn't loud enough for me to hear over the cacophony of my life. I had never confirmed that he should use that name for my writing credit on the film. I had utterly forgotten to confirm the use of any pseudonym. I hadn't thought about *Broken Boner* in decades and decades, though it had only been fourteen weeks since Ken had replaced me because my pecker wasn't leading the pack. Dallas never spoke of it out of fear that reminding me that I had failed as a writer of porn would be bad luck and derail me as the writer of her first legitimate feature film. By all accounts, *Broken Boner* became an infinitesimal part of a distant past that had literally come home to haunt me. I wished I really was Dick Dental and that this wasn't my family in my living room waiting to begin my intervention.

"Mark, why don't you take a seat," Bernie said. "We're way past the swollen genitalia stage, don't you agree?"

My father stepped forward. "He's in shock, Bernie."

"Yes," my mother said. "Maybe we should check his penis first."

"Hello . . . Here I am," I said. "Sitting down. Talking calmly. Surprised, yes. In shock, no." I moved to the sofa and took a seat. If you're ever looking for a sharp slap in the face, have your mother say *"Maybe we should check his penis first"* in mixed company. If that doesn't wake you up, you're not sleeping; you're dead.

"Your family is here because they're worried about you," Bernie said. "They called me after your trip to New Jersey to express their concern. I explained that your erratic behavior was a manifestation of your emotional disorientation resulting from the abrupt and jagged end of your marriage. The legitimate, self-directed guilt you feel from failing yourself and Julie and all those close to you has distorted your ability to behave normally in the world. Your involvement in pornography is the troubling result. The purpose of this intervention is to make you aware of your behavior and our concerns and have you willingly enter an emotional and intellectual detoxification clinic that I run in Chicago. You can see we've packed your suitcase."

He gestured toward the foyer where one of my suitcases was waiting for me.

"Blue jeans, sneakers, and T-shirts, Mark? Isn't it finally time to grow up?" my mother said. "We brought you some chinos, a polo, and a nice sweater. There are loafers too. Italian."

"We specialize in deviant and obsessive sexual behavior resulting from self-inflicted emotional wounds," Bernie said. "Simply put, we help you clean up the scar tissue on your groin and, in so doing, metaphorically reduce it to normal proportions. Do you understand what I'm saying, Mark?"

"Nobody understands what you're saying, Bernie," I said.

"I told you he wouldn't cooperate," Leslie said.

"Leslie, why don't you go first," Bernie said. "Try to remember what we said about name-calling. Keep it to a minimum, no matter how much he deserves it."

While my father and Phil moved chairs from the dining room into the living room and Bernie handled the opening remarks and they all took their seats in a tight semi-circle in front of the sofa where I sat alone, I remembered that this was not the first sexually-motivated intervention for my family and me.

My sister and I spent two agonizing weeks at Camp Waccamaw in the Pennsylvania foothills the summer I turned fourteen. My parents believed it was time for me to broaden my horizons, so instead of sending me to baseball camp in Trenton, they shipped me and Leslie, who was sixteen, to a camp that focused on arts and crafts. There was swimming and camping and singing and hours and hours of arts and crafts. It was unmitigated torture except for Melanie Dasher, the twenty-eight-year-old camp nurse, who was the only reason I didn't drown myself in the lake.

Nurse Melanie was the personification of strawberry pie—a curvy, blonde, sweetheart of a woman, divorced and spending her summer at Waccamaw, earning extra money to supplement her middle school nurse salary.

She was from Pittsburg, and when she wasn't administering allergy shots or passing out pills or taking temperatures, she was an avid swimmer. She would swim in the morning, after her medical duties were complete, then shower and prepare for the inevitable lunchtime arts and crafts bumps and bruises.

Purely by accident, I discovered a peephole on the backside of the women's shower cabin, which was covered by shrubs and brush. I was innocently hiding out to avoid the morning activity—*Drawing Horses is Fun!*—when I heard the shower running behind me. I turned, moved a leafy branch to the side, and was confronted with a perfectly round, two-inch hole that must have once upon a time been filled with a pipe.

I looked through the hole, and there was nurse Melanie, soaping her gorgeous naked body not more than fifteen feet away from my excellent vantage point.

I had recently discovered the joys of masturbation and decided it wouldn't hurt anyone to take this God-given opportunity to jerk off in the bushes while watching the Waccamaw Nurse Goddess rub her breasts with Ivory lather. The fact that I would be doing that instead of drawing My Friend Flicka was icing on the cake.

Larry Loeb, the head drama counselor, a short and fat and bald piano player from Sarasota, New York, where he was a high school music teacher who also ran the after-school theater club, caught me in the act. I was only fourteen, so it never occurred to me to inquire what, exactly, he was doing back there behind the bushes. In retrospect, everyone knew Melanie's routine—there was always a line of counselors wanting some extra waterfront duty when the bombshell nurse went for her morning swim—and I imagine that like me, Loeb was planning to "Waccamaw one off," so to speak. He should have joined me. Two men sharing the same dirty deed behind the bushes. We'd have been friends for life.

Instead, he dragged me to the office, summoned my sister from her sing-along, and called my parents, demanding that they drive from New Jersey to attend an emergency meeting in the camp office. Participating in the assembly would be Loeb, Melanie, my counselor, the group leader, the owner of the camp, the owner's wife, and my family. It was my first intervention.

I had only done it once, and I truly had just stumbled upon the hole, but I was treated as if I were a chronic Peeping Tom masturbating menace.

Leslie suggested that I take everyone to the very spot where I was apprehended, as if the jury needed to see the scene of the crime to make a determination of guilt or innocence, so off we all went to the women's shower cabin, where we retraced my steps behind the bushes. My father peered into the evil hole for a good long while before announcing, "I'm certain it was a hot water pipe that went through here." My mother and sister both looked through the hole. Even Melanie, who gave me several nice smiles throughout the trial, took a turn.

After the summer ended and Camp Waccamaw was an uncomfortable memory, Leslie held the Melanie Dasher Affair over my head until the day I walked into her bedroom while she was masturbating under her life-size Jon Bon Jovi poster while listening to *Slippery When Wet* at full volume, which is why she didn't hear me knocking and also why I walked right in. She was completely naked, her head resting on pillows at the foot of her bed so she could look up at the New Jersey rock star's poster that hung over her white rattan headboard. Even as her furious and mortified shrieking ran me from the room, I knew that the rules of the house had changed.

Our deal was that she would immediately stop mentioning Melanie Dasher or anything about Camp Waccamaw and I would keep my mouth shut regarding Bon Jovi. She was sixteen, and I was fourteen. We were stalemated for decades until now. The scales had once more tipped in her favor.

"I knew there was something wrong when I saw you at Mom and Dad's for dinner," Leslie said. "Remember? You were so pale. I said, 'Isn't it always sunny where you live?' and you changed the subject. Now we know why. You're addicted to porn, Mark. You've been inside writing a hospital porn movie and doing God knows what else for years and years."

"Bon Jovi," I said.

"Melanie Dasher," she said, and we glared at each other like teenagers.

"Both of you stop it," my mother said. "Especially you, Mark."

"Yes," Bernie said. "Only Mark's masturbating is relevant."

Dickhead Phil nodded in agreement. "It can't be easy being a pervert, Marky. We think that's why your wife left you."

"All the telltale signs are there, son—the failed career, the broken marriage, the sallow skin, the teenage clothing. You've been lying to yourself and to everyone who loves you. And now it has to stop," my father said, and he pounded his right fist into his left palm to emphasize his seriousness.

"We love you, Mark," my mother said. "But if you're going to get better, you have to tell us the truth. You have to be honest not just with us, but with yourself."

"You're living a lie, Mark, this whole screenwriting thing. You have to admit it," Leslie said.

"Time to tell the truth, Marky. If you can't do it for yourself, do it for your family."

"*Broken Boner*. How could you, Mark?" my mother said, once more holding up the DVD box for me to see.

My father was red in the face, a signal all my life that things were beyond his ability to straighten out. He sat forward on the very edge of his chair, his hands now uncomfortably on his knees, as if he didn't dare repeat the punching motion for fear that events might spiral even more disastrously out of control.

"There are people in Paramus, yes, even people at the club, who occasionally, not in the least bit abnormally, rent a movie like this, which is to say a pornographic movie," my father said. "Your name is right here on the cover. Did you think your family and friends, my friends, your mother's friends, your sister's friends, Phil's friends, our associates and clients and patients and tennis partners wouldn't recognize your name? I mean this is the thing of it, son. What in the world were you thinking? What in the world *are* you thinking?"

"He needs our help, Arthur. Not our anger, frustration, disappointment, embarrassment, and shame," my mother said.

Bernie lightly applauded my mother. "Thank you, Diane. That was very constructive."

"Though there's plenty of that going around, Marky," Phil said.

"It was my fault," my father said, more sad than anything else. "Those damn *National Geographics*. The naked natives."

"It's important we stay focused," Bernie said. "Here's what's going to happen, Mark. Your family is going to take turns telling you in precise detail all the many ways your behavior is worrisome. I asked them to write a list or an outline or a summary or a framework or an essay, and I believe your mother and sister did all of the above."

Each of them removed a thick stack of paper, reams of paper. We would be here for days on end.

"Before we start, though," Bernie said. "I'm going to give you an opportunity to respond to these opening emotions. Would you like to respond, Mark?"

"How did you get in?" I said.

"Before Julie left for Europe, she gave me a key to your house. We let ourselves in," Bernie said.

"Is that legal?" I said.

"You going to sue us, Marky?" Phil said.

"Only you, Phil," I said.

"It's not about our being here, legally or otherwise, Mark," Bernie said. "It's about our having to be here in the first place. Wouldn't you agree?"

No I wouldn't, I thought. The larger of the issues, though not the largest, was all the people in Paramus and New York apparently watching porn movies on an occasional, not-the-least-bit-abnormal basis.

It was reasonable to think that if my family and friends, my father's friends, my mother's friends, my sister's friends, Phil's friends, and all their associates and clients and patients and tennis partners were porn people, then all of *their* family and friends and associates, clients, patients, and tennis partners were porn people too, as were their golf partners—*especially* their golf partners.

And those people no doubt had friends and co-workers and teammates and neighbors and relatives who were porn people as well. And if all of us were renting or buying *Broken Boner*, then, first of all, it was no wonder that Ken Moynihan was rich, and second of all, maybe I was to be congratulated for helping so many men and women reach their fantastical sexual dreams.

Except for the fact that I had been rewritten by Guy Fuchs and declared a non-porn guy by Moynihan himself, the people of Paramus and elsewhere should have petitioned my parents to hold a parade instead of an intervention.

There were other issues larger than the legality of my family's uninvited presence. My erratic behavior as a manifestation of my emotional disorientation resulting from the abrupt and jagged end of my marriage was one that came to mind. The legitimate self-directed guilt I felt from failing myself and Julie and all those close to me was another. My failed career, broken marriage, sallow skin, and teenage clothing were all issues that jumped to the front of the line for me. But none of these struck me as the largest or even the second largest topic on the table.

The second largest issue that I could ascertain was that the intervention was primarily about them and not me. My mother needed to absolve her anger, frustration, disappointment, embarrassment, and shame. It would be tough to sell real estate in Bergen County carrying those emotions in her purse. My father sought pardon for exposing me to naked African women. The blame for my porn compulsion was his and until he was forgiven, my troubled life would never be straightened out. Leslie came to California to reassert her supremacy in her life-long struggle for sibling dominance. Phil was here to gloat.

Bernie, being a psychiatrist, sought to accentuate and exacerbate my pain so that I would lift my sad-looking suitcase, packed with chinos, polos, argyle socks, and Italian loafers, and travel to Chicago, where he could split my head like a coconut and practice the primary law of psychiatry, which is to make sure the patient knows how deeply and desperately fucked up they are. Whether or not they ever get to the secondary or tertiary laws of psychiatry is one of the great medical mysteries of our time.

That they loved me enough to travel across the country, let themselves into my house with Julie's key, pack my suitcase with country club clothes, and confront me with *Broken Boner* filled my heart with confused happiness. *What a family!* I didn't want any of them to go away hurting. Not even my dickhead brother-in-law. But there was one question that needed answering before I could resolve the largest issue in the room.

"How did you find out about the movie?" I said. As I suspected, Phil shifted uneasily in his chair.

"Phil found it," my mother said as Leslie's husband turned red, then ashen gray, then red again.

"Were you just browsing, Phil? Or was there a specific film you were looking for?" I said.

"I just happened to be in that section of the store, Marky. I was renting *The Rookie* with Dennis Quaid."

"Turn down the wrong aisle? That happens to me sometimes," I said.

"You're a jerk, Mark," Leslie said.

"What did we say about name-calling, Leslie?" Bernie said.

"He's a jerk, Bernie," Leslie said.

"We all know that," Bernie said. "And he may well always be one. It's not something we can fix. But if we all participate in an orderly and adult fashion, he may become a jerk who isn't addicted to porn."

"That's what we're hoping for," my mother said.

"If only," my father said.

Which brought me, finally, to the largest issue in the room: what to do about all this.

50. LYING IS IN OUR DNA

If I acquiesced to their needs and admitted my behavior was obsessively pornographic, that my penis was of magnanimous proportions, and that my skin was sallow, I would be lying my way *into* the intervention.

I couldn't deny that I called Ken Moynihan hoping for work. But after he canned me, it's not like I went looking for other porn gigs. There was also no denying that I had called Dallas Westcott. But when she turned out to be something of a Motor City nut-job, I ended the relationship, even though Dallas didn't (and so far wouldn't).

Porn was no more to me than it was to many millions of other people. Most of the time I would choose a ballgame or a newscast or a sitcom or Jeopardy or even Jimmy Neutron over a porn flick. Not always but almost always. I didn't need an intervention to cure any kind of erratic pornographic behavior. And I especially didn't need to accompany Bernie Bowers to Chicago.

Plus, lying my way into the intervention wouldn't necessarily ease my family's consternation, and even if it did, there would be tears and hand-wringing and painful confessions along the way—theirs, not mine.

Tales of my parents fornicating in the back seats of old model cars at the drive-in, Phil's lurid insurance luncheons with horny old lady clients looking for kinky policy addendums, and Leslie's whips and chains suddenly, literally, out of the closet were all frightening possibilities and family secrets best kept secret.

On the other hand, lying my way *out of* the intervention seemed like the quickest and kindest course of action for all involved.

"It's not me," I said. "I didn't write that movie."

"Oh come on," Leslie said.

"You didn't?" my mother said.

"No. Why would I do that?" I said.

"It's your name on the cover," my father said. "Written by Mark Manilow."

"You think I'm the only Mark Manilow in the world?" I said.

"We called the production company," Bernie said, checking his note pad. "Great Dane Productions. Spoke to a man named Ken Moynihan."

"Never heard of him," I said.

"He's heard of you, Marky," Phil said. "Said you were the writer."

"Obviously, he's lying," I said.

"Why would he do that?" my father said.

"He produces porn," I said. "He has no idea who you are. He said yes to get rid of you. Maybe you were with the federal government; how would he know?"

Bernie wasn't biting. "I spoke to him myself. He knew what you looked like."

"What do I look like? I look like everybody else. Average height, average weight, brown eyes, brown hair," I said. "He probably asked you, 'What does he look like?' and everything you said, he said, 'Yes.' Am I right?"

Bernie's silence said I was. It wasn't entirely a lucky guess. I had written that exact scene in at least two scripts and interviewed three homicide detectives to make sure I had it correct.

"It's not me," I said. "I never saw that movie in my whole life. I don't know anything about it. Besides, I've been too busy working on another project."

"More porno?" my sister said.

"Stop with the porn, Leslie," I said. "I've put up with quite enough, don't you think? It's an independent feature film. Look, I love all you guys a lot, I really do, but you're way off base here. And I mean way, way off." And then I smiled to let them know all was forgiven.

I was an expert liar, as are all professional writers of fiction. As relief began to wash over my mother and she handed the DVD of *Broken Boner* to Phil, it occurred to me that we begin lying as children because we have a deeply subconscious awareness that it is a skill we will need and use for the rest of our lives. Lying is in our DNA. Ask any stockbroker.

"We couldn't have all made a mistake like this, Mark," Bernie said.

"Why not? People make collective mistakes all the time. *Ishtar* and *Waterworld* are a couple of doozies. New Coke. George W. Bush. It's a long list."

"I liked *Waterworld*," Phil said.

"You have terrible taste, honey," Leslie said.

Bernie, feeling the momentum swinging away from him, started to speak, but my father, closing in on the facts, waved him off and addressed me firmly, father to son, man to man. "So you're saying, beyond any reasonable doubt, that you didn't write *Broken Boner*, you've never heard of *Broken Boner*, and *Broken Boner* has nothing to do with you in any capacity whatsoever?"

I will answer this final question, I thought, *and there will be tears and hugs and apologies and we will all go out for dinner in Studio City.* I decided that I would wear the Italian loafers to make my parents proud.

"Dad, Mom, this is the first time I have ever heard anything about this porn movie. You have to believe me. I don't know anything about *Broken Boner*."

At that moment, the front door opened, and Dallas Westcott walked into the house.

51. NOTHING BUT BLOWJOBS ALL AFTERNOON

Ms. Westcott was back from a long day shooting *Big Stick In The Dugout*, a film about an unruly baseball team, their well-hung slugger, the young hot widow of the recently deceased owner, and a few of her baseball-crazy girlfriends.

"Hi, baby. What a day. Nothing but blowjobs all afternoon, then a giant orgy to top it all off," she said as she moved into the living room and kissed me.

She was wearing pink sweatpants and a tight-fitting pink T-shirt that read *100% Pure Goddess* across the front. It was cut short, exposing a piece of her flat, tan, perfect belly. She was wearing pink sandals and her toenails and fingernails were painted pink too. Her hair was pulled back, and her pink sunglasses were up off her eyes and resting on the top of her forehead.

She kicked off her sandals and smiled at Phil, who was staring at her with his jaw dropped open. There was no doubt in his mind that she was the nurse on the cover of the *Broken Boner* DVD he was still holding in his hand. She pulled out a pen from her purse.

"Yes, it's really me. That's so sweet. I'd love to sign it for you," she said, and she took the DVD, signed her name, and passed it back to him. Then she held her hand out. "Dallas Westcott," she said.

Phil glanced at Leslie, who was stunned to silence in a way I had never seen before. My parents were speechless as well, though speechless doesn't fully describe what they were. They were breathless, as if double-punched at the same time in the solar plexus. Cool-hand crazy Bernie was windless with them. Phil shook her hand. "I'm Phil," is all he could say.

I was as flabbergasted as they all were, though for different reasons. While they were thunderstruck to see the star of the movie I had just passionately denied knowing anything about kiss me and call me baby, not to mention tell me (and them!) about her afternoon of blowjobs and orgies, I was staggered by the realization that introducing Dallas to my family might somehow suggest to her that our relationship had taken a deeper, more meaningful step forward.

A voice inside my head screamed, *"Run for it, you fool! Run like the wind!"* but I was stuck in cement of my own pouring.

"Are you friends of Mark's?" Dallas said.

"They're not my friends. They're my family," I said. "My father Arthur. My father, Arthur. My mother, Diane. My sister, Leslie. Her husband, Phil. who you've already met—"

"I'm Phil," he said again, his mouth still agape.

"—and my almost ex-father-in-law, Bernie. They came all the way to California because they think I wrote *Broken Boner*. Can you believe that?" Stunningly, I thought Dallas, possibly by the magic of osmosis, would intuit my desperation and back my story.

"It's the director's fault," Dallas said. "Mark's script was really good until Guy got to it. If he had just shot what Mark wrote, the movie would have been much better. Especially the sex scenes. Mark wrote the best sex scenes. Kinky, but still hot, you know what I mean? Guy's sex scenes are all about how long you can fuck. Hours and hours is what Guy says he wants. Hours and hours and hours. I kind of like the movie, though. I always wanted to be a nurse. I like white stockings." As she finished, she took off her sunglasses, handed them to me, then took off her shirt and tossed it aside.

"I'm going to get in the hot tub. Anybody want to join me?" she said.

My father's eyes shot straight out of his head. The impossibility of the overall circumstances was overloading his orthodontic sensibilities and setting off sirens he didn't know he had. There was no longer any way to straighten this out.

My mother completely stopped breathing. It was as if her brain had sent an emergency message to her lungs that said: *"Don't bother. Air won't help."*

Phil eyes were glued to Dallas's breasts, which were covered with a slinky pink bra. Leslie's eyes shot back and forth between Dallas and Phil, while Bernie checked his intervention notes, as if somewhere on his pad was written the correct response to this kind of situation—if a porn star enters the intervention talking of blowjobs and orgies and begins to strip for the hot tub, say the following: "While your breasts are impressive, it's Mark's penis we're examining now." But apparently nothing like that was written down because he began to nervously hum the opening notes of *The Sounds of Silence* while flipping his pages with futility.

"Well," my mother said, "this is certainly a surprise."

"That's exactly what I was going to say," Dallas said, and she took off her sweat pants and tossed them on top of her shirt. She wore lacy pink panties that matched her bra. She always wore matching bra and panties because she said she was a professional and never knew when she would be called for an audition.

"I'm Phil," Phil said, though nobody had asked him.

"Mark never told me you were coming in for the reading," Dallas said. "Isn't it exciting? Joe said Barry Manilow himself was going to be there. Joe said he's Mark's first cousin, even though Mark doesn't know it. He said it was like a Manilow Family Feud. I really loved that show."

"Barry Manilow the singer?" my father said, trying to act as if the world's leading porn star wasn't standing there dressed in her sexiest underwear.

"Yes. He's doing the music," Dallas said. "Everything's happening all at once. Mark's introducing me to his family, which means he's as serious about me as I am about him." She moved to me, put her arms around my neck, and kissed me on the cheek—I could have knocked my sister over with a whistle. "And the staged reading for my first feature film is tomorrow night. Tomorrow night! Can you believe it? I've been waiting forever to go legitimate. There's a limit to how many times you can have sex on screen. Boy-girl, girl-girl, boy-boy-girl, girl-girl-girl; there's a limit; trust me. I don't know what it is, but I know there is one, and anyway I think I might have reached it because now I'm a legitimate actress with a serious boyfriend, who actually wrote my first real movie. I mean, this all good luck, right?"

She took off her bra and slid out of her panties. A lifetime of pornography had left her entirely bereft of sexual inhibitions.

Phil turned a scorching shade of crimson, as if his face were literally on fire. "Oh my God," he said out loud instead of in his head. "Unbelievable luck."

"Phil," Leslie said, "it's not polite to stare."

Dallas took her sunglasses from me, hugged me again, and whispered in my ear, "Thank you, baby. Your family seems really nice. I guess we have to go to Detroit." Then she turned to my family and said, "I'm so happy to meet all of you, I really am." And to demonstrate her happiness, she hugged each one of them, bending over and down to get her arms around their necks in such a way that her big perfect tits were pushed up against their faces.

My mother and Leslie sat completely frozen while Dallas hugged them, though my mother did say it was nice to meet Dallas too. My father, Bernie, and especially Phil did some variation of putting their arms around Dallas and hugging her in return.

When she had hugged them all, she put her sunglasses on and said, "Nobody wants to join me? Phil?"

Phil looked at Leslie, who smiled and said softly, as if she were kidding, though she wasn't, "Only if you'd like to die a long painful death, honey."

"Thanks, no," Phil said to Dallas. "I didn't bring a suit."

"That's okay, I'm not wearing one," Dallas said, as if no one had noticed, as if she had only now noticed.

"We were just leaving," Leslie said.

"Okay, well, it was really nice meeting all of you, and I guess I'll see you tomorrow night. *Phone Book, The Movie*. Cross your fingers." She turned to leave, giving everyone a wonderful view of her shapely ass all the way through the house until she went out the glass sliders and disappeared onto the back deck.

All eyes turned to me. I sat down on the couch and considered my options. I could pick up where we'd left off before Dallas walked into the house—*ignore the naked porn star in my living room; I had nothing to do with Broken Boner*—but quickly determined there was a low likelihood of success in that direction.

I could concoct a story about being held hostage by Dallas and her evil pornography friends, something straight out of *X-Files*, with brainwashing and blackmail, but that would mean running away under the cloak of night, abandoning my house, my career, and my California life, and assuming a new identity in Paramus.

The good news was that would mean the enforced ending of my Dallas Westcott relationship, something I hadn't been able to accomplish on my own. The bad news was that Caroline Yee had no part in that scenario, so I let it go as quickly as I made it up.

As a last resort, I could try the truth.

"You've got some explaining to do," my father said.

"I know, Dad," I said. "It's kind of a long story."

"I'd like to hear it," my mother said.

But before I could start in on my broken heart, my flight to Newark, and the crazy spiral that followed, Phil snapped out of his coma and said, "*Phone Book, The Movie*? Are you kidding me? You stole my idea. At dinner in New Jersey, when you were visiting, I said it would be a blockbuster, and you said no way. But all the time you were thinking you would write it and make a fortune and cut me out of the deal."

"I'm not cutting you out of anything, Phil," I said.

"It sure seems like you are," Leslie said.

Bernie shook his head with all-knowing psychiatric arrogance, as if he were coming out of a cloudbank that had temporarily obstructed his vision. "You're assuming, of course, that Mark and his naked lady friend aren't lying. Given the lies he's already told and the pornographic nature of her actions, it's possible there is no *Phone Book, The Movie*, and that if there is, it involves degrading sexual behavior of all kinds."

"That's my vote," Leslie said.

"Are you lying about this, Mark?" my mother said.

"No, Mom," I said as Dallas hurried in from the back deck, still wearing nothing but her pink sunglasses, and disappeared into the bedroom. "But I wish I were. There really is a *Phone Book, The Movie*, there's no degrading sexual behavior in it whatsoever, the staged reading is tomorrow night at Colonel Curry's Acting Studio, and I have a ridiculous amount of re-writing to do before then, so have a great day, go to the Tar Pits, maybe Phil will get stuck—"

You'd like that wouldn't you, Marky? Steal my royalties," Phil said.

"—and call me later. I'll give you directions to the reading and you can come see for yourself. After that, I'll tell you about Dallas and *Broken Boner* and anything else you want to know."

Dallas reappeared from the bedroom holding her terrifying jackhammer of a vibrator. She looked at me, smiled, and held the thing up like it was a *People* magazine she was going to flip through while soaking in the hot tub. "The old man's watching me again," she said.

52. TWO PIGS IN A POKE

Contrary to my best intentions, Garrett DeYoung was an asshole. He couldn't help himself. He was too good at too much for too long and was as arrogant as he was accomplished, a self-centered egotistical prick. The enmity I felt for him was matched only by the sad sense of loss I felt for Sam, who had to make love to this jerk three times in the second act. She didn't love him for who he was, I decided, she loved him for who he could be.

Despite detesting my leading man, the rewrite progressed quickly. I slept only two and a half hours, from four to six-thirty in the morning, and finished the third act by ten. I was getting ready to shower when the phone rang.

"Mark, it's Caroline." My head had been hurting since Eddie Gonzalez gave me script notes after detailing my Mustang, but the pounding faded to a very faint throb now that Caroline was on the phone.

"Hi. Did your grandfather decide where we're going this Sunday?" Our outings were the highlight of my week.

"Legoland. In Carlsbad. Three hours south of here. We're going to leave early and come back late."

"Great. Any special music?"

"Barenaked Ladies and Queen."

"I can do that."

"That's not why I called. Some people I know from San Francisco are in town and invited me for lunch. I don't want to go alone. Will you come with me?"

There was a quality to her voice at that moment that I hadn't yet heard, a quaver of trepidation and uncertainty not present even when she'd told me—after we kissed on the Travel Town bench, and she discovered the truth of my relationship with Dallas—that until I resolved the porn star and the juggler I couldn't pursue a romantic relationship with the monkey wrench.

I said yes, emailed the script to Joe, Calvin, and Colonel Bill Curry, showered, and was out of the house before Dallas was done working on her tan.

The restaurant was the California Pizza Kitchen in Canoga Park in the Westfield Topanga Plaza. I took the 101 North (west through the Valley), exited at Topanga, turned right, and drove north for ten minutes until I arrived at the Westfield Plaza. I parked the Mustang and arrived at the CPK, where I met Caroline outside.

"You look great," I said. I kissed her cheek, and she squeezed my hand. She was wearing red capris, red leather Keds, and a black silk T-shirt. A thin black sweater was draped over her shoulders to keep her warm in the chilled CPK air. Her hair was pulled back in a ponytail. She had put on that delicious pinkish-silver lipstick that made me feel flush. I couldn't wait to kiss her again and hoped that day would come soon.

"They're already inside," she said. "I haven't seen them for a while. It's a little awkward."

"It'll be fine; it's just lunch. You'll eat pizza and talk about the old days."

"I know. That's what makes it awkward." Then she wrapped her arm around mine, and we went inside.

The staff at all the many California Pizza Kitchens around the country wear little identification pins that state their names and the cities from whence they came because, apparently, marketing research has indicated that customers will find a way to feel connected upon knowing this information. *"Hey,"* the customers presumably say to themselves as they march through the restaurant to their tables, *"I know a guy named Justin, and I've been to Nashville too. This is really going to be great pizza!"*

Barbara from Portland was our hostess, and she passed us to Tracy from Boise, who was conversing with Caroline's friends when we arrived at the table.

"Hi, I'm Tracy, and I'll be your server," she said.

"I'm Mark, and I'll be your customer," I said, and everybody chuckled. It was a pure Arthur Manilow moment, perfected at countless restaurants in the northeast corner of New Jersey. I hoped he and my mother were at the La Brea Tar Pits with Leslie and Phil, trying without success to drag my dickhead brother-in-law, like a doomed mammoth, from the stinking black goop.

Tracy disappeared, and I faced Caroline's friends from San Francisco. The man was tall and thin and handsome. He had a full head of brown hair that was flecked with silvery shades of gray at the temples and a bushy mustache that was the same color, including the silvery-gray flecks. His eyes were hazel, though greener than they were brown. He wore a gold wedding band on the ring finger of his left hand. He did not wear a watch. He had on a blue and white striped shirt and a blue sport jacket. He stood up to shake my hand and I could see that he was wearing pressed jeans. I had the sense that he thought of himself as a casual person, but there was something deeper that wasn't casual at all, something related to the crease in his jeans, though I had no idea what it was.

"Mark," Caroline said. "This is Walter Rydell. Walter, this is Mark Manilow."

Jesus Christ on a crutch! (Another good time for my father's father's expletive.)

It was the coffee table book writer with a death wish who Caroline had followed to San Francisco only to be unceremoniously dumped for a woman who had previously—and successfully—contracted to kill her husband and served time in prison for her efforts.

"And this is Jenny Brann, his wife," Caroline said.

Jenny stood up to shake my hand after Walter was done with it. She was a redheaded fireplug of a woman. Bright blue eyes, wide smile, firm handshake. She wore a denim skirt with a green sweater. Both she and Walter were in their forties. Though there was a hard-to-put-your-finger-on-it masculine quality to her, there was nothing about her outward appearance that labeled her as someone who had hired a man to drop a steel beam on her previous husband.

"Nice to meet you both," I said, and we all sat down.

"Walter's writing a coffee table book on gun shows, and there's a big one at the Staples Center, and we were in LA, and we thought wouldn't it be nice to see Caroline," Jenny said. "Find out how she's doing. Let her know how it's all turned out for us."

"We heard that she was in LA, and we just thought, wow, kismet," Walter said.

"And now here we all are," Jenny said.

"What a great idea," I said.

"I don't know what Caroline's told you," Walter said. "But once you get past the prison sentence and the death wish, Jenny and I are as American as your next-door neighbor. Two pigs in a poke."

"Oh Walter. Nobody says two pigs in a poke anymore. It's the twenty-first century, for Pete's sake." Jenny laughed and an odd chill went through me. It was a large laugh, generous in its sound, but it was followed by a sharp inhale that made me stop laughing. It was a cold and calculated intake of air that had a voice all its own, as unexpected as the beam that had crushed her late husband.

In an effort to avoid the falling girder that was Jenny's laugh, I sprinted backwards in my mind, past two pigs in a poke, and arrived out of breath at the prison sentence and the death wish. Once you get past them? Was he kidding? You couldn't get past the prison sentence and the death wish with a Sherman tank.

"Would anyone like a drink?" It was Tracy from Boise.

Fuck yes, I thought to myself. *Give me the entire bottle of Cuervo Gold. Don't bother bringing a glass.* "I'll have a Coke," I said.

Caroline ordered a diet Coke and Walter and Jenny ordered iced tea. Tracy from Boise's interruption threw us off track. There was no easy pickup from Jenny's twenty-first century remark. I did the best I could.

"You must be learning a lot about guns, Walter," I said.

"Not as much as Jenny. She's really taken to them," he said.

Jenny nodded her agreement, and her red hair bounced up and down on top of her head. "It's the craziest thing, but it turns out I'm an expert marksman or markswoman or marksperson. Anyway, I can really shoot."

"She's a regular Annie Oakley," Walter said.

"If I had known I was this good with guns—" Jenny said.

"You would never have hired Paulie Petrillo," Walter said.

"—I'd have done it myself," Jenny said, finishing their shared thought.

"Here's to hoping," Walter said, and he and Jenny held hands like lovebirds. "Are you a gun guy, Mark?"

I remembered holding Tango Joe's gun in my office, how heavy it was, how awkward it felt in my hand. I was no more a gun guy than I was a porn guy. "Not really, Walter," I said. "I don't have a good feeling about guns. I'm more of an ammo guy."

Everyone laughed.

"He's funny, Caroline," Jenny said.

"He's very funny," Caroline said.

"Who's Paulie Petrillo?" I said.

"The construction worker who murdered Jenny's husband," Caroline said.

"Not the brightest light in the attic," Walter said.

"Good aim, though," Jenny said.

"No argument there," Walter said. "Lenny was one lucky duck."

"Who's Lenny?" I said.

"Jenny's first husband," Caroline said.

"Are you ready to order?" said Tracy from Boise. She arrived with our drinks on a tray and transferred them to our twilight zone table. We ordered salads and pizzas as if we were just like all the other customers.

53. AND THAT'S WHEN CUPID GOT ME

Jenny Brann was from Merced, California, a western-style part of the state with blazing summer temperatures. She was reared on a ranch with horses and cattle, big barking dogs, and pickup trucks with one hundred eighty thousand miles.

Her father, she said, was a domineering, son-of-a-bitch cowboy, kicked spot-on in the balls by a horse and rendered infertile (and bitter beyond measure) after only one child. Jenny, who was three years old, became all the sons he could never have.

His wife, Jenny's redheaded mother, soon died from the lingering complications of Jenny's birth, and her father never remarried (and never forgave his wife for leaving him alone). Instead, he channeled his grief into an abiding hatred of women, an all-consuming emotional state that Jenny barely escaped by being the closest thing to a boy that she could be without actually being one.

She grew up believing she was gay and had numerous lesbian affairs in high school and community college and then left the ranch after her father died—kicked in the head by the same horse that had crushed his nuts (a mare, fittingly)—and moved to Oakland, where she got a job at Office Depot.

It was in Oakland, after years of living alone, that she met Lenny, a mason who was making copies one day when Jenny was manning the counter. Their courtship was notable because it demonstrated to Jenny that she wasn't gay. She liked men. In fact, she *loved* men. She loved them so much that she hated them because she loved them.

Her hatred of Lenny the mason started as a tiny seed in her left knee, the very place her father had once whacked her with a shovel. From her knee, the hatred spread up and down her leg and then through her body until it matured into an insatiable hunger to murder Lenny in cold blood. There was no doubt in her mind she would do it. It was just a question of when and how.

While she waited, she never stopped loving Lenny. Indeed, the love side of her love-hate equation grew in one-to-one proportion to the hate side.

Walter winked at me at this point in the story as if to say: *Am I not the luckiest duck in the lake?*

She met sad sack Paulie Petrillo at the construction site where both he and Lenny were working. Paulie was a crane operator and a good one. It was, unfortunately, his only shining quality. He was suffering from enormous debt brought on by a terrible gambling addiction, a divorce, a foreclosure, a lawsuit, and the enormous medical bills resulting from his ninety-three-year-old mother's rapid descent into dementia. These backbreaking financial and emotional pressures had snuffed out all his lights but one: crane operation.

Jenny had inherited her father's ranch, sold it for a nice pile of cash, and had banked the money in the hope that she would one day know what to do with it. She offered Paulie twenty thousand dollars to drop a steel girder on her husband, and Paulie agreed.

It was a foolproof plan except for the fact that Paulie had mentioned it to his delusional mother, who though she could no longer brush her own teeth, was able to recount the time, date, and relevant facts of the murder plot for the police. Both Paulie and Jenny went to prison.

"And that's when Cupid got me," Walter said.

He was a high school geek from Baltimore. Well over six feet tall as a ninth grader, he had no desire to play for any of the school's sports teams, though he had the ability and size to make a difference on all of them. Tony Giannascio, a hateful physical education teacher who doubled as the high school athletic director, decided that since Walter wouldn't play, Walter would suffer—not that Walter hadn't suffered all his life.

His birth mother, a sixteen-year-old tramp from Coral Gables, Florida, gave up her twins for adoption (and was pregnant again three weeks later) to a couple that only wanted the baby girl, Walter's sister, but took the boy too because of a legal glitch.

They were Mitchell and Maryanne Rydell, compulsive athletes and executive bankers destroyed by infertility caused by Mitchell's incessant long-distance bicycle racing, Maryanne's obsessive triathlon training, or by God, who thought they were too Type A to rear children. Sports and money were their holy grails.

Margaret, Walter's twin sister, bought into this philosophy in kindergarten with a ferocity that made her parents proud, while little wimpy Walter liked crayons, poems, and pictures of cows.

Mitchell and Maryanne didn't understand their son's artistic bent and wanted no part of it. They put all their parental energy into Margaret, a champion athlete and the most popular girl in elementary, middle, and high school.

Walter was an outsider, both at school (with his superstar sister) and in his own home. And yet he somehow retained the heart of an artist. He tried theater and choir and enjoyed himself, but knew he had no real spark for either one. It was writing and photography that hooked him—he wrote, photographed, and edited the high school yearbook four years in a row.

But he could not escape Giannascio the bully, who tortured Walter, mercilessly questioning the boy's intelligence, courage, heart, and balls at every opportunity, daring Walter to play basketball or football or soccer or even tennis, prodding him to wrestle or bowl or run track for his school, his manhood, and his pride.

Walter didn't fight back because he didn't like the aggressive feelings in his heart, the very same reason he didn't like sports. There wasn't a competitive bone in his body. That's what Walter was proud of, his gentle nature and artistic soul. If he could hold onto that, he would be all right. It was his soft passive heart that kept him sane.

And then one day in the gym, at the end of his senior year, there was a terrible accident that would change Walter indelibly.

It was late in the afternoon, and Walter was doing a story about Giannascio, words and photos, for the school newspaper. It was after a girls' volleyball game and the gymnasium was empty, except for Giannascio, who was under the rollout bleachers, picking up trash and lost clothing.

Walter called out to the unpleasant athletic director that he'd like to ask him some questions and take his picture, and Giannascio, who'd had a particularly lousy day, went ballistic on his favorite target. Walter started to walk away, but from under the bleachers, Giannascio dropped his drawers and dared Walter to take a picture of his dick.

Walter snapped. He ran to the bleachers, smashed into them with the speed and power of an NFL fullback, and pushed them all the way up against the wall, crushing Giannascio to death.

Murder by reason of temporary insanity was Walter's successful plea, and there were years of hospitalization and therapy before he was deemed fit for society. Upon his release, there were two dominant, seemingly irreconcilable streams of consciousness co-existing in his once-more gentle heart.

Because of a lifetime of rejection, he wanted someone to love him for who he truly was and because of his overwhelming guilt for what he'd done, coupled with his unshakable sense of unworthiness, he no longer wanted to go on living. Over time, these complicated, incompatible feelings melded into one heartfelt desire: he wanted someone who loved him for who he truly was to kill him.

Many unsuccessful relationships later, after he was already an established and popular writer of coffee table books, he read about Jenny on the Internet (while researching a coffee table book about murderous women in prison—a book that for some reason never took flight) and wrote to her. She wrote back, and for three years they corresponded, opening their hearts to each other, sharing their stories, and falling in love. If ever two people were destined to be together, it was Walter and Jenny.

The problem was that Walter had met Caroline in New York while writing a coffee table book about boardwalks and things had progressed further than he had intended. He'd liked Caroline too much to tell her that he was in love with another woman, and so the relationship deepened.

Caroline followed him to back to San Francisco, moved into his house near Haight-Ashbury, and thought she was starting a new life with a wonderful man, a tall, good-looking, gentle bear who wrote nice words about diners in Philadelphia and covered bridges in New Hampshire and took pretty pictures of barns in Wyoming and Porsches in Atlanta. But Jenny was released early for good behavior, Walter brought her home, and Caroline was caught flat-footed.

"It was Caroline who forced me to face the truth in my heart," Walter said. "I knew it was in there, but until she followed me to San

Francisco, I couldn't admit it to myself. She made the whole thing crystal clear. As soon as Jenny was released, I knew what I had to do."

"We owe Caroline a great debt of thanks. She'll always have a special place in our lives," Jenny said.

"Except who knows how long that will be for Walter," I said, innocently. That tickled Caroline's funny bone, which unexpectedly led to a quick case of contact laughter and resulted in both of us struggling not to laugh out loud (like Bobby Jensen and me in Mrs. Morgan's class when the witch was reading the piglet book).

"Excuse me," Caroline said, faking a cough. "I'm going to the ladies room."

"Want me to come with you?" I said, and we both laughed out loud this time. She didn't even answer, just headed off to the bathroom, still laughing.

"So tell us more about your movies, Mark," Jenny said. "We know you're a screenwriter, but we don't know what you're working on now."

I gave them the no-huddle version of *Phone Book, The Movie*, up to and including the reading at Colonel Bill Curry's later tonight, in seven more hours, as a matter of fact.

"Can we come?" Walter said, hopefully.

"Oh yes," Jenny said. "That would be great. I've never been to a staged reading of a movie before. It sounds so exciting."

Of course, I should have said no. I should have explained that it was a closed reading and that the actors weren't expecting an audience other than the writer and producer, but I felt an odd kinship with Walter and his death wish.

It occurred to me, as Tracy from Boise refilled our drinks, that I had a kind of death wish for my career in much the same way that Walter had one for his life. How else could I explain my rash and desperate journey into porn, my reckless, discouraging, and mostly miserable excursion into independent film, my endless summer of despondent pitch meetings, my hopeless black hole of story meetings, my mile-high pile of inane notes, my years of writer's block? Didn't I want, like poor crazy Walter, to have someone who loved me dearly kill my career and set me free to live a life with some semblance of sanity and normalcy?

"Sure," I said. "Love to have you there."

I gave them Colonel Curry's address and directions to the former First Church of the Friends of Jesus. Caroline returned from the ladies room, still laughing, Walter paid the bill with his platinum credit card—"I'm here on coffee-table-book business," he said—and we bid good-bye to Tracy from Boise and Barbara from Portland and Gil from Austin and stepped outside into the unrelenting San Fernando Valley sunshine.

By chance, Caroline and I had parked near each other while Walter and Jenny's car was halfway around the world in the opposite direction. As we split up, I said, "See you tonight."

"You invited them to your reading?" Caroline said with astonishment.

"I couldn't say no," I said.

She nodded, somehow feeling what I was feeling. "Once you get past the prison sentence and the death wish, they're as American as your next-door neighbor," she said.

"Two pigs in a poke," I said.

She wrapped her arm around mine, and we walked to her car.

"It was a big favor, coming here with me," she said. "I couldn't have faced them alone. Thank you."

"You're welcome."

"They're pretty out-of-bounds, aren't they?"

"Way out. I couldn't have done it without you either. That's why I'm going to ask you to come to the reading tonight too. I'd like to have my friends there, and you're my only one."

We shared a nice smile, she gave my arm a little extra squeeze, and then she said, "I'm still not kissing you until you figure out the juggler and the porn star. No matter how much I want to."

I nodded and said, "It's okay. This is nice too."

Her arm slid down my arm, and we held hands.

"It really is," she said.

54. LIKE HUMPING RHINOCERI

I decided to take Ventura Boulevard instead of the 101 and got stuck at the light at White Oak when two Mercedes sedans, one black and one silver, smashed into each other, spun around the intersection like square dancers, and ended up limbs akimbo in the center of everything, blocking all access from White Oak and Ventura in both directions.

Two ambulances, three fire trucks, four television news vans, and five police cars filled the intersection, adjoining exits, entrances, and parking lots with personnel and gear.

Traffic was backed up for miles on Ventura, all the way to Sherman Oaks to the east and to Calabasas to the west. White Oak was even more of a disaster. From the intersection heading north, toward and well beyond the entrance and exit ramps to the 101, was a solid block of stopped, stalled, and overheating motor vehicles.

This backed up the ramps in such a way that the long line of cars trying to exit onto White Oak from the freeway stretched for more than a mile onto the 101, causing massive slowdowns and finally a quadruple fender-bender that created a major jam on the southbound 101 all the way from White Oak back to Westlake Village.

Rubberneckers on the northbound side slowed their pace to a crawl, thus causing an interminable stop and go, five-mile-per-hour, blood-pressure-busting slowdown that stretched for miles all the way to Laurel Canyon in Studio City and caused another accident, this one involving a Jerry's Famous Deli delivery van, a pick-up truck packed with illegal immigrant carpenters, an empty school bus, and a four hundred thousand-dollar Rolls Royce.

This negated all the 101 entrance and exit ramps along the way, creating a snarl that stopped all traffic in the San Fernando Valley and killed the canyon roads, thus creating a sorry mess in Beverly Hills.

I climbed out of the Mustang and walked to the intersection, knowing there was nothing I could accomplish. A crowd had already formed, a courtesy to the extra officers, who prior to the crowd forming had little or nothing to do.

The two Mercedes sedans were carnally interlocked like humping rhinoceri. There were cops and cameras and paramedics going through their paces and the drivers were finalizing the all-important exchange of personal information that sets in motion the arcane machinery of the car insurance industry. The driver of the black Mercedes was Ken Moynihan.

His wife and three children, all below the age of six, waited near their car. She was as fat as Moynihan himself, maybe fatter, covered with jewelry, and dressed to the nines. His children were little round balls of puffy flesh.

Ken was conferring with a police officer and the driver of the other vehicle, who was, improbably, Bill Walton, former UCLA and pro basketball legend turned exquisitely honest television color man. At six feet eleven inches, he was hard to miss. As Walton generously signed an autograph for the starstruck cop, I called out to Moynihan. "Ken, over here."

Moynihan saw me, said something to big Bill Walton, and crossed the intersection. He wore a red, custom-made, and very expensive le coq sportif warm-up/sweat suit, which was a good thing, because like all men and women of enormous weight who spend significant time in the hot sun, he was profusely sweating. As he approached, I thought he resembled that giant red ball in the middle of the Japanese flag, if that ball were smoking a cigar while melting.

"Mark, can you do anything about this fucking mess?"

"I don't think so, Ken. I'm stuck here just like you and a million other people."

"Bill Walton. Can you fucking believe it?"

"Was it his fault?"

"Who knows? It's my car on top of his. It was probably my fault. I was reaching back for a bag of chips, grabbing them from my son. He was shoving them in his face like this was the last fucking bag for all time."

"Was anybody hurt?"

"No. Fucking miracle. Spun around three times. Air bags and shit. Kids crying, wife screaming. Fucking nightmare."

"Sorry."

"Who isn't?" Then he took a deep breath and put it all behind him. "We've got a pretty big hit, you and me. *Broken Boner*. That's the good news, right?"

Except for the fact that it had contributed to the ruination of my life, why not?

"Right," I said.

"Dallas told me you wrote her a movie about the phone book."

"It's true."

"I got an idea for a movie about the phone book too. Phone book-related, well, telephone-related anyway. Want to hear it?"

"You know I do," I said, and I remembered thinking I was once going to have coffee and cheese Danish at his kitchen counter.

"It's called *Operators Are Standing By*, and it's about these college girls who start a phone sex business in their sorority. A couple of phone company guys show up to install the lines, big tool belts, if you know what I mean, and you get the rest."

"Yes I do."

"So how's Dallas? She can come on cue, but can she act?"

"We find out tonight. There's a staged reading of the movie at her acting studio."

"No shit. Maybe I'll stop by. What time?"

"Eight-thirty."

"She told me the name of the place once. General Chan's Chicken or something like that."

"Colonel Curry's Acting Studio."

Two tow trucks moved slowly into the intersection. Cops and cameras sprang into action. Moynihan's chubby children bounced and pointed with glee.

"Kids are all excited. Now that it's over, a smashed-up Mercedes is the most fun they had all week," he said. "Probably cost me seventy grand. It's only money, right?" Then he turned, like a giant baked tomato, and started back to his wrecked car, where Bill Walton was posing for pictures with the paramedics. He looked back at me as he rolled away. "Too bad you're not a porn guy, Mark."

Two hours later, the intersection was reopened and traffic resumed. I went home and checked my email. Colonel Curry confirmed that he'd received the script and had made copies for the cast. Calvin Key also reported receiving the script and said he thought Garrett DeYoung was the most exciting action adventure leading man he'd seen in a long time, though he did add that he and Cletus and Gloria and Eddie had additional notes. Joe emailed me back and said he had read all the horoscopes, determined that only Gemini held any promise for our staged reading, and was headed to City Hall to legally change his birthday from October 20 to June 8.

Dallas had left me a note saying there was chicken fried steak in the refrigerator and that she and the rest of the cast were meeting early at Colonel Bill's to rehearse. I took off all my clothes, fed my fish, and climbed in the hot tub.

Immediately upon seeing it was me and not Dallas, the old man living across the canyon abandoned his binoculars and went inside to watch television. I had done all I could do. It was up to the astrological twins to decide the rest.

55. THE HOTTEST UNDERGROUND NIGHTCLUB IN LA

I drove down out of Coldwater Canyon, turned left onto Ventura Boulevard, and headed west toward Van Nuys Boulevard, where I turned right and kept going until I reached Panorama City and Colonel Curry's Acting Studio.

I pulled into the parking lot and recognized the rental cars of my parents, my sister, and Bernie Bowers. I saw Joe Hudson's Mercedes and a massive red Hummer with a license plate that read *I Count*, which meant that Calvin Key and his development team had arrived early as well.

As I entered the former church for the first time since Dallas had surprised me with a visit there, I immediately had the sense that, whichever way the wind was blowing, I wasn't in Kansas any longer.

There were stage lights set up for the reading. Not some half-baked garage band rig, but top-of-the-line stands and trusses and a thirty-foot Lightbridge System holding dozens of ellipsoidals and fresnels and floods and spots. If the touring Broadway production of *The Producers* were playing here tonight, they might not have this many lights. Interspersed between the recognizable stage lights were several larger lighting schemes, elements, and formats that I had never seen before. Large swirling and rotating units with multiple cans and colors and shapes that looked like fantastical components from the space ship in *Close Encounters*.

At the back of the room, a lighting technician named Boogie was reading the script, reviewing his cues, and smoking a joint. When I asked him about his unusual and unidentifiable lighting effects, he said only, "Weather permitting." He had made a major career lighting rock shows and raves, which are enormously insane parties that last until the sun rises or the authorities arrive. "Rock and rave, dude," he told me, offering me a hit of his joint, which I declined.

Though Boogie and the lights were an instant eye-opener, it was the DJ set up just fifteen feet to his right—to provide, I presumed, musical accompaniment for the reading of the movie—that dropped my jaw. He was a black kid, no more than sixteen, who went by the moniker Royal T and claimed he was descended from an ancient line of Watusi kings. Who could argue? He was way over six feet tall, closer to seven feet, skinny as a paperclip, wild as the jungle. Lately, he had been providing the music for the hottest parties in LA.

He told me this was his first film, but he'd read the script and was ready to rock the house. If the size of his sound system was any indication, all of Panorama City would be rocking. The banks of speakers he'd trucked in for the reading—and set up on either side of the stage as if it were a Van Halen concert—dwarfed the mixers, amps, and preamps that allowed him to beat mix the tens of thousands of songs in his collection.

He was playing Roxy Music at a conversational volume, lining up songs for his cinematic debut, and talking music with Bernie Bowers, who was wearing a charcoal-gray three-piece suit with a red tie.

The church itself was transformed. Small metal cocktail tables with black tablecloths and slick-looking black metal chairs with deep purple velvet cushions dotted the floor in front of the stage on both sides of the Colonel's private, (and now) red-velvet-draped, raised recliner platform. Each table was equipped with a lighted candle, a small vase of fresh flowers, and a crystal ashtray in the shape of an open hand.

A full-service bar with a bartender named Angela, who wore a low-cut black top and a micro-mini skirt, was assembled at the rear of the studio, and a flaming gay waiter named Robbie—wearing skintight black jeans, a black tailored shirt and a black tie knotted loosely at the neck—helped Angela wipe wineglasses.

The former First Church of the Friends of Jesus was now the hottest underground nightclub theater in LA.

Gloria and Eddie Gonzales were seated at a table near the stage, drinking cocktails and reviewing their scripts. Eddie had cleaned himself up and was wearing an LA Kings jersey with white denim jeans and white Nike running shoes. He had a white ski cap on his head. Gloria was resplendent in a yellow, flower-print Hawaiian skirt and a matching top.

My sister Leslie and her husband Phil were standing at the bar with Joe, drinking a Napa Valley Pinot Noir. Leslie was dressed for a corporate soiree—little black dress, black heels, and pearls. Phil wore slacks and a sport coat with no tie and loafers with no socks, a New York insurance man signal that he was ready for Hollywood if Hollywood was ready for him.

Joe was dressed for a Brazilian ballroom bash—skin-tight black leather pants, gold silk shirt unbuttoned to his chest, black fedora, and, as always, dark impenetrable shades. His hair was pulled back and under a gold silk kerchief. He had a pearl-handled pistol tucked into his waistband as if it were an accessory, like a pair of cufflinks or a gold watch.

My parents stood at the edge of the stage, speaking with Cletis Oleander about only God knows what. My dad was dressed for a Riverside Country Club Saturday night buffet—colorful sweater with modern geometric shapes, casual pants, and Italian loafers. He was drinking a vodka tonic. My mother wore a pretty blue skirt and a matching silk blouse. She looked great standing beside my dad, and I remembered again how much I loved them both.

They had crossed the country to save me from a depraved life of pornographic behavior, had instead experienced an eye-popping dose of Dallas Westcott, and were now present in what could only be described as a hole in the time-space continuum, talking with an ornery intergalactic truck driver who wore two watches, an unzipped down vest with no shirt, Bermuda shorts, and cowboy boots. Cletis's head was freshly clean-shaven and shiny as a jewel. He held a bottle of Bass Ale in each hand. My mother was drinking a double Johnnie Walker Black.

"Mark, hey, what do you think?" It was Calvin Key. He wore blue jeans, brown Docksiders, a tailored blue-striped dress shirt unbuttoned at the neck, and a casual blue blazer. We shook hands. He was drinking some kind of island cocktail with an umbrella in the glass.

"Did you do this, Calvin?" I said, gesturing at the lights and sound and bar and nightclub tables and chairs.

"Me, Joe, and the Colonel. There's a rumor that some industry people are coming. Based on what the Colonel's got planned, we thought we should dress the place up, make the movie seem as big as we think it's going to be."

"But it's just a reading. Actors sitting around a long table reading the script," I said.

"I don't think so, Mark," he said. "I think it's something else altogether."

56. GOTS TO SPIKE THE KOOL-AID

"Mark, over here," my mother called out from in front of the stage, waving while polishing off her drink.

"I spoke with your parents. Your sister and brother-in-law, too," Calvin said. "They're nice people. Go say hello." Then he walked over to Bernie, Boogie, and Royal T and either answered some light and sound cue questions, discussed where to buy the most potent pot in Los Angeles, or was invited to my interrupted intervention.

I walked to the stage, where my mother and father were standing with Cletis Oleander, who shook his head with disappointment as I arrived. "You late again," he said.

"It didn't start yet," I said.

Cletis made a sound that said, *"Can you believe this chump?"* and addressed my parents. "He always late."

"I'm not always late," I said.

"Since he was a boy," my mother said.

"He be late for his own funeral," Cletis said.

"I guess that's one time it would pay to be late," my father said, and he clinked his vodka tonic glass with the Bass Ale bottle in Cletis's left hand. My parents and Key's butler had a laugh at my expense.

'You right about that, Artie," Cletis said. "I see you after the show. Got to check on the little woman before the lights go down. Don't do nothing I wouldn't do, which means do whatever the hell you want." Then he walked to Gloria and Eddie's table.

My mother kissed me on the cheek. "Hello, sweetheart," she said. "We're having a nice time."

"I'm glad," I said.

"He seems like a good man," my father said, as we shook hands.

If you needed proof that people from Paramus should never stray westward, there it was. The words on the tip of my tongue were: he screws Gloria every afternoon in a different closet. But instead I said, "He is something."

"Used to be a truck driver. Big rigs," my father said, throwing back the last of his drink.

"Interesting outfit he has on," my mother said. "Is that a new California style?"

"I don't think so. That's all Cletis," I said.

"I had cowboy boots when I was young. I'll bet that's something you didn't know," she said.

"That's a good bet, Mom."

"It's an open bar," my father said. "Your executive producer said to put it on his tab. He's got some money, I think."

"Little bit. You want me to get you another round?"

My parents shared a look that was wild for half a second before fading back to reality. "Tonight's tonight," my father said, handing me his glass. "Vodka tonic."

My mother handed me her glass too and said, "Johnnie Walker Black on the rocks."

"Tomorrow, we'll revisit this intervention business," my father said. "But right now, your mother and I are rooting for you as hard as we can. Break a leg, son."

"Okay, Dad," I said, and I headed for the bar.

"Make mine a double, sweetheart," my mother called out behind me. I held up her glass without turning around to let her know she was good to go. It crossed my mind that if I got them really rip-roaring drunk and put them on the redeye so they woke up in Paramus, maybe they'd think the whole thing was a bad dream.

"Hey, my brother. Did you bring the acid? We need the acid, *mon*. Gots to spike the Kool-Aid," Joe said as a way of welcoming me to the group at the bar.

"Hi, Joe," I said, and we gave each other a warm hug. I hadn't seen him for a while, and in spite of every crazy thing in my life, he brought an instant smile to my face.

"Let me introduce you to your sister," Joe said, and everybody laughed.

"Pearls, wow, Les. Really going all out," I said.

"I didn't want Joe to think we all dressed like you," Leslie said.

"Joe and I have been talking about the movie, Marky. Where the idea came from in the first place," Phil said.

"Let me guess," I said. "You want a piece of the pie.

"A finder's fee," Phil said. "What's fair is fair."

"Even if this exact movie wasn't specifically Phil's idea, it was Phil, in a general sense, who created the concept," Leslie said. "You can't deny that, Mark. You would never once have thought of turning the phone book into a movie without Phil."

"He's your muse, *mon*," Joe said to me. "Don't fight the feeling."

In my mind, this had to be the low point of my professional life. Holding my parents' empty cocktail glasses in the Colonel Curry Acting Nightclub admitting to myself that my dickhead brother-in-law was my muse.

Phil nodded at Joe, swirled his Pinot Noir, and said, "I just want to have a voice at the table."

"And so you shall, Phillip. I hereby designate you as associate producer of the independent feature film *Phone Book, The Movie*, written, after receiving divine inspiration from the wellspring of your creativity, by the mad fucking genius known throughout the colonies as Mark Manilow."

Phil smiled like I'd never seen him smile and turned to my sister. "Associate producer," he said.

Leslie put her hand on his arm and said, "I'm proud of you, honey."

Joe nodded his agreement and said, "It's a low-budget film, so the position comes with no salary and last-in-line back-end participation, but you're invited to the set at your own expense and then, of course, there's your credit, which your children's children's children will watch, eyes wide with wonder."

"What do I do first?" Phil said to Joe.

"I would tell your in-laws the glad tidings and drink three large glasses of wine in succession," Joe said.

"Right," Phil said. "We're in business, Marky," he said to me, and then he and Leslie walked across the room to where my parents were waiting for their refills.

"I don't like him," I said to Joe. "Could you tell?"

"Listen to me very carefully," Joe said. "Somewhere in his Rolodex is an insurance agent with ties to the movie business. Do you imagine our insurance costs will be higher or lower with Phillip's involvement?"

"Lower," I said.

"Your sister terrifies me," Joe said. "She's a born proctologist."

I laughed out loud.

"Repeat after me," he said. "Joe, I didn't realize how much I missed you until this very moment."

"It's true," I said.

He put his arm around me and said, "Repay me with friendship, my brother," and then the door opened and the evening took a sharp turn down Insanity Lane.

57. LEGENDS WILL BE BORN

Ken Moynihan walked through the door with an entourage that included Guy Fuchs, Long Ron Dong, Thad Whacker, and three scantily-clad women—one blonde, one brunette, one redhead, named, in order, Penny Polesitter, Kinky Cat, and Tiffany Sin.

Moynihan wore a metallic silver suit, a silver shirt, a silver tie, and silver Adidas running shoes, an ensemble that made him look like the Death Star in *Return Of The Jedi*.

In the darkened former First Church of the Friends of Jesus, Guy Fuchs' white spiked hair served as a beacon of light. He led the porn troupe to the front of the stage, the very first row to the right of the Colonel's raised platform, where they pulled several tables together and took their seats.

Their path took them directly past my parents, who watched them with expressions that said: *We are northeastern New Jersey Jews from the planet Earth. Where are you from?*

"The big silver ball is Ken Moynihan," I said to Joe while handing my parents' empty glasses to Angela and nodding for another round. "He's a porn producer. The guy with the white hair directed the movie I wrote for Dallas. The rest of them are actors with either huge dicks or massive tits that they use as props in every scene."

"I'm not blind," Joe said.

"Friends of yours?" Bernie said as he put his empty glass on the bar. "Tequila and orange juice," he said to Angela.

"Friends of Dallas," I said. "The big one in the silver suit is Ken Moynihan from Great Dane Productions. You spoke to him on the phone. The one with the white hair directed *Broken Boner*. The one sitting to the left of the red head is Long Ron Dong. The guy to her right is Thad Whacker. The redhead's name is Tiffany Sin."

"I've always liked that name," Joe said.

"Joe, this is Bernie Bowers," I said. "He's still officially my father-in-law, but he's also a psychiatrist, so proceed with caution."

"Stay out of my head, *mon*, for your own safety. No one's ever come out alive," Joe said while shaking Bernie's hand.

Angela put my parents' drinks on the bar. I nodded thanks and picked them up. "You have any idea what's going to happen here tonight, Joe?" I said.

"Legends will be born," Joe said.

"Right," I said, and I crossed the room to my parents. A chill ran up my spine as I thought of Bernie drunk on tequila, but I shook it off as the porn table reeled me in.

"You know you're in trouble when the writer's drinking a scotch in one hand and a vodka in the other," Ken said, and everybody laughed.

"Thanks for coming, you guys," I said. "It means a lot to Dallas and to me too." What a spectacular lie that was! Or was it? Were these my friends now? Would Ken, Thad, Long Ron, and I play a round of golf as a porn foursome some day next week? Check out the auto show at the Staples Center? Shop for tight-fitting pants on Rodeo Drive? Drink beers in a Reseda pool hall and yuck it up while Thad clears the table with his dick? *I'm as ready as anybody for an intervention*, I thought.

"You could be a porn guy, Mark. You're this close," Guy said.

"Don't give up, kid," Ken said. "We're all pulling for you."

"When's the show start?" Long Ron said.

"Any minute," I said.

"Can we get a drink?" Penny said. I don't think Polesitter was her real name.

"Absolutely," Robbie the waiter said, as he arrived at the table. He and Guy made an instant connection—like a heat-seeking missile and the flame-throwing engine of a fighter jet. Everyone at the table saw it and approved. "I'm Robbie. I'm your server. I'm also an actor and a writer. I'm working on a screenplay even as we speak."

Those words always wreak havoc with my inner ear, causing instant nausea and a loss of balance. I smiled through them like a trouper.

"I'm a director. I'd like to read it," Guy said. "But only if you audition for the lead."

Guy and Robbie shared a smile that bordered on obscene, and the porn girls giggled like seventh-graders while Long Ron and Thad gave each other and Guy a high five. Ken lit a cigar.

"I have it with me. It's in my car," Robbie said to Guy. "Should I get it?"

"Not until I'm holding a Chivas," Ken said.

"I'll have vodka martini," Kitty said.

"I'll have a black Russian," Penny said. "Although I had one at work today. His name was Boris."

They all laughed, and I gestured good-bye with my parents' cocktails and continued on to where Arthur and Diane were waiting. *Good luck* and *Break a leg* they called after me.

"Your mother and I have a little bet going," my father said as I arrived with their glasses.

"Your father thinks you won't tell us who they are, and I think you will, but you won't tell us the truth," my mother said.

I handed them their drinks, and we all looked at the porn table.

"What does the winner get?" I said.

"None of your business, mister," my father said as if I were twelve years old. But then he winked to let me know that I was a grown-up and the winner was going to get laid or some other sexual reward that I didn't want to think about on an empty stomach or even a full stomach.

"You both lose," I said. "The silver suit is the guy who produced *Broken Boner* and hundreds of other porn films. His name is Ken Moynihan."

"The one Bernie spoke to," my father said, in his getting-things-straight voice.

"Isn't he overweight for pornography?" my mother said.

"The white hair is the director. His name is Guy Fuchs. He's gay as Mardi Gras," I said. "The rest of them are porn actors, friends of Dallas."

My mother took a long hard sip from her drink and said, "They almost look like real people."

"Looks are deceiving," I said, and then Cathy Burns, my agent, walked through the door with Toxic Bob Bloom and a woman in a sharp-looking pants suit who I recognized right away, though I didn't believe my eyes.

58. DISTRACT, DECEIVE, DESTROY

I hadn't seen Cathy in a while, but she looked the same—tailored clothes, two-hundred-dollar haircut, Bluetooth permanently attached to her ear. It was common knowledge in the industry that on her tenth birthday she chose to turn forty-two and had been that age for the past thirty-odd years. With one hand guiding the pant-suited woman, Cathy gave me a wave with her other hand, simultaneously gesturing that they were headed to the bar, an effortless two-in-one signal that she'd learned and mastered in Hollywood Agent School.

Toxic Bob wore a very expensive Armani suit and, to demonstrate the importance of the evening, a full-length Blue Fox fur coat with a matching Blue Fox fur hat and Blue Fox fur mittens. I had a wet and freezing Siberian moment in which an icy winter wind blew through me, but then I remembered we were in Los Angeles and the evening air was 68 degrees and dry as a box of Corn Flakes.

I crossed the room to Toxic Bob even as I saw Joe and Bernie speaking with Cathy and the pants suit. "Do you have an invitation?" I said, less than half-joking.

"I don't need one. I'm one of the producers," he said with an absolutely straight face.

"How did that actually happen, Bob?" I said.

"The same way it always happens," he said and changed the subject without blinking. "Do you know who she is?" he said, removing his fur hat and mittens while gesturing at the pants suit drinking a glass of San Ynez chardonnay. "Here's a hint. Her name is Ally Kramer."

My mouth opened and these words came out: *"Color War"*.

Thirteen years ago, at my very first studio meeting (set up by Cathy Burns, coincidentally), I pitched a coming-of-age drama called *Color War* about four fifteen-year-old boys at a summer camp. The pitch was at Fox, and the development executive was a twenty-two-year-old named Ally Kramer.

My pitch was so immensely painful, so utterly unprofessional and mercilessly long, that during the tortuous second act (thirty minutes all by itself), she gave birth to a child—a miraculous event since she hadn't been pregnant when the meeting began. She had, in effect, as a result of my pitch, suffered through a bad relationship, an unwanted and difficult pregnancy, and a life-threatening vaginal birth without an epidural. In the process, she had aged ten years.

What really happened was that as I started the third act, she stood up and left the room. She utilized this tactic many times throughout her career and became famous all over town for her Unexpected Exit technique, a negotiating ploy that had brought more than one Hollywood player to their knees. She went on to become the president of Paramount Pictures and then opened her own shop on the Universal lot, where her deal was gigantic but dwarfed by the size of the movies she was contracted to deliver.

"What is she doing here?" I said to Toxic Bob.

"Not every movie can be made for one hundred seventy-five million dollars. She's all over this one like white on rice."

"It's a low-budget project, Bob. It's an independent film."

"America's an independent country," he said, taking off his fur coat and smoothing his hair with his right hand. "Let's not sell ourselves short before the opening bell. It's not how we live life in this part of the world. Hollywood history is filled with great men who reached for the stars. Why shouldn't we?"

And so here was the secret of Toxic Bob's takeover strategy: change the subject to something no one can argue. Distract, deceive, destroy.

"Because there is no *we*," I said.

"And there's no *I* in Team. Remember that, Mark. When we're shooting *Phone Book, The Movie* in New Zealand next summer, we'll have a beer and laugh about this conversation. I'm drinking martinis. What are you drinking?"

"Rum and Dr. Pepper. Hundreds of them," I said.

"See you at the bar," he said, walking away.

Cathy Burns, Ally Kramer, Tango Joe, and Bernie Bowers made room for Toxic Bob at the bar. I wasn't worried about Joe. He was armed. If things went awry with Toxic Bob, Joe would shoot him in the head with his pearl-handled pistol, and everyone in Hollywood would swear, though they were nowhere near Colonel Curry's at the time, that it was self-defense.

Instead, I thought it wise to warn Calvin Key about Toxic Bob's hostile takeover. As I walked to the light and sound command post, it occurred to me that Toxic Bob might finally have picked a fight he couldn't win. It's one thing to bully the writer, it's another thing to challenge a man with several billion dollars in the bank. Then again, there seemed to be no limit to Toxic Bob's poisonous potential. His greatest talent was forcing his unwanted way into a project and twisting it into a ballpark pretzel. There was no win-win with Toxic Bob. Everyone loses until the movie falls down dead. If only his father had let him sell shit in Chicago.

Key, Boogie, and Royal T were talking about the script when I arrived. "Calvin, there's something you have to know about the guy who just walked in," I said.

"Does he write the songs that make the whole world sing?" Key said, his eyes looking past me toward the door.

"No, but he wears fur coats in the middle of the desert and—" while I was talking, I saw Boogie and Royal T staring at the door with identical disbelieving squints. I turned my head to follow their gaze, and my voice stopped working in mid-sentence, my eyes involuntarily fell into the same stunned squint, and my brain flipped into fire engine alarm mode, red lights flashing, sirens sounding.

Barry Manilow and his entourage of the ten most glamorous men and women anyone had ever seen crossed the church, right off the casino stage, and took the tables behind Ken Moynihan and his cadre of porn people.

59. AN UNUSUAL WAVE IN THE GROOMED LA SAND

"Jesus Christ on a crutch," I said to Boogie and Royal T. "Do you know who that is?"

"Greenland, Kazahkstan, The Congo, Cambodia. Ain't no one on Earth don't know who that is," Royal T said.

"If you don't know Barry, you don't know shit," Boogie said.

Tango Joe and Toxic Bob left the bar, walked to Barry's table, and shook hands with the superstar and the beautiful people surrounding him, several of whom were of the large and burly bodyguard variety.

Ken Moynihan and his porn people also turned to introduce themselves.

"He's so fucking handsome," Boogie said. "I never saw anybody that handsome in my whole life. And I'm no homo, so don't get no fucking ideas. I mean shit, just look at the guy. He fucking glows."

It was true. A surreal golden glow surrounded him. The only other American who ever glowed like that was Shirley Temple. We were in the presence of some otherworldly kind of greatness.

"He's taller than I thought he'd be," Royal T said. It was an unusual thing for a sixteen-year-old, seven-foot tall DJ to say, but again, it was true. Barry was six feet tall or taller. And thin, almost too thin. He hadn't come from Vegas. He'd come from Olympus.

"This is fantastic," Key said. "He's your cousin, Mark. Don't you want to say hello?"

Boogie and Royal T looked at me as if I'd suddenly grown wads of street-cred out of my ears.

"I see him all the time," I said.

Key nodded and walked to Barry's table. Cletis, Gloria, and Eddie were already there, and Bernie had joined them. To his credit, Barry was patient and gracious and even happy to sign autographs. No photographs, though. One of the bodyguards made that clear when Penny Polesitter pulled out her cell phone and asked Guy Fuchs to take a picture of her on Barry's lap. Barry let her sit there, however, for longer than seemed necessary, which made me re-compute my entire Barry Manilow equation.

My parents stood by the front of the stage, staring at the glowing songwriter with wonder and awe. They weren't as used to seeing famous people as we all were.

Once you've seen George Hamilton buy apples at Gelson's, looking tan and fit for someone one hundred sixteen years old, the thrill dissipates to some degree. But this wasn't just some run-of-the-mill famous person. It wasn't Heather Locklear or David Spade. It was a glowing global legend. My mother was grasping my father's arm with a superhuman adrenaline rush of strength normally reserved for women whose small children are trapped beneath parked cars. I thought to intercede on their behalf and escort them over to meet the man in the flesh, but as thin as Barry was, I was afraid my mother might break him in half.

Ally Kramer's interest appeared to peak now that Barry was here. I imagined calculators clicking furiously in her head. If Barry Manilow was doing the music, she could raise the budget by twenty million. Think of the soundtrack album! Think of the international appeal! Talk about reaching the cabaret demographic! Why make a movie for one hundred seventy-five million when you can make one for two hundred million? I saw her nodding with approval and whispering into Cathy's ear.

Behind me, Royal T and Boogie had sprung into action. Boogie had created a mellow blue hue around Barry's table, dimming the lights elsewhere in the church while throwing three azure pin spots on Barry himself. It was a remarkable effect and I thought if Boogie is this good on the fly, the staged reading should really be something special. To complement the lighting, Royal T had cross-faded Ry Cooder's "Buena Vista Social Club" with Barry's "Trying to Get the Feeling," and the whole room had a sunset on the beach kind of vibe that was warm and electric at the same time.

And then the door opened again and Dr. Alvin Yee, wearing a purple tuxedo and tails, a purple top hat, and purple Puma Clydes stepped into the church with Caroline on his arm, and everything stopped.

My sister saw him first and froze. Phil followed her starstruck gaze and his jaw dropped open. Then my parents saw him. Then Eddie and Gloria and Cletis. Then the porn people. Then Barry and his entourage. Finally, everyone in the Colonel's studio was staring at Dr. Yee and his granddaughter.

Yee's long white beard was done in three separate French braids, as was his hair, which spilled out of the top hat and reached all the way down his back. Caroline was a vision of loveliness in a beautiful blue evening gown, her skin perfectly porcelain, her hair a glossy shimmering black.

For all the money and time and blood and sweat spent trying to catch lightning in a bottle, the truth is that not much magic is found here in Hollywood. It's a town of smoke and mirrors and gummed up gears. So when genuine magic walks through the door—say, dressed in purple from head to toe—legends and losers and icons and idiots alike stop and stare, not exactly recognizing it as magic per se, but sensing an unusual wave in the groomed LA sand.

Boogie dimmed the blue lights on Barry and wrapped a soft white curtain around Dr. Yee and his granddaughter. Royal T, who no doubt had some magic in his Watusi history, cross-faded to Hendrix's "Are You Experienced?" but kept the volume low. Everyone looked at the wizard as if waiting for a signal that all was well with the world.

Dr. Yee stood there for a long moment, letting the vibe wash over him and then held up the peace sign. An audible sigh of relief, or possibly a gasp of wonderment, echoed through the space, Boogie brought up the blue light, Royal T came back with Barry's "Even Now," and Yee and Caroline walked into the room. I met them at a table just beside the Colonel's raised La-Z-Boy platform.

"You look beautiful," I said to Caroline, who smiled and hugged me hello. "Tell your grandfather I'm glad he came."

Caroline translated, and Yee said something in Chinese.

"He says he never misses a coming-out party," Caroline said.

"Tell him I don't understand what he means," I said.

She did, and he smiled, singing his answer.

Caroline translated. "Lucky you. It's a surprise party."

Before I could press him on this surprise coming-out-party business, Colonel Bill Curry strode onto the stage with all the confidence of a madman who has found a way to bend reality to his will instead of vice versa.

"Ladies and gentlemen. You are humbly invited to take your seats," he said.

60. NOW WE'RE GOING TO SEE SOMETHING

The Colonel was wearing a white silk suit with a blue silk tie and no shoes. His golden General Custer hair was blown back, and he looked like the Great God of Theater.

Bernie joined my parents, Leslie, and associate producer Phil at two front row tables to the left of the Colonel's platform, very near Gloria, Cletis and Eddie's table. Dr. Yee, Caroline, and I took a table on the same side of the platform but just behind them. Across from us, Cathy Burns, Ally Kramer, and Toxic Bob Bloom arrived from the bar with Robbie, who carried their drinks on a tray.

As they were sitting, Ally looked my way and shot me a tight smile. She had not forgotten my *Color War* pitch was what her smile said, though it also said that all would be forgiven if *Phone Book, The Movie* became her mega-million-dollar baby. Toxic Bob had ordered three martinis, and Robbie lined them up on the table. Cathy threw down a shot of tequila before taking her seat and followed it with a Tecate chaser.

Behind me, Joe and Calvin took one of the two remaining tables on our side of the Colonel's platform, the side closer to the door, farther from the bar.

"Prepare for lift-off, *amigo*," Joe said to me.

Calvin nodded and said, "Now we're going to see something."

"I recently had the great good fortune to travel deep into the forbidden jungles of the Amazon," the Colonel said, and everyone was silent. Boogie dimmed the lights and put a spot on him. Royal T played a soft string quartet. "It was there, on the hidden border of Brazil and Peru, that I unexpectedly encountered a lost tribe of uncontacted indigenous people living nomadic lives."

I glanced over at Ken Moynihan, Gary Fuchs, and the rest of the porn stars, and they were rapt. Right behind them, Barry and his beautiful entourage were caught up in the Colonel's dramatic delivery as well.

"Distant descendants of the Chachapoya and Djapas, these wild men of the fringe thusly welcome strangers to their village." He spread his arms wide, looked up at the ceiling and shrieked like a wild spider monkey. "Shareeeeeeeeeeebaaaaaaaaaaay . . ."

I had never heard anything like it. I imagined that no human for two thousand years or more had uttered such a sound. It was one part wounded animal, one part ancient warrior battle-cry, and one part totally insane former clinical psychologist.

"Nantooooooooooookaaaaaaaaaaah . . ."

My parents were stunned to their collective Paramus core. Everyone's eyes were wide with a combination of disbelief, confusion, and enthrallment.

"Shashashashashashashashashateeeeeeeeeeeebo . . ."

I thought of that busy day in the Denver airport when the Colonel, then a pet therapist, did unfathomable things with a German Shepherd, his librarian owner, a telephone salesman, and his parrot. I wondered if the Colonel was shrieking on that particular occasion and what those unsuspecting travelers must have thought.

"KareeeeeeeeeeemKareeeeeeeeeeemAbdulJaJaJabbaaaaaaaaaaar."

At this point, I turned to the wings and waited for men in white cotton pants and matching turtlenecks, carrying long poles with large nets, to leap onto the stage, scoop up the crazy Colonel, and cart him off to Atascadero State Hospital, where public safety is one of the philosophical bedrocks of their long-term psychiatric care. No one arrived and the Colonel continued.

"You are about to experience the world premiere of a staged adaptation of a feature film entitled *Phone Book, The Movie*," the Colonel said.

Words are my business. I know words and very often, though not always, I also know what they mean. He had not said we were about to experience a *staged reading*; he had instead used the words *staged adaptation*. He was planning to put on a kind of play, a theatrical version of my script. He had made changes to my screenplay—*adapted it*—in order to present it on his stage.

I looked around the room to see if anyone else had figured it out. No one seemed worried. Only me. Everyone in the church was still staring with wonder at the Colonel, whose charisma quotient was well off the charts at this point. Only Dr. Yee seemed unaffected. He was looking at me, not the Colonel. He whispered something into Caroline's ear.

She said, "My grandfather says this is the lesson you must learn. Everything depends upon it. Your electron river will run straight and true if you can let it."

Great, I thought. Of all the times for an ancient Asian riddle, this has to be one of the worst.

"We shall begin, as is Hollywood custom," the Colonel said, his booming voice filling all corners of the church, rattling Angela's wine glasses and vibrating the cocktail tables, "with the opening credits."

What? I hadn't written a credit sequence. I could feel my chest tightening, my breath coming faster. If I hadn't written it, Colonel Curry had.

"Without further ado, then," the Colonel barked, "ladies and gentlemen, we give you . . . *Phone Book, The Movie*."

61. WHERE IT HAD NO CHOICE BUT TO GO

Curry sprung off the stage and with two ground-swallowing strides jumped up onto his platform and settled on the edge of his La-Z-Boy. He lifted his copy of the script in his left hand and, without turning around, raised his right hand high into the air and made a fist. He held it there for a moment and then dropped it like a hammer, quickly and with great power and purpose, and Boogie and Royal T killed the lights and sound, and the room was thrust into a black and silent void.

Without warning, the hysterical cheering of an arena rock crowd faded up on the huge speaker banks on both sides of the stage and the church was jolted to life with the gut-wrenching opening chords of AC/DC's live version of "Moneytalks."

There was a microphone positioned beside the Colonel's La-Z-Boy, and his voice cut through AC/DC's raucous riot. "Counting Calvin Productions presents . . ." he said.

Boogie bathed the stage in red light with a golden border, and Dallas appeared wearing a skin-tight white leotard, carrying a plastic pistol, and commenced to slinking around the stage, turning quickly this way and that, like James Bond. The leotard showed every outrageous curve of her body. Her hair was as big and blonde as I had ever seen it.

Moynihan and Guy Fuchs and Long Ron and Thad and the girls cheered and whistled as soon as they saw her. They were as uninhibited in the crowd at the Colonel's church as they were on the set at

Moynihan's Encino mansion. Dallas looked at them and smiled. One minute into the show and she had already violated the fourth wall.

"Dallas Westcott as Samantha Barnes and Tyrone Benford as Garrett DeYoung in . . ." the Colonel said.

Tyrone! Tyrone! I had forgotten Tyrone! He was the handsome young black actor from Louisiana who played Rocky Balboa opposite Dallas in the ice skating scene while wearing a pork pie hat and bouncing a rubber ball.

He entered from the opposite side of the stage, also wielding a plastic pistol but wearing a colorful Hawaiian bathing suit and nothing else. He matched Dallas's secret agent movements until they backed into each other and turned and held each other's gaze in dramatic fashion. Maybe he could imbue Garrett DeYoung with a sense of humility. I certainly couldn't.

My parents smiled as if they were at a grade school play while Robbie the waiter delivered another round of drinks. Phil was pounding red wine as Joe had suggested. I had to admit he would make a perfect associate producer.

"*Phone Book, The Movie*," the Colonel said.

Ally Kramer nodded as if to say: Unusual, yes, but promising interracial demographic, sexually suggestive performances, strong gratuitous violence—two hundred mil easy.

Everyone applauded, and Boogie threw a small rainbow of color across the stage. Royal T seamlessly crossed AC/DC with "Fighting In A Sack" by The Shins and I thought, *Hey, maybe this will somehow, in its own preposterously absurd way, come together.* The Shins always make me feel good.

"Co-starring Lorraine Sutter, Sean O'Brien and Turquoise Bell . . ." the Colonel said.

It occurred to me, as Lorraine, Sean, and Turquoise took the stage —Sean in a suit, Lorraine in an evening gown and Turquoise in red leather pants and matching shirt—that my script had included a minimum of forty or fifty speaking roles. The Colonel had eight or nine actors at most.

Dallas, Tyrone, Lorraine, Sean, and Turquoise danced around the stage in ever-increasing sensual fashion, pausing to rub against each other or nearly kiss before pulling away and brandishing their weapons against unseen enemies.

The volume went up a click. Boogie introduced some simple strobe effects.

"Executive producer, Calvin Key . . ." the Colonel said.

Gloria, Eddie, and even Cletis applauded their billionaire boss's name, Cletis with his hands in the air above his head, his dueling watches plainly visible. Key shared a happy glance with Joe and smiled at me too. This is what it was all about for him. He'd bought himself an inward glow. *Money well spent*, I thought.

Steely Dan's "Don't Take Me Alive" replaced The Shins, the volume clicked up again and a swirling laser display shot across the stage.

My heart was pounding, my head was beginning to throb, and I felt the temperature rise ten degrees. Apparently the actors felt it too, because Sean took off his jacket and threw it into the crowd where my sister caught it like a foul ball. Sean unbuttoned his shirt and rubbed his bare chest up against Turquoise, who unbuttoned her red leather shirt as well. Then they removed their shirts and tossed them aside.

Robbie got another round of drinks for Barry's table while Penny, Kinky, and Tiffany cheered. Long Ron whistled with two fingers in his mouth.

"Produced by Joseph Hudson and Robert Bloom . . ." the Colonel said.

Toxic Bob and Tango Joe locked eyes, or at least Toxic Bob glared into Joe's dark shades. A rock and a hard place is what they were, and I was in the middle.

"Associate producer, Phil Hirschman . . ." the Colonel said, and Leslie, still holding Sean's suit coat, and Arthur and Diane and Bernie all clapped harder and louder.

Century City by Tom Petty and The Heartbreakers blasted out of the speakers, and little bullets of multi-colored light exploded all around the stage, blending with a swirling strobe to create a dizzying, battleground-in-deep-space effect.

Dallas removed Sean's red leather shirt and held it like a matador, foreshadowing the climatic skyscraper rooftop scene, where Sam uses her bullfighting skills to rid the world of Marvin Jenkins. Sean, as the evil Jenkins, played the part of the bull while Tyrone did a crazy martial arts dance with Lorraine and Turquoise, who somehow managed to remove their shirts at the same time that they were pantomiming kung fu.

"Written by Mark Manilow," the Colonel said, and Caroline took my hand. It was a good thing she did because I was preparing to stand up, take the microphone, and stop the show before it went where it had no choice but to go.

The volume clicked up and up. Warren Zevon phased in—"Lawyers, Guns, and Money"—and Boogie added more lights, more movement, more shapes, more colors.

The actors were in various stages of undress, mixing martial arts with pseudo sexual acts and non-stop thrusting motions with high kicks and karate chops, all the while firing endless rounds of invisible ammo from their plastic pistols. Dallas climbed up on Sean the shirt-less bull's back and rode him around the stage.

"Directed by Colonel Bill Curry . . ." the Colonel said, and the sound and lights and fantastical acting gyrations became the one and only reality in the world.

Caroline squeezed my hand in what I thought was a gesture of support—we were, after all, still in the opening credits—but instead she was directing my eyes to the one empty table remaining in the room, the table directly between Tango Joe and us. Sitting down at that table, giving their drink orders to Robbie, were Walter Rydell and Jenny Brann.

Perfect, I thought. Now the show really begins.

62. I WAS ONLY KIDDING ABOUT THE ACID

Colonel Bill read the scene description like I imagined God read the Ten Commandments to Moses. The actors held their scripts in hand and pretended they were checking files in Sam's office or eating burgers at Johnnie Rocket's or driving like daredevils through a natural gas processing plant while dodging gunfire or confronting Jenkins at a press conference in the Los Angeles Museum of Modern Art, where the billionaire was donating a wing devoted exclusively to avant-garde paintings of oil rigs.

It was Theater of the Absurd with unexpected animal impersonations and impromptu striptease wrapped in a cloak of flashing-swirling lights and surreal combinations of new-world indie, classic rock, delta blues, and smoky jazz.

The drinks washed over us in waves. Angela was a superhuman bartender, and Robbie was on roller-skates. People who didn't usually imbibe, my parents, for instance, downed doubles and triples of straight alcohol like bottles of Deer Park, and no one, not even Ally Kramer, stood up to leave. None of us had ever seen anything like the staged adaptation of *Phone Book, The Movie* or even conceived that entertainment of this nature was possible.

The story made no sense, but there was the communal feeling in the former First Church of the Friends of Jesus that something cataclysmic was approaching—a meteor, or a collision of super trains, or an Elvis sighting, or something that no one in the audience dared miss.

Penny, Kinky, and Tiffany, already in the first row, slid their chairs right up to the stage and were grooving in their seats, getting drunk, cheering for Dallas, whooping it up when any of the actors removed their clothes, which was often from the onset and more frequent as the play progressed.

My family was loaded. There was nothing like this back home in Paramus. The Riverside Country Club put on a talent show from time to time, but the performers kept their clothes on and Barry Manilow wasn't seated in the crowd next to a table of people who made porn movies for a living.

During the scene when Sam shows off her matador skills to Garrett and their little bullfight-flirting turns more serious, Tyrone and Dallas began simulating sex in such a way that Guy Fuchs yelled, "Don't fake it, baby. Show this boy how we do it in Encino."

Thad and Long Ron got a charge out of that, and Ken turned to Barry Manilow and handed him his Great Dane business card. Though I couldn't hear him over Royal T's mix, I could read his lips. "I'll make you a fortune in money," is what he said.

Gloria, Cletis, and Eddie were wide-eyed. They had felt, I'm sure, creatively connected to the staged adaptation due to the inclusion of their notes in the script. And though none of those notes was apparent in the performance, they were swept up in the bravado of the thing nonetheless, lost in its lights, sound, and naked skin. The story no longer mattered to them—it was the spectacle of the event that had them hooked.

They weren't alone. Behind me, Walter and Jenny were drinking Moet Chandon. They had emptied their first bottle, which was upside down in their ice bucket, and were plowing through their second. Jenny bobbed her head to the music and laughed when Sam outsmarted Allison Bradford, Marvin Jenkins' personal hit-woman, played by Turquoise, by wounding her with a Bic pen (not unlike the one sitting atop the divorce papers on my kitchen counter).

Early in the second act, Calvin Key flipped furiously through his script, unable to find the scene playing out on the stage, a Mormon-like addition to the story created, written, and orchestrated by Colonel Bill, in which Jenkins and his two wives corner Sam and Garrett. The billionaire was adrift, a lone rower in a canoe who realizes he's had no paddle since the beginning and senses that he's approaching the rocky falls. Confusion filled his face as Lorraine, playing the second wife, and Turquoise, playing the first, expressed sexual attraction for Garrett, much to the chagrin of Sam and Jenkins.

While the actresses read their rewritten lines, simulated a catfight, and took off their clothes, Sean and Tyrone, playing Jenkins and Garrett, transformed into a series of wild animals, barking and growling while pouncing about the stage with such emotional commitment that the Colonel left his La-Z-Boy and joined them, reading the screen description while removing his white silk sport jacket.

Joe caught my eye, shook his head, and mouthed the following words: "I was only kidding about the acid, *mon*."

Ally Kramer, Toxic Bob, and Cathy Burns were so deeply wedged between confusion, shock, incredulity, and astonishment that the only way out was to order more drinks. I lost track of Toxic Bob's martinis, and Ally Kramer switched from chardonnay to Jack Daniels straight up.

Barry Manilow was as wide-eyed and stupefied as the rest of us and, in this uncertain state, looked a little like my father, which made me wonder if we Manilows weren't actually distantly related.

Caroline held my hand in a death grip. Like me, she had no idea what the hell was happening. It wasn't a play, it wasn't a movie, and it wasn't any kind of recognizable burlesque or vaudeville either. It was a new genre altogether, one that induced a palpable sense of concern for the safety of the actors, the audience, and any innocent bystanders.

I noticed that Dr. Yee had left his seat and was standing beside Royal T, requesting certain cuts, adding his energy to the musical mix of the movie. He caught my glance and raised his eyebrows as if to say: *Prepare for the afterlife, Mark Manilow, because here it comes.*

And just when I was sure it couldn't get any weirder, when I knew in my heart that we had reached the outer limits of all weirdness, when I was absolutely certain that the weirdest of the weird had already occurred, the actors arrived at the scene where Sam and Garrett surf onto Jenkins' private Malibu beach and battle a platoon of Diversified Propane mercenaries.

To herald them ashore, Boogie laid down a gatling gun of spotlights across the stage, while Royal T and Dr. Yee played "Who's Got The Crack" by The Moldy Peaches.

"Exterior, Jenkins' Private Malibu Beach, Day," the Colonel said. "Sam and Garrett ride the surf to the sand. In the near distance, Jenkins' palatial beachfront home, with tennis court, putting green, and infinity pool is guarded by dozens of mercenaries."

Dallas and Tyrone entered from stage left. Dallas wore a gold, one-piece swimsuit cut way high on her hips with a neckline plunging below her bellybutton. Tyrone wore a tuxedo. Why he was surfing in a tuxedo was a mystery. They had wet their hair backstage to suggest ocean activity, were both barefoot, and were carrying their scripts.

"Garrett, it you really loved me, you'd fuck me silly right here on the beach," Dallas said, reading dialogue I didn't write.

"I've got to battle some bad guys first, and you've got a date with Jenkins, but I promise, baby, when all that's done, I will fuck you coming and going. I will fuck you frontwards and backwards and sideways. I will fuck you inside out and upside down. I will fuck you until the Age of Aquarius and then, when I have most thoroughly fucked you like you have never been fucked before, I will fuck you like a stampeding stallion with his weapon unsheathed, because love is fucking and fucking is love," Tyrone said.

I had given up on the script an hour ago, which is to say sixty pages ago, which is to say on page one, when the actors first started reading dialogue that wasn't mine. Colonel Bill had rewritten me into submission, changed the intent and meaning of my words throughout the script, distorted and bastardized the story, the dialogue, the characterizations, the rhythm, and the tone, yet left enough of my words in place so as to lend a recognizable quality to the writing, as in: *Hey, Mark, if I didn't know you better, I would think you wrote this thing, it kind of sounds like you.*

My parents were smiling in an oddly frozen way, as if they'd been tasered by the words and were simultaneously informing me that they were traveling the fast track from confusion to embarrassment—both for me and for themselves—and were wondering whether they should be laughing or crying. *Both,* I thought, *laughing and crying.*

Leslie looked at me with shock and surprise. I wasn't her little obnoxious loser of a brother; I was something altogether more disappointing. I was her pathetic and emotionally warped little obnoxious loser of a brother.

Others in the crowd, one of Barry Manilow's burly bodyguards, Angela the bartender, and Bernie Bowers glanced at me as well, wondering, I'm sure, how many more degenerate sentiments like those were secretly harbored in my private heart.

I wanted to say something in my defense, tell them that I hadn't written any of those words, explain that Colonel Curry was notorious for not just pushing the envelope, but for setting it on fire and then eating it while it was burning. I wanted everyone to know I was still the boy my parents raised in Paramus, the boy who grew up to marry a woman who left him in the lurch and then got lost finding his way back. I might have stumbled a few steps, but who hasn't?

I wasn't even in the same paragraph as Walter Rydell or Jenny Brann, both of whom seemed transfixed by the performance, swept away in the passionate absurdity of Sam and Garrett. They were holding hands on the table while guzzling champagne, and there were tears of joy in Jenny's eyes. Never before had she seen such an accurate depiction of love. Joe offered her his handkerchief. As he leaned toward her, I saw the pearl-handled pistol in his waistband. If only I could shoot the staged adaptation and drop it to the pavement.

And then Colonel Bill did something that surprised me, though I had long ago come to the point where I was beyond surprising. He tossed the script away. Physically flung it off the stage. There would be no pretense from this moment forward. We were now in a zero gravity zone. Anything could happen.

63. WEATHER PERMITTING

"Sam and Garrett move to each other like wild beasts in the jungle starved for affection," the Colonel said. Were wild beasts in the jungle ever starved for affection? I had no time to consider it. "Like Zulu warriors returned from battle," the Colonel said, "they begin a dance of love on the white sands of time."

Dallas and Tyrone circled each other in a sensual-animalistic-Hollywood-depiction-of-ancient-African-tribesmen sort of way. The Colonel danced with them—removing his pants in the process. Boogie turned the stage a crazy red and rained droplets of sunshine yellow upon the stage while Royal T blasted an up-tempo Ray Charles medley, seamlessly cutting it with Robert Cray's "Smoking Gun."

"Across the dunes, the mercenaries spot them and run to the water's edge, prepared to draw blood," Colonel Bill said, and Turquoise, Sean, Lorraine, and the rest of the Colonel's acting troupe, five more actors dressed in completely incongruous costumes, ran onto the stage, looking their best like mercenaries prepared to draw blood.

"Ignoring the mercenaries," the Colonel said, "Sam removes Garrett's jacket and throws it into the surf, where Barry Manilow catches it and clings to it for life."

Dallas removed Tyrone's jacket and threw it to Barry, who caught it while simultaneously looking horrified, embarrassed, and honored —the first time I'd ever seen that combination together.

"Now she removes his shirt, as does the lovely mercenary with the chocolate skin (meaning Turquoise)," the Colonel said, "all of them dancing like sex-starved slaves in Marrakesh."

Graham Nash's perky "Marrakesh Express" filled the church, and Royal T lit a cigar-sized joint and passed it to Boogie over Dr. Yee's top-hatted head.

Penny, Kinky, and Tiffany stood up and danced at the edge of the stage. My dickhead associate producer brother-in-law gave himself whiplash trying to watch the porn girls while still catching every second of Turquoise removing her shirt. Tyrone removed his shirt too, and Colonel Bill took both shirts and tossed them to Ally Kramer and Cathy Burns, whose minds, no doubt, went utterly blank.

"Mercenaries . . . more mercenaries . . ." the Colonel cried, and he gestured at Penny Polesitter, Kinky Kat, and Tiffany Sin to join the performance.

The porn actresses climbed upon the stage and danced beside the actors. Kinky and Tiffany took their shirts off without any need for further scene description. Penny, who had developed a crush on Sean, focused her dirty dancing on him. Sean, not much of an actor but a big-time heterosexual and an avid watcher of porn, recognized her from her hit film *Firehouse on Fire*, in which she and the firemen and the firehouse sliding pole did amazing things together. He had no problem incorporating her into the moment.

Royal T played "Big Time" by Peter Gabriel, dovetailed it into something by The Flaming Lips, and somehow segued that into Cream.

My parents' eyes were superglued to the stage. Boogie's swirling, strobing, cavalcade of color, Royal T's bombastic score, and the cast's communal dance of wild animal love were blowing their Bergen County brain cells to bits.

"Throw your scripts away, my friends. You'll not need them where we're going," the Colonel said, and Dallas, Tyrone, Turquoise, and Lorraine threw their scripts off stage. Sean had dropped his the moment Penny entered his world. "Join us, my brothers. Join us in this dance of love, this dance of sex and heat and lust." As Colonel Bill bellowed above the music, he gestured at Thad Whacker, Long Ron Dong, and Guy Fuchs, all of who were on the stage in seconds.

"Free yourselves of these earthly garments; we are not bound by the laws of nature. We are actors, and the universe shall do our bidding. Remove your bonds. The war of the worlds is upon us," the Colonel said, and everyone stripped naked.

Caroline's mouth dropped wide open at the sight of Long Ron's dong, but her jaw positively came unhinged when Thad Whacker removed his shorts. Forget clearing a rack of balls, Mr. Whacker could have played lacrosse without a stick.

As soon as Guy Fuchs had his clothes off, Robbie the waiter was beside him, naked and dancing like a harem girl. *He won't have to audition later*, I thought. *He's got the part.*

Toxic Bob drained his final martini and rushed the stage, ripping his clothes off on the way. He was nude when he arrived beside Dallas and immediately began some kind of Midwestern mating dance that seemed to get her attention.

Not to be outdone, Eddie took off his clothes and joined Toxic Bob and Tyrone in a sexual circle dance with Dallas in the middle. Eddie was covered with colorful tattoos.

Gloria and Cletis danced with each other by the edge of the stage. In my heart, I knew Cletis was wondering if the church had a nearby closet.

And then Phil was on the stage, nude but for his boxers, dancing with two anonymous naked acting students. His eyes were on fire, and he was waving his arms above his head in opposing concentric circles to his thrusting hips, his flabby midsection acting as the axis.

I let my gaze drift from Phil to Leslie, who was whistling and hooting for her husband and shaking her booty with abandon. My parents were doing their best country-club version of a rock-and-roll strut, finding their level in the craziness of the moment. I could hear my father's voice ringing in my ears: *"When in Rome, Mark, when in Rome."*

Bernie Bowers was up and moving too, like a break dancer on an urban street corner, sending reverberating waves from the fingertips of one hand through his entire body to the fingertips of his other hand.

Cathy Burns and Ally Kramer were standing at their table, holding the shirts the Colonel had tossed them as if they were the Shrouds of Turin. Both of them were bouncing and jiving to Royal T's beat, which at this moment was "Fall Down" by Toad the Wet Sprocket. I can tell you firsthand that Ally Kramer had no rhythm. I also wondered if they weren't hot for each other.

Barry Manilow and his table were on their feet, and Ken Moynihan was shaking his football field-sized backside this way and that, thrusting his hips and licking his lips in a frightening display I knew, sadly, I might never forget.

On the stage, they were all nude and dancing as if they were having sex or actually having sex, the Colonel in crazy control of the orgy like a Greek God, drunk with obscenity, insanity, and power.

Boogie brought out the big guns. *Weather permitting*, he had told me, and the skies had apparently cleared.

Galactic and Emerald Star laser units bounced beams of light in endless color combinations off the walls in every direction. Egg Strobes and Pin Strobes and Monster Strobes rated at ten million flashes burst across the stage in unique and changing patterns that moved like swooping swarms of magical birds. A Color Wheel and Mirror Balls bathed the church in a flashing-shooting-surrealistic glow accentuated by fog (*by fog!*) that drifted through the church and across the stage into the crowd by means of a Fantom Fogger wired to a Brute Fogger and cross-linked to a high-output Super Fogger.

All of this was inconceivably synced to The Fifth Dimension's "Aquarius/Let the Sunshine In" medley from the musical *Hair*. Royal T blasted it from the speakers, surrounding us with the rhythm, making us clap our hands and stamp our feet while the actors lost their minds on the stage.

Sean and Penny had gone beyond pantomiming sex. Dallas and Toxic Bob, who had won the dancing peacock contest, were into it as well. Lorraine, a closet lesbian, chose this very night to come out of the closet and was all wrapped up with Kinky Cat.

One of the Colonel's mercenaries, a pretty young actress named Madeline, who during the day tended potted plants in hotels and office buildings and was known for her green thumb, had almost as many tattoos as Eddie Gonzales. Eddie found her after Toxic Bob bumped him out of the Dallas Westcott sweepstakes. It was love at first sight, and they each put extra effort into their ritualistic mating dance.

Everyone on stage was bumping and grinding without restraint while the music pounded and the lights flashed and the crowd went mad.

And then Jenny Brann, giddy from the champagne and beside herself with passion, reached into Tango Joe's waistband and removed his pearl-handled pistol. "I love you, Walter," she screamed above the music and pointed the gun at him.

Walter realized through his drunken haze that this was the moment he had waited for all of his adult life. "I love you," he screamed back at her.

The first shot crackled like a thunderbolt. Walter pitched forward and crashed into first Joe's table and then into Cathy and Ally's table. Everyone turned to see what was happening.

Jenny moved over him, still pointing the pistol, tears of joy rolling down her cheeks, the culmination of her emotionally twisted life finally playing out in real time.

Joe, Calvin, Barry Manilow, my parents, my sister, Ken Moynihan, Ally Kramer, Cathy Burns, Bernie Bowers, me, Caroline, Boogie, Royal T, and Dr. Yee, who was suddenly standing beside me, were frozen as she put another slug in her husband.

"Let the sunshine," sang The Fifth Dimension, "Let the sunshine in."

64. WE GOT A CALL ABOUT A FIRE

It was the fog wafting through the open church windows that prompted forty-two-year-old grass cutter Alberto Ramirez to phone the fire department. He was on his way home from a gas station convenience store with a twelve-pack of Miller Genuine Draft when he decided he couldn't drive one more minute without drinking a beer. He pulled to the side of Van Nuys Boulevard in front of the Colonel's church and cracked a can.

Royal T's eclectic mix—Diana Krall to David Bowie, Mozart to Mott the Hoople, Al Jarreau to Alice Cooper—audible from the street, was better than anything on the radio, so Alberto got out of his 1998 Dodge Dart and leaned against the hood, listening to the tunes and watching the lights flash like a carnival in the church windows.

When Boogie threw the three fog machines into overdrive, Alberto pulled his cell phone, dialed 911, and notified the proper authorities, in Spanish, that the former First Church of the Friends of Jesus was on fire.

A pumper, a hook and ladder, three LAPD squad cars, and an ambulance arrived at the Colonel's acting studio in time to catch—and in effect cause—the conclusion of the orgiastic adaptation of *Phone Book, The Movie.*

I can't say with certainty that the show would have stopped otherwise. Though Walter Rydell bleeding on the floor and his crazy wife Jenny standing above him holding Joe's pearl-handled pistol did divert the general attention of the audience, Sam, Garrett, Marvin Jenkins, and the many naked mercenaries on the stage gave him only a sideways glance. They were so lost in the fog and lights and sex and sound that it would have taken more than a couple of gunshots to distract them.

It would have and, in fact, did take the unexpected entrance of seventeen city servants, some with axes and hoses and yellow rubber jackets and tall boots, others with firearms and badges, and three with white shirts, medical bags, and a stretcher.

Even after Boogie and Royal T cut the lights and sound and fog, the actors continued their orgy beach battle. It wasn't until the policeman-in-charge, a large doughy officer, who was descended from a long line of cruel-humored, spiteful men stretching back to the Civil War, named Alan Allan V called out, "Um, folks, hello, we got a call about a fire," that Colonel Curry called a halt to the proceedings.

Walter wasn't dead. He wasn't even unconscious. The paramedics put him on a stretcher and rolled him through the church and out to the ambulance while Jenny, in police custody, walked beside him.

"I'm sorry, Walter," she said over and over, her hands cuffed behind her back. "I'm so sorry."

"It's all right," Walter said, smiling up at her with tubes in his arms. "Next time."

The firemen inspected the church and found no fire. Boogie showed them his super-rigged, triple-strength foggers and his permits and licenses, and the fire trucks pulled away with the ambulance. Four policemen, including Officer Alan Allan V and his partner, Norman Nutt, were left to sort out the circumstances.

The other two officers were fans of Dallas and one of them, an older cop named Marshall Clam, was familiar with the filmography of Penny, Kinky, and Tiffany as well. Officer Clam spent a fair amount of time questioning Ken Moynihan and shaking hands with

Thad and Long Ron Dong, for whom he had special admiration. Dallas autographed one PR photo for him and one for his partner, Officer Franklin Black, who though he wasn't an aficionado like Clam, knew enough to know Dallas and was happy to have her autograph—and an up-close whiff of her coconut oil lotion.

As the police questioned the crowd, unlikely groups formed among us, morphed into other groups, and then divided into different groups again, like amoeba under a microscope. The actors found their clothes and put them on, though in no particular hurry, and everyone had the opportunity to refocus their perspective on the evening because no one was going anywhere until Officer Alan Allan V had the story straight.

65. WE'RE ALL FULL OF SURPRISES

Caroline and I drifted to my parents' table where Phil was pulling on his pants.

"Nice, Phil," I said. "Didn't know you had it in you."

"There's a lot you don't know, Marky. I'm full of surprises," Phil said, slurring his words.

"We're all full of surprises," my mother said, wrapping her arm around my father.

My dad's face was flush with overstimulation. Too much alcohol, lights, loud-lewd music, and strobing, multi-colored, inerasable visions of naked dancers swearing, screwing, barking, and braying at the moon had left Arthur Manilow without any desire to straighten things out. "Yep," he said, for the first time in his life.

"This is Caroline Yee," I said. "Caroline, this is my mother and father, my sister Leslie, my brother-in-law Phil, and Bernie Bowers, my almost ex-father-in-law."

"You have smooth moves," Caroline said to Bernie. "I mean that as a compliment. You were really going for it."

"I was something in my prime," Bernie said.

"This is my prime," Phil said, putting his shirt on inside out.

"Yes it is, honey," Leslie said, giving him a kiss on the cheek.

"Did you really write that, Mark?" my mother said.

"If you take out the sex, swearing, dialogue, naked dancing, and animal improvisations, then yes, I did."

"It was a heart-pumper, son, I'll tell you that," my father said.

"Oh yes. Very original," my mother said.

"Figures you didn't write the good parts," Leslie said.

"Where's the bathroom?" Phil said. "I'm going to be sick."

As Leslie led Phil to the men's room, the room shape-shifted. I ended up with Joe, Calvin, and Toxic Bob, who had pulled his pants on, but was still barefoot and shirtless.

"Great show," Toxic Bob said. "We've got a monster on our hands. Ally and I have a meeting with Sony this week. They're looking for a big budget action romance blockbuster with sex and surfing. They're open to mercenaries as long as there's golf in the movie. We'll change the battle scene from the beach to a golf course. No big deal. We'll fix it on the set. The good news is Gwyneth Paltrow is waiting for my call. I don't even have to say hello. When she answers, all I have to say is *Samantha Barnes* and she's in. I talked to Dallas. She's fine with it. Anything to go legit. We'll write her a new character. Sam's best friend. Sandy Summers. There's nothing they don't do together. We'll get Gwyneth a stand-in for their love scenes. I think they go ménage á trois with Garrett more than once. I have Brando lined up to play Marvin Jenkins."

It was vintage Toxic Bob strategy: put so many preposterous balls in the air at one time that brain freeze is the only outcome.

"Brando's dead, Bob. He died," I said.

"We'll use his digital image. Cut him into the movie. It's all done in post. His estate's on board. They think he'll get a nomination," Toxic Bob said.

"For an Oscar?" Joe said.

"Best Supporting Actor. Big time nod," Toxic Bob said.

"You can't surf on a golf course," I said.

"You can if the boards have wheels and jet propulsion," Toxic Bob said. "Garrett, Sam, and Sandy will figure it out."

"Between ménage á trois-es?" I said.

Toxic Bob made a pistol with his thumb and index finger and fired off a shot. "Bull's-eye," he said.

"It's an indie film. Calvin's financing it. The budget's three million," Joe said.

"We've already spent more than that," Toxic Bob said. " We're tying up locations all over Europe and South America. Did I mention Keanu Reeves is good for Garrett? Neo to the rescue, right?"

Maybe when he's done cutting Alvin Yee's grass, I thought. "Gwyneth Paltrow told you she'd play Samantha Barnes?" I said. I knew he was lying. Everyone knew he was lying. He was an Olympic liar. The Michael Phelps of lying.

"We're tight. She named her son after me," Toxic Bob said.

"Her son's name is Moses," I said.

Toxic Bob put his shirt on and began to button it. "Exactly. Next time you see her, say, 'Gwyneth, who led you out of the desert?' She'll say, 'Bob Bloom.'"

"I'd like to back up to the beginning," Key said. "What do you mean *we*?"

"There's always someone trying to jam up the machine. He's not going to be that guy, is he, Joe?" Toxic Bob said, gesturing at the billionaire.

"I told you, Bob. It's an independent film. Mark's writing it, I'm producing it, and Calvin's financing it," Joe said.

"The train's left the station, it's picking up steam, and I'm already on board. You've been around the block. You know what that means. You can explain it to him."

Joe reached into his waistband for his pearl-handled pistol, but it had gone out the door as evidence with Walter and Jenny and the officers who took him to the hospital and her to the police station.

"No one has to explain it to me. I can add," Calvin Key said.

"Of course you can," Toxic Bob said. "Glad to hear it. Listen, I think we give Colonel Bill a shot at directing this thing, don't you?"

"Is one of you Calvin Key?" Officer Alan Allan V said as he stepped into our group.

Around the room, the amoebas were on the move again, splitting and reconstituting in mind-bending concoctions.

Ken Moynihan, Guy Fuchs, Robbie the waiter, my parents, and Bernie Bowers, who'd been having a cordial conversation, shook hands and said good-bye. The great silver sphere of porn gave my mother a hug, and they both caught my eye and waved at me, arm in arm. It was as discordant a moment in my life as I can remember.

Moynihan lit a fat cigar, signifying a victory of I had no idea what, and rolled out the door like a mammoth ball bearing, Guy Fuchs and Guy's new squeeze in his wide wake.

Just as Officer Marshall Clam had cleared Ken Moynihan of any untoward involvement in the shooting, so had Officer Alan Allan V cleared Barry Manilow. As Barry and his entourage moved to the door, the superstar caught my father's eye and some kind of ancient Manilow magic apparently passed between them because Barry stopped and struck up a conversation with my parents that seemed familiar and jovial at the same time. My mother reached into her purse for family photos.

Toxic Bob slipped away from Tango Joe and Calvin Key to avoid any conversation with the police. A lifetime of passing off lies as truth had left an ugly trail of disgruntled associates behind him, and Toxic Bob thought it likely he might hear—and had no intention of hearing—an officer of the law say, *"Oh, you're Bob Bloom,"* so he joined Dallas, Kinky, Tiffany, and Penny in, I'm sure, a heartfelt discussion of recent global geo-political events and how they would impact world financial markets in the next fiscally-influenced election cycle.

Caroline drifted into a group that included Royal T, Cathy Burns, Ally Kramer, Boogie, and Officer Marshall Clam.

Leslie and Phil emerged from the men's room with Phil looking pale but still game. Phil gave everyone in the church a double thumbs-up upon his re-entry, but only Eddie Gonzales, an apparent sucker for a double thumbs-up, seemed to care. Eddie and Madeline joined Leslie and Phil near the stage and double thumbed up each other some more while Leslie showed Madeline her one and only tattoo: a tiny rattlesnake, poised to strike, hidden just inside her right shoulder blade.

Cletis, Thad, and Long Ron met at the bar, where Angela, who had returned to her post, served them bottles of beer and bowls of pretzels. Cletis showed the boys his watches, and Thad and Long Ron seemed impressed. *There aren't many men,* I thought, *who could match sex stories with Whacker and Dong, but Cletis could any day.*

I ended up with Bernie, Dr. Yee, and Colonel Bill, one former and two current medical health practitioners.

"Dr. Bernie Bowers, this is Dr. Alvin Yee," I said. "Dr. Yee's a new age mental health care professional."

The Colonel made some Asian-sounding noises as if he were translating my words for Yee, who smiled pleasantly and said something to Bernie in return.

"I am most pleased to make your acquaintance and am curious to know what kind of medicine you practice?" Curry said, translating for Dr. Yee, though he spoke not a single word of Chinese and had never met Yee, not even once, before this very night. To speak for the wizard, he used a theatrical accent not unlike David Carradine's on

Kung Fu. Dr. Yee, of course, could have said, *"Wherever you go, don't eat the yellow snow."*

"I'm a psychiatrist," Bernie said.

"He thinks I'm a sexual deviant and wants to take me to Chicago and crack my head open. But he's my almost ex-father-in-law, so maybe he just wants to crack my head open for the hell of it," I said, smiling at Bernie and the Colonel. "Plus he thinks my penis is the size of Mount Rushmore."

"Figuratively speaking, there's an interesting correlation between penis size and sexually deviant behavior," Bernie said. "Head cracking is what's called for."

The Colonel translated again, and once more Yee responded. The Colonel took it all in, turned to Bernie and delivered Yee's response with delirious Asian flair.

"In China, head cracking, as you call it, has been clinically proven to be an ineffective deterrent to sexual deviance, which remains hard to define and ethereal in nature. Instead, psychiatrists in my country lead by example. In this case, Mark would be best served if you would have sexual intercourse with your own life-sized photograph." The Colonel nodded and bowed deeply, as if honored to translate such profound Chinese wisdom. Why he wasn't yet institutionalized remains one of the great American mysteries of modern time.

"I think you might want to double-check your translation. It sounds like the doctor just told me to go fuck myself," Bernie said.

The Colonel nodded sincerely, spoke additional gibberish to Dr. Yee, received an answer he undoubtedly did not understand, and turned again to Bernie, leaning in this time, eyes wide, nostrils flaring, General Custer hair a wild, matted mess. "Figuratively speaking," he said, and he winked at me at the same time.

66. THE AUDIENCE ALREADY PAID

Officers Alan Allan V, Stormin' Norman Nutt, and Franklin Black had joined Marshall Clam and were focused on Caroline, who apparently filled in all the blanks on the Walter and Jenny incident because Alan Allan V raised his hand above his head and said, "Okay, folks. We're done here. You're free to go." However, before leaving, the four officers reconnected and recapped with the Colonel.

After a closing conversation with Joe and Calvin Key, Barry and his beautiful entourage exited with far less fanfare than their arrival. The legendary superstar simply slipped out the door into his limo and was off to brighten other worlds.

Joe joined Ally Kramer and Cathy Burns, who were on their way to the door, and Key entered a conversation with Toxic Bob. Just beyond them, Royal T and Boogie began breaking down their considerable gear.

I was alone and learning to breathe again when my cell phone rang. I answered it without looking at the caller ID.

"Mark Manilow."

"Mark, it's Cathy." I looked across the room and saw Cathy Burns twenty-five feet away. She was looking right at me. Beside her, Joe and Ally were exchanging numbers and prognosticating the cinematic future of *Phone Book, The Movie.*

"I can see you, Cathy. Can you see me?"

"Sure," she said, and she waved to show me.

I waved back and said, "Is there a reason you're calling me instead of walking over here?"

"Yes. The phone is so much less personal."

"Of course. Did you enjoy the show?"

Cathy nodded enthusiastically. I know that for a fact because I could see her nodding enthusiastically. "Absolutely. Nudity, sex, violence, talking dogs, and a story you can't follow, so why bother trying. What's not to like? Ally liked it, too. She thinks it'll do huge numbers in Europe, and Asia will be off the charts."

"She didn't see the second half."

"She never does. She says the second half doesn't matter. The audience already paid."

"It matters to me."

"You're hysterical, Mark. You should be writing comedy. Write me a comedy with nudity, sex, violence, and talking dogs, and I'll sell it for a million dollars."

"Sure. I can pitch it to Ally."

"On a cold day in hell, maybe. You're on her no-pitch list."

"Ally Kramer has a no-pitch list?" I said, not all that surprised that A, she had one and B, I was on it.

"How do you think she got to the top? You were the inaugural name."

"It was thirteen years ago," I said, remembering that day when I pitched her my summer camp coming-of-age movie. "Can't I get off the list now?"

"You can never get off the list. It's this kind of decisiveness that made her who she is today. You were an enormous influence. She respects you for that, and she'll always be grateful."

"But she won't let me pitch?"

"Maybe when pigs fly, though I doubt it."

"I can live with that. So are you my agent again?"

"What do you think?"

"I don't know."

"Let's leave it like that," she said, and she clicked off the call, waved good-bye, and left the church with Ally Kramer.

Joe and Key reconvened with Cletis, Gloria, Eddie, and Madeline. Dr. Yee introduced Caroline to Boogie and Royal T, and Colonel Bill tried on Toxic Bob's Blue Fox fur coat while Dallas handed him the hat and mittens.

The porn people remained at the bar with Angela, and the Colonel's other acting students exited in small groups, as excited as squirrels in autumn, convinced, I'm sure, that their careers had been given a collective boost, the murder attempt notwithstanding. I met my parents, my sister, Bernie, and Phil in the middle of the room.

"You look a little pasty, Phil," I said.

"Careful, Marky. I'll have you rewritten. I'm your boss now. Associate producer," he said, only half-kidding.

He'd been puking for a solid fifteen minutes, and even though he was a dickhead, he was still my brother-in-law, and the father of my beautiful niece and baseball-playing nephew, so I didn't have the heart to tell him that an associate producer wasn't even the boss of the craft service PA. "You got me there, Phil. I'll be careful," I said.

"I need some air," he said to Leslie, his eyes swimming in their sockets.

She took his arm, looked at me, and smiled. I smiled back. She held my eyes with hers long enough for them to say, *I love you, you sick pervert, but don't tell anyone because I'll never admit it.* Then she hugged me, removed her knife from my back, and took Phil outside.

"Mark," my mother said, "we're changing our flight, leaving tomorrow morning."

"What about the intervention?" I said.

"We talked to Mr. Moynihan," my father said. "He told us in no uncertain terms that you're not a porn guy. He said he brainwashed you into writing *Broken Boner*. He said it was his fault, not yours. As for Dallas, he said you never had a chance."

"We're sorry for doubting you, Mark. Aren't we?" my mother said, drilling Bernie with her eyes.

"Psychiatry is an inexact science," Bernie said, "and penis size is a relative measurement. If you find yourself drifting into deviance, call me immediately. I'm experimenting with new therapies all the time."

I'll bet you are, I thought, and wondered if he wouldn't soon be fucking a life-size photograph of himself in Chicago. "Okay, Bernie," I said. "It was good seeing you."

"You, too, Mark," he said, and then he left the building. In all the hubbub, I had entirely forgotten to ask him if he knew where Julie was. Even if he had known, I doubted he would have told me.

"We're some kind of cousins, I think," my father said to me.

"Who, Dad?"

"Me and Barry. We're leaving that door open. Aren't we, Diane?"

"Wide open, Arthur."

"This was a crazy business, this whole thing," my father said.

"The craziest," I said.

"Well, now it's behind us. Smooth sailing ahead, right?" he said.

"Right, Dad. Smooth sailing."

"I don't tell you this often enough, but I'm proud of you, son. I admit I don't know what the hell for, but it's not important. I'm proud of you anyway," he said.

"How you live your life isn't up to us anymore," my mother said. "We just wish you the best so much . . . we forget that sometimes. We love you, Mark. Even if we don't understand you, we love you just the same."

"I love you, too. I can't promise I'll do better, but I can't do much worse," I said, trying to make a joke, but somehow speaking the truth instead.

"It all gets good from here on in, you'll see," my father said. We embraced, and they started for the door.

My mother turned back to me and said, "Lisa Mazer is in town. She's a pediatrician. Divorced. No children. She lost some weight and had her nose done. She's very pretty now. I play mahjong with her mother. Should I say something?"

"Probably not yet," I said.

"You'll tell me when?" she said, hopefully.

I nodded and said, "I definitely will."

I loved them so much that my heart actually hurt as they disappeared from view. I promised myself that I would visit them every year for the rest of time.

67. WE'LL NEED REAL COCONUTS

"Mark," Key said, waving me over. "Question for you."

I joined their group, expecting a query into the nefarious inten-tions of Toxic Bob, who was within spitting distance but locked in a conversation with Colonel Bill, who looked splendid in Bloom's Blue Fox fur ensemble.

"We like the polygamy angle," Key said. "We think it's edgy and hip, and we want you to think about adding a subplot where Garrett is already married to Sam when the movie opens and he adds three or four wives as the story progresses."

After all that had happened, they were giving me script notes. I wasn't the least bit surprised. "Do they fly back to Utah for the wed-dings?" I said.

"Damn right they do," Eddie said. "He got all these wives and shit, he got to save the world in a big way. He at least got to save Salt Lake City."

"So Garrett's a polygamist," I said, "in addition to being a surfing-martial arts champion-secret agent?"

"HBO do polygamy," Cletis said. "Ain't nothing wrong with HBO."

"Can't argue that," I said.

"You can't argue shit," Cletis said, holding up his watches as if threatening me with future accusations of tardiness.

"So what's the question?" I said to Calvin Key.

"When can we see the next draft?" Key said. "Cathy Burns and Ally Kramer had notes, too. We'll add them to the Colonel's notes and Barry's notes and Royal T and Boogie's notes and Joe's notes and our notes and email them to you tomorrow morning."

"Did Bob have notes?" I said.

"He won't be involved," Key said. "So when can we see the next draft?"

"As soon as possible," I said because I didn't know what else to say.

"Excellent," Key said. "You can deliver it in person. Gloria will make pan fried salmon filets with a ginger garlic soy sauce that will make you cry."

"She can cook them sesame peanut noodles to go with it," Cletis said.

Key nodded, and he and Cletis and Gloria and Eddie and Madeline started for the door, still discussing the menu for that day in the near future when I delivered the next draft of *Phone Book, The Movie*.

"Maybe some sweet and sour eggrolls," Eddie said.

"Definitely," Key said. "Smart choice."

"Can we have coconut ice cream for dessert?" Madeline said. "It goes real good with Chinese food."

"Oh child," Gloria said, "you read my mind."

"Good call, Madeline. We'll need real coconuts," Key said. "I own a grove in Maui. I'll fly them in fresh . . ." and then they were out the door.

The billionaire had unexpectedly added a new member to his menagerie. Why not? There was plenty of room at the mansion for a tattooed young actress with a green thumb. Within weeks there would be potted plants in every room. Greenhouses on the grounds would follow shortly and then, possibly, he would buy her a nursery.

He was without doubt writing *Madeline* in black magic marker across the top of a *Phone Book, The Movie* script even as Eddie pointed the Hummer north toward Montecito. I knew that very soon, meaning tomorrow, I would be getting script notes from Madeline too.

I turned to Joe and said, "Sorry about your gun."

"I had a moment," Joe said, glancing at Toxic Bob, who was still chatting with Dallas and Colonel Bill, nearly naked beneath the Blue Fox fur coat, hat, and mittens.

"I saw it. Would you really have shot him?"

"In the knees," he said.

"Would have been nice. I don't know what to say about all this, Joe."

"Words will fail us, as they always do. I'm surprised you don't know that, being a mad fucking genius."

"If you still think I'm a mad fucking genius, then you're a mad fucking genius."

"Madness becomes us."

"Do you really think there should be polygamy in the movie?" I said.

"Do you really think anyone will notice?" Joe said, and we both laughed. It was a nice release, and I thought of how far we'd traveled since that first fateful meeting at Foster's. Joe knew as well as I did how ridiculous *Phone Book, The Movie* had become, how outrageous, absurd, and inane, how unwieldy, unlikely, and unseemly, and yet he approached it with a dancer's ease and grace, moving with the music, never fighting it, letting it carry him wherever until the dance was done. I loved him for it and would follow him into any project, any time, anywhere.

His eyes sparkled, and we embraced. "Next time I see you, there will be hash in the brownies, *mon.* Lebanese Gold. We'll baptize bears and lizards in the river," he said as he started for the door. "You shave your legs, I'll shave mine . . ."

68. I'M A SHOOTING STAR

I went to the bar, waved at the porn players, and ordered rum and Dr. Pepper from Angela.

Royal T and Boogie gave their business cards to Dr. Yee and resumed breaking down their equipment. At the same time, Colonel Bill returned Toxic Bob's Blue Fox fur coat, hat, and mittens and joined Kinky, Penny, Tiffany, Thad, and Long Ron at the other end of Angela's bar. The Colonel wore nothing but the briefest of briefs and seemed as happy as a man can be.

To my dismay, Toxic Bob struck up a conversation with Caroline and Dr. Yee. I could only imagine the lies spewing and spouting from his pompous person. Yee would see through Toxic Bob in a heartbeat. Caroline, too, would sense danger and keep her secrets at arm's length. I had a mind to protect her and her grandfather from Hollywood's largest lying asshole and even put my drink on the bar in preparation for my march across the room, but when I turned around again, Dallas was standing beside me.

"Hi, baby," she said. "Buy a girl a drink?"

"Sure. What are you having?"

"Peppermint schnapps."

I ordered a shot of schnapps, Angela poured it, and Dallas and I clinked glasses.

"What should we drink to?" she said.

"The city of Detroit," I said.

"To Detroit," she said, and we both drank.

"Did you like the show?"

"One of a kind."

"Did I do good?"

Her brown eye was soft and hopeful, eager to please but tenuous and even timid, wanting to know the truth, though fearful of it at the same time. It was the brown eye of a Motor City grammar school cheerleader anxious for the coach, a pretty English teacher and former cheerleader herself, to say, *"Good going, Dallas. That's what I call team spirit."*

Her sky-blue eye, however, was having none of that nonsense. It was distant, waiting impatiently for some other conversation that was next in line. This was the eye that could orgasm on cue, that thought nothing of sharing its world class vibrator skills with the horny old dude living across the canyon, that couldn't hear or wasn't interested in a single thing I ever said that didn't directly relate to the advancement of her legitimate acting career or fucking for luck.

"How do you feel about it?" I said.

She glanced down the bar, where her friends and colleagues were communing with her teacher and mentor. "I don't love you anymore, Mark," she said.

"You don't?"

She shook her head, the beginning of a tear forming in her brown eye only, and said, "I mean, a part of me will always love a part of you, but not the way the other part of me should love the other part of you."

"Are we breaking up?"

"We can't stay together anymore. It would be bad luck."

Though these were the words I had hoped to hear for what seemed like eternity, I was not filled with elation. Before an ending can become a new beginning, it has to exist entirely as an ending for whatever fraction of a moment or longer it demands. Even happy endings are endings, and all endings are subconsciously related and metaphysically tied to the ultimate ending and so viewed as bittersweet at best, with despair and hopelessness at worst.

"I agree," I said. I might have been bittersweet, but I wasn't crazy.

"I'm going home with Bob," she said. "We made a connection tonight. He thinks I'm a shooting star, and all I need is someone to point me in the right direction."

I took a sip of my rum and Dr. Pepper. In the time it took to travel down my throat, I considered the circumstances in the hope of finding the appropriate response.

"He's the one to do it," I said.

"You really think so?"

"Definitely. You and Bob belong together. In fact, of all the people in the world who deserve each other, Dallas Westcott and Bob Bloom deserve each other the most. I mean that, Dallas. I've never wanted anything more than to see you and Bob get together. It's not that I care about you any less, I don't see how I could ever care any less about you, it's that I wish you both many, many years of each other."

She kissed me on the cheek. "You're so sweet, Mark. I know there's a girl for you out there somewhere, it's just not me. I thought it was for a while, but now I think you're right, Bob and I are meant to be."

She told me that Penny or Kinky or Tiffany would stop by to pick up her things. She couldn't bring herself to say goodbye to my fish. She'd become quite fond of them and often told me she thought they had become fond of her as well. She held my hand for a moment and moved close to me, giving me one last breath of her coconut oil body lotion. Involuntarily, my knees buckled.

"I'll miss you, Mark."

"Bob will point you in directions no one's ever heard of."

"I'm a shooting star," she said, and she gave my hand an excited squeeze and walked across the room to where Toxic Bob was waiting for her. Toxic Bob caught my eye and gave me a little salute, as if to say: *The best man won, babe. No hard feelings.*

I saluted him back as if to say: *She's all yours, you Toxic Turd.*

69. YOU CAN PUT YOUR OARS IN THE WATER

Like a ship freed of its anchor, I began to drift in the swift currents of my life. Here was my sister Leslie smoking pot in a giant water bong on the back porch with her high school friends while our parents were in Bermuda and letting me take a monster hit. Here was Gibby with two on and two out in the last inning of the last game of our senior year hitting a fastball into next week to win us the league title. Here was Arnold Schwarzenegger on the set in Canada telling me *Full Force* was the best action picture he'd read in years. Here was Julie throwing her arms around my neck at the farmers' market saying, "I will, I will" after I asked her to marry me at the very same table where we'd first met over a magazine three months earlier. Here was Mrs. Morgan on the first day of first grade, sitting me in the front row, telling the class that she had taught my sister and knew my family and was sure I would set a fine example of good behavior for my classmates. It was a sort of celebration cruise, a sudden rush of good memories to remind me that my life wasn't always like it was now.

Here was the ship of my life unmoored and racing through the rapids when all of a sudden a miniature Chinese man wearing a purple top hat and purple Pumas was standing in front of me, saying something I had no chance of understanding. Caroline was beside him, more beautiful than I remembered (and I had seen her one minute ago).

"He says it's too soon to unfurl the sails, but you can put your oars in the water if you like," Caroline said.

There's no comprehending the psychic upper limits of a man who can map the course of your electron river.

"When can I put up the sails?" I said.

Caroline translated, and Dr. Yee put his left hand on my forehead and his right hand on my heart and said something that sounded profound, even in a language I couldn't navigate.

"When you are the captain of the ship, and the ship is not the captain of you," Caroline said.

He smiled and slid down the bar, joining Long Ron and the porn crew. The Colonel introduced Yee as a prophet and acted as translator as Thad, Long Ron, Kinky, Tiffany, and Penny asked questions about the future. Since the Colonel spoke no Chinese, all the prophecies were his and his alone. I can tell you that the Colonel's vision of the future was worth the price of admission. "Within twenty-five years, an African gray parrot will be elected Governor of California," was one of his forecasts.

"What did Dallas say?" Caroline said.

"We broke up. She's moving in with Toxic Bob. She thinks he's the better bet to launch her legitimate feature film career."

Caroline smiled. "I want to kiss you," she said.

"I still have to work out the juggler before I can pursue the monkey wrench."

"But the porn star's really gone?"

"With the wind."

"He's about as creepy as a person can get."

"The creepiest. What did your grandfather think?"

"In South America," she said, "there is a small, brightly colored, venomous frog called the golden poison dart frog. Its brain is the size of a tiny peanut, but there's so much lethal venom in its body that it can't keep it inside; it secretes the poison out of its skin every day and every night. Lightly touching the back of the frog with the tip of the tongue can be fatal. But the frog is so bright and golden that its predators can't resist it. My grandfather called him the Chinese name for the golden poison dart frog."

"Did you translate that?"

"I told him my grandfather said he had nice teeth."

We were quiet for a moment, watching Boogie and Royal T roll their gear out of the building and listening to the Colonel translate Dr. Yee's prophecies, and Caroline took my hand. It wasn't the first time we had held hands, but there was something significant about her touch this time that I couldn't decipher.

"My grandmother's coming in from China tomorrow. I'm going back to San Francisco."

My heart sank. Caroline knew that's what would happen, so she had taken my hand for the purpose of squeezing it when she told me she was leaving.

"That sucks," I said, proving again that I had a splendid way with words.

"Think of the parts that don't suck. The porn star's gone, and your electron river is flowing again."

"Because of you. When you leave, who knows what will happen?"

She nodded and said, "All we can do is wait and see, Mark. I think that's what messed up your electrons in the first place. The whole wait and see thing. I'm not so good at it either. I don't know anybody who is."

There was a lot of truth and wisdom in this soft and beautiful Chinese woman. How could there not be? She was a direct descendent of the Wizard Chipmunk, who, through the interpretive powers of the crazy Colonel, was predicting for the porn people that as clean water supplies dwindled, humans would crap in the yard with their dogs, creating a stronger-than-imagined bond between the species and a peace of mind heretofore unachieved. All social, psychological, and psychiatric therapy from that moment on would be based upon humans and animals crapping side by side. There would be an end to all world conflict and a sharp decrease in the sale of fertilizer. I imagined that this would be bad news for Toxic Bob's father in Chicago, who had made a fortune selling shit to people who didn't realize they had their own all along.

"What is it we're waiting for?" I said.

"I'm waiting for you, Mark. I don't know what you're waiting for," she said.

70. YOU'RE JUST NORMAL FISH NOW

It was a beautiful night. The air cools dramatically when the sun sets on LA, and all living things, weary and burnt from the unwavering heat, exhale with relief, drink something cold, and contemplate the moon and other things. The item upon which my mind alighted as I left the Colonel's and rolled toward Studio City was a simple four-word sentence uttered by Calvin Key.

"He won't be involved," Key had said when I asked if Toxic Bob was going to give me notes for the third draft.

If there was one inviolate truth of Toxic Bob, it was that he would be involved. He would find a way in and never leave, like a rat in the attic.

Key was not accustomed to being told who was in and who was out. His billions had bought him final say on these kinds of matters, despite the geeky tenor of his voice. He believed that *Phone Book, The Movie* was his project. And why shouldn't he believe it? In any other universe, the man funding the movie makes the decisions. But in the Toxic Bob universe, where distortion is the gravity that holds projects together until total destruction of them can begin, the man funding the movie is just another tongue on the back of the most venomous golden poison dart frog in town.

Their conversation in the Colonel's studio after the police arrived had not gone well, yet both men had come away thinking victory belonged to them. Key had left with high hopes for the next draft, good vibes from Barry Manilow, the tentative attachment of a former studio chief, and a tattooed woman with a green thumb. Toxic Bob had left with Dallas.

I pulled into my driveway thinking, on the one hand, that nothing good could happen as long as Toxic Bob was lurking in the shadows and, on the other hand, that something good had already happened due directly to his propinquity: the sky-blue Jaguar belonging to the leech-like princess porn star was gone, never again to park in front of my Coldwater Canyon house.

As much I despised Toxic Bob, and I loathed him with ferocity normally reserved for invading armies, I owed him a tip of my hat for rescuing me from the hypnotic spell of Dallas's insidious, aphrodisia-cal, coconut oil body lotion.

I put the key in the door, went into the house, and walked straight to my fish. They had seen the last of Dallas Westcott and me having sex in front of their tank. Hopefully, I could undo whatever under-water emotional damage had been done.

"You're just normal fish now," I said to them.

From behind me, I heard, "Were they abnormal fish at one time?" I knew the voice but thought I was inventing it inside my head, so I let it go.

"I had abnormal fish when I was a girl," the voice said. "All they did was float upside down at the top of the tank. Daddy said they were deviant little fish and flushed them down the toilet. No burial, no last rites, just whoosh and they were gone. I got tiny green turtles after that, but they died too. That's why I didn't become a zoo-keeper."

I turned around, and Julie was sitting on my sofa.

"Jesus Christ on a crutch," I said.

"I don't know that one. Is it good or bad?"

"It's just sort of a general holy shit kind of saying. My grandfather used to say it all the time. I just started using it."

"Which grandfather?"

"Shelley. My dad's dad."

"I know who Papa Shelley is. So you're surprised?"

"You might say that."

She stood and moved toward me. "I thought you would be."

We embraced like old friends who haven't seen one another in a while, which is precisely what we were, but did not kiss, not even on the cheek.

"I like what you've done with the house, Mark." She held up the key she got at the closing. "Do you have anything to eat?"

"I'm sure I have something," I said, still processing her presence, and we walked from the living room into the kitchen. "How's your juggling?" I said.

"I stopped juggling a year ago."

I opened the fridge, saw a plate of chicken fried steak, carried it to the garbage, threw the whole damn thing away, plate included, and said, "How come?"

"I was lousy. And it turned out that wasn't who I am."

There was a bowl of cavatelli puttanesca, a scoop-shaped pasta in a sauce of tomatoes, capers, olives, and onions, and a Tupperware container of cold asparagus. I put the pasta in a pot over a low flame and said, "Who are you?"

"I'm a writer for *National Geographic*. I go everywhere in the world and get paid for it."

There was an open bottle of red table wine ($8 from Trader Joe's) on the counter, and I poured what was left into two juice glasses. She was sitting at the table, and I handed her one of the glasses. "With Greg?" I said.

"Sometimes." We clinked glasses and drank wine.

I moved back to the stove, stirred the pasta, opened the cabinet above the dishwasher where I kept my dishes, and took down two small bowls and two salad plates. I portioned out the asparagus on the salad plates.

"Why now, Julie?" I said. "I mean, I'm happy to see you; I've spent most of the last three years either trying to find you or trying to figure out why you left, but why are you here tonight and not two years ago or next Thursday? Why now?"

I can't deny that there was an awkwardness between us—certainly there had to be, and I always imagined there would be some hemming and hawing—but there was also a directed sense of ease, as if our subconscious minds had agreed in advance that something would be settled regardless of any clumsiness or discomfort.

"My father told me your family was having an intervention. He said it was related to pornography and the size of your penis. I thought I should probably be here, since I might have had something to do with messing you up."

"Up, down, and all around. When you left me . . . I just . . . I had no idea a person could feel that lost."

"I didn't want to hurt you, but it was either leave or die."

There was no underlying drama to her words. They were simple and clear and immediately recognizable as Truth with a capital T.

I nodded and said, "I know that feeling. I'm sorry I had to be a part of it."

"You know, Mark, you can be angry at me if you want to. I'll understand."

Her hair was slightly longer than I remembered, but it was still soft and gently pulled to the side where it was clipped with a jade clasp. She wore minimal makeup because she didn't need any. That hadn't changed either. She had on blue jeans and a white cotton dress shirt, which she wore untucked and with the sleeves rolled up, giving her the casual yet neat and tailored effect I had fallen for at the farmers' market on Fairfax. Her fingernails were manicured, but not painted. She was not wearing her wedding ring, but neither was I.

In my two-year tailspin—between the end of *Full Force* and my fated flight home to Paramus—in which I pretended to live life normally, I had scaled mountains of anger, crossed oceans of despair, and traversed vast wastelands of depression only to arrive at a state of emotional abeyance, where the ownership of my feelings was decidedly undecided. But for nearly six months now, that main stage of confusion had been curtained while the vaudevillian procession of *Broken Boner*, Dallas Westcott, and *Phone Book, The Movie* played on the apron. As I spooned the puttanesca into the bowls, I had the sense that the curtain had risen with Julie's appearance, and I had no idea what feelings were still on the stage.

"I was angry for a very long time," I said. "It's exhausting, being angry like that."

"You're not angry now?"

I put the pasta on the table, and we sat across from each other. The steam from the bowls curled into the air between us.

"No. I'm past it," I said, and I knew why. Caroline Yee.

A broken heart is nothing at all like smashed glass, where you look at the thing on the ground and say, *"Okay, that's a lost cause. Time to sweep that shit up and get a new glass."* I wish it were like that, but it's much more like a feather pillow that's been sliced open with a bowie knife, some feathers flying around the room, others staying in the sack, giving you hope that if you could just scoop up the lost feathers, stuff them back in, and sew the damn thing together, everything would be all right again.

It is a false hope, for even if you manage to gather a few feathers, more have blown away when your back was turned, the pillow is deflating, and there's nothing you can do about it.

The ensuing frustration, depression, and rage are all a result of not letting go, of holding on to emotions that offered comfort in happier days, despite the fact that there's a deadly gash in your heart that's bleeding you to death one feather at a time.

Caroline Yee—and to some extent her wizard grandfather—changed all that for me. I wasn't yet in a place where I understood why, and right now I didn't care. It was time for me to toss the whole slashed pillow of my marriage to Julie into the trash and think about something and someone else.

With that revelation, my head utterly and completely stopped hurting, and I felt myself smile for the first time in three years. I had smiled, of course, but this was the first time I felt it run through me from head to toe, and I knew what that meant: my electron river was flowing without impediment. *My God*, I thought, *I'm actually happy*.

"You found someone else?" she said.

"Maybe," I said.

We ate together and drank our red table wine, and I told her about the intervention introduction and subsequent cancellation of the main event. I told her about Dallas Westcott and *Broken Boner* and *Phone Book, The Movie*. We talked about my writing, my car, and my haircut—she thought I looked quite handsome with my hair longer. I had simply forgotten to get it cut.

My experience at Ken Moynihan's porn palace made Julie laugh out loud. It was wonderful to hear that sound again, but it did not make me want to be in love with her, and I knew, finally, what had happened to us.

"We weren't really friends, were we, Julie?"

"I always liked you."

"It's not the same thing. I always liked you too, but what I mean is that we sort of fell in love before we knew why."

She nodded. "Two souls who liked to laugh at strange things and had great sex."

"Was it really great sex?" I said, hopefully.

"Sometimes, yes. But it was never less than good sex."

"What a relief."

She told me about her juggling journey, her new career with *National Geographic*, and her on again-off again relationship with Greg, her photographer and travel companion.

"What are you working on now?" I said.

"Bees," she said. "Colony Collapse Disorder. Since 1971, almost half of the U.S. honeybee colonies have vanished. Now it's spinning out of control and no one knows why. Pesticides, pathogens, parasites, viruses, bad weather, cell phone signals? All of the above? Basically, without bees, no pollination. Without pollination, no life. Einstein said that after the bees disappear, we'd all be dead within a decade. So if there's anything you wanted to do, now's the time. This pasta's really good, Mark."

"Thanks. You working with Greg on this one?"

"Like we did the penguins. Yes."

We finished the wine and all the food and put the dishes in the sink. I had ice cream sandwiches in the freezer, and we each had one of those as well.

She called a cab, which is how she'd arrived, and while we waited, outside in the cool air, leaning against my Mustang, I said, "So what now?"

"You mean us?"

"You, me, us, now what?"

"I think we should be friends. I think I could be a good friend, if someone gave me half a chance."

"That's all I'm giving you. I don't think either one of us could survive a whole chance."

She laughed out loud and said, "You're a very silly man, Mark Manilow."

The cab arrived, and we embraced again, this time without holding back. I suspect it was as good for her to see me as it was for me to see her. If that's not the start of a friendship, I don't what is.

I watched the cab depart, waving to her while she waved to me, then went into the house. As I passed the fish, I realized I had forgotten to have her sign the divorce papers. I ran to the kitchen—as if running to the kitchen would do anything—and grabbed the papers off the counter. She had already signed them. Apparently, she had found them while taking a self-guided tour of my house, clicked the point of the pen, and signed Julie Bowers in all the indicated places. I put the pen in my pocket. I was divorced.

I wasn't sure what to do after that. It had been three and a half years of cataclysmic confusion and now it was settled. Just like that. Ten strokes of a pen. I walked to the hall closet and pulled a suitcase off the top shelf.

I carried it to my bedroom wondering what advice I could offer myself after living so long without wind, adrift under a thick and infinite cloudbank, no stars by which to navigate, destination unknown, bleeding feather by feather below deck while writing bad porn and movies about the phone book.

There's a mirror above my dresser, and I caught my own eye as I opened the drawers and considered my clothes. At long last, I had some advice for myself that made sense. *Bring a sweater*, I said to myself. *San Francisco can be chilly in the summer.*

71. THEY ARE MADMEN AND NOT TO BE TRUSTED

Julie had said the bees were collapsing and humankind had ten or twenty years left, and I wanted to spend every one of them with Caroline Yee. I left the next morning after arranging for the fish to be fed and the grounds to be watered. I called Caroline, who was still at her grandfather's house in the Valley, and said, "I'll be waiting for you in San Francisco." You know what she said? "You'd better be."

Just north of Monterey, my cell phone rang. It was Tango Joe delivering the denouement. He told me that Toxic Bob's lawyer, a mean-spirited prick named Chandler Downing, messengered letters to Calvin Key, Joe, Barry Manilow, Colonel Bill Curry, Ally Kramer, Cathy Burns, me, and even Ken Moynihan, suing us all for untold sums of money under the pretense that Toxic Bob had tied up the film rights to the phone book, and no project could proceed without his attachment as producer.

Calvin Key, who, it turns out, could be one heck of a belligerent billionaire when backed into a corner, put a dozen lawyers into reflex motion with a solitary intent: no one would ever, for the rest of time, make a movie about the phone book if Key couldn't, especially Toxic Bob Bloom.

"Are you okay, Joe?" I said.

"In spite of the death of our independent feature film, today I am particularly chipper."

"Why is that? And where are you, what am I hearing?"

Joe laughed and said, "I am in a hot air balloon looking down upon Camarillo. You are hearing gas jets, they tell me, but I cannot be sure because they are madmen and not to be trusted. I am chipper because Calvin Key is buying a television network in Mexico and wants me to produce a series for him. Something with police and half-naked women, possibly a Spanish-speaking horse. Are you ready to work?"

"I don't know, Joe. I was thinking about writing a novel."

"Are you insane? No one reads anymore. No one has read a book since 1981."

I laughed and said, "They read the phone book."

"There's acid in your orange juice, *mon*. What will your novel be about?"

"A juggler, a porn star, and a monkey wrench."

"Yes, yes," Joe said. "Walk into a bar and then what?"

I lost his signal before I could answer, but what I would have said was, "And the bartender says, 'What is this, some kind of joke?'" which is funny, I think, but not as funny as the truth, though it wasn't until I reached San Francisco that I'd realized it.

ALSO BY RICH LEDER

Workman's Complication
Kate McCall dreams of basking in the bright lights of Broadway. But after her PI dad is found dead in a New York City elevator, she has no choice but to split time between show business and the family business. When her vampire musical fails to pay the bills, she accepts a workman's compensation case that's sure to put her acting chops to the test. On her way down the trail of clues, she can't help but get sidetracked by her father's unsolved murder. Will Kate crack her cases before playing detective becomes a role to die for?

Swollen Identity
Kate McCall hopes she can balance her passions and her PI practice. Struggling to keep both on stage, the way off Broadway performer finds herself in the deep end of a billionaire's allegedly stolen identity. But her role as a super-sleuth takes center stage when a corporate crime scene replicates her father's unsolved murder ... Can Kate shine a spotlight on the killer before she loses her part for good?

Emboozlement
Kate McCall dazzles audiences on stage by night, but by day she searches for her father's killer. She seems to gain ground, until the man who pulled the trigger sends texts that prove he's one step ahead. While investigating the murderous messages, she takes on an embezzlement case from a handsome sports bar owner who might just be her top suspect ... If she can't close both cases, Kate's next intermission could be permanent. Will Kate's latest song-and-dance deliver justice or a fatal review?

Let There Be Linda

Dan Miller may be a smooth-talking swindler, but he's still in the hole. So when his malicious moneylender comes to collect, digging up $75K is going to take a miracle. Lucky for him, his latest client can breathe life into the dead. Reunited after their mother's passing, Dan and his strait-laced brother hatch a lucrative plan to resurrect a coke-addled dentist's beloved poodle. But when the undead dog goes bloodily off-script and a wannabe-comedian cop starts chasing them, the Miller brothers discover a trouble shared is not a trouble halved. So they bring back their mother to clean up the mess. Can they get their hands on the cash before the loan shark renders them deader than mommy dearest?

Cooking for Cannibals

Carrie Cromer pushes the boundaries of science, not her social life. The brilliant behavioral gerontologist's idea of a good time is hanging out with her beloved lab rats and taking care of her elderly mother and the other eccentric old folks at the nursing home. So no one is more surprised than Carrie when she steals the lab's top-secret, experimental medicine for aging in reverse. Two-time ex-con Johnny Fairfax dreams of culinary greatness. But when his corrupt parole officer tries to drag him from the nursing home kitchen, the suddenly young-again residents spring to his defense and murder the guy—and then request Johnny cook them an evidence-devouring dinner to satisfy their insatiable side-effect appetite. As their unexpected mutual attraction gets hot, Carrie and Johnny find themselves caught up with the authorities who arrive to investigate the killing. But even more dangerous than the man-eating not-so-senior citizens could be the arrival of death-dealing pharmaceutical hitmen. If you like fast-paced plots, unconventional characters, and humor that crosses the line, then you'll have a feast with Rich Leder's wild ride.